RESONANCE

A.J. Scudiere

GRIFFYN INK

For further information, please contact:
Griffyn Ink
www.GriffynInk.com
MediaRelations@GriffynInk.com

Cover design by Joanna Leverette

Book design by
Arbor Books, Inc.
19 Spear Road, Suite 301
Ramsey, NJ 07446
www.arborbooks.com

Printed in the United States of America

Resonance
A.J. Scudiere
1. Title 2. Author 3. Fiction

Library of Congress Control Number: 2007936753
ISBN 10: 0-9799510-0-3
ISBN 13: 978-0-9799510-0-8

For Eli
without whom none of this would have been possible

Human life is important only to humans.
—author unknown

Man's greatest triumphs stand no chance
against the whim of nature.
—author unknown

Twelve years ago, airline pilots had to recalibrate their compasses. This was because the exact location of the magnetic poles had drifted, and it was a first in aviation history. Six years ago, the poles had drifted even further, causing the need to again reset the compasses. They recalibrated again three years ago, then two, then one, and are currently realigning every three months.

Approximately 200 million years ago, map north was magnetic south. But ten million years later, the poles switched places. They've traded again approximately every sixty million years – the last of which was sixty-five million years ago.

It is theorized that the dinosaurs achieved such great size due to the slightly larger magnetic field of their time. Today, some living things, like homing pigeons and honeybees, are highly dependent on the earth's field. Even those creatures that don't seem to notice it are in jeopardy if it changes, since we don't know how they use their internal magnetics, only that they have them.

Like us.

And the earth we are sitting on is five million years overdue…

Chapter 1

Stupid paleontologists, he thought to himself. Didn't know how to grid a dig properly. *Morons.*

What had he been thinking? Sharing a site with the dino boys? And now he had chunks of strata strapped to his waist, each meticulously labeled in the dino boys' lazy scrawl. Each clearly mislabeled for direction or depth of find. They had acted like they understood the dip and the horizontal. But the markings were clearly honked up. Yet, some of the rocks looked right. Which was the ultimate insult – David couldn't even count on them to be wrong.

Maybe they were fucking with him, he sighed into the deep night, that was a sincere possibility. There was nothing like envy laced with continual disagreement to drive a wedge of dislike between two people. Those two people being him and anyone else on the dig. Your choice, as it was pretty much unanimous.

The paleo guys were all out for drinks and a discussion of the day's successes. There was that one big heap of bones, and oh yeah, that other big heap of bones, then there were the bone chips.

Using the winch and harness system they had set up, David lowered himself down the incline, tiptoeing and letting out line as he went. Not because he couldn't have scrambled his way down – he could have, the slope was a just walkable 45 degrees – but, in order to go on foot, he would have to dig in with his toes to get purchase and the dig would have been forfeit. Couldn't have that. At least he and the dino boys agreed on this one thing.

The other thing they had agreed to was not to hang out in the dig alone. That, of course, made sense. No one wanted to be the one left at the base of the site with a broken leg while everyone else ate lunch, or worse yet stayed out all night drinking. And no one wanted to be the one who mucked up the site, with no one around to say what went where.

But just because he had agreed *to* it didn't mean that he would *do* it. And, well, if David was being honest, they had already ruined the site, what with all the mislabeling and everything. Therefore the only thing he was risking was his own night out under the big black sky with a few broken bones. So he slowly kept letting out the line, getting a little further down the slope each minute. He didn't go too fast, for God's sake he wasn't stupid, and the pitch here was a bit on the sharp side.

His foot hit the first grid line. A thin white string wound round a short post hammered into the ground denoting the edge of the official dig area. David swore a few times under his breath, sure that he had scuffed a few loose pieces of rock into the dig. And that would earn him nothing but verbal and social hell come tomorrow morning. He decided to take it all a little more carefully. Besides now he was far enough down the backside of the slope that he wouldn't be spotted. The camp was on the other side of the crest where it wouldn't interfere with the dig, and no party-poopers making their way back early would see his beam as long as it was a small one. And that meant no bright headlamps. So he pulled the flashlight free, slipping it from the carabineer on his belt with a flick of his wrist.

Crap, he had shoved some pieces under the grid edge. Softly he stepped down and began flinging the loose gravel away. After five minutes at it, he figured that he had covered his tracks well enough for a man who was probably going to get caught anyway and he decided to get down to brass tacks.

Pulling one zipper bag from its carabineer at his waist, he tacked his line and used both hands to pull the rock from its baggie. Tilting his head, with the small Maglight firmly between his teeth, he read off the coordinates, then picked up the line. David let himself down a few more feet and high-stepped to the right about fifteen yards, watching carefully for the meter lines that ran the grid. They had originally been only a few inches off the surface, but as this dig had progressed they had altered the smooth plane to extremely uneven, leaving the ground anywhere from just a few inches to just over a foot below the grid lines. The perfect heights for getting an ankle tangled and then bashing into the slope of the dig. And, oh yeah, breaking said ankle and mucking up said dig while you did it.

He moved slowly and carefully, each footstep set methodically into the loose ground, so as not to grind or scour any of the precious soil or bone chips out of place. He lifted his foot high with the same care. Right foot right, find footing, left foot follow, set down carefully.

It seemed to take an eternity to get to the other side of the fifteen yard grid to the labeled home of his rock. As he landed, finally, in his square, he tacked the guide line again, allowing his weight to sit back against the taut rope. With the light in one hand, he held up the baby rock and turned it over.

It was sedimentary, full of fossilized organic matter and exactly what anyone would expect of a layer from this location. His eyes perused all of this, reading it the way you would read a newspaper, for the whole story and never one letter at a time.

This piece had clearly belonged to an ancient streambed. From what the dino boys were finding, the water had nourished a whole bunch of critters up until the very last moment. What caused that last moment was David's job.

He liked the rocks, and it was natural to assume that he had gotten into this profession because of his father. The layers reminded him of his Dad a lot: cold, hard, and unreadable to all but the most trained of observers. David was an expert reader of both. Although, in his estimate, the rock was always easier to get a bead on at first and easier to get along with. Also, the rock always gave up the whole story eventually.

The streambed and sediment were ABCs. What David was reading as he rotated his chunk of old earth and his flashlight was the tiny shiny chips in his piece. Now they were talking. And they said that the Paleo boys were retarded.

Shaking his head, he used the letter and number code on the tape to line the rock up with the direction and pitch it was supposed to have come from. Letting a little more slack into the line, he leaned down and placed the rock into the spot it supposedly called home for eons, until yesterday.

David's head tilted. His Maglight circled, and he studied the lay of the strata in the bed and the rock. It looked a little too damn good. Not to mention the remaining side of the bed from which the piece he held had been chipped. The two sides fit together like a puzzle piece.

Shrugging, David slipped the rock back into its baggie and pulled the permanent marker from his back pocket. He checked the upper right side of the label and clipped it back to his pants just as his stomach let a loud growl. His head perked, just as it had when he was a boy afraid of getting caught. But no one appeared to have heard. Hell, no one appeared to be within fifty miles of the site.

Cursing silently to himself, he wondered why it would have been so hard to slip a piece of jerky into a pocket, or for god's sakes, make a sandwich. It wasn't like he didn't have a belt full of zipper baggies already. But he didn't have time to go back. He needed to check his pieces and not make more enemies on the dig than he already had.

So he pulled the next rock from its zipper pouch and carefully began making his way to another grid square. Lift foot, set foot, lift other foot, set foot.

Four hours later, he hadn't tripped at all, which was a miracle since he was silently swearing a blue streak. The dino boys hadn't mislabeled a single rock, which only made him more furious. Hell, you couldn't count on them for *anything*.

And if the rocks were all aligned right, then the rest was all aligned wrong. An eddy in the stream could explain one spot, maybe even a few, but not the consistency of the whole dig.

A bright light shone into his eyes, blinding him more easily than the dark of night ever had.

"Hey, pretty boy!" It was Greer. David had always figured that 'pretty boy' was the best Greer could come up with since he wasn't one much inclined to the use of the more apt *asshole*. "You done checking out our grid markings? You didn't break any bones did you?!"

"No, Fuckwad, I didn't." David held his hand up in front of his face. He was going to catch hell for this. He knew it now.

"That's too bad." Greer directed his five-billion megawatt stadium light at the ground and slowly David's sight came back. He started climbing the slope cautiously and methodically, as Greer taunted him all the way. "Well, seems we disappointed you didn't we? You thought we had mislabeled all your stones."

"They're not stones." David growled as he climbed.

"Too bad. Now you're going to have to do some real geology work – not just come out and wave your hand like you always do and spout off what's *just so obvious* that the rest of us must be blind."

"Congratulations, Greer. You are right on so many counts. My rocks were in fact labeled correctly–"

"How many of them?" Greer taunted.

"*All* of them."

"Uh huh."

"And I do in fact have a little bit of work to do when I get back to the tent–" He stopped climbing.

Greer spotlighted him again. It would have blinded him, but he wasn't looking in front of him, just staring into the space ahead. If it meant what he thought it meant…well,…

"What is it David?"

"I want everyone off the site tomorrow. Just you and me. I need to check all other possibilities."

"Everyone off the dig tomorrow!? Jesus, David, do you know what you're asking? Is your Daddy gonna pay our salaries?"

"No, but the royalties off my paper will. Dammit, Greer, clear the site tomorrow."

If it was what he thought it was…well, he might just prove that the David Carter II geology center had been worth its money.

God, what was it that made her feel like such a fool? All that school, all that 'prestige', and yet she stood there like a moron. Eyes wide, 'yes' 'yes' monosyllabic answers to each question. The horrible, lost feeling of being in an unfamiliar institution.

"So you two are the new peons."

Jillian nodded. "Yes." There it was again. The idiocy.

The guy beside her – Jared? Jeff? Jacob? – was cool and only raised his eyebrows to the question.

Dr. Landerly was hunched over his desk and had whitish hair that stuck out in about fifty different directions and looked as though it hadn't made friends with a brush in a lifetime or so. He had male pattern balding and probably arthritis, judging by the way he held his pen. Whether he didn't look at them because of pain or out of sheer rudeness was anybody's guess. "You two turned in all your documentation and fingerprinting crap down in HR?"

Jake? flicked the new badges hanging from their pristine white jackets, "Yup, hence the ten a.m. arrival."

"Ready for the tour?"

At the sound of yet another one word answer, he finally looked up at them. For a moment he simply looked them both up and down, taking their measure. Jillian did the first proactive deed of her day and sized him up too. Landerly's face reminded her of a grandfather, not her own, but that old man look, crossed with a little mad scientist. With his focus turned on them, she felt the same intensity that the papers he was marking on must have felt just minutes before. She was surprised the pages hadn't burst into flame before she and what's-his-name walked in and pulled a little of the good doctor's attention from them.

"Well, you must be Jillian Brookwood, and you must be Jordan Abellard."

Jordan! That was it.

Landerly tapped his forehead, "Deductive reasoning." And despite the insanely poor joke, she began to like him.

He simply turned and began walking down the hallway, talking as he went and expecting them to keep pace behind him. He never checked. "This is your office." He pointed to his left into an open door and what could only be called a large cubby. He was already walking away. Jillian had to nearly run to catch up with him, already midsentence.

"-that whole half of the building is I.D. That part you'll only go in on an 'as needed' basis. Which basically means never. Unless you get promoted, or we decide we don't need you or don't like you, but can't think of a better way to get rid of you."

For the first time, Jordan turned to her, his eyebrows raised until she shrugged in return. Dr. Landerly's voice trailed off as her focus slipped to the signs on the wall. Every etched plate had the tiny inscription on the top: *Centers for Disease Control and Prevention.* But Landerly was old-school and still referred to it as the CDC.

Not ten minutes later Jillian realized that they had walked a short circle, and Jordan wasn't missing that fact either. "That's it?"

"Sure." Landerly fixed them with another stare. "If you want to see the Infectious Disease side, you can go get your own tour. I told you, you're peons."

"I'm a–" Jordan stopped himself. "We're physicians."

"Yes, and you're underlings. At the CDC. On my team you'll be spending a lot of time drawing blood and writing reports."

Which, Jillian admitted, had been exactly the job description. So she wasn't sure where Jordan got off being upset. In truth, it had been just that part of the work that had made her apply. She had spent all that time and money on medical school, only to find out that she hated the endless churn of minor complaints that flowed through a doctor's office. This job had been her proof that she hadn't chosen the wrong profession.

Landerly had disappeared back into his office, and by craning her neck she could see him scrubbing through the most disorganized desk ever. But he held out two identical key chains and spoke again. "Keys to your office and your lab next door. Go check it out then get cracking. You've already got three cases sitting on your desk."

There was no other dismissal, no wish of good luck or welcome, just the turn of his shoulder and the intensity of his focus directed elsewhere. The two of them no longer existed to him.

Turning, they silently followed Landerly's instruction, walking two doors down to the plaque that read *G-1763 Lab 13, Landerly.*

"Hi." Jordan's voice filled the empty space around a young man with inky hair who stood at the basic black lab island dialing the micropipette to a new measure.

"Oh, Hi. You two must be the new docs. I'm your tech." For a brief moment he held out a gloved hand before realizing what he was doing and withdrawing the offer. "I'm Mark. I'm prepping slides for Landerly right now, but let me know what you need. My desk is in the back." He pointed to the corner, to a table piled with skewed stacks of loose papers and file folders of various colors.

"Nice to meet you." Jordan pulled back out of the doorway and wound up leading her back to their office, where they spent four minutes choosing which side of the large desk they each wanted, then another hour exploring the file cabinet they shared and finding out what the previous occupants had left for them. Which turned out to be an odd mix of pens, pencils, microtest-tubes and pipette tips, and one stick of mint chewing gum.

After a half-hour of hardly speaking she finished up organizing her drawers and labeling her hanging files, only to look up and find Jordan watching her from across the desk. "It's two-thirty, are you hungry?"

She nodded. But he spoke again before she could get in a word edgewise. "You find the cafeteria and I'll treat."

She would have rather paid, but she held her tongue. She could do this, right? On the 'tour' Landerly had pointed down one corridor and mentioned food and vending machines. With a deep breath she marched off in the general direction they had started, and faked it to the best of her ability.

Two corridors later she could smell that she had found the right one. Then, after they ordered, she completely disoriented them on the way back. After they got situated and endured a few minutes of silent chewing, Jordan leaned forward. "Since we get to stare at each other until one of us goes insane or gets promoted, why don't we get started with the usual stupid questions?"

She almost smiled. Almost. "The usual ones?"

"Like 'Where are you from?'" He leaned back and Jillian barely covered her gasp at realizing the vast majority of his lunch had already been reduced to empty wrappers. "I'm from Lake James, North Dakota. Where it's colder than a w-…well just about anything, and there's really a lot more bible thumping and militia than you might guess. College and med school at UCLA. Your turn."

"Emory Med, but I grew up in Chattanooga. Same town through undergrad." She smiled from behind her limp cheese-burger. "Favorite fast food? Mine is Chick-Fil-A nuggets."

"What's Chick Fillay?"

"Ahhh, I'll take you tomorrow."

Jordan shrugged. "Favorite burger is Jack in the Box Bacon Ultimate Cheeseburger."

"Jack in the Box?" She supposed that's what happened when you met someone from the opposite end of the country.

"Ahhh, good, cheap food. College student fare. Too bad I can't return the Chick Fillay favor. Jack-in-the-Box is mostly out west."

Satisfied that she had the basics, Jillian figured it was time to start earning her keep. "We should get to work on these cases."

"Can I just guess now? Botulism, gas leak, and Salmonella."

"Really?" She put her hand to her hip. "I would have had you pegged for a 'secret government weapons being tested on our own people' type."

"Nah, I'm a realist." He picked up the folder and started through it, while she made a thinking noise. He laughed. "Do you realize that you even 'hmmm' with a southern accent?"

She nodded. "Can't be helped."

Jordan was pissed. The cases in their box this morning had turned out to be botulism, botulism and botulism. One, he was mad that his guess was wrong. Two, he had skipped the invite to UCLA's PhD program to come here and do research as a physician, even though he would only occasionally be putting the vast majority of his med school skills to work. He had thought that this would be more exciting than telling mothers that their kiddies had ear infections or strep throat. Three, they hadn't even had to leave their desks to figure the damn thing out. Four, Miss Jillian had turned out to be anal retentive. Although 'turned out' was being generous. She had looked the part from moment one.

Aaaaaaaack. Where was the next AIDS when your life needed a spark? Miss Jillian was sitting across from him, diligently making notes in the two files that she held, while he scanned the new one that had turned up in their inbox this morning. Jillian gave him a dirty look that he wasn't helping her write reports, and it occurred to him that Landerly had done this on purpose. Jordan was to be the forward thinker, the one who would make those reasoning leaps, and Jillian was the workhorse.

Her nose wrinkled and she brushed her hair back again. Not that it accomplished anything other than her getting to move her arm. The hank of hair fell right back over her shoulder. The phone buzzed, startling him about three feet into the air, and he was already trying to cover that fact before he was even back down. "Landerly wants us."

Jillian stared a brief moment through not entirely open eyes. "That was so not smooth." But she followed him next door and graciously didn't mention it again.

Landerly stood as they entered the office, his attention a physical sensation as it turned from the phone to the two of them. "This is why I created you guys."

"Like God?" Jillian's voice was dry and Jordan wasn't sure if she was kidding or what. But Landerly was, and he laughed a good guffaw and responded with "Maybe a demigod," before continuing.

So Jillian was already his favorite. How could two people on this earth have that same sense of humor?

The older man held up a file before speaking. "I've got a little girl in Deltona, Florida with a spider bite reaction that the local docs say doesn't look like your basic anaphylactic shock. They think the spider has some new venom or maybe is a vector carrying something else. She's all yours." He handed the file to Jillian just as Jordan decided that there wasn't anything he could do about it. And maybe he hadn't been hired to be the brilliant theorist. Which, of course, meant he would have to get his butt in gear and do some work.

"Anne in reception will have your schedule. You need to leave this evening to see the reaction and do anything before it gets worse." And like turning off the light, his focus was off them and they were expected to find their own way out.

By now Jordan knew his way around and he certainly knew Anne. She was the adorable blonde in reception, and he had made those thoughts clear to her this morning. Anne handed each of them an itinerary, but it was Jordan her eyes remained on. Not that he was going to dip his pen in the company ink, but there was a certain warmth in knowing the ink was receptive to being dipped. Jillian was walking away before he realized it and he smiled good-bye to Anne before turning to follow his cubby-mate down the hall.

At their desk, Jillian turned and stared at him, leaving him ready for some scathing remark about his behavior, but instead, with no preamble, she asked about Landerly. "Do you think he's just too old to go off gallivanting around the country? Why do you think he set up his team of two here? Why us?"

Jordan had no good answers, and he told her so. But he did offer to make up for getting lost – no less than three times – on the way to lunch yesterday and asked where he could find this Chick Fillay. "We have time to do fast food, right?"

"The 'fast' part is the part you seem to be having trouble with." She didn't look up and he couldn't decipher the dryness in her tone. He had heard it several times now and he truly wasn't sure what to make of it. That scared the crap out of him. And given that they were on their way out the door for a company road trip, and since she was a co-worker, he figured he'd better find his footing right away.

"Are you mad at me because I got us lost yesterday? Or for something else?" Her face was unreadable. Well, he thought it was. She just looked a little confused and maybe perturbed.

"No, I'm not angry." After tilting her head to the side for a moment, she nodded. "You're worried that I'm one of those 'my feelings are hurt' girls. Well, I'm not."

"Then why no fast food?" She was still looking at him and Jordan figured that was the best way to read the book: when it was open. But Miss Jillian seemed to be written in a foreign language, one that he only understood in random phrases.

Her words were slow and methodical. "Because I want to have time to pack. And because you got lost the last time the directions were 'three miles, then turn right.' I just don't have time."

Before she even finished the sentence, her purse was over her shoulder and she was heading out the door, "See you at the airport."

He was still looking confused when he heard her footsteps change directions and saw her head reappear in the open doorway. "Should I pick you up?"

Again she read his expression before he got his words together. "We'll both get there, and only one parking charge."

"I can drive."

She nodded. "So can I. And I know my way around. If you want to contribute you can pay the parking fees."

"They're reimbursed." So that wasn't much of a contribution at all.

"I know. I just hate expense reports." She disappeared beyond the opening and this time didn't come back even as he muttered to himself.

"And here I thought you loved paperwork."

In a few minutes he had cleared his thoughts and headed home. It took him a while to locate things from the boxes. Jordan had lived here all of one-half a day longer than he had been working at the CDCP, and it showed. He found his only two suits – one still in the dry-cleaning bag. Scrounged up socks, without holes. Underwear, also without holes. Then went in search of his hanging bag. This, of course, was pristine. It had been used once, for his interview here.

He pushed that thought aside and turned back to his packing. There was no way of knowing how long they would be there. He had to plan for the possibility of a full week, so he stuffed all the spare pockets and pouches with extra clothes and, in a glimpse of reason, all seven of the ties he owned. After staring at the bag and waiting for it to tell him what else to pack, he finally realized that it would say no such thing, and so he threw in a few pairs of khakis for good measure.

The last step was to change himself. Jeans, tee, a sweatshirt, and an old pair of sneakers seemed the best bet for flying. They'd go see the little girl after they got settled in a bit, right? He decided to believe what he wanted and pulled the sweatshirt over his head, just as his stomach grumbled and the doorbell made the horrid high-pitched noise that the manager had called a chime.

"Coming!" Jordan crossed the short distance from the very back to the very front of the apartment and pulled the door open. "Hi."

"Hey!" Jillian walked through the open doorway and past his open mouth. "I think you actually have a bigger place than me. You ready?"

"Yes." Getting his bags took less than half a minute; his thoughts would take a little longer to gather. What was up with Jillian? She looked all of nineteen in her jeans and small white t-shirt, what with her dark hair pulled back in that ponytail. If she was in the airplane seat next to him, people would think he was a dirty older man.

But none of it even registered in her expression as he grabbed his luggage and trailed her down the stairs and out to the eerily quiet street. She simply popped the trunk of her little white car open and let him throw his bag on top of the two she had stacked back there.

"What is this?"

"Rav-4." She slid in behind the wheel, no longer Miss Jillian of the CDCP, but a complete stranger. "It has its quirks, but it's reliable and, one day, when I get a dog, she'll go in the back."

She was quiet most of the way to airport, navigating into long-term parking with ease. Her matching carryon was slung over her shoulder and she wheeled her hanger bag behind her, never fussing at the long wait at security. And when the plane took off from the runway at Atlanta International she was already asleep in the seat beside him.

Becky sat knee deep in shallow, muddy stream water, her long bangs falling into her eyes. Melanie wasn't listening to her,

Brandon had wandered off somewhere, and her mother was going to be mad. She was wet, a little on the cold side, and she was the only one who hadn't caught anything yet. She raised a hand to push her hair out of her face, not remembering until she felt the cold that her hand had just been in stream water that was *not* clear. Oh well, the muck would help plaster her hair out of her eyes.

For a moment she gathered her breath, then she yelled, "Brandon! Mom's gonna be angry if you don't stay with me. Get back here!" But Becky didn't wait for him to show up. He would, and so she turned back to searching the running water for the small frogs she wanted. One jumped in front of her container and with a quick movement she completely missed it.

With a deep sigh she lifted her head up, and let out another long yell. "Brandon!"

"I'm *right here*, Becky." He shook his head as he looked down on her, holding the bottom of his shirt in front of him making a scoop in which he piled all the containers he had filled with one frog each. Just like she had asked.

And to think biology had seemed like such a great field to go into. She had her doctorate, and yet her little brother and sister put her to shame at 'obtaining specimens'. The only consolation she had was that Brandon and Melanie had also seriously shown up every other biologist and assistant she had brought out for the job.

"Becky, look."

"Yeah, you did great."

"No," He scooted closer. She knew that he would have grabbed her arm. He had tried, but his lightning reflexes had him straightening the tumbling containers before they got too far. "Pick up that top one, he's the biggest."

With a smile of pride on her face, she held the clear tupper up over her head and let the light shine through on a good size rana. One of the larger ones caught here, but certainly not the largest. "He is pretty big. You holding out for more money?"

"Becky! I thought you were smart. *Look* at him! He's got four legs, you retard!"

Melanie also looked up at the underside of the container, although what she could see from about three feet away was anyone's guess. "Frogs all have four legs, retard."

Becky shifted to give both of them dirty looks about the name calling, but left it at that, knowing full well she couldn't win.

Brandon rolled his eyes with all the meaning a ten year old could muster. "Four *back* legs."

"Huh?" Becky held the tupper aloft again, this time higher to catch rays from a break in the tree cover. Frowning, she looked him over, and she didn't see it until he jumped: four hind legs, two per side, coming out of the hip flexor joint. Holy crap! She shook the plastic container a bit. Yup, all functional. "Okay, I'll give you two bucks for him."

Brandon still clutched the edge of his shirt, keeping the ten containers stacked precariously in there, but his expression said that he wasn't moved by the two dollar offer. "They're all that way."

"What?" She reached down and pulled another container from his clutch. Holding it high, she gave it a slight wiggle and watched the small frog try to rebalance itself. Four hind legs. All functional.

She quickly set it down and grabbed for two more. Both had a second pair of jumper legs. In under a minute her breathing had sped up and she had ascertained that Brandon was correct.

But that would be wrong. Very wrong. With her brows pulled together, she went over to check the row of tuppers that the kids had caught here. It had been hard to see those spare legs at first. Maybe they just hadn't noticed. But her little sister was a sharp one, and she'd already checked the locals out. "They're all normal."

"So, Brandon, there were..." she counted, "eight six-legged frogs where you were? And you caught them all?" He was a good catcher. Once he spotted it the frog didn't stand a chance.

"No, they were all like that. At least I think they all were. Almost. There are more. I just ran out of lexans."

"Where!?"

Brandon took off with Becky right behind him; Melanie would catch up, she knew. The trail was well-worn and well-known from her own childhood days, and they bounded down it, anticipating every fallen tree and protruding rock. She just kept running after Brandon, never having heard of anyone finding a full clutch of six-legged frogs before. A tree branch that Brandon had held out for himself came slapping back at her, but even without her conscious thought, her hand was there to catch it.

Six legs occurred in nature, and didn't kill the frog most of the time. Usually they were slow and so predators got them. But it was a *growth* mutation, not a genetic one. It also usually resulted in just one spare leg, a five-legged frog. These *all* had *six*. So how would you get a whole clutch of them? Unless something was wrong with the site…

There was a nuclear reactor program a little west of here: Oak Ridge, where they had built the A-bomb. There were always stories of Melton Lake Dam being shut down for mercury levels being too high. But this?

They had run a long way before Brandon finally stopped. He pointed to a section of the stream. There was absolutely nothing out of the ordinary to the human eye. Even the trained human eye. "I caught them all here."

Becky slowly walked to the stream edge then kept going right in. Her shoes were already caked in mud and silt and of absolutely no concern to her. "So would you say about a third of them were that way? Maybe a tenth?"

Brandon shook his head, "No, I'm telling you they *all* are."

Slowly she squatted down, getting a good focus through the running water. There were frogs here, lots of them, but with the movement and the refraction, those back legs were hard to distinguish. Hell, they'd been hard to spot at first in the lexans. *Shit! She had run to the site with no tuppers!*

Becky swore at herself a little more, then went back to peering through the water. But it wasn't helping. She needed to see these guys up close. Looking back at Brandon she asked the sixty-four-thousand-dollar-question, "Do you think you could catch one bare handed?"

Small deep breaths came from just behind her; Melanie had caught up to them. "You...don't...have...to."

Becky turned to find her baby sister, leaned over, huffing for oxygen, but in Melanie's outstretched hand was a tall stack of tuppers, with all the lids shoved down in the top one.

Becky shrieked. "You are a genius!"

"I...know." Job done, Melanie sat back to watch Brandon get frogs and Becky try.

Becky held each new catch aloft, the fifth came up with normal legs, prompting a question. "Brandon, how many normal frogs did you throw back?"

"Two."

"*Just two?*"

He nodded.

The sun was setting by the time Melanie arrived from her return trip to get the wheel barrow. As Becky had ordered, each of the frogs from the other site bore a scrap of masking tape across the lid. And all the lids bore a single digit – the number of legs on the contained frog. There were so many 6's that Becky had to look again. Each time she thought the numbers must be off. But they weren't. She stacked the five four-legged frogs from this site in one spot, thinking they would be as useful as all the sixes. Why hadn't they changed, too? And how did their numbers get to be only one out of ten?

Becky was frantically writing on the scratch pad she had brought along in case any question popped into her mind. She was beginning to think that today the fifty sheets the pad claimed to have weren't going to be enough.

She just couldn't detect anything out of the ordinary. It was your standard East Tennessee summer day by all measurable counts. So what was up with the frogs?

Eventually she had to give up. She had no barometer, no litmus paper, and no Geiger counter, so there wasn't much more she could measure, even if she wanted to. The Geiger counter gave her pause. What if there was some sort of radiation leak? If the government had buried some sort of waste here? Wasn't it possible? There were always news stories about plutonium being flown in and out of the labs. Could it have gotten here? And had she exposed her brother and sister to it, for…she checked her watch…four hours? God, her lack of protocol had been horrible.

Chapter 2

Jillian closed the door behind her. No longer 'Miss Jillian' in his mind. My God, she was a little chameleon. In the airport she had looked like a kid, ponytail and all. And less than fifteen minutes after they had arrived she knocked on his hotel door, business professional from head to toe. In a deep teal suit that looked like it had been cut just for her and brought out her eyes. He hadn't realized there was so much green in them.

She had, of course, immediately told him to quit staring, that yes, she did in fact own several suits and he needed to get it together. Jordan had never had a woman beat him at getting ready before. And certainly not look so good doing it.

She had thrown her lab coat over her arm then peeled off her jacket just like he had in the stifling Florida humidity. He had sweated buckets just on the drive over. She had looked cool, "I'm from the south, remember?" All he could do was swear to slap anyone from LA who ever bitched about the 'humidity' again. And ask God's forgiveness for all the times he had done it himself.

He pulled his jacket back on to cover his sweat stains as they entered the hospital flashing their CDCP credentials. Jillian clearly actually owned some of the adult faculties he was pretending to. Everyone spoke to Jillian, wanted her opinion first. She was smart, confident, and on top of it. A million miles from the woman who poured over paperwork, pulled her hair back in a barrette, and had that weird flat sense of humor. It almost pissed him off.

It also lent a lot of credence to his new hypothesis that he wasn't the brilliant theorist. And if that were the case, why was he here? He'd made his own diagnosis. But Jillian had given the same one, and they had all asked her first.

She followed him out of the little girl's room to confer in the hallway. "What did you think?"

He shrugged out of his lab coat. "Same as you."

"It makes sense, doesn't it? West Nile with anaphylactic shock caused by the spider bite."

"So we're here for another two days at least."

"Why?" She looked perplexed and he had the feeling he was about to be shown up again. It didn't sit well.

"Because you can't tell West Nile from Yellow Fever or Dengue Fever without a viral analysis or waiting out the symptoms." By his count, two days was the least amount of time they might need to see the distinction. He waited for her to tell him all about the new reasons he was wrong.

But she didn't. "What's the difference?"

"You don't know?" He was shocked.

She shook her head, her expression suddenly clearly belonging to the girl who had inhabited the other side of the desk from him. It just pissed him off. "I hate you, you know. You walk in there, all confidence and knowing all the answers then only confess out here that you don't."

Her head tilted, and she smiled, "No one wants to believe that it isn't an exact science. And that family has had doctors telling them that they have no idea what it was and that they called in the experts. That's us, Starsky."

He sunk into one of the doctors' lounge chairs. It was unfamiliar, but so much like every other hospital's lounges. "The way I'm feeling, I think we should go by Bonnie and Clyde."

She laughed, lightening the load on his shoulders. "Nah, Bonnie and Clyde actually knew what they were doing."

"Yes, Mom, I'm home." Jillian had the phone wedged between her shoulder and ear while she folded her clothes.

"How are you feeling?"

"Like crap, Mom. I just walked in the door twenty minutes ago." Well-trained girl that she was, she was already putting her clothing away. And calling her Mother.

"So now you've been with this job, like, a week? And you haven't had a day off. What are these people doing to you?" Jillian heard the slight intake of breath and she knew what was coming. "I just don't see why you couldn't have gone into private practice...why you didn't–"

"Mom." The sigh behind her own voice was deeper and well worn. "I never deluded you about wanting a private practice. I never intended to come back to Signal Mountain and check ears and throats for a living. I don't have the touch for that. Nor the desire."

Nor was her mother getting the everyday prestige from having her little girl go off to Emory for medicine and come back to help serve the community. But her mother's high hopes had been just that. And they belonged entirely to her mother. So, as far as Jillian was concerned, her mother could figure out what to do with them.

"So you enjoy traveling all over the place with no days off?"

"Mom, I have days off." Then, just to be a little facetious she added, "You know, saving the world doesn't happen on a nine to five schedule."

That managed to shut her up for all of the three seconds it took her to shift gears. "So are you meeting any nice doctors?"

Her shoulders ached. Slowly rolling the one that wasn't cramped up under the phone, she gave the same answer she had been giving for two years, since the end of her last major relationship. "No, Mom, they're all assholes."

There it was, the expected intake of breath, but she spoke again before her mother could criticize her language. "But I did meet a really nice janitor, and he wants to take me out on Thursday – Oh Mom! That's the other line! Maybe it's him. I'll call you next week! I love you!"

She barely waited for the resulting "I love you, too" before hanging up the phone and tossing it on the dresser. God hang her for using her mother's prejudices against her, but…she just couldn't put up with it any more.

The bed beckoned. She was tired of being good, tired of putting her clothes away, tired of explaining her life choices to her family. In Chattanooga, smart girls married men with money. Even in this day and age. She knew three girls who attended one semester of freshmen year, just to say they did it, before they went off and married their much older boyfriends. Jillian had wanted her own career, and her own life, and apparently you couldn't have both.

She flopped back onto the comforter – tomorrow she had to go into the office and they had to write a report on the spider bite, and then there were four glorious days off until Monday again.

She had been in the apartment for all of two and a half weeks, and since starting her job she estimated that she had been here maybe twenty-four hours total, including sleep time. Shaking her head, Jillian decided to pass out.

After half an hour of staring at the ceiling while her thoughts ran rampant with her, she finally accomplished her goal.

"This is silly, Rebecca."

Ooooh, Dr. Warden had downshifted to 'patronizing'. As her boss, his only real function seemed to be the monitoring of anything he deemed to be under his control – which included employees, discoveries, and even paperclips. Becky just knew she wouldn't last three minutes without actually hitting him.

Taking one deep solid breath, she nodded. "All right. I understand. My resignation will be on your desk in fifteen minutes."

"Rebecca, where would you go? You can't just resign."

She faked a startled look. "My parents live down the street. And I'm sitting on a huge discovery that will pay off in a little while. I'll be fine, but thank you for worrying about me."

Turning, she began to walk out of the office. His voice caught up to her quickly. "That's my paper. Those frogs are university property."

But she was done. She squared up to face him, as he towered over her tall frame, making her feel small, but she knew she was in the right. "No, it's not your paper."

He started to talk but she held up her hand. "Just because three of those frogs are sitting in my office, doesn't make them university property. I would point out that my purse also sits in my office. Most of those frogs are still at my home. Sitting under a lamp I bought. They were caught in tuppers that I purchased with my own money. I have a receipt." She grinned, then continued, even as she talked this was getting better. "They were caught by my siblings, on land owned by my parents, and since you haven't anted up a penny for them yet, I'd say you would be pretty hard pressed to prove that I don't own–"

He interrupted, as she knew he would. "In your contract with the university it says that all related discoveries–"

She laughed; God, her day was getting better. She had come for a reward for her brother and sister, and when he'd childishly refused, she'd upped the stakes. Now she was going to walk out with a paper. "Doctor Warden, *your* contract might stipulate that, but mine doesn't. I crossed those lines out, on the advice of my brother. Harvard Law, ninety-eight."

Warden paled, and it was all she could do not to dance a little jig right there in the second floor J hall of the Reynolds building. She forced a smile and continued. "You can sign reward checks for my brother and sister, and my paper will have your name on it.

Or I'll go draft my resignation, effective immediately, and you can explain to the higher-ups why this doesn't say 'University of Tennessee' all over it."

He didn't say anything. Just turned and went back to his office.

Becky tried to keep her voice light. "I'll be back for those checks in an hour."

"But—" He didn't finish and she just smiled.

It was down the corridor, around a corner, and through another lab that her office sat. Definitely out of the way. She went in and started writing up the findings, but after starting with the date, time, and location, she realized that she couldn't do anything. Not *anything*. Not until Warden put it in writing that the paper belonged to her and anyone else who she chose to have on it.

If she used university equipment or wrote up anything, the frogs and the paper could legally become property of the UT Biodiversity office. And, since finding new and unusual species and behavior was what the Biodiversity team did, she would be hard pressed to prove it was a personal project. So, for the moment at least, her hands were tied.

The ranas stared at her from their tuppers lined up on her shelf. Three of them. All in a row, all looking right at her, their little throats bobbing as though with their breathing. One big, one little, one medium. There was nothing extraordinary about any of the three, other than the obvious extra legs.

Becky was suddenly extremely grateful to Aaron – that he had chosen law school and in his own arrogant way had decided that no man was complete without some knowledge of the law. He said she'd be thankful when she was in her first car accident or bought her first house. Neither of those things had happened yet. But she sent up a silent acknowledgement as she sat there.

She was also grateful for her own error, remembering how frustrated she had been, making an extra trip to the restaurant supply store for the lexans she had forgotten to bring home with her. It was all lining up. If she jumped ship she wouldn't regret it. And if she got fired…well, she really still wouldn't.

She filled her time reading emails and doodling, before finally gathering the lexans into her arms. The water sloshed as she walked, the frogs trying to stay motionless out of fear, but constantly having to squirm to correct their balance.

Warden looked up as she entered. "You're leaving?"

"Yes."

"I have your checks." But he didn't hand them over.

If she was fired, it would be worth it just to spend this minute watching the prick squirm.

"Do you have your resignation?" He eyed her, and leaned forward but didn't ask again.

"No. Not if I get my checks now and tomorrow morning I have it in writing that the paper is mine and mine alone." She took the checks and balanced the frogs in one arm while reaching into her pocket to pull out a sticky note. "Here's my home phone number so you can call me and tell me when it's ready." Already knowing he wouldn't take it, she stuck it on the nearest bookshelf.

Against the ropes, he nodded, swallowed a bit, then reached out. "Mind if I take a look?"

Just before his mealy hand closed on one of the tuppers, she turned away. "Yes, I do. These are still my frogs."

It was two city blocks to the parking garage then up two floors, and all the way to the back. And this was privileged parking. She was only allowed here as an employee. Students had to park even further away. Her jacket was cloying and constricting, but she wouldn't set down the frogs. They were her future right now. And something was very wrong with them.

Her folks' home was a ways out in the county, it was the only way they could have all that land. It just wasn't as far out as it had been when she was small. Several of the neighbors had parceled large properties and housing developments now stood where nearby farms and fields had been.

She followed the local school bus the last few turns to her home and met Melanie and Brandon as they leapt down to the gravel roadside. "No one believes we caught six-legged frogs!"

The wail was that of a plaintive seven-year-old who was about an inch from a seriously good pout.

But that telling everyone part made her nervous. Becky scooped up her little sister and asked Brandon to grab the tuppers out of the front seat. "Let's not tell people just yet. They'll believe you when they see your picture in the paper, even if it doesn't happen for a while."

Melanie consented, and after a slow evening her father showed up and her mother took advantage of adult company, pouring them three glasses of wine from the box in the fridge, if it could be called 'pouring'. But it wasn't bad, and partway through nursing her drink and contemplating how she had destroyed her future and was now the proud owner of forty-three frogs she couldn't investigate any further than a good once-over, Brandon called up from the basement.

"Becky, your frogs are all staring at me! They're weird!"

Her mother yelled back, but didn't move an iota. "Of course they are, they've got six legs for chrissakes!"

"Becky, can we rotate them?!" Melanie wanted to torment the frogs, and Becky wished she hadn't started those early biology lessons with her little sister. The girl was too bright – it would be great if she forgot something just once in a while.

"No!"

"But it's fun!"

In a low voice she spoke only to the table. "Can't argue that." The frogs had a lot of built in responses. When put on their back they would flip upright and get ready to jump. If you rotated the ground beneath them, they would turn to stay oriented to the original direction. And it was all reflex. The frogs would do this in the lab even if they were decapitated. Of course that response only lasted a few seconds before the dead frogs would jello-out and lose all muscle tone.

But it was enough to make the squeamish lab students jump and scream, and the more sturdy-hearted spend good lab time just rotating the dissection trays watching the beheaded frogs reorient one way then the other. In a few live frogs the responses could entertain a couple of elementary school kids for hours. For the frogs' sakes, Becky regretted showing it to her little siblings.

It was quiet for a few minutes. Well, maybe more than a few minutes, her wine glass was empty. They all turned at the sound of footsteps on the stairs. Brandon and Melanie emerged on the landing, arms full of little clear lexans.

"Becky, they keep orienting themselves." Melanie put one tupper on the table with a small *thunk*. "Look." She turned the tupper, and sure enough the little rana moved his front legs hand over hand and shuffled his back feet as the container moved, constantly keeping his nose pointed in the original direction.

"Melanie, I told you not to rotate them." Looking to her parents for backing, Becky sighed.

Before her folks could put in their two cents, Melanie continued with her mini-lecture on the orienting process of frogs. She picked up the lexan and softly but quickly shifted it onto its side, leaving the inhabitant on his back. She put it on the table again, and up the little guy went, onto all six legs, squat and ready.

"That's exactly what they're supposed to do. So stop tormenting my frogs." And to think she had spent this morning arguing for bonuses for the little Dr. Moreaus.

Melanie ignored her. "Now the four-legger." She scooted over the container marked with the normal masking tape from its spot at the end of the table. Now center stage, the little rana performed, hand over hand, back legs shuffling, while Melanie rotated the container. Then she flipped him onto his back and set the tupper upright in line with the three six-leggers.

And Becky saw it.

What Melanie and Brandon had seen. She barely paid attention to the little guy as he flipped himself up off his back and into 'ready' stance. It wasn't what he did. It was what he *didn't* do.

The difference was obvious. This time Becky grabbed one of the downstream frogs, flipping her softly onto her back, and as the little rana struggled briefly then expertly flipped herself upright, even Mr. and Mrs. Sorenson were getting onto their feet.

Her Dad spoke first. "Are they supposed to do that?"

"No, Dad, this is definitely new."

When the four-legger hopped up, he faced whichever direction was easiest. No matter what she did, each time the six-leggers came to a stop, they faced the same way they had previously. All three of them, always the same direction, all the time.

Without speaking, each family member grabbed one lexan and separated them to different rooms, hollering out. "Same way!" "Toward the bed!" "Facing the sink." It didn't matter though. All the phrases meant the same thing.

She left the tuppers on the floor while scrambling down the stairs, her family close on her heels. With breath held tight, Becky flipped the light switch. All the little six-leggers were staring straight at her – oriented the same direction as the ones upstairs. Her voice was weaker than she meant it to be. "What direction are they facing, Daddy?"

"Northwest, looks like."

Greer walked into the lab like he owned the place. Which was silly, David thought, because *he* did. "Hey, pretty boy, what's up with your stones? Tell me something interesting, because I'm footing a helluva bill for that shut-down day."

"It's good." It was better than good, but David went back to perusing his pieces. He didn't even bother to correct Greer about the 'stones'. It was just said to annoy him anyway.

"Dude, you've got to give me more than that."

David didn't even look up. And that was the wonder of Greer. He always meant what he said, just as he said it. You never needed to see his face. "All right, you are on par with Hell Creek."

"*Excellent.*"

Yup, he didn't need to see Greer's eyes to know that the sarcasm flowed in rivers.

"Now how about something I can use?" His friend prodded. "I want information that I'll find worthy of shutting down my dig for a full day, and I want it in complete sentences."

He looked up, gauging what to give away and what to keep. "Well, you've got the iridium layer at the KT boundary, just like you were hoping. Only here, it's better than Hell Creek because you've got a rapid lay down. Which gives you as close to full-on proof as you'll ever get that the dust cover directly coincides with the dino die-out. It's real thick at the KT, tapering off over the next several hundred years. No glass or ash content that the lab can discern–"

"You just said 'the lab', that means you didn't do my analysis yourself."

Shit. Explain, explain. David took a steadying breath. "Well, I couldn't get it done in the time frame you wanted. The lab here did it and I oversaw it. It's good work."

Greer nodded slowly. "Our agreement was that *you* do the testing, but you farmed it out. So tell me what was so hellfire important that you shut down my dig and then blew me off for it?"

This time David looked up. "You don't tell anyone."

"Fine, but you tell me."

Making his way into his office, he closed the doors behind Greer.

"Your dig is a hotspot. A magnetic jump point."

Greer raised his eyebrows, "Do go on."

"Every so often, a long time, even by geological standards, the earth's poles shift…swap places. It happens that certain spots shift first. Then, the theory is that when a critical mass of hotspots, or altered areas, is hit, the poles snap. Bam! And it's all over. North is south, south is north and all that, magnetically speaking. But no one's seen a magnetic hotspot on the KT before. It might explain the slight discrepancies in die-out times better than the asteroid theory alone."

"And you weren't going to share your *dinosaur theory* with me?" Greer leaned forward on the desk, eyes blazing, and David wasn't quite sure how to fill in the empty logic hole he had left. He was going to share, just not now.

"Listen, Greer, I'm still not positive. These rocks are good for it, but I need to get more. You know, most geologists never see a hotspot like this. My Dad was one of the few who did. I always look for it—"

"Jeez, Carter, that chip on your shoulder must've been what stunted your growth."

"Thanks, fuckhole."

Greer smiled, "You're welcome." It would have sounded very genuine if not taken in the context of following the word *fuckhole*. "What are you going to do when the old man kicks off?"

He shrugged; it had been a question that plagued him for many years. "Same as I've been doing. Sit around, live off my Dad's money and his name."

"Dude, I'm going to let you in on something, because I think I'm the only person who likes you enough to tell you." Greer shook his head, but David knew that last part was true. "You are the only one who thinks you're getting by on your Dad's name."

"Yes, but you don't have all the facts. My Dad bought my way into Princeton when my grades weren't good enough."

"Oh, so sad, and boo hoo, and suck me. You've proven your worth on your own since then." Greer sighed, and that meant that the conversation was finished. "So when are you going to get positive about this theory and let me in on it?"

"I have to go to the Appalachians next."

"Pray tell, why?"

"Because, I was scrounging old files, looking, and three years ago there was a KT dig there – just outside a nowhere town called McCann. Wharton took his top dogs and then got furious when they got back because the specimens were all mislabeled. He even dismissed three of his graduate students over it. But, I'm guessing now that it might have been another hotspot. And that, my friend, would make a great paper."

"Who are you taking on this secret dig?" Greer's arms were crossed over his chest.

"I don't know. I only just started thinking about going back to check it out this morning. Those are the specimens I was looking over out there. By the way, they have the same iridium strata as your Warren Fault pieces. –Hey, do you want to go to Tennessee with me?"

There were three slow blinks of his eyes. "I'm a black man. Why in the hell would I want to go to Tennessee?"

"Greer, this is the new millennium. No one's going to make you jump down, turn around, and pick a bale of cotton. I'm pretty sure they've gotten rid of that 'separate but equal' stuff, too."

This time the eyes blinked once.

David smiled, "What you really have to be afraid of are the cabbages."

"I need to fear leafy greens now?"

David shook his head. "It's the name for the inbred, back-woods folks. They were called cabbages because the inbreeding led to large heads and equivalent mental capabilities." The more he tried to convince Greer to come the more he realized that Greer was ideal for the spot. "Come on. They found bones…" He trailed off, using something Greer would enjoy as bait.

But Greer sighed. He was a smart fish, and he recognized that the worm had a hook jabbed in its back. "Haven't your paleo guys checked it out yet?"

"Nope, there are just bits and pieces, and because they thought all the specimens were mislabeled, when they got back Wharton was furious and just threw everything into storage, calling the dig a complete waste."

"What kind of bones are they?"

That question began to make David hopeful. "I don't know, I'm not a paleontologist. But you're welcome to look them over, they're sitting right out there on the lab table." He stood and opened the door letting Greer out into the main lab again.

They didn't speak. Working side by side, they shuffled around the lab, getting a book or a test kit here or there. After a deep intake of breath Greer uttered the first words in two hours. "Damn, this could be crap or it could be a goldmine."

Carter just nodded. He'd had the exact same thought.

"All right, answer me honestly." Greer squared up to David, a good nine inches taller and with all the dignity David felt lacking in his own moral fiber. "Is there a chance that these are just mislabeled specimens? That the students didn't know what they were doing and none of this info is correct?"

David shrugged. "I wasn't on the dig. I didn't know any of the students other than a few faces I saw in class as undergrads. I'd have to say that there's a possibility it's not even KT. But it appears that *all* the specimens are mislabeled. I have to go check it out."

Greer nodded slowly then pulled out his palm pilot. "How long do we need?"

"Two to four weeks. No telling 'til we get there." Carter went back into the lab for his own schedule, cool as a cucumber, but inside wildly excited that it was Greer going with him. No one knew his shit like Greer. "The major work is already done. But the site's three years old. It'll take some reworking and we won't have any students."

David looked for a reasonable chunk of time when he could go. Most of these digs were planned months in advance. "If we just need to confirm what we have, it'll be short, but if we find new pieces, we'll be longer, you know how it is."

"When?"

"A.S.A.P."

"Then I have to head home now. Explain all this to my ever-so-understanding wife. Find a way to make it up to her. Then I can leave two Mondays from now." His head was bent low over the palm pilot and he tapped at it rapidly with the little stylus. "But I have to be back at my place one month later."

David picked up his red marker and drew a line through the dates Greer mentioned, noting that he had drawn through two staff meetings and a dinner with the head of the department, and all sorts of other stuff that would have to be moved. "Looks great."

"Are you expecting U Wisconsin to kick in funding?"

David shook his head. "This is a private venture. It's the only way I know to not have to write a paper explaining my suspicions and then wait an eon while they decide to give it back to Wharton who fucked it up in the first place."

"Daddy?" It didn't sound as snotty as it could have. It was from Greer and there was no malice behind it.

But David shook his head again. "Nope." He took a deep breath. "I'm touching my trust fund for this one."

"Really?" Greer's eyebrows rose. "Then I'll fly in baggage and try not to eat."

"Nah, we're going nice all the way. Once I touch it, it's touched. It's about the principle, not the amount. But this will be worth it."

Jordan let the water sluice down over him. He had been right, which usually made him pretty happy. Except when his prediction had been a solid ass-whupping. When he had gotten to town, even before he had unpacked, he had driven in ever-widening circles from his new place, looking for a gym.

The first evening after joining, he'd met Martin. So they had signed up for racquetball together, and every Wednesday, except when he'd been in Florida, they had played. Jordan had come close quite a few times, but he had beaten Martin only once. The workout was good and the challenge and standing date was better.

If he was ever going to be in good shape and have a healthy sex life it would be now. He had avoided relationships through med school, focusing on his studies and what few one-night-stands he could manage. It worked well and didn't distract much, but didn't keep the johnson as happy as he'd have liked.

He cranked the water hotter, something he hadn't done before receiving his gas bill just yesterday. He could afford it. And today he had earned it. God, he ached. So he stood there, hands flat on the slick tile, one leg straight, the other bent in calf stretches. After a few seconds he switched legs.

His mind wandered to Jillian in her tub, surrounded by white bubbles. He'd seen her place. Her tub probably had the same yellowing tiles with cracked caulking that his did. But in his imagination it was a pristine white claw foot.

It got bigger. Room for two. He added Marla from UCLA. One of the other med students. Two years older than him and hotter than hell. She hadn't had time for any of them, as she was hell-bent on a surgeon out of residency and with his loans already paid off. But she was in Jordan's tub right now in his head. With Jillian nonetheless.

By the time the shower water turned colder, the tub was a hot tub. And included his high school crush, but with bigger boobs, Angelina Jolie, and Marcy, the tech from earlier today. All kissing each other. And…

Shit.

He had to face two of these women tomorrow. The water was cold and he thought that the phone was ringing anyway. So he cranked the faucet off and grabbed for one of the two towels he owned. Wrapping it around him as he ran, he dove to catch the phone before the machine picked up. He didn't get to look at the caller ID even, "Hello?"

"Jordan."

It was his Dad. And that in itself was odd. They weren't estranged, just not close. If it wasn't a holiday, they didn't talk. So instantly he was alert for problems. "Hey, Dad, is something going on?"

"Yeah," It was a sigh, low and long, like when his dad talked about Mom. "Eddie died."

"Oh, no." The weight in his chest took him by surprise. He and Eddie had rarely seen each other since they were children, and Eddie had always seemed ill at ease after Jordan had gone off to pursue medicine and Eddie had left high school early to go into construction. In the ten years since he'd been out, Eddie had made a name in Lake James, built himself a nice house, married a cute girl and had a daughter. Then got leukemia. "I thought he was in remission."

"Well, they thought he was better, that he was going to make it. He put the weight back on. Grew some hair, was fine. ...we thought."

Jordan wracked his brains. He couldn't talk medicine with his Dad, but he had with Eddie. They had finally seemed to be on more even footing, and Eddie now spoke some med-lingo from his time in the 'slammer,' as he referred to the hospital. He had seemed fine at the family Fourth of July picnic, only a few months ago. "So, do you know what happened?"

"Don't think anyone really does. He got some stomach flu. Next thing you know he's in a coma and then this morning he died."

That didn't sound like anything Jordan had ever heard of. He wanted to drill his Dad. Get answers. Because that sure didn't make a shitlick of sense.

"Funeral's Friday. You should be here."

"I will. I'll be there sometime tomorrow. I'll call and let you know when I get in."

And that was the end of the conversation. He stood with the cordless phone loose in his hand, shoulders slumped, one hand running down his wet face.

In a few moments he was on the line with Jillian, briefly wondering if she was also wrapped in a towel, bothered mid-bubble bath by his call. But the thought was momentary at most. Her sympathies were heartfelt and he was told in no uncertain terms to leave for the funeral right away, she'd be fine inspecting the latest staph infection by herself. She even offered to drive him to the airport. He almost told her 'no', then thought better of it. Between low level pay, student loans, and now a last minute plane ticket, he could use the savings from not parking.

Next he called Landerly and left a message. Then hopped online, and even called the airline, getting all the requirements for the grievance discount. Thank god for credit cards. Lord knew, none of it was in his account right now.

Becky protested. "You're trying to distract me from my frogs." She sounded like a petulant teenager and she knew it. But that was the politics of the professional academic world. Gain your footing and hold on for all you're worth.

"Rebecca, what, really, have you found out about those frogs?"

"Nothing unusual–"

"Exactly. So I don't understand why you are so determined to miss out on this great opportunity." Warden sat back in his chair. If he was the villain in a film, he would look just like this. Only creepy music would be playing in full digital surround sound.

She hadn't told any of them about the directionality of the frogs. Probably because she couldn't explain it. And she didn't want anyone else explaining it before she found a suitable solution. Not that she had found even an unsuitable solution in the last week. Her mouth opened, but there wasn't anything to come out. She closed it again. Biodiversity was her job. She traveled all the time to collect and study animals. She would pack all her frogs home first. They would be in better hands with Brandon and Melanie, even if they would be slightly tormented.

"All right. Where are these birds, and why do I need to see them?"

"I knew you would realize that this is the right thing, Rebecca."

That's Doctor Sorenson to you was the first thought that entered her head. He called her by her birth name, Rebecca. Which she thought sounded far too mature for herself, yet he treated her like a child. An idiot child at that. The second thought that went through her head was, *Bite my ass.*

"It seems there's a flock of warblers in Dalton, Georgia."

She waited the briefest of moments. "This is an odd time of year for them. Did they just never leave? They should be in Canada."

"They did leave. But the local birdwatchers say they're back, *and* they're nesting."

"Nesting?" This was maybe as interesting as the frogs. "All right. I'm hooked. What do I do?"

"When can you go?" His fingers still steepled in front of him. His hair was still on the greasy side and she still trusted him about as far as she could throw him.

"Tomorrow."

"You'll drive down, make a preliminary assessment and let us know if we need to assemble an ornithology team, or if there's a fluke or an obvious issue." He handed her a three by five lined card. The cheapest paper for making small notes on, by his own statements. "Call this man at this number when you get in; he'll be more than happy to show you the birds and their newly chosen habitat." Warden dismissed her with a disdainful wave of his hand and gave her his back even before she could have possibly started out the door. But that was okay, his front wasn't his best side.

Chapter 3

Jordan looked around the living room. It was cozy and warm, and the deep-toned plaid couch screamed everything but 'Eddie' to him. Kelly must have done all the decorating.

The room was a definite step up from his own place. One, that it was in a house, on a lot with a yard and a swing set even. Two, the carpet was lacking in the stains his had come with. Three, the kitchen was fully functional.

He'd never been here before. After all the time he and Eddie had spent blowing things up together as kids, somehow he had never seen the house his cousin had built with his own hands and his own construction crew. It seemed a shame to see it only now that Eddie was getting buried.

Kelly sat on the couch, taking all of it much better than Jordan had expected. So when Aunt Agnes left her alone, he tried to casually saunter over with his soda in hand and position himself next to Kelly.

"How are you holding up?" It was her voice asking him that question before he could ask it of her.

"I'm all in one piece." And before he could ask anything, she started in.

"Eddie was always telling me stories about the two of you and the M-eighties, or the illegal fireworks. Were they true? Could he have really walked into your medical school and convinced them that you had a sordid past and shouldn't have been admitted?"

Jordan laughed. He hadn't expected laughter and not from Eddie's widow. "Yes, it's all true." And Jordan tried to use his opening. He had to know. "What happened? I thought he was in remission."

"He just caught this stomach flu. It got worse and worse. The E.R. and his regular doctor told us that it would pass. Then he passed out, and by the time they admitted him he was in a coma." She took a sip of the gin and tonic that she was holding in both hands, unaware that it had sweated a ring onto her linen skirt. Jordan waited, seeing that she was just steeling herself for something important. "Before…with the leukemia…he had made me promise to pull the plug. But I couldn't. I couldn't do it. I just knew he'd come back around. But three days later he flatlined and there wasn't anything they could do. He was gone."

For a moment, her hand shook, rattling the small cubes of ice exposed above the level of liquid in her glass. But then it stilled.

"Kelly, I don't get it. That doesn't sound like Leukemia at all. And I never heard of a stomach flu that put anyone in a coma. How was his white count?" He had leaned forward, elbows on knees, soda clenched in both hands.

This time when she looked at him her eyes saw his face, but no further. "Jordan, what are you doing?"

"I just want to find out what happened." He reached for her arm, but she was already jerking it back out of his way, standing in one fluid motion, her hands raising.

"Why!?" Her voice was as loud as it was high pitched. "Why! What can you do? He's gone. Just when I was getting comfortable with the thought that I might get the forever I signed on for. In five days he went from healthy to dead."

Jordan opened his mouth to apologize, but she didn't let him.

"Can you bring him back? I know that he's dead. But stop asking me these goddamn questions. I don't know what his blood count was. I just want him back." She dropped the glass then. It fell in almost slow motion, and even as he was aware of everyone in the room staring at him like the leper he was, he reached for Kelly and set her back on the couch to keeping her from falling. "I'm sorry. I'm sorry." She was in tears now, full streaming tears, the fallen glass unnoticed.

Even if everyone else hated him, Kelly didn't seem to. Although he would have understood. He shouldn't have pushed her like that. With a great sigh, Aunt Agnes picked up the glass, luckily still in one piece, and sent her husband, Bill, running for paper towels. Kelly stayed there, crying into his shoulder, while slowly, everyone around him went back to their business.

He had forgotten the cardinal rule – that these were people. He could always remember that when it was strangers. But with his own family he pushed. And he shouldn't.

And he had ruined it. As much as he regretted hurting Kelly, and pushing her past whatever safety barrier she had found, he more regretted that he wasn't going to get his information that he wanted.

They were all still looking at him. Why had he done it? He could answer but they wouldn't like it. They were all blue collar by choice, and he had gone out and paid through the nose to educate himself, to do what he wanted. But he had learned a whole new language, and they didn't speak it. Jordan didn't fit. And he'd upset one of the people who did. One at the center of the circle.

He rode home with his Dad in silence. Anyone else would think his father was carefully schooled and stoic in his lack of expression these past few days. But Jordan knew better. Dad simply hadn't had it in him since his Mom had died.

He was in his old easy chair within moments tonight. There was no reproach for Jordan's behavior, as he might have gotten when his mother was alive. Even though he knew his Dad didn't approve, he didn't hear about it. "'Night, Dad."

His father didn't answer. Just a quick look in his direction and a nod let him know he had even been heard.

Jordan lay on the bed, his hands laced behind his head as he stared at the ceiling. His thoughts turned to Jillian briefly, wondering if her day at Grady Hospital had been horrifyingly long. But he realized that she had probably done just fine without him. A small smile played across his lips before it was erased by his medical mind.

Eddie had died of the stomach flu and a coma. And none of it added up. If anyone here would know that something was off with Eddie's death, it was Jordan. But no one was listening.

Kelly's words haunted him.

Why! What can you do?

In five days he went from healthy to dead.

He couldn't bring Eddie back. He just wanted to understand. But there wasn't even an autopsy. Not for a man who had leukemia for five years.

His lids slowly gained the weight of sleep, and within moments the glare of bright light. He blinked against the harsh sun through the windows he hadn't bothered to close, because he hadn't believed that sleep was coming. He was still in his slacks, his shirt, and his tie. All of it formerly pressed and Sunday best.

He had the whole day to contemplate his horrible behavior from the evening before. The idea that God was punishing him for it began with the taste of old gym towels in his mouth.

With only a few blinks in a lazy attempt to clear his head, he pushed his way off the bed and into the bathroom. Relief surged at the flavor of mint replacing the gumminess of sleep. Jordan reached into the stall and flicked the shower on, the sense memory of where exactly to turn the dial remained even in this blurry state. Within a minute the water was a decent temperature, and he had yanked his tie loose and proceeded to strip. He almost fell back asleep standing there naked under the ancient showerhead.

By the time Jordan was downstairs, his Dad stood at the stove, his one concession to real-life cooking was the electric griddle that was perpetually on the counter top. The smell of Bisquick pancakes brought Jordan back to every other weekend he and his Dad had spent since his mother had died. He sat down with no conversation and ate until he was near bursting. Wondering all the while, as he always did, if his father made the pancakes even on weekends when he wasn't home. He'd never had the heart to ask.

Just as Jordan set down his fork, the phone rang. His father motioned with the spatula that Jordan was to answer it. In China, children cared for their parents unto old age. In Lake James, Jordan saved his Dad the social effort involved in answering the phone. "Hello?"

"Jordan?" The voice was soft and sweet and he couldn't quite place it. "It's me, Kelly."

"Oh, hi–"

"I wanted to apologize for my behavior yesterday. We all need to make sense of it in our own way." He could hear her breath across the line in the sharp inhale she needed before she continued. "You need to know. I don't want to. I don't care what you find out, but I signed a release to the hospital and told them you were with the Centers for Disease Control and Prevention and that you needed them to cooperate."

"Kelly..."

"No, It's okay. If it had been you, Eddie would have found the answers leveling a field with a caterpillar and a backhoe. This is how you find yours. I'm just sorry I wasn't more under-standing yesterday."

"Kelly." He took a deep breath. "Thank you, and I'm sorry I upset you. I just..."

"It's okay. Don't worry."

"Listen Kelly, I wanted to tell you that Eddie once told me that he was the luckiest guy alive to have you."

"Liar."

"No he did. He then told me what a pansy-ass I was with my nose in books all the time."

He heard her sniff even as she laughed. "Thank you… have a good flight home tonight Jordan."

Great, he had made her cry. Yet, she had given him access to Eddie's medical records. He wanted to jump up and down and cheer. He hated himself for it. But he had nine hours at the hospital until he had to leave for his flight.

Becky wasted little time unpacking her duffle bag and simply splashed some water on her face. The hotel was covered by the Amateur Birdwatchers; it was far nicer than anything Warden would have approved of her staying in.

She pocketed her room card and slipped her purse over her shoulder. Making certain that her door locked behind her, she found her way back to the elevators and wondered what she was getting herself into. She spotted Marshall Harfield easily, mainly because he was the only person actually sitting and waiting in the lobby. He had told her that he had dark hair and dark eyes, and that he would be wearing a blue ABA jacket. What he had neglected to tell her was that the dark hair was thinning and the ABA jacket was bright enough to scare away all kinds of wildlife and that it was struggling to stay closed around the wide girth of his belly.

He neglected to tell her that he was nervous and that he would startle when she approached him. Wiping his hand on his pants, he held it out while he greeted her. But she couldn't very well refuse to shake his hand. He led her out to his car, plastered with ABA and various other bird bumper stickers. Some even thought they were funny.

As they left the parking lot, he began a stream of nervous chatter. Becky, of course, listened with half her thoughts to Marshall, and the other half wondering what she'd gotten herself into. Her heart leapt when he reached into the backseat, but all he produced was a series of marked volumes on the Georgia Spotted Warbler.

Within moments, he had her flipping pages, finding out details and seeing that everyone who had ever printed anything about the Georgia Spotted Warbler agreed that they were only Georgian during the winter months. If it was true, then these birds were way out of sync. And Marshall Harfield had found his groove and a warm smile that he shared with anyone who could get excited over an unremarkable brown bird.

Her whole attention was turned to him as he continued, and she didn't even notice the drive. They were pulling up to a farm-house outside Dalton and four people were standing in the middle of the front lawn, their bright blue ABA jackets giving them away. They all but pulled Becky from the car and smiled and shook her hand in turn as Marshall introduced *Dr. Rebecca Sorenson* around to the lot of them. They were polite enough to make it through introductions, then they were all speaking on top of each other.

She posed the question to the group in general as she was getting the hang of understanding them. "So last year the birds flew in the proper pattern, and they left last spring at the appro-priate time…but now they're here way too early."

"Yes."

"No."

"Not exactly."

Becky decided to go with the kid, Weston, who had said 'not exactly'. "Explain please."

"This is the nesting ground for this flock – every year they're here in Mrs. Chesterfield's orchard. Well, last year they didn't arrive on time. And two weeks later we found them while we were out looking for spotted woodpeckers over at the Dalton Arboretum. They were there, the warblers, and they were nesting. So we thought that was weird–"

Becky's brows knit with questions. "How do you know it's the same flock?"

Anne, the older woman, spoke up this time. "I've been watching this flock for years. The birds come and go, but there's a consistency. You'll see the same birds for quite a few years. We named the ones we can positively I.D. There's Marsha, Jan, Cindy, Greg, Bobby, and Alice. Sam, Peter, and Tiger didn't come back this year."

Clearly no one else in the group thought anything of the names that Anne was rattling off. Marshall smiled again, his big beaming smile. "That's why we called the Biodiversity lab. Last year our birds were a bit off. But this is way out of our league." He grabbed her by the arm, but by now she took it as a good sign, "Do you want to go see them?"

She nodded, and Weston rummaged through his backpack to come up with a bright blue ABA hat, which he held out to her. "I thought you might like a hat. We have Lyme ticks."

"Thank you, Weston." Before she knew it, she was in the back woods of Georgia, in eighty-five degree heat, and eighty-five percent humidity, trailing a team of birdwatchers. They laughed, and she didn't even ask as they pointed out Boss Hog and Roscoe, two woodpeckers who were squabbling over a nearby tree.

It was two a.m. when Jillian spotted Jordan at the airport curb. He stood with one bag over his shoulder and a carry-on just clinging to the tips of his fingers, looking much worse for the wear than she was.

Pulling up, she spilled out of the car, her arms offering up a hug, and immediately she saw the awkwardness of the move, but it was too late to stop herself. He was a co-worker, and not family. Even if she was here in the middle of the night.

Jordan was startled by the move, but he hugged her back, maybe even just a moment too long, clearly out of it, and she wouldn't have been surprised if he passed out right there in the pick-up lane. But he simply threw his bag into the backseat and slid, bone weary, into the passenger side. "Thank you…"

If he was going to say something else, it was lost in the moments between starting the car and her intense scrutiny of the few other vehicles in the pick-up lane while she tried to find her way back to the freeway. From the expression on his face and the way he hid it behind spread fingers, his cousin's death had been hard on him.

When he finally looked up, she handed him the extra soft drink she had gotten for him. "I don't know if you want this, maybe you just need to go home and pass out, but I was getting one anyway."

"No. I'm starving, actually. Thank you." He sighed, sucked down a good portion of the soda, and two seconds later started talking again. "I can order a pizza right now, right? Will you come up and share it with me? I need your help."

That pulled her brows together. He was tired and not in there. And he wanted her to come up for pizza in the middle of the night? But again she didn't get to say anything.

"Eddie had leukemia. But he died of a stomach flu that put him in a coma." Frustration carried bell-clear in the soft deep timbre of his voice.

"What? I don't know of any stomach flu that does that." She pulled up to the curb in front of his building.

"Exactly." He popped open the car door and retrieved his bag. "I alienated my family asking questions. All they know is that he's gone. His wife is right, I can't bring him back. But I can't answer any of the questions either…. And you probably really want to go home and get some sleep."

"Actually, I'm wide awake now. Buy me a pizza and tell me all about it." She closed her car door and turned the key, managing only a small wince in the still city night air as the horn beeped that the alarm was engaged.

In the elevator he rummaged through his carry-on bag, producing a heavy folder that looked at once brand-new and well-worn. Jillian took it from him, while he entered his unit and went around the small living/dining area, opening windows, and turning on lights and the fan. The first slight breeze hit her face and it occurred to her that it was stuffy in here, even for the middle of the night. She turned the file over. "This says the file was released to Dr. Jordan Abellard of the CDCP.... Did you use the CDC to get this?"

He shook his head. "I went in with Kelly's release form, she had put CDCP on it. I had my badge and they never questioned it."

"That's not really—"

"I know," He put his hands up in the air. "What do you want me to do? I never said anything, they assumed. And I had the complete file in my hands in under twenty minutes."

Jillian couldn't smother her smile. "I'm fine with that; I was just curious if you knew that it was against policy."

His stance relaxed. "So what do you like on your pizza?"

"Canadian bacon and pineapple—"

His face immediately told her that he didn't feel the same way about toppings.

So she continued. "But I'll eat pepperoni, or sausage, or olives, or peppers."

He paced while he was on hold and she thumbed through the huge file; it would take hours just to see what was in there, but it wasn't like she had a busy social life demanding her time. After a few minutes she had found nothing unusual and Jordan was ordering. A few phrases broke through while she was reading. "...two-liter coke...large pizza...half Canadian-bacon and pineapple the other half..."

She smiled. By the time he was sitting next to her at the old coffee table, she had made a once over. "It looks normal – for a leukemia patient – up until that last stomach flu. So fill me in on the rest."

"You got the basics from the file. There were a few scares, but he kept pulling through. He was in remission since this time last year." Jordan shoved his fingers through his hair. "It was the longest remission he had maintained over the five year course of the disease. His white count was normal up until the end. It was fine when he was brought in. It sounded like flu, but everything sounds like flu."

Her heart ached for him. It wasn't just a medical mystery he was trying to solve. Jillian couldn't remember him ever mentioning his cousin, but clearly Eddie's death had shaken him up. "You know, there may not be an answer."

"I know. It's just so odd. If it's a disease that took advantage of his weak immune system...I work for a company that has the foremost technology to prevent these kinds of things from happening." He shrugged.

Jillian began dismantling the large folder into sections by visit and series. She handed one chunk back to Jordan. "Tell me about him."

He shook his head. "Twenty-nine year old, Caucasian male, mild smoker, mild drinker–"

She cut him off. "No, really tell me. Where did he live? What is his place like? His family?"

Two hours later, she was exhausted.

Jordan probably would have been asleep except that he was pacing tracks into the carpet. "What do I do, Jilly?"

"Let's sleep now, and at noon, when we get in, we take it to Landerly."

David pushed his hair back off his face. In the wet wool of the thick air it clung like spider webs, giving him willies as he imagined the one thing he was really afraid of.

Greer laughed at him, his usual low chuckle when David's harsh personality amused him.

"What are you laughing at? You're okay because your people are from here, you darkie!"

"Dude, you are way messed up. My people are from Africa. Trust me, we aren't built for this kind of humidity." Greer never stopped his careful chipping at the rock beneath him.

"At least your hair sticks up and out of the way."

"Yup. Which is the reason my race is superior and yours felt the need to better yourselves by enslaving us."

David also never took his eyes off the ground layer beneath them. There was no good comeback, and so he avoided one all together, the conversation trickling off to nothing while they worked.

There was water making constant background static nearby, and a damned obnoxious bird that had a call that just never quit. God had been laughing when he put the lungs on that thing. Just as soon as it shut up another one would answer it.

Evidence of deer had been all over the first few days, and it had taken nearly a week to push back what time and the East Tennessee climate had done to the abandoned site.

It was slow going in the back woods, with the rustles of forest and the slope of the Appalachians beneath them. The only sound that broke the peace was the two men calling each other names and the high 'ching' of the tiny picks striking rock. Neither of them had the easy swing of a student, so the calls of the birds were periodically interrupted by the sharp screech of metal glancing off rock followed by a colorful string of swear words. Then, after a brief pause, nature would resume its noise, hiding their presence here from the cities and homes not that far away.

"Greer, this one's for you." Carter brushed off his knees, and stood, not cursing out loud this time. The pain in his joints that told of age was not anything he wished to acknowledge to the world.

"What is it?"

"Fuck if I know. It's a bone, maybe it's a damn trilobite. If you're lucky, it's one of your lizards."

He heard the edge in David's voice. "Dinosaurs aren't lizards. You know it, I've told you that."

"Ah." David stood and stretched his hands over his head, taking in the thick mass of tall trees and virtually untouched wilderness that enclosed them. "That would imply that I listen to you."

He tried not to let his legs give him away as he moved to a new spot that had looked interesting. But, even from where he was bent over his dig, Greer saw it. "Well listen to this, my honky friend: I'm bigger than you, and stronger than you, and–" he pointed his pick at David's knees, "not nearly as arthritic as you. So don't call my dinos lizards. It's insulting."

"Hey Greer, you do know that all your dinos died, right? That means that you're studying an animal that is gone, gone, gone, and won't ever come back. You have a totally useless profession."

Greer snorted. "Dude, you think the limestone you hold is going to reveal anything other than what happened a zillion years ago?"

David held up one chunk that he had extracted, and smiled. "This baby can tell the future."

"Well, you just tell me what your Magic Eight Ball there says."

"We're headed for another polarity shift." David smiled. There. He'd said it, out loud, even if it was only to Greer.

But Greer snorted again. "Yeah, in another million years." He pushed himself to his feet and dusted off. "Be sure to let me know how that pans out for you."

David started carefully picking his way through the grid lines. "Just go play with your petrified lizard."

But Greer was already standing over it looking down, trying to figure what the piece that David's pick had revealed might be. He turned his head one way then another, before sliding the instrument into the hammer-loop of his carpenter jeans and pulling out a smaller, lighter one from a deep pocket somewhere. His voice was no longer the one that insulted David, but a little more thoughtful. "There's a good chance this dig will help us solidify the dinosaur-therapsid link."

"Us? *I* don't need a link."

"Us paleontologists." Greer knelt down and spoke to the small whitish smooth piece buried within the packed limestone, "Come to Papa." He took a few small swings at the peripheries before speaking to David. "Actually, you do need a dino-therapsid link. The therapsids were dinosaur-like pre-mammals and warm-blooded to boot. Which means they are absolutely pertinent to you, Mr. Mammal."

"Like I care about the distinction between dinos and lizards and theradons–"

"Therapsids."

"Exactly, *I don't care*. My kind survived. Me and my mammal friends."

David could see the edges of Greer's smile even though he was bent over, softly chipping at the rock. "Come to think, I'm not so sure that you are a mammal. Mammals are warm-blooded."

"Ohhhhhh." David drolled out the monotone. "That was low, Greer." Then he smiled. "Congratulations, I didn't think you had it in you. I thought maybe 'honky' was the best you could do."

"At least I don't have to carry limestone in my pockets. Seems to me that's the only rocks swinging in your pants."

David turned to look at his friend, but Greer was on his hands and knees, and all he could see was an eyeful of upturned ass. So he looked away. "You're sooo funny."

But Greer didn't seem to hear him. At least, he didn't respond. So, bending over, David went back to reading the tags hanging off the intersecting lines in the grid he and Greer had painstakingly mapped. They had tried to match it to the original site that Wharton had laid out, and they'd gotten damned close as best as they could tell.

He turned to find the specimens that matched this location and came back with a few zipper baggies heavy in his hands. Wharton would kill if he knew that Carter was at this site. More specifically, he would kill David. And bring shame upon his father. Ah, well. Wharton could go to hell. He was the one who had missed the geologic hotspot here. More the fool he.

Turning the baggies over in his hands, David read the markings through the clear plastic. The KT boundary here was much closer to the surface, much of geological evidence of the past washed away by wind and time. The Appalachians were much older than the Rockies, the fault lines here all but inactive, and so they had been worn smooth and low, exposing things to the surface, or hiding them just barely underneath. For him and Greer to come and pick at.

"Sweet!" The exclamation came from the spot he had abandoned to Greer moments before. "This was worth leaving my pregnant wife at home."

"That ain't saying much." Carter could hear the drawl developing in his voice, not that they spoke to much of anyone around here. But like the humidity, the accents were so thick in this part of the state that you couldn't help but absorb it. Like some communicable disease. "What'd you find? Petrified turd?"

"Dude, you have no sense at all. It's an egg, maybe a whole nest, so back off." The steady sound of the light pick striking stone picked up again as Greer tried to unearth his find.

For the briefest of moments David wished for a team, where he and Greer could lead like they usually did, and have other people do the labor, the intensive and time-consuming picking and brushing and getting things out. But then he remembered why they were here alone; they had to be.

Another baggie with another set of markings was telling the same story. The polarity here was reversed. This specimen from just at the KT boundary had a clear magnetic direction. But when it was lined up with the site, north was south and south was north. Wharton had fucked up. And David was more than certain that he had dug up another hotspot. He tried to keep his breathing regular even as he felt his stomach roll over.

Greer let up a cheer as he unearthed something that would interest only him, so David just pressed his hand to his middle hoping to quell the churning there and did his best to ignore all of it. Damned birds started up again, and to add insult to injury a woodpecker started in on a nearby tree. He was only familiar with the Woody Woodpecker variety. So with a great sigh of misery, David lifted his head to see if he could see the thing. Sure enough it was racking its head at jackhammer speed against a trunk, but luckily no obnoxious laughter emerged.

At this point the Deep South was so disturbing to him that he wouldn't have been surprised if Injuns had popped out from behind the tall oaks, wearing feathers in their hair and looking for scalps. Or maybe the deer could just come out and do a tap dance.

He had his hotspot, he knew it. Soon he'd be able to leave the land that time forgot. He just needed to unearth enough evidence so that there could be no argument. If Greer found a tie between the hotspots and the die-out times, well…there was no telling where it might go. Except that they would get themselves immortalized in every high school science textbook.

Carter needed more evidence. The rest of the world might not know what he knew in his gut. It was here and he was standing on top of it.

So he lowered himself to his knees and hunched-over again, and began wounding the earth beneath him, just a little more.

"Botulism, botulism, and botulism" had been Jordan's guess on the caseload that morning. Yesterday they had arrived at two in the afternoon, squinting in the bright sun and trying to look like they hadn't slept sideways on his couch, Eddie's file dangling from their sleep slackened fingertips.

So the guess hadn't been very exuberant. It hadn't been creative. And it sure as hell hadn't been right. Jordan figured one of these days he had to hit. But then he began the worrying: Would he die of boredom writing reports about food poisoning while he never figured out what happened to Eddie?

And why the hell did old man Landerly have to pick this week of all weeks to leave town? He was barely able to get around the office some days, so what was he doing climbing on a 747 and hitting the beach? Just when he was needed, too.

He hadn't said anything, but Jillian's voice cut into his thoughts, so accurate that for a moment he wasn't sure that she was actually speaking, "He'll be back in a few days. Eddie's file won't change in that time."

He did look up to nod and force a small half-smile as thanks for her concern. Today she was well put together, her dark hair drawn back away from her face in a tight clip. Her usual look for the office. Her clothing was getting more casual, and she was questioning him less and less as she worked. She churned out files like she was writing emails to friends. And she didn't question why his pace had ground to a near halt.

A few blinks and he tried to clear his head. A quick scan down to the bottom of the front page showed that it was not, in fact, anything like botulism. He had a clear cut case of Legionnaire's Disease in his hot little hands and he had stared at it blankly for half an hour.

Something pestered him while he began to slowly type, tabbing across the open fields on the computer screen, inputting bits of information here and there. And...

Jilly was watching him. Her keys didn't click, they had stopped some time ago, and that's what was bothering him. Just as his eyes lifted to meet her gaze, she spoke up. "Let's go get lunch. My treat."

He shook his head. "I'm not keeping up. I'm just going to eat out of the vending machines. I've got to get back into the groove of things." Why he wasn't already in the groove of it, after a full day, was beyond him though.

"No you won't–"

"Thanks for the vote of confidence, doll." But even though he had refused verbally, Jillian was walking around the large desk, shedding her labcoat and dropping it onto a hook on the old curly coat stand shoved into the corner of the room. But their cubby of an office was so small it was all in arms reach.

"You need chicken nuggets." Her smile got wider. "You're frustrated because you lost someone you've been trained to save, and not only weren't you there, you still can't figure out what went wrong. And I can't figure it out for you. And to make matters worse, Landerly is suddenly out of town, so you can't get answers from the one person who might be able to provide them. But I can buy you chicken nuggets and I can help take up the slack a little so you can figure things out." With a small shrug she dismissed her own generosity for nothing.

She had his hand in hers, although he was unsure when it had gotten there. And suddenly it seemed like a rather intimate gesture. When added in to the fact that she had just put to words what was eating at him, he couldn't stop the curl of his fingers around the heat she offered with just her hand. He couldn't stop the first smile he had formed all day, and he let her lean her full weight back as she made the motions of pulling him up from his seat.

They didn't speak on the way over, and he let her order for him, not surprised that she knew exactly what he wanted; they'd been here at least six times in the past month and he hadn't varied his order at all. So he tried not to dwell on Eddie. And three empty sauce containers later, he asked her, "So what did you find in the reports today? Botulism?"

She shook her head, knowing that she had blasted his predictions all to hell. "Salmonella–" Her voice kept his mind from wandering too far astray, "Then there were the three old people in the nursing home. Some sort of vague guess at a staph infection. It killed them but there was no real conclusive evidence–"

He looked up because her voice had just trailed off. Jilly's mouth hung in a small open 'o', her blue eyes focused somewhere beyond his shoulder. The gears working in her brain were visible and he waited her out. The tension he hadn't realized he was carrying tightening in his muscles every second. But he didn't push her to voice her reasoning.

Briefly it flashed across his thoughts again that he hadn't been hired to be the brilliant theorist. And if she was both the workhorse and the genius then perhaps he was just window dressing. Her lip turned in, and just as he had leaned all the way forward, waiting on edge for whatever she was going to announce, she looked at him and spoke. "Jordan, we have to go back and double check that file."

Chapter 4

Becky sank into her wooden swivel chair with her head cradled in her hands. Warden hadn't let up on her regular load because of the frogs. Never mind that investigating animal oddities was what the Biodiversity lab was set up to do. Never mind that she had stayed and kept the paper with the university. Warden seemed to begrudge her the find because it had been hers. Angry birds here, creepy frogs there, it was all too much.

But–

Her head snapped up. Maybe…

Maybe there was a connection between the screwed up frogs and the screwed up birds. She worked on it for the rest of the day, trying to come up with some sort of link. Then drove most of the way home until her little Jetta sputtered and died on her. She trudged the last mile, and arrived weary in her soul, brain, and body. From where she threw open the front door, Becky could see that her mother was in the kitchen and Brandon and Melanie were playing with two frogs loose on the living room carpet. "Those better not be my frogs." It was meant to be a threat but she didn't really have the energy to back it.

"They are, but I'm supervising." The voice sounded so much like her Dad's that her head snapped up.

"Aaron!" She felt the smile spread across her face as she launched herself into his arms. Only two years older, Aaron had been her god since the day she was born. In her early teens, she had suffered through the indignities of having to share him with her friends. And later with having to share him with the town. Knoxville was like every other southern town. There were three religions: 'Baptist,' 'Football,' and 'Other,' in order of their like-lihood of gaining you a spot in heaven. And Aaron had led the town to a state championship.

"Hey, Becky." His hair was blonde and short but his eyes were green moss just like hers. "Long time, no see."

"What are you doing here?"

"Just drove up for the weekend. And come to find out you've got yourself some weird little frogs." He looked over her shoulder, his eyes snapping wide. "Hey! Melanie! I told you two hands!"

That made Becky jerk her head around. Only to see Melanie roll her eyes and hold the frog out at arm's length, wrapped in the short fingers of her right hand. She shook the frog slightly for emphasis as she spoke. "This is how you're *supposed* to hold them – with only *one* hand. Back fingers hold their legs down. Top finger and thumb hold their arms out, and they can't get away!" She rotated the frog to upside-down and back upright. It waved its hands but didn't accomplish much else. "Tell him, Becky."

Forced to display a small smile to Aaron, she conceded. "She's right." But then she turned back to her sister and with two hands slipped the frog from Melanie's grip into her own identical hold. "But you aren't supposed to flip them around like that."

"Whatever, they're so creepy anyway. I was just getting a lexan." With that the reprimand was dismissed and the little girl wandered off to get the plastic container. In a moment, she held it up for Becky to slide the frog down in, head first, then snapped the container back closed.

Becky started when her mother spoke suddenly from directly behind them, and turned to find the woman using the same emphasizing hand gestures her younger daughter had just moments before, only with a spatula not a frog. "We're really looking into sending her to that gifted school out in Cedar Bluff. They just opened that new Magnet Program out there."

"*NO!*" It was earshattering and they all turned to stare at Melanie who had gone red in the face in the space of a breath. "I won't go! I don't want to ride the *short bus!*"

Becky shook her head, far more used to their little sister's antics than Aaron ever would be. He had moved away to college the first chance he had gotten, his status of 'Golden Boy' eating at him in a way even Becky had never understood. He had been out of the house before Melanie came along and had never really gotten to see her full-fledged personality.

Letting herself sink down into one of the dining room chairs, Becky toed off her thick sneakers and let the feeling of relief soak into her feet. She leaned back and almost closed her eyes before she realized that Brandon was standing right beside her, clear tupper in hand, the frog inside pointed toward the window. Becky raised her eyebrows; too worn out to voice her question, she let it show on her face.

"Melanie got too mad to tell you what we discovered. Watch." Brandon walked over to the refrigerator. Becky tilted her head to see, but expected nothing other than the appearance of a moldy ham sandwich. He placed the lexan flush against the fridge and waited.

Slowly, the frog turned to face the old white unit. When he pulled the container away, the little fellow re-oriented to his original direction. He put it back and the frog turned again to face the fridge. Waving his hands like some demented magician, Brandon declared it "Cool, huh?" then gave his theory. "I think he's hungry see…Melanie says that's not it, but she'll see. Can I give him pizza?"

"No!" But her brows were pulled together, and she was out of her chair in her bare feet, traipsing over to where he stood, her fatigue dismissed in the wake of her growing curiosity.

Trying it herself, Becky kneeled in front of the fridge and moved the container slowly towards and away from the white door. Her frown deepened as the frog made the same subtle adjustments every time.

"For god's sakes Becky, I need to get the margarine." Her mother tapped her foot impatiently behind her, not at all moved by the new level of oddity displayed by her catch.

Obligingly, she stood up and went in search of other objects the frog might turn to. She started toward the TV, which Brandon pertly informed her wouldn't work. He grinned like a praised puppy when it didn't. "It's just the fridge."

But Becky didn't believe that. There had to be something else. But she just wasn't sure what. She traipsed through the house, testing every large object she could think of. Aaron dogged her heels, for once following *her* to see what she would come up with next.

They were all three piled behind the front door watching the frog shuffle uncomfortably, waiting to see if it would change direction or settle into its familiar line. None of them heard the door click and all three fell into a startled heap when Mr. Sorenson opened the door onto them.

Melanie came bouncing over the pile of struggling bodies, "Daddy, Daddy, you're home!"

"Yes, I am." He grabbed up his youngest and stepped gingerly over his other children, trying to gracefully right themselves. "Were you all so anxious to see me?"

Aaron shrugged, and Becky was amazed to watch the transformation from grown man to child that was so rapid across his features. "We were just checking out Becky's weird frogs."

Her father's eyes caught her gaze. "Is it something new?"

"Yes! Daddy, Yes!" Melanie bounced in his arms. "They turn toward the fridge!"

Becky decided to be grateful her sister was no longer sulking in her room, withholding what might be valuable information, and she held the frog next to the oven. It stayed in its normal direction. Becky swore under her breath, dropping her behavior marks another few notches. But at the top of the oven, the little guy turned. He turned toward the washer and dryer, too.

"I know what it is!" She yelled out as she turned and smacked squared into Aaron's chest.

"Where's Landerly's signature?" Anne shook her pretty little blonde head as she poured over the forms in front of her.

Jordan smiled and pointed. He was afraid his expression screamed '*It's a forgery*'. He had vetoed Jillian standing beside him at this point, so she didn't have to be here for this display of fraud. Also because she was a really terrible liar.

Anne giggled. "The way you're grinning at me, and the number of times this thing's been through a fax…you could have forged this."

"I didn't forge it." The irritation that the difficult-to-read signature was his work was genuine. He hadn't forged it. Jillian had.

But Anne just giggled again and entered the data. "It'll be about half an hour."

He raised his eyebrows, not giving voice to all the questions he desperately wanted to ask, but couldn't because they'd give him away like a neon sign. Was she going to call to corroborate with Landerly? She had already made a comment about forgeries. Was she going to run it by the higher ups?

"Yeah, I can't whip up a plane ticket out of thin air." She giggled again, and as much as it reassured Jordan that she was dumb enough that he just might pull this off, it also was beginning to annoy the hell out of him.

"Thanks, babe." He turned and walked away, not getting to see her response. *Babe?* He winced inwardly and went back to his desk. He already knew what would happen if they were found out. Landerly had told them that first day that the CDC would just send them into the Ebola lab without suits. His breathing picked up.

Just as he entered his cubby hole of an office and leaned wearily back against the inside wall, his leg vibrated, scaring the shit out of him. But it was just his cell phone, and as he held up the display panel he realized that it was Jillian. "Hi."

Her panic radiated through the phone even before she spoke, poor thing. "Jordan, are you okay? They didn't find out did they?"

"No. Our flights will be ready in about half an hour."

"Where are you going?" The voice was masculine, and coming from behind him. In that first split second Jordan schooled himself to a calm response.

"You startled me." Turning, he saw it was Mark from the lab. "We're going to Florida."

Mark nodded in understanding, although just what he understood was beyond Jordan's capabilities. "Spiderbite-girl having a relapse?"

"Nope, something new…" He stopped himself before launching into an explanation; it would just be more to get tangled in later. Offering a smile, he turned his attention back to the conversation with Jillian and ended it as quickly as possible in hopes of avoiding other such scares.

Mark simply wished him good luck, and turned to go. Or so he thought. Again the voice startled him. "Is Dr. Brookwood going with you?"

"Hm?" It came out before he put the pieces together. Jillian. "Yes, she is." As he went back to his sorting, it occurred to him to add up Mark's actions over the last few weeks: it equaled a crush on Jillian. But Jillian would never put up with that shuffling walk. No authority.

The desk phone yelled at him, an angry electronic buzz that was supposed to resemble a bell ringing. He answered it gruffly just to stop the noise. Realizing only as he got the phone to his ear, that there was every possibility that it was Landerly, calling to check up on them. Perhaps having noticed the, oh say, *thirty* fax pages he had received from them before they went about forging his signature.

"Dr. Abellard." The wispy quality and lilt of the voice dispelled any of those fears in less than the time it had taken them to form. "This is Anne, at reception. Travel has confirmed your flights. You leave in three hours."

"Thank you, Anne." He pinched the bridge of his nose, glad that the one thing keeping him here was finished. He wanted to get away and hide from the people he was cheating. Maybe he could be on the plane before anyone figured out what was going on. "I'll be by within the next ten minutes."

No, they wouldn't get caught. Landerly wasn't going to be back for another week and they would be back before then; no one would be the wiser. And even Jillian thought she could justify the trip after the fact. Landerly listened to her.

He grabbed his briefcase and hefted it to the desk, stuffing in the extra files. It brimmed already with all the paperwork he could find on Eddie and Lake James' medical history. He gave only the barest of smiles to Anne as he breezed by the front desk. Her voice trailed him down the hall like so much cheap perfume, "Have a good trip Dr. Abellard!" Jeez, could she yell it next time? *Hope that forgery pans out for you!*

But he stuck his badge on the reader at the front door without unclipping it and waited the short eternity for the computer to decide that he deserved to leave and then actually slide the glass doors open. It was all he could do not to squeeze through sideways the instant a crack appeared.

The afternoon sun hit him full force, blinding him almost as thoroughly as it would after a matinee movie. He blinked rapidly to clear his vision, knowing full well that his sight adjusting was a matter of time and not moisture. He was basically tear free by the time he popped open the door of his overly blue Cavalier. He should get a better car. But that would happen a lot easier once his student loans were paid off. And that was a minimum of a few years away. He shoved the car into drive and left the building that was threatening to reveal his secrets to his bosses.

He dug his cell phone out of his pants pocket and depressed his #2 speed dial while he was waiting to merge onto the freeway. "Hi, Jillian… I'm out. Our flight is at seven-fifteen.…we get into Sarasota-Bradenton Airport at midnightish,…yeah, I'll come by your place…. All right, Bye." Traffic was getting heavier and he was glad to hang up.

But a conversation would have been preferable to the thoughts running through his head. Landerly would call from Hawaii. Or he would see his pager had gone off and all the numbers were the same. And when he did finally call in, Jordan and Jilly would be gone. Bad move.

He pulled out the cell and held it at arm's length in front of him, carefully feeling his way around the number pad. "Hi, Anne, can I ask you a favor? Can you forward all the calls to my office to my cell phone?"

"What about the calls for Dr. Brookwood?" He could hear her eyelashes beating a steady rhythm just from her voice.

"She'll be with me, so they can all come to my cell."

And he gave her the number and hung up feeling much better, until he realized that he'd given Anne his personal number. He just prayed that he hadn't given her any ideas.

His apartment seemed to be about ten miles further away than he remembered it. Crime sure did find a way of turning you upside down. And once he was there he wasn't really sure what to pack. So he threw in all the same things he had packed for his earlier trip to Florida and headed out to Jillian's.

He parked on the curb and buzzed her apartment, leaving his bag in the back seat. She didn't even answer the ring. Instantly the door began to buzz, and he followed the sound inside. Jordan jogged up the stairs, hoping to burn off some extra energy. It didn't work, and coming face to face with Jillian, her hall door flung wide, didn't help him calm down either.

She was taking deep breaths and talking. Almost to him… maybe not. "Landerly told us that when we found an answer we would know it. And that he would back us when that time came. He wasn't available. No one else would help, we knew that. We can ask each of them in turn if they would have signed off on it. They'll say 'no'."

So he took her by her upper arms and guided her back into the small apartment, "Jillian, calm down. We're going to be fine. We aren't going to get fired, for all the reasons you just listed." He breathed in. "Take a deep breath." And he waited until she did, "Now, we have to leave. Are you ready?"

She just nodded and started to reach for her bag, then fumbled with the lock to her front door.

"Jillian, if you don't calm down, they're going to detain us at the airport for being suspicious."

"Huh?" Her whole body stilled. "I was a cheerleader and a girl scout. I couldn't possibly be a terrorist."

He laughed. "Actually that would make you the ideal terrorist. So pull it together."

She laughed with him, the first easy, relaxed sound he had heard from her since they had hatched this horrible plan over lunch. And she managed to keep herself steady and calm, even when security did an open check on her bags. For the briefest of moments Jordan wondered if they would pull out anything good, like a vibrator or a chain of foil condom packets. But no, there was a novel and a bunch of photocopied files that he was pretty certain represented cases that she had searched and pulled together.

They made it to the terminal just as loading was beginning and joined all the other fliers funneling themselves down to the gate like so many cows to the slaughter. Once they were at their row, he made Jillian give up the window seat, arguing that she had slept through every single flight the last time. He didn't add that he had never gotten to fly until he was an adult paying his own way. The window still held a kind of magic for him that had worn off most middle-class kids by the age where they could read the take-off time on cartoon watches. And sure enough, even as he watched the houses and freeways below getting smaller and smaller, he felt the soft weight of her head settling on his shoulder, and the swish of her hair, unbound, falling across her face.

Becky's eyes adjusted to where Aaron swung the highbeam, lighting the whole area in front of them to ghastly shades of bright and black. All the shadows of midnight remained, just thoroughly delineated by the overpowering light. It became even creepier when they entered the woods at the back side of the field.

She started talking just to quell the feeling that she was walking where she didn't belong and where she was unwanted. "So how has–"

So did Aaron. "How do these frogs do–"

They laughed together, then she let him finish asking about her catch. "These are *rana*. A genus that really includes all your garden variety frogs, no bullfrogs though. They're indicator species – really sensitive to the environment. They'll mutate, like my little guys, really quick, if anything is off. You know, radiation, pollution, that kind of thing. Or magnetics."

"So, what is this then? We're visiting a polluted frog spot in the middle of the night that might be loaded with radiation from the power plant?"

"I thought of Oak Ridge, too. They actually do grow some creepy frogs out that way sometimes. But they're on the other side of the town from us, and they tend to hop down towards Chattanooga."

"How comforting." He muttered.

She maneuvered around behind him, disliking how her own shadow gave her such a case of the creeps. "I checked them all out at school with a Geiger-counter and got nothing. Like almost zilch. I mean *you* would register on these meters, they're that sensitive."

"All right." He raised the light, letting her decide which path to take, and even though it didn't look anything like it did during the day, she instinctively knew which way to go.

"So, anyway, other than the fact that they have spare legs, and are all from this one spot, I've got nothing." She took another long pull on the coke she carried with her. "That is, until tonight I had nothing."

"But what is it? Are all frogs magnetic and yours are just backward?"

"Nope, I've never heard of it in frogs." They were getting close, the tiny creek making burbling noises even at this late hour, and the local frogs raising their voices in a hellish chorus.

"So why would these frogs be magnetic?"

"Other animals are." She raised the compass in her palm, angling it to catch the light, and read it. Still in the right direction. No worries there. Yet. She kept up her chatter with Aaron, they were getting close and she was nervous about what she might find out. "Bees are, and so are homing pigeons."

"Not enough to stick to the refrigerator."

"You're sooo funny – Aaron, look!" She held up the compass. The needle had flopped to the opposite direction. She stepped backwards retracing her steps out of the area where she had first found the freaky little frogs. The needle swung back to the correct orientation.

"Sweet Jesus." As she walked back and forth, it changed. To exactly the opposite direction. Sure she wasn't seeing it right, she lifted her head to ask her brother to shine the light over her way and was met with a blinding glare. For a moment she had visions that the sheriff had found them and was going to haul them in, cuffs and cruiser and all. Although they were on their own property and all they could be cited for was leaving the car by the side of the road.

In a second, Aaron was at her side and the blinding glare was gone, directed down at the face of the compass, leaving her completely unable to distinguish anything beyond the borders of the light. Back and forth they walked for a minute or two, mesmerized by the swing of the needle. Then Becky pulled him forward to the edge of the stream and the spot where she and Brandon had caught all the frogs.

The needle stayed re-oriented. North was south and south was north. "This is where we caught them." She shoved up her sleeve and slowly bent over, sinking her hand into the cold water. The forest around them was now quiet, except for the wild trickle of the creek. It had no instincts and didn't know that something was amiss with all this bright light in the middle of the dark. But the frogs knew, and Becky could spot their shapes under the edges of the bumps and eddies. Their little noses and eyes stuck up above the surface, trying to catch a breath, and yet be still enough to thwart the predator.

But Becky got lucky, and in a moment she had reached down and slowly wrapped her hand around one of the little guys thinking he had it made by being motionless. She held up her catch, even as the nearby frogs scattered away from the site of the latest loss of their brethren. "Look Aaron, four back legs."

When she finished pulling up several six-legged frogs, she wandered the area using the compass as a guide, certain that some large object was buried here. Sighing, she was grateful again that Aaron was a lawyer. "What if whatever's here is government? Can they keep me from publishing my findings?"

"Huh?"

"If this is a dump site, you know, for some magnetic ore, or there's a secret lab under the ground," Okay, now she was getting really far-fetched, "would they be able to stop me from writing this up and letting the world know?"

He thought for a moment. "No, we're on our own land. I don't think they have any legal recourse. But if you have skeletons in your closet that they might blackmail you with, who knows?"

She laughed with him. "I don't have a boyfriend. I don't even steal paperclips from the school, and I've never made one of those freaky sex tapes."

"Don't let Mom and Dad even know that you know what those are."

"No joke." She crossed the stream on large stones that she had put there years ago and wandered through the woods, crashing through underbrush and sounding much like the Jolly Green Giant. She was half trying to convince herself that it was just the unearthly silence that made it sound that way. If Satan himself rose up before her, she couldn't say that she would be too shocked. But just then the compass needle jumped.

Becky startled, then walked back and forth a few times, using the sway of the thin red magnet to get a feel for the edge of the spot. "Aaron."

"Hm?" He looked up from his musings. "What?"

"We need to go get stakes and a…that yellow police tape stuff. There's a clear boundary here. We can mark it."

"But not now." He refused, and once he shined the light back the way they had come, she had no choice but to follow or be abandoned to the noise and the blackness.

"Oh we weren't expecting you." It was Maddie, according to her nametag.

Jillian just smiled. She wasn't half bad at this lying. "Really? I'm sorry. Our secretary was supposed to let you know that we're following up the interviews done by Drs. Smith and Webber." Maddie was Maddie Levinson. She and her husband owned and ran the Levinson Home for the Aged.

The round-faced woman just smiled and stepped back, holding the door open for them. "Well, you're here now." She seemed perfectly content to let them come in and reassess the place. Which clicked in Jillian's mind as a good thing. If they were trying to cover up elder-abuse or something, the case for a new disease would never hold.

Jordan trailed her in and she introduced both herself and him to the woman's husband, who was just as round and polyestered as she was. They had the same pie-faced smiles that ultimately seemed kind and gentle. A visual sweep of the area made it clear that this was a home that had been converted to a care facility. She'd read beforehand that these two lived here, twenty-four seven. "We would love to comb through your patient records, if we could. Maybe we could just stay out of your way."

But she had barely gotten the last word out when Jordan started speaking over her. "We just think that there might be something new here, and we want to be certain that it gets identified and stopped. I know the last CDC team suggested a staph infection–"

And for the first time the sweet moon face looked disgruntled. "I just don't know how that could have happened. We're so…it sure hasn't happened again, if that's what you're afraid of."

Jordan stepped close and put his arm on the woman's shoulder, leading her to sit at her own breakfast table where he pulled a seat a little closer. "When Dr. Brookwood and I reviewed the file, we didn't feel it was a staph infection at all. There wasn't any evidence of it; they just couldn't find anything else." His hand covered the older woman's, calming her immeasurably by that simple, unforward touch. Jillian watched the changes in her with awe. "Jillian is right."

She couldn't believe he had used her first name. Not that she was angry, but she didn't understand. It was all about being professional, right? And having no clue where he was going, she decided to step back and let Jordan ride the wave he had created.

"We'll want to go through all the old records like the other team. But beyond that, we'll need some time to talk to you. Maybe you can tell us something that isn't in the records."

Maddie balked a little, "We keep very thorough records."

Jordan didn't even try to argue that one. "I've seen them. They're some of the best in the business, but there are other things that you'd never think were medical, things that only a close caretaker, like yourselves, might notice. Any information you can give us would only help."

Arthur Levinson, 'Art' by his nametag, finally spoke up, but only to talk to his wife. "Honey, why don't you help them get the files and I'll serve breakfast."

And with that Maddie led them down the hall and unlocked a large, very neat office with mauve frills above the windows and ducks walking around the border at the top of the room. Walls of cheap, black file cabinets surrounded them, each carefully labeled and clearly locked. Mrs. Levinson let them know they were welcome to anything they wanted to peruse and, smiling at Jordan, handed over the small key ring labeled 'office' and asked what she could bring them to drink, or if they wanted a danish?

God, that was Jordan for you. Five minutes and any woman would be eating out of his hand. Look at the way he had worked over Anne at the front desk. Jillian was glad she wasn't that kind of girl. But here they were – in the office, with all the files at their disposal. And coffee on the way. Sweet deal.

She took a deep breath. "Let's get to work."

"Roommates?" Jordan asked, not looking up from the labels on the file drawers.

It was Maddie's voice that answered. "The roommates of our members who got sick? Well, there's Mildred Hartford. She's still here in the green room." She paused while Jillian started scribbling furiously on her notepad, "third down the hall on the right. She was Joseph Finklestein's roommate."

Maddie continued – the second roommate was in the hospital in Sarasota with a broken hip. And the third roommate had moved to another home after developing a more severe case of emphysema. But Mrs. Levinson said she had numbers to reach all the current caretakers. Then she named names and rattled the numbers off from memory, impressing the hell out of Jillian.

Three hours later, Jillian had about thirty folders pulled and open in various states of disarray around her. Jordan had about twenty more. They were getting somewhere. But God, if she had to look at these cream-colored walls for five more minutes she was going to spontaneously combust. "Jordan?"

"Hmm?"

He didn't look up from where he hunched over the files on the floor. He had graciously insisted that she take the only desk space. But in the hours in between he had sprawled, his jacket getting hung up over the inside doorknob, his tie loosening then disappearing. Now his sleeves were rolled up and he was in some unnatural position, chewing on the end of his red pen.

"I don't know about you, but I need lunch." She stood and stretched, ignoring the fact that her suit was wrinkled. That was okay, it wasn't designed for stretching either.

When they finally pulled out of the driveway, they both began talking at once. "I think it's a–"

"I'm positive it wasn't staph."

"Me, too." She sighed, running her hand over her hair, smartly pulled back into a ponytail that looked as professional as a ponytail could.

"There's no positive culture and nothing to link the three patients. No chain of infection." Jordan looked out the window at the passing communities of cookie-cutter bungalows, all labeled as "Sunset" this or "Retirement" that. "And I don't know if you've watched these guys…" he trailed off and waited for her to shake her head. Of course Jordan had observed them in action. She wasn't sure why the thought hadn't even occurred to her. "They are fastidious. Every injection clean. Every surface wiped down. Hugs and touching all the time, but I have never seen two people wash their hands so much." He sighed, slumping a little lower into his seat.

"Do you think it was all just for show?"

"No way." He turned to look at her, not doing his part to help find food anymore. "We walked in here, unannounced, just as we planned. There were already hand sanitizer bottles everywhere, sharps containers in every room, and if you noticed, both the Levinsons have very chapped hands, indicating this handwashing was going on long before we got there."

Of course she hadn't noticed.

What she did notice was a small sub stand with a name she didn't recognize, and she pulled into the lot and climbed out. "None of the roommates has anything even resembling this. I called the nursing home and the hospital for the two that are gone. The hospital is ready to send the broken hip back to the Levinsons for the remainder of care." She didn't stop talking while she read the menu up and down. "So there's nothing there to indicate it being airborne."

Jordan sighed and pushed both his hands through his hair, adding his order right on the tail end of hers. Only his was twice as big. "They have all the same symptoms that Eddie did. I don't get it."

Jillian waited until they were seated and Jordan had his head turned sideways, taking a huge sharklike bite from the sub. "They were the three most immuno-compromised patients in the home at the time."

That made Jordan look up. But she still didn't pick up her sandwich. "And get this: Bertha Martin was a leukemia survivor."

Becky thought they probably looked odd, marching across the field, dressed for camping, snapping photos while they went. Melanie had suggested the disposable camera from the checkout at Home Depot this morning. And Becky had gotten two. You just never knew.

The real work was in getting all the equipment out there. Aaron had taken that upon himself; he looked like a hiker gone mad – or a serial killer – with the lumpy bags, the pack and the shovel. She, Brandon, and Melanie followed like ducks, holding clear lexans of frogs that were finally returning to their home. But just to visit.

Once they arrived at the site, the frogs were set down and they all went to work with the compasses they had picked up. Melanie swung her little hammer, pounding a stake meant to hold garden edging into the soft ground near the stream. With the small mallet, she hit at it until it was low, or until she mistakenly whacked some part of her body and swore a word that Becky wasn't aware her sister knew.

Brandon was a more efficient force; he and Aaron both having seen the need for method early on. Baggy army pants oozing garden stakes, both guys walked a line designated by the compass in their left hand, periodically pulling a stake from some previously unused spot on their person and pounding it into the ground with one swift stroke. Of course, Brandon pulling stakes out of his pockets resembled a gunslinger, with a swagger and a little preening where Aaron was all efficiency of movement.

Aaron looked up at her right then. "Hey, Doctor Smartypants, get in here and help."

"Aye, aye!" She crossed the creek on the old stones and set about mapping the other side. Within half an hour, all the loose ends had met up and they had an oddly shaped circle. Becky set Melanie to winding the tape from spike to spike, clearly delineating the magnetic boundary, while the rest of them wandered the site, eyes glued to compass needles, looking for any smaller spots of greater activity.

That was an exercise in futility. There was nothing. Well, it was all or nothing. No one spot that gave a greater reading, or even caused the compass needles to jump or shimmy. No such luck.

"Okay, guys." They lifted their heads from whatever they were meddling around with at the sound of her voice. "It's hokey pokey time. Put all the frogs in the circle."

Even Aaron got into it. Each of the four eagerly grabbed a lexan and walked inside the orange boundary. They each set down the tupper with a flourish and waited for…nothing.

"Anyone?" Becky whispered.

"Nothing." Aaron told her. His voice strong with certainty.

"Nothing." Brandon repeated, bell clear.

Becky felt her heart sink. She had thought surely bringing the frogs back here would accomplish something. Melanie's voice called out next. "Nothing! Nothing!"

That was a little too chipper. Wasn't it true that the really smart ones always cracked?

"They aren't doing anything, Becky!"

"Duh, Dorko." Brandon sneered, standing guard over his frog, legs spread, fists on his hips, sneer worthy of the schoolyard. "They're just acting like normal frogs."

"And they *aren't* normal frogs!" Melanie was at a near fever pitch.

"Holy shit." Becky whispered. "She's right." The frogs were no longer orienting. Reaching down, she turned the container. Aside from the usual the-world-is-rotating-under-me shuffle that all frogs did, this one didn't do anything. It didn't re-orient northwest. "Turn your frogs!"

This time even Aaron and Brandon caught on. "Okay, this is just too freaky." Aaron looked up at her. "I like things neat and understandable. This is beyond my boundaries. Can I have these little green guys arrested for disorderly conduct?"

Becky laughed to herself. The disorderly conduct was what they were *supposed* to do. It was the lining-up-in-one-direction that was creepy.

She took a moment to write notes. Then had everyone take their frog out of the circle.

Alignment.

That got noted too.

Into the circle, in new spots, this time.

Disorder.

Out of the circle.

Alignment.

But this time there was more.

"Everyone, back in the circle." At least they didn't look at her like she was crazy. Something was drastically wrong in the spot where they were standing. Her breathing hitched.

"Okay, we're going to take our frogs and walk out a bit." Three nods. "Every one has compasses?" Three nods. "Good, now start walking, *carefully*, away from the site."

She had lined each of them up in a different direction, so they backed out like four corners on a compass until Becky couldn't see any of her siblings anymore. But, loud bunch that they were, vocal contact wasn't an issue. She yelled out, "My frog is facing southwest. Aaron?"

"North-north-east."

"Brandon?"

"South-east."

"Melanie?"

"West!"

She hollered out to her sister, whose little voice was coming through the thick trees from somewhere on the left. "Melanie! Have you figured it out?"

"Yes! They're all facing the site!"

Chapter 5

Jordan scribbled furiously on the pages of loose leaf paper spread out on the floor of the office with the awful mauve accents. He and Jillian had been here for two days, and he was never happier to not have a laptop. He had survived med school, ridiculed for his handwritten notes, but remembered everything far better than if he had typed it. And now this chart was taking over its eighth page, and he never would have accomplished this with the best notebook program.

Jillian watched while he organized and wrote and drew arrows in multiple colors. He started thinking out loud, "Okay, recap: Joseph Finklestein had lupus, Bertha Martin was a leukemia survivor, and Beatrice Weitzman had a kidney transplant and was on immunosuppressive drugs."

Jilly picked up. "No other transplant patients here, according to files, the Levinsons, and patient report. No HIV positive patients. No one even close in immuno-status. So that gives us a set-up, but what *is* it?" She chewed on the end of the marker she was holding. Normally that would have driven him nuts to watch, but he was too keyed up. He couldn't sleep last night. And now he was running on pure caffeine.

"Go over Eddie's case with me."

Jillian nodded and started rattling stats again. She was better at that than any doctor he had ever met. "Stomach ache, reported by wife, at seven days prior to death. Vomiting at six days,"

Desperately, Jordan tried to push it out of his mind that this was Eddie she was so carefully reducing to a series of numbers and isolated incidents. But that was what would solve the case. "Admitted for dehydration, in E.R., at day five. Given IV fluids and Raglan for nausea. Seemed to be doing better but was mildly disoriented and complaining of sleepiness. Nurses report that he was very sleepy and slept a good portion of his time in the ward. Nothing unusual there.

"Files indicated normal white counts. CBC and full Chem Panel show nothing out of the ordinary. In fact, all numbers are very normal. Day three, patient goes to sleep and wife reports that he's difficult to rouse. After medical intervention, a CT scan is performed and it is determined that the patient slipped into coma during sleep. On day one, patient is put on ventilation due to oxygen sats being under eighty-four percent, and on day zero, all brain activity stops, and staff performs heroic measures to no avail. Patient dies at 2p.m."

Jordan sighed.

There wasn't much he could do at this point except sigh. He had arrows drawn to and from what he knew. Joseph Finklestein hadn't had vomiting. His decline had taken nine days from first complaint to death. He had died at the home, with a very short delay between slipping into a coma and simply passing away while waiting for transport to a full medical facility.

Jillian opened the reports again. "Aaagh."

He looked up, hoping that it was a good 'aaaagh', but apparently it wasn't. "These guys were on so much medication that you can't tell what changed and what didn't. Just tracking their medication would take a whole flow chart like that!"

"Then we do it."

Her eyes widened, and she almost looked scared, which was about the funniest thing he had thought in days. Jillian scared of paperwork.

She begged, "Only if you do it. I can't do that...whatever you're drawing. I need a spreadsheet."

"Can you do this on a spreadsheet?"

She shook her head, her mouth moving to the straw of the supersize coke she was drinking, while she rubbed the sides to remove the sweat. Her scrubs bore the stains from the water drips where she had rested the drink on her leg earlier, and in this heat he didn't blame her that she didn't care.

He sat up to be close and spoke low; he didn't want the Levinsons getting tipped off that this wasn't an official investigation. "We still have to get Landerly's signature on this. The only way I feel relatively assured that that will happen is with a solid diagnosis."

She nodded.

Her voice pitched lower as well, but for an entirely different reason. "Do you think we're seeing SuperAIDS?" She didn't want to scare the Levinsons.

"Shit." He barely breathed it. "I hadn't even thought of that." His pushed his fingers through his hair and looked again at the gaily colored chart. Immuno-compromised patients.

She shook her head. "The set-up is right. But the play-out isn't."

Jordan waited for her to continue. He agreed, but wondered if she was following the same angle as him. "Flu-like symptoms at onset match, but not the lack of time lag, although that's always been hypothesized as the new trick up the virus' sleeve. Then coma and death. The issue is, those cultures should have shown not just something but *everything*."

"Right, HIV doesn't kill you. It's what AIDS allows to get a foothold that kills. So, no superAIDS." He was on the floor again, spread out with his paper. He'd been here for their whole stay, getting more and more ragged looking. Jillian had stayed up at the desk, but her posture had gone to hell in a handbasket. She was slumped in the chair, bringing her head to the coke instead of vice versa. Her knees pressed together, and her sneakered feet turned at odd angles resting on the shaggy caramel carpet. Her right hand played incessantly with her ponytail and if her mouth wasn't speaking it was gnawing something – the straw, the poor pen. He'd never seen her like this.

Then again, they hadn't yet had anything they couldn't solve with a report and a spreadsheet before. The only real trip they had taken had involved a case with clear answers once they looked at it from a few angles. This they'd tipped over, looked underneath, and shaken down, and only the barest of glimpses of ideas were falling into place.

"Okay." It was just a small statement, made on a tiny breath, but it was the beginning of a change. He sat patiently while Jilly straightened herself and pulled a well worn folder off the desk. "Clear out some papers, flow-chart-boy, here goes."

And she rattled off a list of about thirty medications, making him mark in a different color any that had been prescribed within the last month prior to death. Joseph Finklestein had two. Increased dose of Lipitor and Prescription Naprosyn for pain because Ibuprofen was upsetting his stomach. Bertha Martin had one, Cephalexin for an imagined ear infection. And Beatrice Weitzman had no new scrips in that time. Between the three of them they were on forty different medications, and the number was only that low because so many overlapped.

Jillian set down her soda with a clunk and opened Eddie's file, her fingers expertly shuffling through reams of loose paper, never letting any fall or even slip out of place. "Ready?"

She rattled off a short list. When she closed the file, Jilly joined him on the carpet, scanning the flow chart. She watched and pointed a few times while Jordan cross-referenced and drew marks and asterisks between any duplicated medications that showed up. But they didn't seem to yield any new information. So the nursing home victims had been old? They knew that already. Not a single medication or even medication category cross referenced to Eddie. Eddie was close to med free. They checked lifestyle markers then. But as expected, the three Levinson Home victims all cross categorized nearly perfectly. Leaving Eddie the outsider, and thus the key to the whole thing.

Jillian ran her fingers down the list again. "Cephalexin." She pointed to Bertha's quadrant of the chart. "Why was she on it?" She fingered open the chart and looked puzzled. "Ear infection. That's probably what tipped them off to staph." She thumbed through the tome, coming up with the prescription date. "No good indication of an ear infection though. 'Mild redness' that's all."

Jordan frowned. That bothered him for some reason he couldn't put his finger on, and he followed a hunch out to the courtyard where Maddie Levinson was hosing down the plastic furniture. She smiled when he approached, which he had to admit was a very magnanimous gesture at this point. He and Jilly had taken over her office for three days now. But she just offered him lemonade and asked, "What can I help you with?"

"Do you have a minute? I'm looking for some of that personal information that I thought might not be found in a medical file."

Her eyebrows raised, but she quickly set aside the hose and wiped down two chairs offering him the first before settling her large frame into the second. She still seemed wary until he asked the first question. "Bertha Martin was prescribed Cephalexin for an ear infection she didn't seem to have, just five days before she died. Do you know why that was?"

Maddie laughed. A clear vibrant sound accompanied by her slapping her thigh. "Yes, I know why." She wiped at her eye where a small tear had formed, although he wasn't sure if she missed her houseguest or had just laughed too hard. "Bertha was ornery, at times. And she insisted she had an ear infection. Wouldn't quit her caterwauling until the doc gave it to her. He finally relented. She'd had enough ear infections that she probably knew."

"And Joseph Finklestein. He was changed from Ibuprofen to Naprosyn also within the last few days before his death. Why was that?"

Her expression sobered right up, and Jordan didn't doubt that her answers were as accurate as any could be. She knew each of these patients, and he'd lay odds that the woman couldn't do simple algebra but could rattle off every dose of every medication every patient here was on, and put even money that she still knew the old doses, too. "Joseph started getting headaches right then. We didn't think anything of it at the time."

"So he said the Motrin wasn't really helping?"

She sighed, her shoulders doing a soft heave before she went on. "He didn't really say it. He didn't communicate well for the last several months. But he kept grabbing his head, rubbing his temples, and…" She couldn't find the words so she showed Jordan. She shoved her shoulders up under her chin and put her hands behind her ears, shoving them forward rubbing the bone where her skull met her neck.

He watched.

Headache, maybe. Ear pain. Maybe.

"Thank you, Maddie." He stood and offered his hand, which she shook politely.

When he entered the office, Jillian looked up at him, and Jordan launched into a shortened version of his discussion with Maddie, ending it punctuated by Jillian's "Wow."

"Will you call my cousin Kelly and ask her if Eddie had ear pain?" He continued. "I think we can safely say that we have something new, that isn't airborne, and we've been sitting in it for three days."

David hung up the phone. He had to. His ears were ringing. If Greer so much as got one iota more excited, the earth was going to shift on its axis. The eggs were a true find. A full clutch, almost all intact. Yada yada yada.

And McCann, Tennessee was a hotspot.

He turned over a specimen, eyeing it carefully. His old man would love to get his hands on this piece of history. But that was too damn bad.

The testing was showing up just like the Warren Fault pieces. Heavy iridium layer at the KT boundary. Reversed magnetics in all the pieces. What was killing him was the size of the spot. It seemed so small.

From his father's work he had believed, as his father always had, that the hotspots had to have a certain size, a critical mass, in order to carry a reversed magnetic field. Something there had to support it. Had to keep it out of alignment with the field of the earth as a whole. That implied some level of size.

But this didn't come anywhere near close.

He and Greer had practically gone door to door asking if anyone had an oil rig in their backyard, which had sounded retarded as all hell the first three times he asked. But sure enough, folks were friendly, and by the end of day three, they had awful stomach aches and forty-two core samples, giving David a nice view of the strata around his dig.

And here he sat. Wishing that he had stayed longer. That he had known the horrible nausea and vomiting would disappear the next day. Because every oil well sample had come up negative. No magnetic reversals in any layer.

Add in that the lab staff had done the experiment blind. None of them knew what he was looking for. Just the series of tests, and that was it. So he sighed at the core samples. They had given up all their secrets like cheap whores. And he was done with it. Depressed almost to the point of tossing it at the trash.

While he had his hotspot, none of this was going to accomplish much more than reminding everyone that his father had seen it first. Damnit.

Jordan pulled his decrepit Chevy into the CDCP lot right behind Jilly's pert Rav-4. They had stayed at her apartment last night, still going over the paperwork. Landerly would be back in a day.

They had to get prepared to explain. To make their case and make it stick well enough to *not* get fired.

Together they had hovered over Jillian's computer, filling in the codes for the visit and symptoms. They labeled and sorted and listed evidence. They spent hours searching for linked cases and only came up with three in addition to the four they started with. And even those only *looked* similar. There wasn't any evidence that was close to conclusive. Then they wrote a paper for Landerly explaining why they had forged the signature. Documenting how many times and when they had tried to get it legitimately.

And here Jordan was: pulling into the parking lot, papers printed and sitting on the passenger seat beside him. Whether or not they would save his ass was still up in the air.

He and Jillian met again in between the cars where they parked. Took deep breaths together, and then walked down the hall. Reaching the office felt like they crossed a finish line. Jordan wanted to hunch over and gulp air. He wasn't cut out for lying. Within a minute they silently took their seats and turned on the monitors on the desk, pulling up their files. Jillian looked up at him and smiled, her nod indicating that they were going to be okay.

The movement in his peripheral vision caught his attention just seconds before the loud clap of their door slamming open caused all his muscles to instantly clench. His heart plummeted when he saw that Landerly was standing inside their office. Well, those were his feet anyway. It took Jordan to the full count of ten to force himself to look up to Landerly's face.

The voice was old and soft and anything but calm. "You two have some serious explaining to do about a signature of mine that I don't remember being on the continent to sign for."

The world was going to hell.

There was a long lull, then they both began speaking. "Dr. Landerly, we had so much evidence–"

"We tried so hard to get in touch with you–"

His leathery hand, palm out, put an end to the words frothing from their mouths. "I'll talk to you separately." He pointed to Jillian. "In my office, now."

As Jordan watched, she stood as though pulled by strings. Her expression that of sheer horror. And then she walked out the door followed by Landerly, who didn't so much as glance Jordan's way. For long minutes, he sat there, unmoving, still digesting what had happened. Landerly shouldn't have gotten in until tomorrow. Had someone tipped him off? Had he come back early to corral his renegade peons?

Jordan knew he was going to get fired. That was all there was to it. He considered himself too much of a man to get up and start packing his belongings, not until he was actually told that he was fired. But it wasn't beneath him to let his gaze wander around the office, falling on various objects and cataloguing what was his.

The phone buzzer shocked him to life, his heart missing several beats before picking up a steady rhythm again. Gingerly he lifted the receiver from the cradle, "Hello?"

"Abellard. Get in here."

He winced, "Okay," but it was too late. Landerly had already hung up, and Jordan was holding a phone that was softly buzzing a dial tone at him. He hadn't been this afraid of getting spanked since elementary school. At least then he had put smoke bombs behind the toilets in the girls' room and the whole thing had been fun.

The hall felt long, and Landerly's office was closed, forcing Jordan to grip the knob and open the door on the scene of his own demise. Jillian sat in the visitor chair across from where Landerly lorded behind his desk. She was ashen and looked like she had early stage Parkinson's – fine tremors snaked their way down her arms and out her fingers. Anger broke in a tidal wave as Jordan looked her up and down. Landerly had tormented her. He turned to let the old man have it, but was brought up short by the bark that Landerly leveled at him. "Is it true, what she tells me?"

He had to force himself to take a deep breath. "I've never heard Jillian lie."

That put the old man's eyebrows up. "So you orchestrated all this? By yourself?"

"I realize that I am not the genius here, and that this ploy may seem a bit above me. And, no, I didn't 'orchestrate' the whole thing. But Jillian didn't speak any lies to anyone. Jillian has many talents. Lying isn't one of them."

Landerly snorted. "Forgery apparently is."

"Apparently." Jordan knew he was shoveling the hole he was standing in. But he couldn't stop himself. "Tell me if that paper was three years old you would have recognized that it wasn't your signature."

Jillian gasped, but at least it earned him a respectable nod from Landerly, who then began talking right over Jordan's thoughts. "If you'd like to not get fired, effective immediately, you had damn well better explain this and why you couldn't wait until I got back. And it had better match Dr. Brookwood's story exactly."

Jordan thanked God Jilly couldn't lie worth shit. He knew their stories would match word for word. So he took a moment to gather himself, watching her visibly relax as he did. They would be here a while.

Eventually Landerly interrupted. "Same thing she said. The two of you using company policy to support your illegal trip…"

Jillian paled a bit at that, and Jordan put his hand over hers where it gripped the spindle arm of the chair. They'd at least be fired together. "Are you going to hear us out or not?"

Landerly nodded and managed to not interrupt again for the remainder of the story. He was silent for several minutes after Jordan finished. Finally he placed his soft leather hands on the desk and leaned forward, somehow managing to invade Jordan's personal space from over three feet away. "One: we never had this conversation. I don't know about that signature. I assume someone else okay'd your trip. Two: one slip from either of you and I will suddenly find that paper and recognize the forged signature and you'll be out so fast your head will spin."

Jordan digested that. It actually sounded like they weren't getting fired.

"Three: you drive out tonight. There's another case that sounds like the same thing in the Appalachians. You're going to an area just south of Knoxville – McCann County."

"Another case?" It was Jillian's voice, though hard to recognize, it was shaky and soft and lacked all her normal confidence.

"Yup." Finally Landerly leaned back, "We'll name the disease after you two as punishment for this escapade. Now get out of my office. Go home. Pack and get your asses back here by five so I can hand you the paperwork."

"Yes, sir." His voice was strong, even if his belief wasn't. And Jilly was falling all over herself to thank the man whose name she had so expertly forged less than a week ago. She was gesturing wildly and Jordan reached up to pluck one of her hands out of its flightpath and used it to drag her out of the office.

She trailed him down the hall, hand still tucked in his, getting tugged along. When they got to the office, she released herself from his grip and sank like pudding into her wooden swivel chair, leaning it back and bringing her hands to her head as though she could hold all the thoughts in. "I can't believe he didn't fire us."

"Yes, and we're not waiting around to let it happen either." Jordan grabbed her purse and handed it to her, before yanking her up out of the chair. "I'll drive, you're in no shape."

In seconds he had pulled her down the hallway, waving the ID card miraculously still in his possession at each coded entry and finally emerging into the bright sun. Jilly raised her hand to shield her face, then pawed inside her purse for a moment before producing sunglasses and keys.

He pulled the keys from her hand and dropped them back into the leather bag. "You shouldn't drive. I'll drop you off then swing by and get you on the way back."

"No, really, I'm–" She cut herself off when she saw how badly she was shaking. "All right, thank you."

He settled her into the passenger seat of the crappy little Cavalier, then closed her in and jogged around to the driver's side.

"Do you think–"

"Landerly said–"

"You go first." He braced his arm on the back of her seat and looked out the rear window while he backed out of the spot doing all he could not to lay some serious rubber on the pavement in his hurry to be away.

"Do you think we're really onto something? That there really are more cases?"

Jordan sighed. "It has to be. The only alternative I can figure is that Landerly is sending us into the mountains and a hitman will follow us. You know, so no one will ever find the bodies."

"So, we're going up into the Appalachians."

"I have to say I'm freaking out about that."

Jilly looked sideways at him again. "Why?"

"I've seen *Deliverance*."

Jillian listened to the deep sigh Jordan heaved into the door of the car. In sleep, he had wedged himself between the seat and the window, stuck at an awkward angle that seemed to bother only her.

His remark about being sent to McCann County to meet up with Landerly's hitman ricocheted in her brain. But it morphed as it went. Landerly wouldn't need a hitman; McCann was itself Purgatory, or so it would seem.

The Rav-4 bounced along the horrid road, and Jillian had thoughts about not getting reimbursed for the damage to her car. She tempered them with thoughts about not getting fired. Darkness had come to cover them like smog while she drove along roads that needed little instruction. Blinking to keep her eyes open, she was assaulted by the bright glare of a green interstate sign bouncing her brights back at her. McCann, 1 mile, population 232. That was telling. That they included the population on the sign. And that the population included a significant digit in the ones spot. Ouch. Jordan had been right about *Deliverance*.

Jillian looked at the glowing digital numbers on the dash, they were going to arrive early, and she wondered how that could be possible. The drive had seemed interminable; she couldn't even sing to the radio to stay awake, not with Jordan sleeping in the passenger seat.

Their turn was highlighted by a small brown sign atop a metal post, with one word "McCANN" and an arrow pointing the only direction there was to go down the dirt trail. She had the distinct feeling she was entering a land where a sixth grade education would be considered worldly.

Jordan bounced around in his seat, his shoulders and head periodically knocking about. Surely he would wake right up, keep her company. But he didn't. When she felt the frown cross her face, she realized that she had been anticipating his presence. Landerly had done a good job putting the two of them together. They communicated well about what needed to be done, and they worked well together to be certain that it was achieved. She hadn't ever felt that Jordan wasn't pulling his own weight, nor had she felt she'd been carried. And he was good company, which was more than she had expected. Most people had found her cold and distant, and she understood that. Pretty much she was cold and distant; she lived in her own world where the need to achieve drove her every waking moment.

Funny how Jordan had become her personal life now. He had other commitments and friends in the outside world of Atlanta. In the few weeks he had been here, he had made more connections than she had in all her five years at Grady and in Atlanta combined. On the way out, he had taken time to call his friend Martin and cancel his Wednesday night racquetball game. For a brief moment she had regretted that she didn't have anyone to call.

The road went on forever, made worse by the fact that it was little more than ruts in the hard-packed earth and any sort of speed was an unattainable goal. At least it had been used recently. Small bushes and grasses had been flattened in the middle of the parallel ditches that had yet to pop back up and look alive. Beside her, Jordan finally stirred, his eyes opened, his jaw worked and his voice uttered a soft, *What?* Before he shook himself fully awake and realized that he knew exactly where he was. In that moment he began apologizing for sleeping through such a long portion of the ride.

"So make it up to me by checking out the map to James Hann's place so we can get the key to the house where we're staying."

Jordan complied, looking over the hand-drawn lines that Hann had faxed to Landerly earlier today. Google had come up with nothing. Not surprising since McCann itself didn't register on most maps.

According to the shakily scrawled fax there were five roads in McCann. Parson, Main, Lintle, Shields, and Squirrel. Jillian had to admit that 'Squirrel' bothered her. And that, of course, was the road where the rented house was marked with a wavery X on the map.

Jordan turned the map one way then the other, "I take it we're on Main."

"To the best of my knowledge." Her casual shrug was lost in the movement of the jostling car.

Trees had closed in over the road, overgrown and hanging low, scraping the top of the small car. It was either romantic or horrifying, and Jillian squashed the urge to look into the backseat for stowaways. She was searching desperately for road signs, and when she was ready to sigh with weariness and frustration, Jordan pointed low. A hand-lettered wood two-by-four was nailed to the base of an old tree. *Parson Rd.*

That was good enough for her. And she cranked the wheel of the Rav-4 hand over hand, wishing that she was already at the house on Squirrel.

The road was even worse than Main, if that was possible. Branches whipped the windshield at a ferocious pace, slowing them even more. Just when she was ready to comment, Jordan broke the nearly rhythmic *thwapping* sound, "Landerly hates us. He does not expect us to return."

Jillian had to laugh.

It was that or cry. She'd had no more sleep than Jordan, and while she was glad they weren't fired, never had she imagined this kind of sick punishment.

Just then the trees broke, and a small house stood probably a half mile back off the road. No front lawn or porch lights illumi-nated the outside, but lights were on in the windows, and given that it was approaching eleven, Jillian was willing to turn the car down the gravel driveway and take her chances that this was the Hann residence. A porch light flashed on in welcome even as she pulled up next to the garage.

In the dying residuals of her headlights, Jillian noted the dilapidated horse barn and matching shed tilting precariously in the background, but her attention was diverted by the older man walking down the stairs. He looked nicer than what she had expected in these parts. His jeans were clean and unpatched, like his red plaid flannel shirt. And his face was just enough weathered to appear kind.

She plastered on a smile and threw open the car door. But he spoke first. "You must be Dr. Brookwood. Miss Greene didn't tell me you were so pretty." His smile reached his eyes and he held his hand out to her, somehow managing to convey comfort and friendliness with his remarks.

He held out his hand again as Jordan approached. "I'm James Hann. And I have a set of keys to our rental house. Just come inside and Melissa will get you a drink."

Jillian started to protest, "Oh, thank you, but–"

Jordan's elbow in her lower back cut her off and his voice overpowered her own, "That would be great. It's been a bit of a drive."

So she bit off her retort and followed the two men up the short stairs. The inside of the place reminded her of her Aunt Lenora's house. There was a whipstitched cover for the Kleenex box in the shape of a church, complete with a steeple and open doors. Sampler pillows dotted the old brown couch in shades of pastel, broken only by the hideously yellow crocheted throw.

James introduced his wife Melissa, a woman who appeared to be in her fifties like him, who brooked no protest about popping out of her seat to get drinks even as he settled in. Jillian let Jordan handle all the talking, since he was the one who had accepted this invitation anyway.

She felt herself drifting asleep with her eyes open until James Hann's voice cut through the filters she had thought were turned off. "Y'all are married, right?"

While she tried to hide the startled look she was sure had materialized on her face, all thoughts vaporized at Jordan's immediate smile and knowing nod. "Of course we are."

Snapping her jaw shut, she turned to stare at him – then worked furiously to cover the expression that she knew had clouded her eyes. If there was one thing she had learned at the CDCP, it was that Jordan said some wild stuff, but he could be trusted. So she forced a grin, praying it looked less demonic than it felt.

His smile was far more genuine, and he reached across to lightly brush her fingers. "Jilly decided to keep her last name. Dr. and Dr. Abellard...well you'd never know who was who."

Hann accepted the iced tea his wife was holding out to him without even acknowledging her presence, which of course prompted another negative reaction that Jillian fought hard to tamp down. Then she was discretely passed a bumpy glass full of tea and garnished with a lemon and a mint sprig. Garnish! At eleven thirty at night! And Jordan smiling and talking about them being married. It was the damn twilight zone.

"I noticed you don't wear any rings."

Jordan held out his hand for Hann to inspect. *Could the night get any weirder?* She just couldn't wait to hear this. "I've got a bit of a mark from it."

Jillian couldn't see anything but a pristine ring finger, but she kept her mouth shut.

"We can't wear our rings when we work. They get caught on the gloves." He smiled at her again, and she saw genuine humor in his eyes. He knew that she had no idea where he was going with this and he wasn't going to explain. "And Jilly here won't let us bring them on trips. They might get lost."

So she turned back to Mr. Hann and nodded as if she agreed. "You know. They're too important."

James nodded to her conspiratorially. "Melissa would have my hide if I lost mine."

In a few minutes she had guzzled her tea, far thirstier than she had known she was. Then Jordan was taking her hand and pulling her up off the couch. He had the keys to the house on Squirrel firmly in his other hand and the Hanns' blessings.

Mr. Hann watched from the doorway while Jordan folded her into the passenger seat of her own car, then smiled as he held his hand out discretely for the keys. She slipped them to him, wondering even as she did it why she was going along with it all. A smile and a wave later, Jordan had them turned around and bouncing back up the driveway, and Jillian could keep her mouth shut no longer.

"We're married?"

He laughed. "This is not like Atlanta. They just rented us a house and they'd probably rescind the offer if they had known we weren't married. Sin is sin."

"What?"

"Did you see all the God stuff in there?" He looked both ways for the non-existent traffic at the end of the drive, "They would have insisted that you stay with them. Is that what you wanted?"

"You're serious."

He just raised his eyebrows and held up the keys to the house. The keychain read *With Jesus all things are possible.*

"Well, holy Mary, mother and Joseph." She hated when he was right and she didn't have the wherewithal to even catch on.

It was fifteen minutes of relative silence later that they parked the Rav-4 in front of the rental. Jillian fought the urge to cry. It was straight out of the Apple Dumpling Gang. Weathered wood siding, hanging loose in several places, the porch had a slight tilt to it, and in the windows she could see curtains with red roosters prancing back and forth.

She prayed that the beds didn't sag too much.

Jordan hopped out and reached into the backseat to grab both duffle bags and headed to unlock the front door. Following right behind him, she was assaulted by the stale smell and stagnant air in the place. Jordan made a face that must have mirrored her own and immediately dropped their luggage and went around opening the windows. The night air was a welcome addition into the house.

Jillian wandered the place, snapping on lights. The kitchen was a countrified hell – roosters covered every surface. Wire mesh lined some of the cabinets in a way that could have been charming were it not part of the whole overdone theme. The hallway boasted a linen closet that was stacked with chenille throws and a variety of outdated floral print sheets. The one bathroom was cramped and pink, but Jillian thought the sink looked about as good as any could right now.

The faucet handle didn't give when she turned it. And so, with a much harder crank, she sent the thing spinning and started a horrifying series of moans and gurgles that culminated in a brown thick liquid spewing from the faucet.

"Now that's what I call hard water." Jordan laughed from behind her.

Jillian spun around, furious not at him, but at the fact that things could be this bad at midnight when she hadn't slept in four days and hadn't even begun to unpack. She started to turn off the offending spigot, but Jordan's hand on her shoulder stilled her, "Let it run, it'll clear up."

With that she turned and left the faucet to its own devices and started opening the doors at the end of the hallway. One was a master bedroom, if the term was applied loosely. The bed was queen-sized and looked like it had been furnished from a barn somewhere. The other bedroom sported a single pressed into the far corner with only a lone pillow and no headboard.

"I'll take this one." Jillian went back for her bag, but Jordan beat her to it and argued chivalrously that he would take the smaller room. In a few minutes she got him to concede and he lowered her bag to the floor, then called from a little further down the hallway "The water's good now, bathroom's all yours."

She'd have to see that clean water to believe it, but sure enough, when she re-entered, the water ran clear and pristine. Except for a smudge in the bottom of the basin there was no evidence of the sludge it had been turning out a few minutes ago.

Rapidly she brushed her teeth and scrubbed her face before heading back to her room and changing into her flannel pajamas.

The bed both called to her and repulsed her. But exhaustion won out over unfamiliarity and she lifted the layers of sheets and blankets to slide beneath. She was rolling over to punch the pillow when the world dropped out from under her.

Eyes wide, she sat up and promptly slid off the end of the bed where the foot of it had fallen out from under her. She just gave up. Mumbling swear words, she yanked the covers off, and tromped down the short hall dragging them after her. Jordan's door was ajar and he was centered on the large bed in a draping sprawl, t-shirt and sweatpants bunched in a way that would be uncomfortable to all but the truly tired.

Jillian sighed. "Scoot over."

Chapter 6

David reached into his pocket and felt like a fool. But he smiled at the stewardess and ordered a scotch even as he corrected his mental error to 'flight attendant'. His fingers tightened around the three inch wide cylinder he had shoved there earlier. There were four more in his carryon, each with one end covered in plastic and tied down with a rubber band. He figured if he made so much as a false move he'd be shot by those plainclothes police officers that were supposed to be flying around as protection for regular US citizens these days.

The core sample he had taken from the McCann hotspot was hardly a weapon, unless someone used it to publish his data before he did. But he had watched the guy in front of him in the security line get a travel shampoo bottle confiscated and get rebuked for trying to get 'these things' on the airplane. How was shampoo even dangerous? Yet here he was with a solid, eight inch long piece of hard rock in his pocket. That could do real damage upside someone's head–

"Thank you." He accepted the scotch from the smiling blonde in the navy suit with the tie neck cloth that reminded him of his cousin Ester's Girl Scout uniform. He shouldn't even be *thinking* about the damage he could do with the rock-club. He just prayed they didn't arrest him when he hit the ground.

Removing his fingers from the core sample, he aligned his napkin with the edge of the tray, then the glass into the corner created by the scalloped edges pressed into the paper of the napkin. It was a habit he had inherited from his father – that and the habit of picking up rocks and trying to hear them speak. This one was begging him not to let it get confiscated. This one, compared with the four nearly identical pieces in his bag, was why he was on this stupid flight. Why he was headed back into McCann County again.

He brought the glass of scotch to his lips, glad that it had been a smooth ride, and that no one had caught his error in bringing the rocks on board. At least, not yet. The top layer of each was made of looser dirt, not packed in by eons of hard rain and pressure and walking animals. Yet it still had the tiniest amount of scrap iron in it. Not as reliable as the riverbed sediments. River silt would line up as the poles dictated. In water, the magnetic shards were free-floating and excellent indicators even hundreds of thousands of years later, but these loose pieces should have had just an overall trend that was statistically significant.

These had far more than that. No one had to crank the numbers to see it. Students had pointed it out as they analyzed layers for him. "Wow, Dr. Carter. Where'd this come from? Near an MRI machine?" The cores were from Wharton's dig site; they showed hotspot activity from sixty-five million years ago. And today. The mystery kept growing the more he looked at it.

After he got off the plane, it was only thirty minutes before he was on interstate 75 headed north. It was all getting too familiar, and he found himself at the little run-down motel on the outskirts of Farragut, which was on the outskirts of Knoxville. The Whippoorwill Inn sported a sign that clearly revealed it had once been a Best Western. David was certain that the Best Western Corporation had disowned this bastard stepchild a long time ago.

The man behind the counter remembered him though as he walked up to the front desk and inquired about a room. For a brief moment he panicked that maybe they were full, and then what would he do? But he almost laughed out loud as the thought slipped away. Farragut was hardly a convention center. The only thing that might fill this place up was a wedding, and he had serious concerns that most of the weddings around here involved shotguns and noticeably pregnant brides, so he pushed that idea out of his head.

His watch said it was barely 5pm home time, and he was already exhausted. He shook his thoughts out as he turned the key and let himself into the room. It was as stale and washed out as he remembered it, and he decided that he should take his luck escaping the airports with his specimens intact as a sign from the Gods. He would only do what the Gods told him to do for the rest of the day, and right now they were telling him to get some sleep.

He had just stepped out of his shoes when his cell phone rang, the clear digital tones strangely discordant in the time capsule room. When he didn't see a name on the panel he almost refused the call, only his close co-workers and a few friends knew this number, and the phone should have recognized them. But he let the phone go through another whole cycle of ring and wait before he remembered that 865 was the local area code, meaning someone here was calling him and that was just too freaky to not answer.

"Hello?"

"Yes, I'm looking for a Dr. David Carter the second."

"This is he." *This is weird*. The combination of his personal line and formal name. The tight, upper-classy sound of the female voice speaking to him.

There was a soft sigh on the other end of the line before the voice resumed the formal words that weren't telling him much. "My name is Dr. Jillian Brookwood. I work with the Centers for Disease Control and Prevention, and we're running a survey regarding McCann, Tennessee. There are credit card receipts and several residents that state that you visited recently."

She paused and David realized that he was supposed to fill the space with an affirmation or rejection. He cleared his throat. "Yes, I was there."

"I'm going to record this call if that's all right with you?"

The CDC was on the phone with him and wanted to record the call? And weren't they in Atlanta, not Tennessee? So why was the call from a local number? He felt stupid saying it, but rather than badger her with his misgivings he just said "sure." If it was a prank, he would have detected that thick southern accent in the air, right?

There was a small click and she resumed speaking. "One moment. Dr. Jillian Brookwood of CDCP Lab G12067..." Her voice faded away from him as he realized that she was recording all the information for the call. It was about as interesting as the legal disclaimers after commercials, but he snapped to when he heard his name. "Dr. Carter, you were recently in the town of McCann, Tennessee, correct?"

"Yes."

"What was the purpose of your visit?"

That made him pause. This was likely someone trying to get information out of him regarding his dig. "It was personal."

"About how long ago were you here?"

Here. She was in McCann.

"About three weeks."

"And how long was your stay?" Her voice came over the line cool, professional, detached.

"About three weeks." He barely paused before speaking again and making a point to interrupt her. "May I ask what this call is about?"

"Certainly. Have you had any nausea in the past few weeks?"

"Wait. What is this about?"

"We're doing a survey–"

He cut her off again. "Why don't we do this face to face?"

"I'm sorry, sir, I won't be able to get to Chicago in the near future."

"I'm in Farragut."

"Now?!"

He almost laughed at the surprise in her voice. With just her tone, she seemed to agree with his feelings, *Who the hell would want to be in Farragut?* "Yes. I'll be in McCann tomorrow."

"I can come to you, tonight even. Where shall we meet?"

He only knew of one place and it was a hole in the wall right next to his cheap motel, so he gave her an apology before he gave her the address. She told him she'd be there at eight and she hoped he was staying close to his hotel. Then he hung up and lay back on the old creaking bed. That was just too weird.

What the hell did the CDC want in McCann?

Probably a brain scan of anyone idiotic enough to visit. Probably they had classified living there as a disease and wanted to isolate the gene. See if he was maybe a carrier or something.

He closed his eyes and the alarm immediately malfunctioned and went off, causing him to swear. He smacked it and got up, going into the tiny bathroom to retrieve an alarm that actually worked. He pulled it from his bag and stared at it for a moment. 6:50. That was…7:50 local time. *Shit*, he'd actually been asleep. A lot of good it had done him, too.

He had all of ten minutes to get himself together and go convince the CDC lady with the tight-assed voice that he was not diseased. At least she had sounded offended about being in McCann. That was a definite bonus in his book.

David set the clock back down and looked into the mirror. That was all it took to convince him that he needed to wash his face, if for no reason other than to wake himself up. If this CDC chick was the real deal, then maybe there was something interesting going on and he should pay attention, and he headed next door to the greasy spoon.

When he entered, an older woman said hello to him. Clearly as friendly as she could be, but she didn't offer him a seat or ask what he needed. He was expected to seat himself. Each seat looked about as appealing as the next, and that wasn't a compliment. David crossed the small room and pulled out a vinyl covered chair that allowed him to see the door. By the time the lady had walked up to him and asked, "Unsweetened tea, right?" and he had been shocked that he was remembered, a woman was walking in the door who looked as out of place as he did.

The waitress smiled her toothy grin and said, "Hi, honey," to the woman, then walked off to get his tea. David stood, surprised by what he saw. As she came closer, clearly unsure who he was but guessing correctly, she tilted her head and examined him. She was much younger than he had expected, and while her voice had been all authority and questions, now on sight she was unsure, clutching the notepad and pen she held to her chest just a little too tight. "Are you Dr. Carter?"

"Yes, I am." He stood up and stuck out his hand in a gesture that was way too formal for the setting. "And you must be Dr. Brookwood."

"It's nice to meet you." She shook his hand, a firmer grip than he had expected from someone so young. They settled into a formal position, looking ridiculous, trying to keep an air of business decorum over a plastic tablecloth that looked like it had lived a past life as an abused picnic blanket.

He was going to say something, but the waitress lady, who still had yet to introduce herself, turned up at his side, and asked Dr. Brookwood, "What can I bring you, honey?"

The doctor's black eyebrows went up. "Do you have any bottled water?"

"Sorry, honey. But we got bottled coke." The waitress didn't even have the wherewithal to be offended by the unspoken suggestion that the water should be imported.

"That would be great, thank you."

He glanced at his own glass of tea, a tall old yellow glass that had the lemon pre-squeezed into it. The CDC chick wasn't drinking anything handled here, and suddenly he wasn't quite so thirsty.

David swished at the tea, wondering what came next. But he didn't wonder for long. Dr. Brookwood opened her pad and spread out a few sheets of a questionnaire. He was having trouble reading it upside down, and was interrupted by her voice, softly clearing her throat. "Shall we get down to brass tacks?"

And that was it. The good doctor was in her element and was off and running. She started up a tape recorder, a small silver thing that looked like a missing part from an alien space ship in this out-of-date setting. She re-questioned him about his where-abouts and the reasons for his visit. He re-lied about it being personal.

Then she asked him all kinds of questions about his feelings. Fever? Nausea? Dizziness? Disorientation? Gastrointestinal upset?

Within three minutes, the woman who looked and acted as though she was anywhere but Podunk, Tennessee, knew more about him than his mother ever had. Then she started asking him more and stupider questions. "Has your stomach felt queasy in the past several weeks, since you returned?"

David felt the frown move into place on his face. "Didn't you already ask me that?"

The professional mask broke form and the side of her lip curled just the slightest amount. "You wouldn't believe how many people can answer the same question five or six times, but on the seventh try, they suddenly remember that yes, they do have a life threatening allergy or yes, they did have exactly those symptoms. My favorite thing to hear when I'm interviewing someone is: 'come to think of it…'"

He almost laughed. Then he heard the words coming out of his mouth and was powerless to stop them. "Come to think of it, my friend and I did feel a little sick to our stomachs just before we left."

"This would be…" She flipped back through her paper-work, scanning for the answers she had jotted down earlier. "Dr. Greer Larson?"

"Yes."

"Was it mild or severe? How would you rank it?"

Dear God, she was insane. All this writing, and she wouldn't tell him what was going on.

He sat at the table, studying her intently and answering all her questions as best as he could. While she looked up at him only to ask another stupid question and another, and furiously recording his answers. Finally she thanked him as she stood up. "Please stay in touch. And *please* call daily with an update on your condition if you do go into McCann city. Thank you."

He glanced down at her card, making sure he had enough information, and looked back up to ask her if McCann actually qualified as a city, but she was gone. There were a few bills on the table, and the bell that had been hung over the door was letting the world know that someone had left this little hole.

Becky knew in her heart that the birds were the next in line to be magnetically freaky and that the project was no longer hers. She could only hope that they would recognize her efforts and give her a good billing on the paper that likely she would write every word of.

She drove herself to work in the old Jetta, hearing the wheezes from the engine that was never quite fully repaired. Her office smelled just a little stale, and she wondered for a brief moment if any of her colleagues had been in. But she pushed herself down into the wooden rolling chair and leaned over the desk. U.T. had sent her to Georgia, and several birds had been brought back to the school labs, using school equipment. She would call the birdwatchers from her U.T. phone, providing a record of the conversation. It was officially out of her hands. Marshall Harfield answered on the first ring. And he recognized her name right away.

"We were wondering when we would hear any news about our Bradys."

She tried to keep her voice light, even though she already knew what he would find. "I actually have a task for you if you can help us out. Then I'll be able to give you more information."

The man was overly eager to help in any way he could, and it brought back memories of being in the woods surrounded by the ABA group, all talking at once. "I need you to gather your birdwatchers and give everybody a compass and check out the areas where the birds first migrated and where they're settled now. Do you think that you can get everybody together for that?"

"I can do it today." She could almost see him puffing with pride. The manners her mama had drilled into her told her to let him know that it wasn't necessary, no matter how much she was anxious for the results. But he stepped in before she could have gotten a word in edgewise anyway. "We're having a meeting at three, and we can just change our agenda a little bit."

"Is that okay? I don't want to bother–"

"Just tell us what you want us to do."

Becky was glad that he was so happy to help. She felt a little less like she had put a chore on him. And she spent a good while explaining how they should map and record the electro-magnetics of the area and what they were looking for.

Mr. Harfield concluded with a sniff and a "we'll know it when we see it, right?"

"Yes, if there is any activity, you won't be able to miss it."

"I don't suppose you can tell me why it is that we're looking for this?"

She smiled. The man was a goon and always overeager, but he was a sharp tack. "I can. I hope it will be within the next several days. And the information you get this afternoon will help me gain the authority to share what I know."

Becky hung up with a sigh, dragged herself to her feet and gathered a few supplies. The walk to visit the Warblers wound down a long hallway and around behind several labs. An undergrad was hunched over, muttering to himself when she entered. It took only the briefest of explanations to get him to agree to a break from mucking the crates. "I'm trying to figure out why they're so creepy."

"Well," He laughed, "that's a noble endeavor. But one I doubt you'll be able to solve."

"Why is that?"

"Because Dr. Jenkinson has been at these guys since you brought them in. We've been testing them with everything we know and can't come up with squat."

"Ahhh," Becky sighed. "But I have the inside track." She went back outside the doorway and gathered up the magnets she had set down just before entering, in a few moments, he had one of the warblers out and Becky had the magnet in front of it. It turned when the magnet was moved.

"Ho-lee shit. You win. You do have the inside track."

They tried bird after bird and then finally entered the room with their pockets loaded with as many of the magnets as they could find. The birds followed their movements, becoming obviously agitated when they separated, taking the magnetic pull in two different directions.

"So that's why they were all staring at me when I entered."

Becky nodded. "Actually, they stare at the door all the time. What direction is that? Do you know?"

He looked around a little, orienting himself inside the building as the thought clearly formed for the first time. After a few motions that Becky couldn't decipher, his brows knit together and he said, "West northwest."

Becky was ready to smack herself in the forehead. Why hadn't she brought the compass? There was something about the way she had come down the hall. The undergrad followed patiently while she mentally retraced her steps backward from the birdroom, winding up in her office. Sitting in her chair with the empty shelves behind her.

The shelves are empty. Becky sighed. And only as he responded did she realize that she had spoken.

"Why are they empty?"

"Because I took the frogs home." The breath rushed out of her. "The frogs were facing the same way."

"Jilly."

Jordan's voice broke her reverie and she snapped to with a feeble excuse. "I was just thinking…"

Jordan waited, looking at her, watching, as though he might see her thought process. She knew she was a mystery to him, how her mind functioned, what she saw, and how she lived with such a singular drive. But at times like these, he sat, waiting for whatever she would come up with, and she felt the pressure of him expecting more of her than she was probably capable of producing. McCann was turning out to be more than she could handle.

She shrugged at him, giving up. "I don't have any idea what to tell Landerly, but we have to phone this in. We hit criteria."

Jordan nodded. "Do you want to make the call or me?"

"Are you serious?" She would have laughed if she hadn't spent the day fielding the six new patients down with this illness – two already at a coma state before she and Jordan got to them. All their families had said was that they were 'under the weather' or 'feelin' a little down'. Good God, one family seemed to think the father would just come out of it.

Jordan had sent her back to re-dress the first morning when she had declared herself ready in her suit and labcoat. He had said the good people of McCann wouldn't tell her *anything* if she dressed like that. He had made her dig through her bag until she produced jeans and the oldest looking top she had brought. What Jillian understood was that people would open up to Jordan no matter what he was wearing. Dirty little children just asked if they could hug him.

She looked around the makeshift lab in the bedroom with the broken bed. Her bag was stashed in the corner; the slanted bed wasn't even good as storage space, everything just rolled off. James Hann had offered to come over and fix it. So she had waited until he declared that he needed a 'part' and that he would come back with it in a few days.

Jillian wondered what 'part' one needed to fix an old wooden slat bed. A nail? A screw? She stared around the obnoxious room feeling desperate. She couldn't come up with a solution or any idea of what they had. She wasn't even sure if it was viral, bacterial, or chemical. All she knew was that the weaker your immune system was the more likely you were to get it. And that they'd been living in 'it' for days. Bathing in it? Eating it? Breathing it?

And that wasn't anything more than they had known in Florida. Except that here they could trace a link. In Jordan's bold print, it graced the wall – the connections from patient zero to the other locals who had come down with 'it'. Not that there was a standard incubation period or anything. Jillian couldn't wrap her mind around it. No matter how patiently Jordan waited on her. And she didn't want to have to tell Landerly that.

So Jillian forced herself to trail behind him to the kitchen where the old yellow phone was mounted on the wall. The push buttons were its only bow before modern technology. If it had been dial-up…well, she didn't think the CDCP even accepted dial-up calls anymore.

Jordan smiled at her, the large ugly receiver held against his head, the short coil holding him captive against the far wall of the be-roostered kitchen. "Hey Dr. Landerly."

Breath pushed into her lungs. She would never have addressed him with 'Hey, Dr. Landerly.' But then again, she wasn't Jordan. She listened, waiting for the screech that was sure to come. The questions as to why their assays hadn't showed anything. The makeshift desk top in the 'lab' was covered with test plates. But nothing had turned up.

Jordan nodded, knowing full well that Landerly couldn't see him. "Yessir. Problem is – we hit criteria for quarantine…about fifteen minutes ago…19…down or deceased…well, yes, but here that's the necessary 8 percent of the population…do it our-selves?…" His eyes looked up finally meeting Jillian's. He looked bewildered.

She was certain his expression mirrored her own as she imagined the two of them rolling yards of yellow tape around the outskirts of town.

"I thought we would call in a team. How do we hold quarantine with just two people?…" The pause seemed interminable. "The law enforcement? This place isn't a city, so there's no police… sheriff?…" He looked at Jillian, eyebrows up waiting for her to provide the answer.

So she did. In a situation like this at least she was useful as a storage and retrieval center for seemingly useless trivia. "Just one man and his son. Jerome Beard."

"How many exits to the town?" Jordan beseeched her again, and while she got the original faxed map that James Hann had sent them, she heard Jordan becoming irked with the old man. "No, I do not think better when I repeat your questions like an idiot. Jillian thinks better when I repeat your questions like an idiot."

She tried not to laugh as she held up the map. His look shut her up. Jordan's face clearly displayed that she would be the one making the next of these phone calls.

His shoulders slumped and his free hand went to his eyes. "Yessir. It looks like four exits. But that's–"

Jillian waited while Jordan's teeth clenched, her own lower lip folding in to be chewed on, a habit she had thought she had broken years ago.

It sounded a bit like Charlie Brown's schoolteacher was on the other end of the line. She could only make out that Landerly was speaking, and since she hadn't heard anything before, she gave serious thought to the possibility that he was yelling at Jordan. If she was braver she would have grabbed the phone out of his hand and told Landerly where to stuff it. If she hadn't landed her dream job with the CDCP right out of her residency…well, she had to admit to herself that there were enough ifs to leave the phone right in Jordan's hands where it already was.

Finally, Jordan spoke again. "It's a hand drawn map sir. It looks reasonably accurate but to be truthful checking out Mr. Hann's cartography skills wasn't on our list of things to do. So there may well be undrawn roads or paths…well, we're in backwoods Tennessee. And these people walk or even ride horses a lot of places so there's no way we can cover all the exits…"

Jillian stood there for forever while Jordan talked about the fact that they had checked every criterion they could think of. They were almost out of needles and reagents. All they had achieved was that they could reasonably predict who would come down with it next. Jillian's money was on Mr. Parson. He was married to a victim – exposure was strike one, was old – strike two, and his Chem panel showed that he had a very low TSH – strike three.

But that was morbid.

And probably correct.

Jordan looked ready to explode. So Jillian stood nearby to offer support, but made a desperate effort to drown out what was actually being said.

How long she stood there like that, watching Jordan move his hand from his hip to his temples, switch the phone from one side to the other, talk about McCann and how little information they had, she had no idea. The first thing that registered was "Jillian and I thank you, sir." as he hung up the phone.

His stance slugged even a little further down. His eyes all but closed. His back found the wall and he looked up at the ceiling, though Jillian had to wonder what he was looking at. She stepped forward to give him a hug, to thank him for handling that…monstrosity of a phone call.

For a brief moment she thought he didn't see her, and she saw her arms extend to him and she saw an awkward moment in the immediate future. But he was Jordan. He saw her coming and alleviated any tension by reacting. Just loosely draped his arm around her waist in a limp return-hug and mumbled 'thank-you' into her shoulder.

Her own voice was stronger, having not just been through the wringer with Landerly. "So, what? We just go to BigLots and buy about thirty rolls of 'quarantine' tape and make some makeshift roadblocks?"

Jordan chuckled a little. "Something like that. We try to keep the people contained as best we can. More recording than anything else. The backup 'rural' team will be here in two days."

"Two days!" She stood up straight, planting her hands on her hips as she removed herself from his embrace.

"Yup."

"Well…how…oh, fuck it. I'm not even going to try to figure that one out."

Jordan's eyebrows raised again, and his blue-green eyes rolled her way.

She pressed her lips together. "Yes, I know the F-word." Then she shrugged. Perhaps the best plan was avoidance. "Thank you for fielding that call. Landerly is going to kill us one of these days."

Jordan shook his head. "No he won't. He's just going to name this disease after us. So whenever anyone feels nauseated they'll think 'Brookwood-Abellard'. It's how I always imagined my life." His tone changed to a little more wistful. "People will say, 'oh, Abellard, like that horrid disease that makes you vomit and die?'"

Jillian was trying to get the picture. "Why isn't it 'Abellard-Brookwood'?"

"Doesn't sound as good."

"Oh, and there's a law about discordant names for vicious fatal diseases."

He finally looked up and smiled at her, a real, full-on Jordan smile, and she was grateful that Landerly hadn't been too much of an ass.

"We should call and see if we can interview David Carter again."

"We do need to see him. We need to get him quarantined. He's been in McCann, right?"

Jillian stilled. "In and out. Repeatedly." Then more quietly "Oh, God."

Jordan took her hand, pulling her behind him and out the door. "Not 'Oh, God'. Everyone's been in and out of McCann. And there's no way to track it or to have prevented it."

Jillian nodded, guessing that he was right. Her imagination that they were responsible was only partly true, and it was impossible, not to mention improper, to impose quarantine without the proper criteria. Still, Oh God.

Chapter 7

There was a knock at the hotel room door. David opened his mouth to yell that he didn't need room service, before realizing that room service didn't exist here.

And that meant someone was really knocking on his door. He was hardly awake and barely moving, given that he had spent the day climbing trails in the mountains. He'd been taking topsoil samples and testing them as best he could out in the middle of nowhere. But now he was sore, and slow, and he pushed his hands against the cheap paint job of the door and stuck his face flush against it before realizing that there wasn't even a peephole.

Well, there was a chain lock, not that that offered him any real protection…So he turned the knob, while muttering something about 'coming' and looked out the crack that the chain afforded. Not anyone he knew. Just some guy with a sweatshirt on.

"Are you Dr. David Carter?"

David nodded, still trying to clear his head, and a slightly familiar voice gave her name before he could place the melody and cadence in his memory.

"I'm Dr. Jillian Brookwood, we spoke a few days ago–"

He nodded and closed the door on the young man, jerking the chain out of its slot and letting the door swing freely this time. "Come in." He smiled and pretended he was awake. "What can I do for you?"

For a brief moment, he considered apologizing for the state of the motel room. But it wasn't messy, just…awful. He remembered that the good Dr. Brookwood had mentioned that she was staying in McCann, so his accommodations were probably better than either of theirs. He finally realized that the thing nagging the edges of his conscious thought was her voice, offering pleasantries and introducing her partner, who was scowling at David who was eyeing Dr. Brookwood. "-Dr. Jordan Abellard."

So David stuck his hand out and pretended he'd heard the whole thing. "Nice to meet you, Dr. Abellard. Are you staying in McCann as well?" See, he could fake it with the best of them. He'd had whole conversations with his father where he hadn't paid attention to one piece of the shit his father was trying to feed him.

"Yes, Dr. Brookwood and I have rented a house there."

A house? "Oh, are you married?"

"No." Her voice.

"Yes." His.

But then Dr. Abellard looked sideways at his partner and laughed. Raising his eyebrows and putting his hands up like he'd been caught, he confessed. "No, we're not married, but the people who own the house are very religious. So we told them we were."

"Ahhh." So the Doc was off limits. That was a damn shame. But David just smiled and waited.

It was Abellard who caught on first. "May I sit down?" He motioned to the end of the unused queen bed near the door. "Jillian's report stated that you were doing research in the area and that you had come back for a personal visit."

David nodded. *Yeah, get to the point.*

"I have to tell you that this doesn't look like a personal visit. We haven't seen you in town at all."

David started to protest, but Abellard raised his hand. "Hear me out... people are getting sick."

David raised his eyebrows in surprise, before cursing himself for giving away his hand. Dr. Abellard nodded at him, acknowledging his slip. "Yeah, I didn't think you knew."

Jillian looked as surprised as David felt about Abellard's accusations. But she had the grace to sink down beside him on the green and gold-ish comforter and look up at David questioningly.

With a sigh, he fessed up. "You're right. What do you want?"

"People are dying in McCann."

This was just getting too weird. The CDC was sitting on his crappy motel bed telling him that people were dying in the town he was researching. "What is it that they have?"

Abellard's lips were tight. "That's just it. We don't know." He opened his mouth but no sound came and he closed it just as fast. Making David wonder what the doctor wasn't telling him.

But he wasn't about to find out.

"We do know it starts with a stomach upset. And you had that, but you have no other symptoms."

"So, I don't have *it*, right?" David felt the worry festering in him.

Jillian nodded. "We'd like your permission to run a series of assays on your blood, testing for the profile we've seen in the victims." She pulled a rubber tourniquet, blood vials, gloves, and a huge needle from her jacket pocket. Unlike her partner, she went straight for the punch, her eyes looking into his waiting for his yes/no response.

His chest moved. It was a gesture of resignation. They hadn't mentioned the odd piles of stones stacked in the corner or asked him anything about his research. They only wanted his blood. "Sure. Just leave me enough to get a good night's sleep."

Dr. Jillian popped up off the bed with a surprising amount of energy, and she was shoving up his sleeve and had the rubber strap around him before he even had his arm fully extended to her. Her fingers were quite gentle given the amount of enthusiasm she had for getting his blood sample. Her gloves slid into place with seemingly no effort on her part, and she pushed the vein with her finger before sliding in the needle that he hadn't even seen her attach to the vacuum tube. He felt the pinch, then watched as his blood pumped into the vial.

After a moment she jerked open the tourniquet allowing him feeling in his lower arm again. Then held a cotton ball over the needle while she quickly slid it out of his vein without him feeling a thing. Only after inspecting the blood in the vial and turning it one way then another, did she look him in the eyes. "Thank you."

Yea, she could poke him in the veins anytime she liked.

David pushed back a happy thought that she was over eighteen, and he couldn't suppress a smile, "Is that all you guys came for?"

"No." David followed the sound of the voice and stopped his musings about the raven-haired Jillian, remembering that the two were probably involved.

Abellard spoke again. "If your business here isn't personal, then what is it?"

Damn. "Well, actually that's personal." He saw Jillian's lips press together, like she'd been hoping he'd just tell them everything. *Too bad, honey.*

"All right." Dr. Abellard stayed in his seat on the bed, his head two feet lower than David's standing height, but not show-ing any sign of weakness. "Let me take a stab at it then: you and your colleague came here to do some clandestine research. And you found something."

Shit.

He turned to see if Jillian had that *I'm close, aren't I?* look on her face, too, but she didn't. She looked surprised, her atten-tion finally pulled away from looking at the blood vial as though she didn't need the tests but could just read the red ooze itself.

Abellard continued. "You came back here to do more research–"

"Listen, I don't know what the two of you are doing here, but I don't need people prying into my life like this." Whatever blood that bewitching little vampire had left him raced faster, flooding his face with his anger.

Abellard held up a hand, palm out. "If I'm right, then you've stumbled onto something you aren't sharing with your university." His expression stayed David from kicking them both out the door right then. Barely. "And you know something very unusual and significant about an area where people are dying of a disease we know nothing about… we don't want to interfere with your research. We just need to know if the two are linked. We need to save lives."

Bastard. Abellard had him by the short and curlies.

Becky sighed, watching miles of interstate roll by and gallons of gas get guzzled on her MasterCard. She had gone around the area west of home yesterday with her compass and her frogs along for measurement. But nothing had happened. The frogs always faced the same way. Just like they had when she had traveled the area south of home the day before. Today was east, and she could see that she wasn't going to open up any new discoveries to take back to the team and impress Warden.

She *had* been paying attention to where she was headed, but somehow she was out on highway 144, heading past the old route to the airport. She drove five more minutes with no real movement from the frogs before she gave up. And she didn't know how in hell she was going to explain this in an expense report to Warden. Hell, he wanted her five-dollar dinners pre-approved before he'd reimburse them.

"Aaaaagggghhhhh." The sound of her frustrated voice startled the frogs in the seat next to her. She had meant to just think it. The little harbingers of the apocalypse looked at her. All three of them, so sweet and froggy and innocent looking. But wasn't there a bible passage about that? *So beware evil. The wolf that comes as sheep in wool…* Then, of course, there was that whole *rain of frogs* stuff.

"Stop staring at me!"

Yeah, that was mature. Yell at frogs. So she growled at them. And the far one diverted his eyes. Then his head. Then he began a slow shuffle to facing away from her.

Becky almost stood on the brakes. She did slap on the blinker and pull off on the shoulder. One of the other frogs shuffled, too. Just a mild reorienting, but way more than these froggies were supposed to do.

"Holy…"

She slammed the old pile of parts in gear and pushed back out into traffic, cutting someone off. He flipped her the bird, but she quickly asked God's forgiveness; she knew she'd never get the other driver's.

The frogs' noses were all pointing off to the south by now. They faced an area that looked about as well traveled as the moon, and she had been on some of those back roads. She'd be stranded and eaten by cougars, or bears, or worse. She knew one man up there who swore the scientists in Oak Ridge had coordinated the whole thing with the aliens.

With force, she shoved her brain in gear. Her frogs should be re-orienting at the magnetic halfway point. That meant they were either very close to a smaller site, far from a big site, or exactly as far away from a site of the same size. Becky turned the wheel and followed the frogs' noses.

Jordan looked at the page from the cheap printer they had brought along to spit out test results. It seemed a shame to get the scoop on whether you would likely live or die from a $79 printer that wheezed and beeped like an abused photocopier when it ran out of paper.

Dr. Carter's results rested in his fingertips at the moment. The only person that they weren't sure of until just now. His white count was textbook, and he didn't test positive for anything else interfering with normal immune function. Meaning it was highly unlikely that he'd be in the next batch to come down with Brook-wood-Abellard, as Jordan was already calling it to himself. It also meant the geologist was likely to come around trying to read the slopes on Jilly again. Maybe he just shouldn't start 'David' on the supplements yet, give him a little time to weaken up.

While it was supremely tempting, it did violate that whole Hippocratic Oath thing. Jordan scowled to himself.

Instantaneously, Jilly's voice reacted to his expression. "Does David have something?"

"No, David doesn't." He forced a smile and forced down the thoughts that were bubbling up about Jillian. He set the printout aside, stacking it on top of the pages of blood tests from every person in McCann. His and Jilly's were at the bottom of the pile, along with a flood of nerves. "What we need to do is go out and get the good sheriff and his boy to help us set up the road blocks."

Jillian's giggles mingled sweetly with the harsh ring of the old yellow phone and, covering her mouth, she ran off to the kitchen to answer it.

Jordan knew what she was laughing about, too. In an earlier attempt to find the appropriate methods of shutting down the town, they had set up your basic D.O.T. barricades. Only McCann wasn't a town. So they set up James Hann's two sawhorses at the east entrance of Main, and Sheriff Beard produced a real barricade from the trunk of his cruiser, only it said "City of Kingsport" in black, sprayed-on letters. Neither Jordan nor Jillian had questioned the sheriff on that.

Sheriff Beard was McCann born and bred, and he'd informed them in a deeply twisted drawl that 'them bear'cades ain't gone keep anyone . Folks'll just pick'em up and go on by.' So they had hopped into the Rav-4, desperate for a trip out of town anyway, and searched every store they could find, finally stumbling across some old Halloween barricade tape reading "Beware. Beyond this point lies certain death". Jordan had wound up being the voice of reason on that one. Jilly had begged him to get it and laughed herself into tears. And Jordan knew then that it was true: when the serious ones go, everybody better watch out.

She came back into the room now, all trace of laughter gone from her face. She took in a deep breath to help expel the nasty thought she was about to speak. "Jeb Parson's daughter just found him on his living room floor."

He bit his tongue to keep from making the inappropriate response that Jillian should claim that ten dollars she had wanted to bet. She had the first piece of her Trifecta. Jordan pulled up to the conversation on a medical level instead. "He's in a coma?"

Her head shook slightly. "He was dead when she found him."

It was only then that he noticed she was fingering the rolls of yellow 'do not cross' tape that had arrived via one very perturbed FedEx driver this morning. His truck was splattered in mud unbecoming a professional. Still, he had delivered thousand-foot rolls of bright red biohazard and yellow quarantine tape, warning signs and corrugated waxed paper road barricades that assembled like cardboard dinosaurs. None of it would keep out a scooter, but it looked pretty official.

"We need to go to the Parson's house then and–"

"We need to seal up the town." Jillian's firm voice pushed his concern down deeper. "Mr. Parson went down fast. We need to keep everyone who's in in and everyone who's out out. Until the men in suits get here tomorrow. Then we need to visit Sandy Parson and…" She turned around to walk out, but he heard her voice from the hallway. "-pray."

They didn't bother to unpack the remaining two boxes of barricade supplies, just shoved back what they had already inspected and threw the boxes into the trunk of the Rav-4. They would have what they needed when they got there. Jillian tossed Jordan the keys and was already flipping open her cell phone and dialing up some number she knew by heart. She paid little attention as she climbed into the passenger side of her own car. "Yes, David please."

David please. He tamped down the urge to tell her that the polite form of address was 'Doctor Carter'. Then he spent another round of thought on the fact that she had known the number by heart, and even if he was beginning to think something, he was too late. *Too bad, so sad.* And he'd better shove it down quick. If Jillian wanted to monkey around with someone, it would have to be David Carter the second. Jordan had critical work to attend.

The conversation was brief and, since the cell reception was so horrible, Jillian had to repeat everything she said at least three times. So Jordan had the whole conversation by the time she hung up. David Carter was not to leave his hotel room unless he spoke to her first. Not them, *her.*

It took fifteen minutes to drive the less-than-mile to the edge of town where Parson became Main. Hann's sawhorses were still there, but true to Sheriff Beard's prediction, they had been moved. Whoever drove through must have stopped to put them back, the gap wasn't wide enough for a car.

Jordan parked the Rav-4 right in the middle of the street after abandoning the idea of pulling over and was greeted by a series of fresh hoofprints, dead center of the slightly widened gap. And he didn't have a guess as to who the hell they belonged to. At this point in the game, he wouldn't have been shocked if a Conestoga wagon full of settlers showed up.

Jillian joined him and silently they each grabbed both red biohazard and yellow 'Do Not Cross' tape rolls and handfuls of wire. They separated and went about a hundred yards out from the road, winding tape around trees and wiring it to branches, sealing off the place at waist level. Jordan added tape and wire to hold the sawhorses into place. Someone would basically have to rip his work down in order to cross. *Or jump it on their horse.* He put his hands on his hips and went about adding another level of tape at eye height. The yellow and red barricade looked flimsy but the tape was strong and wouldn't rip. A good pair of shears would make short work of it though.

He wished that just for a moment he could tip his head back and be blissfully unaware and enjoy the weather and the coming season. But he had worked hard and was still paying good money for the privilege of having his ignorance stripped away. So he simply opened the driver side door and she followed suit. They drove along, neither of them saying a word until they hit the west entrance of Main. The Kingsport D.O.T. roadblock still stood where they had left it, and Jordan looked specifically for horse tracks this time but saw none.

Meticulously laying out yards of the tape, Jordan hoped that being this far backwoods they wouldn't wind up with a bad case of media crawling all over them. He and Jillian were both trained in what to say and how to refuse interviews should the news vans appear like vultures circling the town edges. He also knew how to keep things quiet and pray.

He was winding the last piece of red tape around the orange and white barricade, when he heard the gasp.

Knowing it didn't sound right, but having no other explanation, he looked up at Jilly, who was looking straight at him. They both turned to find a redheaded girl wearing jeans and low pigtails with a smattering of freckles just across the bridge of her nose. Jillian's expression gave away that she was rapidly searching her brain for a hint of recognition. Jordan knew instantly that he had never seen this girl before.

"Um?" Even with just that sound, it was clear that she wasn't the girl he had first thought her to be. After her next sentence, it was clear from her accent that she wasn't a local and she was well educated. "I think you just taped my car in...I...I have lab specimens in the front seat." She looked back and forth. "Oh dear God, what's biohazardous in there?"

Jordan's eyes narrowed, she didn't sound scared. But excited. Intrigued. And she was carefully trying to cover it. Jillian didn't catch that. She offered her most soothing tone, a mother to her child after a bad round of nightmares. "Oh, that's just to keep people out."

As the girl wiped her hand off on her jeans, he watched her stance shift. She knew what she was about and she held the cleaned hand out to him. "Dr. Rebecca Sorenson, UT

Biodiversity Laboratories. And you are?" She said it with a lilt – that upward turn at the end of all sentences that females used to play inferior to their male counterparts. And she used it very well. Jordan heard the confidence behind it. She had known she didn't look the part. And he glanced down at his own sweatshirt and now dirty sneakers just briefly before sticking his own hand out to take hers.

He spoke quickly enough to divert the doctor's eyes from Jilly's surprised expression. "Dr. Jordan Abellard. CDCP Atlanta." He motioned to Jillian, who thankfully now had it together. "This is Dr. Jillian Brookwood, my colleague."

"Becky." Dr. Sorenson corrected as she slipped her grip out of his and transferred the handshake to Jillian. And just as quickly as she gave a good, hard, quick stare, indicating that she knew the score and she'd play fairly, she spoke again. "I won't go to the media."

"Thank you." Jillian's voice held unknown volumes of relief.

"Are people sick?" Becky looked them both in the eyes again. If he didn't answer her straight, he would have to simply say he wouldn't tell her.

So he gave her one word. "*Dying*." and ignored Jillian's combined look of surprise and disapproval, but he saw that disappear even as he looked away and ignored her.

Becky turned the conversation toward him. Like Jordan, she knew an ally. "Why aren't you in full suits?" Then she answered her own question. "We've already been exposed."

She didn't show the emotion he expected.

But he nodded, confirming her answer.

"It's contagious." Her eyes wandered, focusing far away, and in a moment he realized that she was listening. She frowned. Becky mumbled a word that sounded like 'warblers' but he didn't know what that meant. She looked him in the eyes again. "Wanna share?"

"Yes."

Jillian hid her shock better this time.

Becky sighed. "I have a series of mutated frogs and other species. You're standing in a spot that I just realized today when I came in has a reversed magnetic field."

Jillian's voice finally cut into the conversation. "We know."

Jillian paced the room, finally keyed up enough to ignore her hideous surroundings. The bed still had not been fixed. And she desperately wanted to sit on it, lay back and maybe even cry. But she knew from experience that that would lead to rolling off. Which led to humiliation and frustration. Still, she couldn't sit in that horrible little ladder-backed chair for another moment. So she forced her feet to keep going. At least she would sleep at the end of this interminable day.

The motion served another purpose, siphoning off energy that she would gladly use to fillet Jordan alive. He had simply opened his fat mouth and spouted off to some girl with no ID a good portion of what the CDC knew, and what they didn't. And Jillian had no idea what reasoning he had. If any.

Not that they had been able to talk. Jordan had brought the girl back with them, and even called James Hann to see if they had a spare room for Miss Becky. Dr. Rebecca Sorenson and her mutated frogs had just left, finally, headed out to the Whippoorwill Inn, and Jordan sat in the wooden chair, re-reading printouts like the case was closed.

Jillian bit her tongue. She swallowed repeatedly. She pressed her lips together, as though that might keep it all down. But she knew better, and of course it all came out anyway, with all the harsh air she had been holding back. "How the hell did you reason out telling her all that?"

Jordan looked up at her, not at all startled by her outburst. "She's not going to the media. She's with UT, and Biodiversity could be a big help."

Jillian's mouth hung slack for a moment before she put it in gear again. "She had no ID on her. You didn't even call UT to see if someone by that name works there!"

"She's trustworthy." Jordan remained calm.

Which just served to send Jillian rocketing to the other end of the spectrum. "Trustworthy!? How would you know? You just met her!"

He clenched his teeth, then slung it right back at her. "Would you accept an argument from a blind man about the color of the sky?"

"Uh!" She knew she looked and sounded stupid standing there with her mouth open again, but she couldn't shut it off. The offended part of her brain stepped in to fill the void. "Blind! Well, I'm so sorry I wasn't born with your handy trust-o-vision, but you don't just blurt out classified material like that."

She had done it. She knew it. Jordan snapped, and came up out of the chair at lightning speed. He towered over her, his face close enough to fill her field of vision with the anger and hurt in his eyes, with his chestnut brows drawn tight together, with the clench of his jaw. "If we don't solve this, it's going to be named after us. And *other people will die*. What would you have me do, Jillian? Refuse help?"

Her teeth clicked, she brought them together so hard. She turned away out of his space in order to breathe in. And slowly out. It wasn't enough, and she forced herself to do it a second, then a third time. When she had pulled the pieces of herself together enough she spoke again, but she didn't look at him. "I may not have that intuition you do, but you should still consult me before you decide to spill secrets."

She felt his sigh even though her back was turned. "There wasn't enough time."

This time Jillian squared up and looked him directly in the eyes. "Yes, there was. And if you believe there isn't, then you need to find the time."

He took a small concessionary step back as his hand came up to comb his fingers through his already rumpled hair. "You're right." His voice washed over her again a heartbeat later. "I'm sorry."

Jillian blinked in surprise as she felt all the support leave her, and she sank back onto the tilted mattress, knowing even as she did it that it was a mistake. She spread her knees, planting her feet firmly to brace herself against near-certain humiliation, and sunk her head into her hands. "What if she screws up the investigation?"

She heard the chair scrape up beside her before she felt the heat of his arm around her shoulders. "She won't."

She sniffed, and even as she did it became mortified.

"Hey, don't cry. We'll figure this out."

With his acknowledgment, it became impossible to hide the tears. "How am I going to figure this out when I can't even remember not to sit on this stupid bed?"

She felt the deep rumble in Jordan's touch long before she heard the sound of him laughing, and slowly she, even though her left leg ached from bracing herself upright.

Jillian finally gathered herself, the one concession to her tears a brief wipe with her sleeve. And she pushed herself off the bed and away from him before she faced him, unable to hold back a final sniff. "I need ice cream."

She rambled into the kitchen with Jordan following and pulled the carton out of the fridge, ignoring the roosters staring at her while she did it. She fixed two bowls and sat down, "We know that it isn't airborne. The chain of infection just doesn't make sense."

"If it's viral or bacterial, it doesn't match with anything known. So it isn't contagious. And that leaves environmental as the best guess."

She sighed, trying to enjoy the food, and grateful it was created outside the town boundaries. "But…we've checked everything. We have no standard radioactivity. No toxic chemicals. We've tested the water, the meat Parson's has been getting, the air, the soil. What the hell else do we test?"

"Both Carter and Sorenson say we have a magnetic anomaly in part of the town." His spoon scraped the bottom of the bowl.

"Yeah, that magnetic reversal. It's weird, but…let's face it, an MRI is about a thousand times stronger than the earth's field. And that's an entirely enclosed magnetic field. And we put people in those every day, some people repeatedly, and aside from it yanking off your jewelry, there are no harmful effects. Certainly not vomiting and coma."

She let a few bites melt on her tongue before she started thinking aloud again. "It makes more sense that it's immuno-logical. Like AIDS was when they first saw it. It attacks people with weak systems."

Jordan stood and politely rinsed out the bowl, which she was relatively certain had a pig staring up from the bottom. "But those people tested positive for everything. Ours test for nothing. Is it the weakened immune system combined with the magnetic field?"

Jillian shook her head and waited while she swallowed down the pat of ice cream she had just fed herself. "Immuno-compromised patients go into MRIs at five times the rate of non-immuno-compromised patients, without these effects."

"How the hell do you know that?" He put his hands up. "Those cancer patients are often nauseated anyway, maybe the MRI compounds it and we just don't see it."

She shook her head in time to the thoughts churning inside. "It's chemo that makes the patients nauseated, and there're tons of immuno-compromised patients that don't have chemo. But even then those patients still don't exhibit ear pain, or coma and death. And if that is our culprit, those people ought to be going down fast and furious because they have far weaker systems than Mr. Parson did… What's actually more than likely is that the magnetic reversal mucked up the machinery or assays and we have something standard, but our results aren't printing out."

Jordan's grin crossed his face like a wash of brightness. "That's my girl."

"Have you measured the strength of the field?" Becky rubbed her palms across the knees of her new jeans. Her bank account was now over two hundred dollars lighter due to four days of new underwear, two new pairs of jeans, t shirts and a sweatshirt. All from that fashion bastion WalMart. Never mind that she was on lockdown with men in her age range. Men that she'd never met before. Men with PhDs and MDs. Here she was dressed head to toe in cheap, yet she'd just come over and knocked on David's door.

"Yup." He shook his head at her. "And I got nothing interesting. It's the same as the field anywhere. No Bermuda Triangle-like force to explain any of this."

She laughed, for a moment forgetting the roach that had scuttled out from under her bathroom linoleum and prompted her to knock on David's door, suggesting a professional discussion. One that involved her being part of numbers greater than the roaches. "So you're saying Atlantis isn't beneath the Appalachians?"

His eyebrows raised at her, blond and skeptical.

She had already topped the money she'd lost at WalMart with a very expensive phone call home, and she would have to call Marshall Harfield and tell him there were out-of-season warblers here, too. She changed the subject with little tact or concern. "So how long have the doctors had you holed up here?"

"Only since yesterday." He turned away, then back. "Are we all sharing here? And no one will be stealing or leaking anything until we all go public with it?"

She shrugged. "As long as the government doesn't declare it all classified and shut us down." David nodded. Looking every inch the son of the Senior Dr. Carter she had met three years ago. And every inch unconcerned about a penny of this trip. He sat on the edge of the gold polyester bedspread that reminded her so much of the one on her parents bed back home and ran both hands through his hair, showing her for the first time that the gold strands were thinning just a bit at his crown. "Okay, just outside of town, there's a geological hotspot we found on a dig. When the last polar shift occurred the polarity reversed there first. Maybe as little as a thousand years before the poles swapped on earth. There's another hotspot in Montana. And they're at the KT boundary."

"The dinosaur extinction." Becky supplied. When David gave her the slightest nod, she kept going. "Do you think the pole reversal is tied to the die-out?"

He put his hands palm up as though asking for divine inspiration. "My partner, Greer Larson, is a paleontologist, and he thinks it may be, but we're still not sure."

"So, do you think we're on our way to another pole reversal right now?" She spoke in that slow southern fashion she knew belied her education and, at times like this, her concern.

"I don't know." He was upright again, unable to contain his nervous energy, his docksiders wearing a circular pattern on the already threadbare carpet.

"But you have a gut feeling...? You look like that's your professional opinion but not your personal one."

David faced her, his eyebrows up again, his mouth quirking, but only on the one side. "You and Abellard ought to get along great with your little insights." David sank next to her on the saggy bed, and when he stilled, it lowered the tension she didn't even realize she'd been building.

"So?"

"The short answer is 'yes'. I do think we're sitting on the next pole reversal. But according to our past data, it may take a few thousand years. As best we can tell, we're due in any day now. Of course, even our best estimates are give-or-take fifty thousand years. But within the past years the poles have begun shifting. We don't have any historical evidence–"

"Excuse me?" Becky leaned toward him. "The poles are shifting now? Our north and south?"

"Yup. About twelve years ago it was discovered that magnetic north had moved. Just a little, but enough. Four years later it was even further off. It's sliding fast these days. Geologically speaking, of course."

"Wow." She breathed in, aware of her own functioning just for a second, absorbing what he was telling her and shuffling it cleanly in with her own information. "They just slide right around?"

"No. The theory is that they start sliding slowly, but individual hotspots reverse first. Weird little pockets of backward magnetics. Like here. Then as the hotspots become more numerous, they meld and, eventually, in a bang, the poles snap. Instantly magnetic north is south and south is north."

Her own backyard would then be a 'hotspot' as David put it. There really might be the rain of frogs the scientist in her was so skeptical of.

"You don't have to look so disturbed. It's all just a theory."

"Of course." Her whole life was based on 'just theories'. "And the competing ideas are?"

He ticked off the possibilities on his fingers as he rolled his eyes. "Our data sucks. All the samples were actually from riverbeds – meaning a meteor could create that pull. Or an Atlantis-like anomaly. Or we're all retarded and we're just so anxious to see something that we're fucking up our samples."

"Yeah, I'm sure that one went over well with your Dad."

David made a hard choking sound. And Becky continued. "I met him once. He was a nice man, but he didn't seem the type to take that kind of disparagement from anyone."

David went back to talking rocks, brushing aside her reference to his father. "Then the last alternate theory is that we're right. That's exactly how it happens, except we've got our dates off by, oh say, twenty million years."

"I see."

He scrubbed his face with his palms, blinking a few times with the rush of red he had worked into his features. "I was going to go the Montana site, where the KT hotspot was to see if there's a hotspot there now. But I'm quarantined, and United Airlines doesn't give a 'detained in quarantine by the CDC' refund." He turned and looked her in the eye for only the second time since she came here tonight, and she sensed it coming. Her turn. "So what's your story?"

Chapter 8

"Shove over!" It was tired and drawn out, and Jillian pushed against his back with all the strength in her arms. It wouldn't have been enough even if she had been fully awake, completely stress-free, and stronger. Jordan asleep was a rock not worth her effort. "Jorrrdaaannn."

It was the wail of the insomniac. She had heard it on her rounds as an intern and now regretted that she hadn't found more sympathy for the sufferers. And now her mind wouldn't shut off. They had called FedEx at midnight after frantically separating portions of the blood samples to send a full set of all they had collected to the Atlanta Office for re-testing. Just in case the machinery was warped by the almost non-existent magnetic field. Mike should be faxing them the results this morning and then Landerly and the quarantine crew would arrive later this afternoon.

Becky wanted to spend the day catching frogs. Jillian desperately wanted to inspect these biological specimens Becky was going to get. Check out the habitat. See if there would be any clues to the mysterious Abellard-Brookwood disease.

But in order to traipse through the woods, she would have to get a good night's sleep. And in order to get that, Jordan would have to shove his lead butt over a few damn inches! She gave another heave against his back and accomplished only the barest of deep sleep acknowledgments from him.

She'd stopped asking James Hann to fix the other bed. How could she push him to repair it? Tell him that she didn't want to have to share a bed with her *husband*? She punched at her pillow and tried to find comfort and sleep on her small wedge of mattress. Forcing her thoughts to her puppy George from childhood, she willed sleep to come and found herself thinking of her mother instead. What would Mrs. Brookwood say if she knew her daughter was in bed with a man she wasn't married to? Hell, her Daddy might just jam the business end of his twelve gauge into Jordan's back and walk him to the altar. She was too exhausted to decide if that thought should make her laugh or cry.

At last, as the light brightened, sneaking around the shades and further into the room, Jillian felt the heavy weights of rest pulling her eyes closed.

"Jilly." The soft whisper was accompanied by a warm hand that fit on her shoulder and rocked her gently. She felt the low tetany of a 'hmmmmmm' tremor through her chest but didn't care enough if she actually made the noise.

"Jilly, baby, I need you to wake up just a little."

This time the shake was firmer, and this time she made sure she was heard. "No thank you." She rolled away. The hands rolled her back over. Her eyes popped opened and her features scrunched against the piercing light.

"Baby, Mr. Hann is checking the pipes in the bath." Jordan's face was only inches from her, and she felt the wash of jealousy over his chipper alertness. Until she remembered that she was the one who had paid for his heavy refreshing slumber. And then she hated him for it.

"*Baby*," She forced her voice, now that she knew why he was being so oddly affectionate. "You almost shoved me out of our bed last night."

"I know. I'm sorry." He sat on the edge of the queen-sized mattress, taking up the space she had occupied just a few minutes ago. "That's why I let you sleep in so late." He pointed to the clock and the blurry red digits proclaiming it was already well past eleven. "Why don't you go back to sleep? I just didn't want you to wake up and be startled, or walk into the bathroom and find Mr. Hann in there."

"Huh?" She shoved up, leaning back on her hands, unconcerned that she could hear James Hann in the other room futzing with the broken bed. Or that she was in a sleepshirt and the covers were rolling away. Her face felt pushed and shoved in wrong directions and her eyes still didn't open all the way.

Jordan's hand cupped her shoulder again. "Why don't you just go back to sleep? I just didn't want you to wake up and be startled, or walk into the bathroom and find Mr. Hann in there."

"I'm awake." But the thick slurring of her words said otherwise. Her movements were slow and awkward. Jordan was able to push her back down without much resistance.

He pulled the covers up, tucking them around her shoulders in a gesture that almost made up for the bed being taken over last night. When she felt his hand brush her hair back off her forehead, she understood with certainty why the spider-bite girl in Florida had loved him so much.

Her eyes rolled open and shut a few times over the next several hours, and only on the surface of her mind was she aware that Mr. Hann had left. Jordan's footsteps were carrying to her more as vibrations than sounds while she tried to find the will to get up.

"Jilly? You do need to get up now." In dim light, she saw him check his watch, though she hadn't been aware that she had opened her eyes. "Landerly will be here in about an hour."

Cold water could not have been more effective, and the insulting remark to ask why he had not woken her sooner was barely stopped in its tracks by her brain. By force of will, she pushed out the words she really meant. "Thank you for letting me sleep in this morning."

"It's the least I could do after playing hostile takeover in my sleep last night." She glanced back at him and held her tongue again, but only because he had the decency to look sheepish.

She was in the bathroom before she called back to him, "Did Hann get the pipes all fixed?"

"No. They still squeal but they work."

"Well, it'll wake me all the way up at least." She started to close the door but his voice stayed her hand.

"I got a call about fifteen minutes ago. Gemma McKnight went down this morning."

She stepped back out of the bathroom, concern on her face as her arms folded across her chest. "Dead?"

"Only comatose." He looked away, sadness painted on his features. They both only knew of one way out of this coma.

She breathed in deep of air that felt fresher than almost anything she'd inhaled in her life but was probably deadly. "Gemma was only borderline on her labs." She turned to head off to the bathroom, but stopped just short and whipped around, excitement bringing her back to the living. "Unless, of course, they were wrong."

He just shook his head. Jordan didn't look like he was going to say much more, just planned to stand there with the borrowed coffee mug complete with rooster tail handle. She waited him out while he sipped at it, until he finally conceded to her stare and explained. "Mike faxed the results in this morning. Number for number they are dead on to ours."

"Nice choice of words."

The shower was less than refreshing, and she found herself on the edge of being flat out angry. There was nothing in this godforsaken house that was comfortable, and every time she encountered another person in this town of the damned, things went awry. They got sick. They delivered the news that someone else was 'down'. Seven people had died and fourteen more were comatose.

Wrapping herself in a towel, Jillian peeked out to find the room vacant and closed the door tightly before dressing. She hadn't worn jeans this often since she was an undergrad. Leaving her hair hanging wet down her back, she padded out into the kitchen to find Jordan at the small round table eating a bowl of frosted flakes. Giving in to the urge to make only the most minimal effort, she grabbed a bowl and spoon. Then she lined up a row of eight pills of varying sizes and shapes, and one by one washed each one back trying to ignore what they meant.

They ate quietly, Jillian certain that Jordan's thoughts mirrored her own. Landerly was coming. And they had nothing good to tell him. No leads. Every road a dead end. And townspeople dying. One by one. Her thoughts strayed to the CDC vans that might even now be turning off the interstate and she prayed they had the wherewithal to arrive in differing unmarked cars and at different times. Even just that many normal cars headed into McCann could raise someone's suspicions, but a white CDC caravan would have the press on them like flies on dead meat.

She started at the sound of a car pulling into the driveway then bouncing the long distance to the house. Jordan's gaze caught hers but they still didn't speak.

Landerly was here.

Jillian abandoned her half finished cereal and hit the front door, coming to a dead stop when she spotted the yellow space suit climbing out of the van and approaching her.

What had she been thinking? Of course they were in full suits. They had no idea what this was. She might have been showering in it. Or sleeping in it. Or inhaling it. If not simply getting it from touching and being near those who had it or had already died from it.

She stood in the open doorway, feeling Jordan just behind her, only he didn't give off the waves of shock she was sure she emanated. "Landerly." His voice was strong and she could feel the heat from the coffee mug he again cradled.

"Abellard. Brookwood." Landerly's voice from inside the bubble hood was distorted. As though it had been yelled through a pair of paper cups and a string. "We have a full DeCon tent set up at the perimeter."

"Are we clearing the town sir?" Jillian upped her volume, even though she knew he had a microphone to collect sounds from outside the muffled interior.

"Not yet." His head shook, even though the bubble-faced suit did not. "We talked with Drs. Carter and Sorenson on the way in today and we have them running a full magnetic check of the town. Then we'll clear anyone we can out of the reversal area."

Jordan's voice carried from over her shoulder. "Do you think it will do any good?"

Landerly held back a sad smile. "No. But we need to do it anyway."

Jillian fought the urge to defend their work, but she wished suddenly that she hadn't found the excitement that she had come to the CDC searching for. "Do we need to go through DeCon? Get suits?"

"No suits."

She should have known it. They'd already been exposed to the point where Landerly didn't see the need to waste money on them.

But he kept talking, interrupting the morbid river of her thoughts. He was looking at the house. "Damn, this thing is ugly."

"You should see the inside." Jordan's grin was evident in his tone, and Jillian wondered if he really thought it was funny or if it was a set-up on a cruel practical joke.

"All right, you two need to pack everything that's personal. Leave the CDC set-up and gather all the paperwork. Do that first." He turned and walked slowly and painfully to the van.

When it became clear that Landerly had explained everything he was going to, they simply headed back inside to begin their first assignment of packing up the files.

"What the hell is this–" Jordan pulled up short at the door to the 'lab' bedroom. A suit stood in the center and pretended not to hear them or actually didn't. His back remained turned and he snapped photo after photo, inspecting each one on the small screen on his digital camera before turning his focus to the next thing.

Jillian pressed up on tiptoe to spy on the rendering of the most recent photo and was startled to see that it was of the wall charts, and clear enough to read every word. She grabbed a set of papers and when she turned, she smacked into Jordan again.

"Hey."

"Sorry." But she didn't look up, focused only on the pain in her nose and holding the tears at bay. Although if they were from the sting to her face or her pride she was unsure.

She felt her arm jerk in the socket before she realized Jordan had a death grip on her elbow. "It's not that." He stayed still and silent until she acknowledged him with a clear gaze. "Don't be sorry. People are dying here. Just don't go tripping and breaking a leg or getting an open wound. Now's not the time to stress your immune system in the slightest."

"Oh yeah. Landerly sending in the suits and giving us crazy orders that we don't understand doesn't stress my system at all." Only to herself did she admit that her sarcasm masked a very real fear.

Jordan still didn't loosen his hold on her arm. "I'll get the rest of the papers and you start packing. You have more to pack than I do anyway."

She resented the underlying sexism in the remark, until she admitted that it might not be biased but simply truthful. When Jordan finally freed her arm, she didn't look up, but concentrated on the ground in front of her as she headed off.

Her hands and feet worked independently of her head, folding and rolling her clothing and stuffing it back into the duffle bag while she remained silent. Jordan appeared at her side with his own bag and together they went to the front door, encountering Landerly coming up the walk. His gait in the suit gave away his age, and Jillian wondered what it was about this case that got him out and about. Wasn't that what she and Jordan had been hired to prevent?

"I was just getting ready to see what was holding you two up."

Jillian opened her mouth to protest that it had been barely fifteen minutes since they had been ordered to clear out, but Jordan's hand grasped at her wrist. Not that it mattered anyway, Landerly was talking again without paying the slightest bit of attention.

"We've got teams checking out the three cases you pulled as evidence – two of them appear to be the real deal. And there're another two cases in Florida in that nursing home that I *authorized* you two to visit while I was in Hawaii. You're going back."

Jillian's mouth hung slack, but she managed to keep it from gaping. Her eyes went wide with real fear. None of the ideas she had had about Landerly's packing them up had to do with the possibility of further outbreaks. She had almost forgotten the Florida cluster. The entire nursing home had been exposed. She shook her hand, loosing it of Jordan's now tighter grip that had threatened her circulation.

Landerly kept talking as though neither of them could possibly need a second or two to assimilate the damage and possibilities he was laying at their feet. "You'll pick up Dr. Carter en route. He's already back at his hotel packing, as he'll be going with you to check out the area. Dr. Sorenson is staying here and will be working for the CDC obtaining wildlife specimens. We need everything you can gather on the Deltona cluster. See if we can crack this thing. It's getting ugly."

He turned away, finished.

Two suits emerged then from the back of the van, and from the looks of the gesturing all of the files had been duplicated. Jordan took her duffle bag from her nearly slack wrist and went to throw it in the back of the Rav-4, only to be stopped by a suit. Jillian's brain was working too fast to think about where she was going. So she set herself behind Jordan and followed like a little duck wherever he went.

The cluster in Florida was growing. That indicated either contagion or…continued toxin exposure or…or a bizarre vector or…or…long incubation period. And that was the worst. That would mean far-reaching spread. The way AIDS was all over before anyone knew it even existed. Lentiviruses, or those that remained inactive long after infection, could be serious to society simply because the spread was undetected for so long that tracing the path from victim to victim was nigh unto impossible.

With a start from her morbid thoughts, she realized the afternoon sky was a shade of blue you couldn't see in the city, and the autumn trees were alive in reds and golds she hadn't seen in a long, long while.

"I'm sorry, you're going to have to fill me in on what the fuck you two are babbling about." David leaned forward, saying what he wished he'd said an hour ago.

Jillian and Abellard had sat with their heads tucked together speaking English with enough Latin thrown in to be damned obnoxious. It was giving him a pounding head and shoulder stress. And worse, it made him feel under-educated.

When they looked up at his comment as though only just then realizing that he was on this plush flying den with them, he almost stood up and walked to the back of the room again. He could just help himself to another scotch. Or he could stand his ground.

"What can we tell him?"

Jordan spoke as though he wasn't there. That cretin had the hots for Dr. Brookwood, too. But the more David watched, the more certain he was that there wasn't anything actually going on. What he was uncertain of was whether the hot doc returned the feelings.

She shrugged and frowned and pursed her lips, and if they weren't flying straight into the pits of hell – retirement haven, Florida – he would have been turned on. "I don't know." She looked away from Abellard and up at him, causing him to realize that he had in fact stood up.

The CDC had appointed their private Lear jet quite nicely. The seats were pale leather and cushy as hell. And in the back was a full bar that he had been the only one to avail himself of.

For a brief moment, he entertained the thought that Jillian wasn't yet old enough to drink.

"David, what level of security clearance do you have?" Jillian's voice was sweet but off, a perplexed honey bringing him back to the bizarre reality he was in.

He smiled a smile that spoke of the scotch he'd already had and the one he'd like to have next. "I have no idea. Let me know when you can speak to me."

It was Jordan who proposed an answer to the dilemma. "He must have some sort of emergency clearance. Landerly sent him with us." He looked up, not having moved from where he had swiveled his own seat to sit all cozy with Jillian. "Landerly is nothing if not logical. I'll take the heat for whatever we share with you. He can't mean for us to keep you in the dark."

David took the seat next to Dr. Brookwood, willing to give up the scotch in favor of a little maneuvering. He was upset to find that he liked Dr. Abellard, but that didn't mean he wouldn't steal sweet little Jillian right out from under him. Well, from the looks of things, she hadn't been under him yet. With effort, he redirected his thoughts and focused on Jordan. "What is it that I need to know?"

"We have a spot of reversed polarity, which is weird as hell, and people in that spot are dying of something we can't classify. All our tests are coming up negative. If it's a virus, it's got a protein coat unlike any we've ever seen before. All the assays are missing it."

Jillian's voice broke in beside him. "We can't find anything with microscopic analysis either."

"But you couldn't have had the best equipment there in McCann, right?"

Jordan nodded, "True, but we've been sending samples back and forth. The Atlanta office can't find anything either, and they've got the best machinery anywhere."

David soaked in that for a second. "It sounds like you've got your hands full, and I have to say that I have no idea why I'm even here."

Jillian had stood and was stretching, the only one of the three of them to be able to reach full extension in the plush but midget height fuselage. "You're convenient?"

"You wound me."

"Yes, but I'll bring you another scotch to soften the blow."

So he asked it. "Are you even old enough to serve scotch?"

Her eyebrows quirked, but Jordan's voice carried to him, over his shoulder now because David had twisted as Jillian climbed over him and made her way back to the bar. "She's a physician, you know."

He twisted back around, "Yeah, but maybe she's really accelerated. It happens."

Jillian interrupted them to ask David again if he was going to take her up on that scotch. Right as her hand appeared over his shoulder handing Jordan what looked like a gin and tonic that he hadn't even asked for. Jordan smiled and said thank you, before meeting David in an eye lock that said he had some idea what the geologist was about.

Whatever.

In a minute he had his scotch and Jillian settled in beside him with a margarita.

"So? Upset stomach? Then coma, then death." David thought that was way too simple a way for a person to die. No bells, no whistles, no grand symptoms. "Are you serious?"

"As a heart attack."

"And it's contagious?"

Jordan shrugged and lifted his drink in a long swallow that revealed more about his tension than his words or manner. It was Jillian who stepped up, filling in the holes.

"We can trace transmission from person to person. But with a small town like McCann that really doesn't mean much. At this point, quarantine is mostly to keep tabs on everyone who's been exposed. We can't begin to hope to control spread at this point. Jordan and I are headed to Florida to pool the new data with what we have."

"Are they evacuating McCann?"

"As we speak." She said it like it was somehow her fault. So he changed the subject.

"What if the Florida site is a hotspot?"

"Then we've got some serious problems." Jillian set the unfinished drink aside and pulled a blanket out from under the seat, as though she had known all along that it was there. Covering herself, she turned away, tucking her feet up under her.

Jordan swiveled sideways and pulled out a sheaf of papers to leaf through, leaving David with his own thoughts. And David didn't like them very much.

He'd had an upset stomach when he had visited McCann the first time. So had Greer. And it had passed. Did that mean he'd been exposed? Was he now immune? The CDC didn't seem to be worrying too much about these two docs, although they all had been put on a regimen of medications. Then again, maybe it was just too late to do much more than medicate them and pray. Then again, David didn't put much stock in prayer. It hadn't yielded anything of value for him before.

He tapped Jordan's shoulder, impatient for the millisecond it took the doctor to acknowledge him. "Are there carriers for this disease?"

"We have no idea. We can't figure out anything except that we've never seen it. The symptoms aren't like anything we know so we can't even assume it will act like other things of the same family." He looked back down at his papers, then up again, "Why?"

He almost couldn't say it. "My friend Greer had upset stomach. Worse than me, when we were here the first time. He's gone home to his wife, who's pregnant. Could he pass it to her?"

"I have no idea. I'm sorry." Somehow Dr. Abellard managed to look like he actually *was* sympathetic. Yet within a second he was back to thumbing through his papers and jotting down numbers on a miniature legal pad.

David sank back in his seat. Inadvertently swiveling it, he let it rock gently back and forth, sustained in an almost harmonic motion by the flight of the plane. His scotch turned wet and slippery in his hands, leaving him no choice but to polish it off before the ice melted and it became even more of a soggy mess. He reclined the chair and, in minutes, sleep rolled over him, taking him to a foggy place with gravitational forces from all sides, and fossils that contained writing instead of bones.

"Mom, I'm good." Becky shoved a hand through her hair, realizing that she was overdue for a shower. Her mother had started with 'I'm afraid that you're going to get sick.' And like a well written essay, all you needed was the topic sentence. The rest was just the jabberings of a mother well practiced in the art of worry.

Becky listened with only half an ear, waiting for a break in the tone or speed, hoping to get a word in. "I'm eating, Mom. In fact, the CDC is monitoring my diet. Even you aren't as strict as these guys." Becky left out the part about the medications they were feeding her and the men in the yellow space suits. "I need to know about the frogs. Are Brandon and Mel taking good care of them?"

"Yes. They went out and caught a few more just yesterday–"

"No! Mom, don't let them out there!"

"Why is that?"

Becky felt the gloved, yellow hand on her shoulder. They were monitoring the conversation, as Becky was still waiting for an emergency clearance status. The agent listening in was one of the conditions of phone privileges, lest she spill the scary beans.

"Mom, that area mutated the frogs." She didn't lie, she just didn't tell the *whole* truth. "I don't want the kids out there without me. And I need Aaron's new cell number. I tried his place a few times and got no answer."

She pressed her mother to go just a little faster, without revealing that an agent was standing over her shoulder, or any other little tidbit that would scare the woman even more. Becky spoke about three more words before artfully extricating herself from the conversation, a skill perfected out of necessity.

The space-suited alien didn't comment, he simply took the portable phone out of her hands and walked out of her tent, locking the 'door' behind him. Her bizarre forced vacation was turning into the equivalent of Siberian work detail. She had actually been digging in the hard earth with a pick earlier today. If she had worn metal ankle cuffs with links leading to the next digger she couldn't have felt more imprisoned.

At least the CDC had seen fit to send her three little *rana* along with her. The poor frogs were even more incarcerated than she. Each in its own little terrarium, always facing the heart of McCann. Becky hadn't learned much from her digging. The underground species seemed unharmed. But the local amphibians were whacked out, the newts and salamanders suffering the same kinds of fates as the local frogs.

The frogs she had pulled here were, in general, four-legged, but not any luckier than her first batch. The majority of these guys were blind, and many were pale in color, making it a wonder that so many existed. Pale wasn't a good camouflage color, so animals like that were often picked off by predators first thing. And the sheer numbers of these guys that were bordering on white made her wonder if they tasted bad or something.

Good, another thing to do tomorrow. And here she'd been afraid she'd get bored.

Tamping her internal sarcasm back down, Becky made the mental effort to realign her thoughts. First she had to call Aaron while it was still early enough that he would answer his cell. She stuck her head out the door and asked for the phone again. The guy looked at her like she was a bother, and Becky had no doubt that she was.

Aaron answered on the first ring. And she explained more than she had to her mother. "Don't let Mel and Brandon back there. I know they want to play…but…"

"But what?" Aaron had never settled for the 'I'm the authority, do as I say' answer, which had rubbed one person in town the wrong way over and over – their father. But now, Becky wished he'd give her a bye just this once.

But she gave him a little more information instead. "Frogs develop *after* they're born. So the environment affects that.

Clearly *something* is wrong there. And Brandon and Melanie are still developing themselves. So please, just keep them out."

"Sure, sis." There was a pause, and even over the phone she could hear his brain gearing up to ask a harder question. "Does this have anything to do with the other area you found and your little 'extended research trip'?"

Becky sucked in a breath. The yellow suit sitting and listening in this time wasn't the same as a few hours ago. So she risked that they would cut off her phone privileges and just said, "Yes." And before he could ask anything more, she jumped in again. "I need you to do me a favor."

"Is this one of those 'no questions asked' favors? And when the bodies start piling up, I'm going to get disbarred kinds of things?"

Becky wondered why he'd had to use that reference to bodies. As if he knew more, or could read more from her tone, than he was letting on. So again she just said "Yes." She tried to put a little laugh in it, but she wasn't that good of an actress.

The yellow suit man gave her a stare, but she shrugged at him, like *what was I supposed to say?* And she asked Aaron to go out and recheck the boundaries of the site.

"Becky, are you in trouble? Am I going to regret this?" His voice was a hiss and the irritation and tired humor that had spun through his words even just a few exchanges ago was gone.

"Aaron, I'm okay." It was the best she could tell him, not knowing if she was sitting around waiting to die. "And you might help a lot of important research with this. Thank you."

He said a quick good-bye and hung up.

Looking up with a conjured smile, Becky handed the disconnected phone back to the suit, knowing they'd return with it when Aaron called her back. And she waited.

An hour later, the suit came back in with the phone. "Hello?"

"Becky? Why the hell did I have to go through some sort of security check to get to you?" Aaron was clearly worried. And there was nothing she could really do about it.

"Because you did. How's the site?"

"Nothing." She could hear the chirping of cicadas in the back ground and the usual woods noises. He was there now.

"So it's all the same." She let out a breath, startled by its release.

"No, there's nothing here. The compass needle doesn't move at all. I walked the whole boundary twice."

Her brows pulled down, and her fingernail tried to compete with her words for space between her teeth. "So north is north and the whole site is just a staked out boundary?"

"Looks like it to me…wait. No, north is still south according to the compass." He sounded as perplexed as his words were making her. "But it's not changing at the boundary line. Not like before. It was real clear, now…nothing."

Her heart raced, throwing a lump up into her throat. She couldn't even think of the implications of what Aaron was telling her. So she asked the obvious, "Can you find the edge?"

Through the cell phone connection, she could hear his boots crunching through the undergrowth. "Already looking for it… wait. Got it!"

"Where are you? Where is it?"

"About ten feet out."

"God. Aaron, just get out of there. Go home."

Chapter 9

Jordan woke to the sound of sledgehammers keeping cadence inside his head. It was their third day here, and nothing was new. Oh, except the mysterious Brookwood-Abellard had struck Florida again. One of the coma victims had slunk off into quiet death yesterday morning. And fate was claiming another. Maxie Londers had only had ear pain prior to this, but quickly the vomiting that had begun at four a.m. had changed. Maxie was now on a ventilator, awaiting her turn into the kingdom of whatever god she chose.

He ached for the Levinsons. Art was less obvious in his grief than Maddie, but maybe more touching for that exact reason. Rolling his face into his pillow, Jordan made a half-assed attempt at self-suffocation. He should get up and brush his teeth and get dressed like every other day of his life. But unlike every other, he would breathe a little harder down David's neck, begging and praying for a resolution to this thing.

On the one hand, he wanted the problem to be the magnetic reversal. Problem solved. The bug they couldn't find didn't exist. Not their fault. But that would leave holes of uninhabitable space on earth. Surely all the hotspots couldn't be in North America, right? There had to be others elsewhere, right? And at that point the problem went way out of his scope. Hell, it had been out of his scope from the start.

David was trying. Becky was trying. Jilly's fingers were about bare to the bone and his own back was about to break. He could simply cry foul and give up. He and Jillian had kept sharing a room, leaving the second free as workspace. So he could just not go into the workroom again. Simply ignore all of it.

"It's like there's nothing here to find." Her voice was soft in the false darkness created by the blackout curtains. It came from over his shoulder and the rhythm and timbre told him she'd been awake for at least a while. "I've kicked myself a dozen times this past week for not being a pediatrician."

He couldn't suppress the small laugh, and he finally rolled to face her. Somehow she was bundled under the covers with the look of a child huddled against the cold of winter. "What do you say we just leave and go set up a practice together? We'd be good."

"No, we're just missing something. I know it."

He sat up, letting the sheet slide down him, fully awake. If Jillian thought there was a connection they were missing, if it was niggling at the corner of her brain, then he trusted that it was there.

She sat up too, holding her head as though to keep the information from sloshing out. "There's a numbers issue that we're missing here."

Jordan's feet hit the less-than-plush carpet and he started pacing, energy renewed at even this slight prospect. "We aren't at quarantine, and we're way too populated here. It's too high profile to swarm down in yellow suits."

"No, it's not about quarantine. It's about numbers I *saw* somewhere."

They needed to be up and dressed and in the other room where all the numbers were lined up in neat rows and gathered on charts waiting for them. He forced a deep breath into his lungs. "I'm going to get dressed and go down and grab some food, then I'll bring it back–"

"No." It was positively frantic. "You can't leave me alone. Just keep talking to me. It's like a word on the tip of my tongue." She was throwing off the covers and stepping out in her shorts pajamas that sported a squinty-faced red-head and the words *bad hair day*. At another time, it would have made him laugh.

"Okay." And even as he extracted himself from her grasp she re-clung to him. "What's wrong, Jilly? Are you all right?"

She waved her hands in front of her face. "It's here. And if I don't solve it, people will die!"

The starch left him. Perhaps Jillian didn't have any answers. She just had fear and guilt the same as him. "Let me go into the bathroom and get dressed. Then we'll go down and get breakfast." He didn't mention numbers again or solving anything. He didn't really think they would.

"I'll change out here while you're in there."

He nodded. Even in a panic, and buried under a brickload of guilt, Jillian was efficient. Closing the door behind him, Jordan allowed himself a brief measure of time where he could ignore the fact that Jilly was close to tears just beyond the wall. That the hallway door would only open to a host of other responsibilities and problems.

They wandered down for the continental breakfast and were heading back, food balanced in their hands when she stopped, almost causing him to put steaming coffee down her back.

"Room numbers." She pointed at the numbers they were passing with each door down the hallway. "But not numbers." With no warning she went from 'off' to 'on' and started back down the hall. "Not numbers." Again she muttered, and Jordan knew that he would be the one to set down his carefully balanced breakfast and fish out the magnetic room key.

She was passing him into their room when her head snapped up. "Room colors!"

He nodded, his brain catching on to her excitement. As though he, too, could now see light at the end of the tunnel. He just didn't know what was producing that light. "The Levinsons color-coordinate the bedrooms so the guests don't have to remember anything but their color."

She ungraciously unloaded her food onto the side table. "All the patients were in color coordinated rooms, and if we go back and check, I'll bet they're all at one end of the house. Or clustered."

He mentally tabbed through what he remembered of each of the patients, calling up a face, and a mental picture of the room. One blue, one pink, one purple, all at one end of the long house. "They were at the north and west ends. Even the new ones."

They nodded at each other with Jordan supplying the words. "Another physical anomaly. But then why hasn't David found anything?"

Heavy breathing sounded in the open doorway over his shoulder and Jordan leaped around to find David hanging in the gaping space, sucking in air even as he spoke. "David has."

"What?" Jordan took in the wrinkled and filthy khakis and the bags under his eyes. Whatever David had been up, to he hadn't been dressed for it.

"There is just now a start of two reversals – at the north end and west of the kitchen. Small spots. With small fields."

"Why didn't we see it before?" Jillian walked toward David, but it was Jordan who handed over his coffee with an "I didn't drink any of it" to a grateful David.

"I'm used to seeing this stuff in deep layers. There's a history of reversal here, but no one ever recorded it before. All the strata tell the story. But, right now the top layer is showing the shift, too. Not my forte, but I found it." He took a sip of the steaming silt water and had the wherewithal to thank Jordan.

"So why are you just telling us now?" Jillian shook her head, still looking inside, not focused on either of the men in front of her. Jordan knew the signs.

"Because, sweetcheeks, I was up all night playing in the dirt."
Yup, Jordan thought to himself, *that matches the appearance.*
"And I only just now found it." He tipped up the cup, draining the last of Jordan's coffee. "So you two can call the old doc and tell him it's high time to move these people out! And I am now going to sleep."

With that, he practically rolled out of view and Jordan heard the metallic click of David's door closing just a second later.

Jillian stood stock still, thinking. "We're missing somebody."

Not able to help her think, Jordan called Atlanta, but not Landerly. "Mike, it's Jordan."

"All our numbers exactly match yours." Something about the tones in his voice made Jordan sure that Mike was in the lab.

"Yeah, I figured they'd match." His hand went automatically through his hair, a gesture of frustration. "But I've got another set of info for you to run."

"Lay it on me, I'm going to be sitting on my assays here in a few minutes."

Jordan laughed. "That's funny."

"What?"

"Sitting on my *ass*ays."

"Oh." He could hear the shrug in Mike's voice, as though the thought had never occurred to him. "What do you need?"

"I need you to do a statistical comparison of the numbers we're getting for our people and the general population."

But Mike was Mike, and in a minute he got it. "What are my controls?"

Jordan rattled off the stats, then Mike was gone, his hands no doubt resuming their usual speed as he plated samples and provided numbers for them.

Turning, he found Jillian watching him. "Was that Landerly?"

That showed how long she had been paying attention. "No, Mike. He's going to run a standard deviation for us. See if the reversal is lowering people's immune systems so they get sick, or if it's making already weak people sick."

He could see her absorb that in a lightning flash, and as she made eye contact with him, he realized her eyes were bright. He was opening his mouth to ask, but she beat him to it. "I know what we missed."

"Yeah?" From the look on her face he was certain he didn't want to hear it.

"Eddie."

Becky sat on the edge of her cot with her legs apart and her elbows balanced on her jeans-covered knees. No one was dying anymore. In fact, everyone who'd been in quarantine had stayed healthy for five whole days. According to Jillian and Jordan things hadn't been going anything like that before they were all moved out of town. So good news was coming. Certainly.

And with the little blind amphibians she was picking up here, along with some seriously disturbed insects, she was certain that the environment was to blame. Amen to that, and here were the men, no longer in their yellow suits, approaching her. She just knew that they were ending the quarantine. Becky stifled a 'Halleluiah!'

Two of them walked up in jeans and t-shirts looking very unlike the CDC scientists they were. But then again, they were in backwoods Tennessee, and not their offices in Atlanta. She hazarded a glance down at herself and thought she didn't look very scientific herself. One of them nodded at her like he knew her, which was only confusing, until he opened his mouth. From his voice, she could tell he was the one who had brought her the phone, consistently listening in on her conversations for the past three days. Briddle.

"Quarantine's over?" She looked up expectantly, praying for an okay to return home, and check out her own backyard.

"Yes."

She didn't wait to see his reaction. Just jumped up and started packing her things. Becky had forced herself to hold off 'til now, because she just knew she would have entered clinical depression if she had to unpack.

"We wanted to let you know that we've removed the project from Dr. Warden and the University of Tennessee's jurisdiction."

Her busy hands stilled. "What?" They were taking her frogs?

"We would like to offer you the opportunity to stay with it, with the CDC. Of course, you'll be compensated if we all survive."

"*If* we all survive?" Her mouth hung open. "Is that supposed to be a joke?"

Briddle looked perplexed. "Was it funny?"

The man behind him shook his head and rolled his eyes. "No, it wasn't."

Becky's gaze snapped to him, recognizing the sound if not the face of the biologist who'd been working with her in the makeshift lab occasionally. "John!"

He stepped forward, taking over the conversation for the un-funny Briddle. "There's a lot of work still to be done. You know the animal species are going to help us suss this thing out. Plus there's enough material for about, say, a billion papers." His lips pressed together in what was almost a smile.

"Papers?" *A job? With the CDC? Chasing frogs?*

Inside a few minutes Becky had voiced all those concerns. Her packing remained forgotten as she sat back on her cot, suffering a mild case of shock. She *had* to go with the CDC or hand over her frogs. They were government property now.

She heard other voices outside. A sound she hadn't heard before. The people of McCann being set free. Almost. "They can't go home, can they?"

"No." John shook his head, his face unshaved for what must have been a good four days. "The government will have to relocate them."

"What do we do next? Do we set up a lab in Atlanta?"

"Eventually. But right now we need to go do tests on a new location in Florida."

"Florida?" She said the word as though she'd never heard of the state before. Her brain really was on overload, and she'd ruined her routine and hadn't eaten any breakfast this morning because she'd been too excited.

"Can I go home first?" That was what was making her a mess. Her mom and dad were worried, Aaron thought she was on the run from the law, and no matter what the CDC was offering her, she wouldn't take it if it meant she didn't get to show her family she was okay.

"We need to head right out. They want us on site by tonight. Brookwood and Abellard are already there. And they're seeing the same kind of magnetic anomaly."

"You can't tell her that!" Briddle stood over them, looking like he was going to wire John's mouth shut. "She hasn't signed her paperwork; she isn't cleared yet!"

"She has emergency status." John just looked up to where Briddle had planted himself in the corner of her tent. Again his face showed his dissatisfaction with the teetotaler. "Besides, she's going to sign."

"You're right, I'm in." She stood and stretched. "But on one condition. I'm going home first. I'll call my Mom and tell her to have everyone there so I can see them."

John looked up at Briddle, still not standing, not giving the man any of the respect or formality he seemed to want.

"Oh, all right. But no talking to them about any of this, and you're still on emergency status until we get the paperwork through." He handed her a clipboard and she quickly read and signed everything – basically accepting a probational position and agreeing to defer to her superiors' judgment of what she could and couldn't share. But she knew what Aaron had said about government contracts. Your signature meant everything and then some. Theirs meant nothing.

Briddle left with his precious paperwork tucked under his arm and she looked back at John. "You'll want to come home with me. When's our flight?"

"They'll put us on something this evening." He, too, finally stood. "I need to go with you? I'm not much for carrying luggage."

"I have forty of the frogs from my site at my house."

She almost laughed as she saw his jaw drop, and re-phrased her thought. "I guess I should say 'we' do."

Jordan stilled. Standing in the doorway, his question was answered. He hadn't told his Dad that he was coming to Lake James. Yet here he was on a Sunday morning and the smell of pancakes was weaving through the house he still had a key to. "Dad?"

"Jordan!?" His father came through the opening from the kitchen, brandishing his spatula like a weapon, hope and fear both written plainly on his round face. "What are you doing here?"

"I needed pancakes?" He shook off the burdens of the flight, and the sound still in his head of Jillian giggling and the sheen in her eyes. David was with her and they would handle the stress they were all under together. Jordan had his Dad. Not that his father spoke much.

Case in point, his father simply grunted and pointed with the spatula to a vinyl seat at the old scarred table and brought Jordan a plate and fork while the griddle sizzled. It seemed not only did his father make pancakes on his own every Sunday morning, he made enough for Jordan who wasn't there, and maybe even his mother, too.

He caught his Dad up on things while the pancakes cooked, his own voice the only thing easing the sounds of his father's rhythmic work. "We're here to examine Eddie's case. A team of us. But I can't tell you much more than that."

He saw the nod from the back of his father's head.

"I just wanted to come visit."

Again the small nod.

So he ate. Better than he had eaten in weeks. Fresh, hot pancakes. With syrup from the plastic bottle with the grocery store brand label across the front. Nothing fancy at all. But the kitchen and the food and the smells – it took him back.

And something must have showed. Because when his father finally sat down he took one look at Jordan and asked, "Who's the girl? Jillian?"

"What?" His face lifted from his plate and his heart kicked up a notch. How had his Dad seen what he was only just admitting to himself? And just a few days too late, too. Late enough to begin with the serious self-ass-kicking.

"That doctor you work with. You mentioned her last time you were here." It was more words than his Dad had strung together in years, to him at least.

"How did you know?" He spent time cutting the pancakes and shoving another bite into his mouth to hide the expressions he was sure were giving him away.

"I've seen that look. Almost identical. On my own face, when I thought your mother was going out with someone else."

Jordan almost laughed. If his mouth hadn't been full, he might have. "That bad, huh?"

"What's this other guy like?" Mr. Abellard held the fork as though it was a laser pointer and he was giving the latest Power-Point presentation.

"Dad, you haven't said this much to me in forever."

The older man shrugged and ate another bite of the pancakes. For a full minute, Jordan was certain that he had effectively shut down the one open communication he'd had with the man in years. And it hadn't been worth it. So he followed suit and shoveled in more food.

But his father surprised him. "Didn't know what to say to you." There was a shrug, buried in the beefy shoulders and in his voice. "You went off to college. I'd never been, didn't know what any of it was like. Didn't have any friends who did. And ashamed because I couldn't pay for it for you."

"Dad—"

"But I *know* this." He jabbed his empty fork at his son again. "I've heard about this Jillian. But what about the guy?"

Jordan's brain churned, doing the thing that probably separated him the most from his father. The constant reassessment, the continual striving for more information. "How do you know there's another guy?"

"No good excuse for you not to have her if there isn't." His Dad didn't look up from his plate. There was no expression or any sign other than the words showing Jordan that his father held him in higher regard than he had ever known. "So what's he got on you?"

"Blond hair, good build, smart, little bit older, stable."

"He a doctor like you?"

Jordan sucked in a snort. "Try: world renowned geologist...And he's rich."

"Hm." He sounded like the same old Dad. "Well, what do you have on him?"

Again Jordan snorted. "Obviously not enough."

But his father waited. Eating his pancakes, and occasionally looking up, until it was clear that his father would think less of him if he didn't at least give it a shot. So he did. "I'm taller...and I still have all my hair."

His father laughed. A serious belly full of laughter, and it was worth the flirt in Jillian's eyes when she looked at David just to hear his father laugh like that.

He waited, eating more than he should have, until he hit his threshold of pain. Thinking that if he ate enough his father would spill the secrets of the universe. Or at least how to undo the innuendo and whispers that he had heard from their heads tucked together when he woke up on the plane.

They had flown in first-class this trip. Time was less of the essence. Jillian, having seen the connection at the same time as Landerly, had Mike plowing through back cases to discover Eddie and one other death in Lake James from five years ago. The fact that Eddie's last name was Abellard and the date of death hadn't escaped Landerly in the slightest. The phone had rung just moments after Jilly had spoken his cousin's name. Those two scared him more and more. Another good reason to skip out and come visit his Dad.

David had insinuated himself next to Jillian, and should have passed right out given his night in the dirt. But no, he swore it must have been the coffee Jordan had given him – perked him right up like he'd slept all night. Damned coffee. And the next thing he knew, Jordan found himself dozing across the aisle while Jillian and David talked about all the things they could. Anything but the purpose of the trip. Anything but the fact that three scientists were on the next flight to Minnesota for the CDC.

Despite the pancakes and the ugly turn of his thoughts, his father shared no more wisdom with him. Just a bear of a hug and hardly a word as Jordan said thank you for the breakfast and headed back to his hotel room – the one between Jillian's and David's.

When he finally slid the key through the lock to his room and flipped on the lights, he found Jillian curled up on his bed still asleep, but starting to blink at the light, so he slapped it off. The flutter in his chest betrayed him, happy at seeing her in his room again. "I'm sorry, I didn't expect you in here." He almost kicked himself for saying it.

Her voice came out of the depths of sleep, "I just thought we'd set up the same. I can move if–"

"No, stay put. It's fine."

She sighed, and he recognized the sound as that of her falling back deeper asleep. The last thing he heard from her was a mumble about a 'wake-up call' and 'another hour'.

Becky had hugged her whole family and thanked them. She said she didn't know when she'd be back, and folded herself into John Overton's car.

"So your sister freaked me out with her Oak-Ridge-radioactive-waste theories."

"Yeah, well…" Becky didn't know what to say to that.

"That bit about the other spots with the frogs and *were people sick?* and was that why you couldn't talk?…" He trailed off only to come back full force, this time looking at her instead of the road. Both of which she wished he wouldn't do. "Did you *tell* her?"

"No. She's just that good." Becky sighed and spoke to her hands twined together in her lap. "She's really gifted, and she makes the rest of us look like idiots a lot of the time."

He nodded, and with a quick bite to her lip, she purposefully changed the subject. "So when your guy comes to get the frogs tomorrow, he needs to get other specimens from the UT lab. The American Birdwatcher's Association has a North Georgia branch that contacted us. They have warblers migrating out of season and away from their usual nesting sites."

He didn't ask, but she knew he didn't see the connection yet, so she fed it to him. "I tested them with magnets. They rotate to them just like the frogs do."

She grabbed the door and the edge of her seat with white knuckles as he yanked the steering wheel to one side and peeled into a car dealership before slapping the gearshift into park. His stare was leaden. "You have other species from sites in Georgia?"

She nodded.

He might as well have had the word *incredulous* typed across his face. "And you're only just now telling me?"

She felt the starch sneak up her spine. She was giving him gifts and he was mad? But she didn't fight back, just held some quiet dignity. "I've only known that I was your employee for about four hours, and my parents were around for most of it, so I didn't think I should say anything in front of them."

His hands covered his face for a moment. "First, you aren't my employee. We both work for the CDC and we both push our papers for Briddle." He dragged in a breath as though it would help, but clearly it didn't. "Second,…people were dying and you kept this kind of information to yourself?"

She felt like she'd been slapped. "I…I…" *Calm yourself Becky.* She took a slow, sobering breath. "You guys have had me doing tech work – out catching amphibs. No one asked me about any of it. No one wanted my theories and no one came to tell me when it was confirmed that the magnetics were causing the illness. I've been so stressed out that it didn't even occur to me. And no one lives on these sites. It's like the one in my backyard!..."

She stopped because she simply ran out of things to say, and so she said the only thing she could think of next. Nothing. But she reached for the door handle, figuring the CDCP had already released her from her UT contract and they were about to release her from this one too.

Overton's hand on her arm stopped her, "You're right. I'm sorry."

She remained suspicious of him for a minute.

He opened his mouth once and closed it before opening it again and actually having sound come out of it, "We still haven't confirmed the magnetics theory. No one thinks it makes any sense. Just correlation, not causation."

When he saw that she wasn't planning on fleeing the vehicle anymore, he started to back up and pushed the gas pedal, waving at the car salesman who was just now walking up to the car and grinning at them, smelling a sale. "So some of these warblers are at UT?"

"Yup, all of them. And they really should be part of this study. Warden doesn't know about the magnetics." Her chest constricted as she was telling him about her subterfuge. "I just found out before I left and was trying to gather more evidence. I figured he would have laughed me out of the building if I told him."

"Thank God you didn't tell him."

Well, that wasn't what she'd expected to hear. Since she couldn't think of anything else to say, she changed tacks. "There are also some bees in LA. UCLA has a cluster there, too. And a definitive reversal spot. Where State Road 134 crosses I-5."

"L.A.?" He slapped the wheel. "Holy shit."

Becky didn't think shit had ever been holy, but if there was ever a time for that expression, it was probably now. "It's the Biodiversity lab. I travel a lot to study unusual animal behavior. UT got a call from UCLA about three weeks ago. They have bees swarming in columns. Weirdest thing I ever saw. Their bee dance is messed up too. No turn and circle moves." She paused waiting for him to ask her questions, but he didn't.

John watched the road and Becky watched John, then continued. "So we wound up going out to the site to collect, and we took some amphibs, too. Blind ones like in McCann. And the bees have some sort of magnetic issues too. But UCLA is doing that testing."

"Crap!" He slapped the steering wheel again, and she wondered if it was a tic, if he might start yelling out swear words randomly at any minute in a rush of spontaneous Tourette's.

John pulled into the airport, taking the route labeled "rental returns" and shifting back to Becky. "You! You keep talking! *You* are a fountain of knowledge."

"But I just ran dry." She turned to the window, disappointed that she didn't have anything else to give. "I've been on this case for almost two months now, and I don't have any other information. All I've gleaned can be summed up in the half hour trip to the airport."

David stood awkwardly in the front entrance of the yellow ranch house. This house was warm. Even in the front entryway he could see that a little girl lived here. His mind swept briefly back to the house where he grew up, where it wasn't apparent that *any* humans lived there. But here a toy barn and a handful of odd plastic horses gave testament to this child and her life.

He shoved it down in a way only the truly practiced could.

The wife of the dead cousin was emerging from the kitchen, wiping her hands on a small towel and calling back over her shoulder to a child "Wash your hands honey, we have company." Then she saw the three of them, people that she had hollered out to, to come into her house even though she didn't know who they were, and had never seen two of them before. "Jordan!"

She walked right up and, ignoring her flour stained apron, threw her arms around him in the kind of hug David had read about in books. "What are you doing–" But she cut herself off, noticing the flour she had left on her cousin's front and immediately began apologizing and dusting him off in a way that almost made David uncomfortable to be standing there watching.

"Kelly." It was Jordan, grabbing her arm, ignoring the last traces of flour on the front of him. "I don't know how to say this…" His hand came up and went through his hair.

And while he wasn't paying attention, Jillian stepped into the gap, filling in the story. "I'm Jillian Brookwood. I work with Jordan." She shook hands with the blond woman who was growing warier by the moment, but she kept talking right through the woman's expression, not missing a beat. "We've found other cases like Eddie's. We think there may be an environmental link."

Kelly stepped back, her hand clutching at her heart, although she seemed unaware of the action herself. Her eyes darted from one to the other of them . Her other hand waved behind her until she stumbled back far enough for the couch to materialize behind her and she sank onto the arm, dark circles appearing under her eyes as she started to frown.

But Jillian kept talking, leaving no time for the widow to form a sentence, let alone a full thought. "We have a good idea what it's linked to, but we need to run some tests." Turning slightly, she motioned to him, bringing him into the fold of the conversation for the first time, "This is Dr. David Carter. We want him to look around the house, to see if what affected Eddie was here."

With a wave of her hand she dismissed him, to start wandering around and see what he could find. So he did just that, not wanting to stand there like a moron any longer and see the blonde's eyes cloud over, or her hand clutching for things that weren't there.

Pulling a tiny meter out of his back pocket, he began pacing his way around the perimeters. They had started this crap with compasses and such, but had refined their choice of equipment as they better knew what they were looking for. The meter read normal. The field lay in the right direction, with the appropriate strength. And he felt like an idiot walking around this tiny middle-American house, with the little black box in his palm, getting nothing.

He had done this as a kid – took one of his mother's jewelry boxes and cut a rectangle out of the top with a paring knife from the kitchen and taped in a white piece of paper with red block letters and numbers written on it. He had walked his whole house reading the 'meter' that was so much like the ones his father used. Much bigger and less useful than the one he held today, but he had been so excited to do what his father did. Back then he had been a fool, but in his childhood hadn't felt like one. Today he sure as hell did.

He called back, "Mrs. Abellard?"

The house wasn't big, and she was all of fifteen feet away. Jordan's arm was around her and the hug was almost too familiar, as though those jokes about small town families being too close were true. The blonde looked up at him expectantly, a sheen of tears covering her eyes.

It was all he could do to keep from telling her that those tears wouldn't work on him, and this problem wouldn't be solved unless she could get it together. "There are two closed doors at the end of the hall. Can I go in?"

She nodded, and he realized how much he hated getting permission. What if she had said 'no' then died? Well, at least it would be her own fault. The first room he went into was the little girl's. More of the creepy, plastic horses covered the available surfaces of the bedspread and the white, standard issue, matching dresser and canopy bed, complete with pink ruffles. For a moment, all he could do was stare at the girl-ness all around him, too frozen to do his job. Sure this house was warm, but tasteless. He'd be damned if he didn't vomit from all the ruffles around him before he left. Or was it the magnetic field? Either way he was bound to puke.

As he ran the meter next to the wall, he began picking up a level change as he approached the corner.

"Sonofabitch."

It wasn't much. Not even a reversal, but at this point he'd seen enough to know it was coming. This was either the top edge of a coming bubble or the side edge of an already existing bubble.

The normal field gave way, over a distance of about five inches. First weakening, then, if you could locate the exact spot and hold steady, you could find it – where the field went to zero. A phenomenon that should not occur on this earth.

He had zero.

Far in the back corner, right at the floor.

And he had a wall in his way.

The mother's room was at least more tasteful. Though it looked like the Dad was still here, too. David didn't analyze that any further, just headed for the corner that abutted the other room, where he had to move furniture and get down on his hands and knees.

It was here, too – the edge of an already existing bubble – and the thing was decent in size. A good part of the bedroom was affected.

"Sonofabitch."

"What is it?" The voice belonged to Jordan.

"Got one."

Even in the space of the two words, Jordan was at his side, kneeling, reading the meter over his shoulder. "Bet this is what got Eddie." His voice had trailed off at the end of the sentence.

David knew he should be sympathetic. But he wasn't. He was having the time of his life. His old man had *never* seen shit like this. And there were going to be papers until pigs flew out his ass. And Greer was going to ride that dino theory all the way to the bank. "Yeah, it's great."

"Thank you."

The sarcasm wasn't unnoticed, but David left it to sit, un-responded to. It's why he wasn't a preschool teacher. He heard the widow in the doorway, but didn't look up, didn't care to see that he had offended her. Let Jordan soothe the woman and explain to her that she needed to pack for herself and her daughter and that the CDC would be putting them into a hotel and starting them on medications.

"Lindsay was sick yesterday morning." There was a sound to the voice such that David wouldn't have been surprised if he turned around to find the woman actually wringing her hands.

"Vomiting?" Jillian's voice broke in, and he closed his mind to all of them. They voluntarily cleared themselves from the room, leaving him with his bubble anomaly.

He smiled. The swap was coming. Like nothing any of them had ever seen before. And he was sitting right on top of it.

For a brief moment, he pictured his father's face when he heard.

Chapter 10

Jillian stared at the wall, suffering the strange sense of déjà vu she had. She had stared at walls just like this. In three cites that looked just like this. Well, from the inside of a hotel room, they all did. The only difference was the handful of medications she swallowed. The carpet was the same, a bizarre floral pattern that was created just for this hotel. They were all in reds and browns and creams, though, and all just as ugly.

Designed by the humans that she was trying to save. Looking around herself, she shook her head. Maybe she should be trying to save Becky's amphibs. It might be a more noble cause.

Landerly had called again.

The four bubbles here were to be abandoned. Again there was another team coming up behind them, and Jillian had to wonder where and why they were being moved. It seemed all they could do was show up and say "there it is." And steep in it a little more.

Becky had found another spot on the side of a freeway in LA. Jordan should have been happy about that, but Jillian knew that he was worried about his family. He was sworn not to say anything. They couldn't start a panic.

Well, no, they *could* start a panic. A damned good one too, if she put her mind to it. David had already popped up with an excited grin and told them he was trying to calculate when the shift would occur. He was looking at the number and growth rate of the reversal spots. He was calculating in the historical data from the KT boundary, the evidence that he and his paleontologist friend had been on the phone for hours discussing. Jillian, for the first time, realized what it felt like to be her family listening to her talk. God, it was boring.

Then he had told her Greer's reversal/dinosaur die-out theory.

Jillian still got cold inside when she thought about that conversation. "David, all the dinosaurs died. There was mass extinction. There were volcanoes, which you are now telling me might have been triggered by magnetic reversal? The kind that we're looking at seeing here in the next what? Year? Month? Are we talking of going the way of the dinosaurs?"

"Well," Rather proud of himself, he had looked her in the eyes and almost smiled, "most of the mammals lived through it."

She wanted to scream until her throat hurt too much to ever talk again.

But she didn't want Jordan to come running. Or admit her to an asylum.

Then again, there was comfort in just sitting in a corner, rocking on her heels and mumbling about human extinction and magnetic poles, while nurses soothed her and gave her medication to make her happy and calm. But the phone rang.

"Brookwood." She held the receiver to her ear. It was a CDC phone, and the damned thing was a secure line. What the hell was she doing with a secure line? She was supposed to be writing reports on other doctors' evaluations of things as simple as E. coli and botulism.

"Landerly."

She snapped to and didn't say anything. Landerly would just start talking when he was ready, and there was a certain charming efficiency to it.

"You're not going to LA."

Yea! Follow-through. Finally they could stay in one spot and–

"There's a prison at the Nevada-California line, and they have a bubble, too."

He paused. Jillian absorbed. And waited.

"We can't move them. There aren't enough facilities, and these are maximum security prisoners." He sighed and Jillian knew what was coming, but she let him say it. "Our deadline for solving this thing just bumped way up. After the AIDS debacle, the CDC can't afford to let prisoners die. Start packing. Your tickets are waiting for you at the airport."

And with a sharp click in her ear, he was gone.

Jillian stood, the phone still clutched uselessly in her hand, her brain churning. The CDC had suffered from the AIDS issue. No one had cared enough, no one had done enough, because those suffering were gay men. It wasn't all the CDC's fault. They had actually done a lot. Private funding had failed to foot the necessary bill until grandmas started getting AIDS from blood transfusions and Ryan White became a tiny mirror with a big reflection of America's ugly underbelly of prejudice.

And the CDC wasn't about to be on the short end of that stick again.

So just in case Jillian didn't feel enough pressure, there were now politics involved. Suddenly she understood physicians who medicated themselves. Demerol, Statol, Percocet all sounded fantastic about now. She allowed herself the dream of a good drug addiction for a brief moment before she hollered out to Jordan. "We're not going to LA."

She didn't move from her spot, couldn't bear to see his face. Not when she knew that he looked happy, and she was about to open her mouth and dash it. "There's a maximum security prison in Nevada that has a reversal and we can't move the prisoners."

"What!?"

She could hear his feet hitting the floor. That meant he'd been leaning back in the chair, thinking. For a moment she was glad that he hadn't fallen backwards. Although she could have used a good laugh right now. Jillian started to yell out her response, but Jordan was capable of movement and his footfalls were pounding her way from just beyond the open door.

So she sighed. "We're on a plane out tonight. We have to solve this thing and quick."

"Why us?" His feet caught up to his head and he stood upright, shoving overworked fingers into undertended hair. Pieces of it stood straight up. And his blue eyes blinked slowly, like a man told that he'd just been sentenced to the electric chair.

Her voice was softer than she had intended. "It's punishment."

"For what?"

"Forging Landerly's signature? I don't know. We must have been very bad in our past lives. Do you remember torturing puppies or something?"

Jordan shook his head. "Very funny, Jilly."

"Hey don't mock me! I ran out of 'very funny' about two weeks ago." She finally found the source of energy needed to move herself to the nearby desk and she plopped down into it unceremoniously while Jordan melted onto the bed. He rolled all the way through, onto his back, as though there was something to be learned from the ceiling.

After a minute, Jillian interrupted the hum of the air conditioning. "It's because of Eddie."

"How is this because of Eddie?"

"That's why we went to Florida, forged signature and all. That's how we found those cases and linked it all together. Eddie was the start of it. If he hadn't been your cousin, I don't know if we would have been this far along."

"Fat lot of good it's done us."

"I know." She resisted the urge to go to him and offer a hug. Although that wasn't hard, given that the phone call from Landerly had drained her of all her energy. With an effort far greater than should have been necessary, she pushed herself up out of the chair and plucked the hotel phone from the cradle, punching the four digit code to David's room.

Only it wasn't David who answered.

She mumbled into the black handset, "Sorry, wrong number." Then stared at it like it had bitten her. How was that not David? She thought back through the code –

"You're probably dialing his number from the last hotel we were in." Jordan's voice came over her shoulder, indicating that he hadn't taken his cue from her and hadn't moved an inch. "I bet you remember them all. All the room numbers and the layout of each place…"

Jillian was just happy that he couldn't see her blush. The poor boy had been subjected to Jillian-24-7. She could be her own sad reality-TV series. She punched in the code for David's current room and he answered on the third ring. "Carter." She curled her lip at the phone.

"David, it's me, Jillian." *Well, that was a hell of a lot more human than 'Brookwood' barked out like an army order*. She had to get a new 'hello'. They were all such techies. "We're on the move again. To the Nevada-California border."

"And what's there?" She could hear him rustling in the background. He was probably already starting to pack.

"Maximum Security Prison. With a bubble." Stopping herself, Jillian realized she was starting to sound like Landerly. Subject-Verb, minimal clauses, and don't bother with articles or adverbs. And she seriously doubted it sounded charming on her. So, with a sigh, she started again. "They can't move the prisoners. Right now the CDC is still keeping the media out, but there's no telling how long that will last. We've got a tight deadline."

Jordan's whole body was leaden; the bubbles had grown black and faster moving. One was going to overtake him, but he couldn't force any more speed from his legs. Jillian and David had been running with him, but they had both disappeared along the way – David into thin air, and Jilly, smiling and waving, had been happily engulfed by one.

Although Jillian had gone willingly, Jordan knew there was no good in the reversals. It was certain death. In testament to that fact, there were lifeless, rotting bodies strewn around him on the street. The smell was overwhelming. And the rumbling of the bubble was freight train loud as it got closer. The ear pain and nausea overtook him, as he knew they would.

"Jordan."

He looked, still running, for the source of the sound. The second time the voice said his name, he recognized it as Jillian's, but he couldn't find her in the black.

With a jolt, he slammed into the cushioned seat of the airplane as though he had been dropped from a high place, his eyes opening as the vicious dream faded into the back of his head. But the ear pain and nausea were real, surely byproducts of the rapid descent they were pulling.

He felt himself sinking through the seat, giving up and giving in, when Jillian grabbed his arm again. "You have to wake up. David's up. We're landing in two minutes."

They would call Landerly when they got in the car and got the secure line set up. They would tell him all they knew, and all they had seen, and wait for his mind to churn. Not that Landerly had been a banner help lately. That he was as stumped as they were had been a small comfort.

Jordan blocked all else from his mind and thought of the hot tub and the pool that would await them where they would stay near the state line. It was cheaper on the Nevada side, and that would mean gambling and lights and noise. But that would be all right he supposed; it might keep his mind off what he had left behind, and how Lake James was doing.

Kelly and Lindsey had been evacuated right away, in a bald and scary attempt to save them from the reversal that was growing in the corner between the two bedrooms, creeping a little wider each day like an infestation of mold in the walls.

Lindsey had already been sick, stomach ache and ear pain that same morning they had arrived.

And that had scared the crap out of Jordan. Lindsey was the only living proof of Eddie's existence. Everything else would fade with time. He soothed himself with the thought that it seemed if they were able to pull a person out of the reversal in time, before they got too sick, they wouldn't have any effects.

On the flip side, if they didn't get the person out in time, there was only one course – the victim always ended up dead. And no one had any idea what the cut-off point was.

In his head, he counted out the death tolls. Florida was at seven. Lake James at five, and maybe more. Twenty total in McCann, although no more since they had figured out to get people out of the area.

Both McCann and Florida had traceable paths – a patient zero, the look of contagion. Lake James didn't. The bubbles were cropping up all over the place and taking out random people. Or at least it seemed that way now…Jordan desperately wanted Jillian to have an epiphany. He wanted to interview someone, anyone, who would give him that last shred of information that would allow his mind to grasp the picture in the puzzle even though they were nowhere near complete.

If Lindsey had truly had *it*…Well that was another story. He had seen her labs himself. And she was a perfectly healthy kid by all known measures. It would have almost been easier to take if she had been sick and nobody had known it. But if this thing was taking out healthy people now…there really wasn't an answer.

And why wouldn't it take out healthy people? Diseases killed without prejudice or forethought. They could wipe out entire populations without conscience. And even if this was simply an environmental hazard then, what would they do when David's predictions came true and the poles swapped? When the whole earth was a reversal field?

He knew he was possibly looking at the end of 'life as we know it'. If it wasn't disease that did them in, then they would have to stand on their Darwinian principles and die the brave death of the non-fittest.

Becky trudged through the high grass in the far back of her parents' property, hiking boots laced tight, stomach full from the family breakfast her mother had insisted was necessary because her oldest daughter had returned home the night before. And Becky had let her do it. Since she was heading back to Atlanta and the bio lab right after she packed her things. Which was right after she assured her parents that she wasn't going out to the frog site.

Which was a bald-faced lie.

She was heading crosswise through the property, toward the back corner fence, carrying a walking stick with a mounted compass. Her backpack full to the brim of lightweight CDC equipment and empty lexans. By necessity, she was out here alone. Was that a stupid thing? Probably. Who knew what this site would do to her? She might go into a coma and die right there on the spot. But something told her she wouldn't.

Jordan and Jillian and their infectious disease cronies hadn't told the biodiversity team any more. They hadn't found out if the illness was caused by one-time long-term exposure or if all the little exposures added up to get you sick. If that was the case, then she had been plenty exposed, and just walking into a site like this was asking for trouble.

The trouble was that the docs had no real theories. No one could tell if the older sites were stronger, or if the newer ones were. Or if size mattered. No, the one thing they had told her about that was they were counting on *her* to sort that thing out. No one felt the need to evacuate the animals from the sites. So it was Becky and John Overton who were supposed to be exploring those possibilities.

The boundary tape was dirty now. Little leaves clung to it. The bright color faded away. Maybe they shouldn't have put it so low to the ground. Maybe tent stakes hadn't really been the best idea. What if an animal tripped and injured themselves? What if a person did?

Closer up, she saw pink tape. It wasn't staked but wound around tree trunks and draped across low lying branches. It was brighter, newer. The CDC had tagged it but not marked it 'keep out' or 'biohazard'. God only knew if the neighbor kids crept over the fence to play.

About ten feet from the tape, she saw the compass jump. *Dammit.* She knew this site was growing and she hadn't been paying attention.

Fingers of sun came through the tall trees now, and winds found their way around the trunks. Becky pulled up her turtleneck, glad now that she had dressed a little warmer. Starting back again toward the site, this time she kept a clear eye on the compass. Strands of her hair slipped across her face and into her mouth right as the needle jumped.

This time she set down the backpack and pulled out a rubber-banded bunch of weighted flags, CDCP DO NOT TOUCH emblazoned in repeating letters across the orange streamers. She dropped one where the compass started to bounce.

The red needle danced in every direction, unsure which way was true north, confused by the one thing that was supposed to keep it constant. She dropped another flag where it became steady again. Of course, this time it was pointed south.

Standing several feet inside the site now, Becky looked over the two dropped flags. The fuzzy edges were getting larger as the bubble grew. Her brows pulled together against the thoughts in her head, even as her shoulder blades pulled together against the wind that had picked up again and was biting at her exposed skin.

Becky breathed deeply, concerned about just what it was that she was breathing in. Unsure if the reversal caused the problem or brought the problem or fed the problem. God, they didn't know *anything.*

She thought she should feel something different. That her body should instinctively know she was somehow being exposed to something deadly. Her heart did beat faster, but Becky had no doubt that was due to her own adrenaline surging rather than any external force altering her heart rate.

In that instant the sun disappeared, causing her heart to speed up as her head snapped back. She saw the cloud dusting its way across the sky even as her brain reminded her there was, of course, a logical explanation.

But chasing the cloud was a jet. Probably taken off from McGhee-Tyson and headed into Nashville.

Her breath sucked in, and she stood, trapped, mesmerized, petrified, as the jet blazed a trail toward where she stood. In the clear sky, it took almost two full minutes for the plane to reach a point directly overhead, and for the entire time she simply stood there, tense as a piano wire, adrenaline keeping her whole body on high alert. Her brain flipping and discarding thought after thought about where to run and how to escape if the plane came tumbling down out of the sky.

Somehow, no one had thought to check the height of the bubbles. A possibly fatal error – if the plane flew low, and if the bubble reached up that far. The bee columns from LA indicated the reversals things could and did achieve some altitude. What would the pilot do if all the dash readings went suddenly out of whack? If the compass started jumping? If they looked down and saw they were headed east when they should be headed west? Would they change altitude, to avoid a crash, only to lead them head first into another plane *actually* traveling east?

But the jet passed over without any events, leaving Becky sucking lungfuls of the air inside the site. This job was going to kill her. Well, that was if it didn't kill the whole planet first.

She shoved her thoughts to the back of her brain – the disturbing ones anyway – and focused on the frogs. They would be harder to find this time. It was later in the season. There might still be a few straggling tadpoles. And that, she suddenly realized, was why she was here. Those stragglers would grow in the site as it was today, this week. And they would tell its story now. Probably the same one. But they would give her and John a better idea about long term exposure to the site.

Her stomach rolled alarmingly, and she refused to even begin to calculate how long it would take the reversal to reach the edges of her parents' fenced yard or, god forbid, the house.

Again she forced a tight rein on her thoughts to keep them from running away. Counting backwards would indicate that the bubble had been 'born' about two months before the first time Becky had encountered her own little 'Apocolypse Now'.

Becky faced the task at hand – spotting the tiny ranas darting among the refractions in the creek and peeking out from under crunched leaves. Within an hour, she had populated fifteen lexans, and she lined them up for a good-looking over, which was about as scientific as she could get out here in the woods. Her fingers ached from plunging them in and out of the now cold water, from bumping and grating her fingertips and knuckles across the smooth looking rocks. Her brain ached, too, and she feverishly prayed it was from effort and stress and not the environment.

But all her frogs were normal legged. Just two hind jumpers. They were pale, not whitish, but not the healthy greens and browns of the earlier batches. Six were blind.

Dear God. They looked more like the batch she had hauled from McCann than the batch from here.

Information was pouring in. David had been shocked that it had started so fast; Jillian had barely plugged in the fax machine when it started beeping and spitting out ink strewn papers. All three of them had forgotten to unpack and had sat, silent, in the supremely uncomfortable chairs around the nice cherrywood table in the corner of the hotel room. They had simply read and passed the pages, each of their faces knitting deeper into concern the further along they got.

About an hour into it, Jordan had stood and stretched. Throwing a handful of worn and smudged papers on the table top, he declared he needed a break. David had almost hopped up and agreed, until he saw that Jordan's idea of a 'break' was to stop reading the fax pages and to start reviewing and hanging the hand drawn charts. Personally, he'd been thinking more along the lines of a steak and a hot tub himself. But as he watched the butcher paper go up, revealing its colorful circles with links and lines and notes, he kept his mouth shut.

The fax pages were coming in from all over. Suits were crawling the country, and worse yet, the World Health Organization was starting to collaborate their findings of a 'new disease' in India and Africa. David shook his head to himself, things were in the crapper when even the geologist could see what was happening.

The fax beeped, and gurgled, and whirred, and then started spitting out another black and white missive. David grabbed it even before the machine was fully done with it. Which was his plan, as this little portable shitbox had a tendency to hang on to the page once it was finished printing, and then, at a random interval later, release it, sending the paper flying out away from the table and sending three very stellar scientists scrambling like fucking idiots to fetch it.

He turned to Jordan who was standing back, fists perched on his hips, and way over-admiring his thumb-tacking job. "Listen to this."

Both the docs stopped what they were doing and gave him their attention while he went over the major, if blurry, points on the page. "They have an animal link between the Knoxville site and the McCann site. They think the McCann site may be a few months older..." That was as far as he'd gotten but while he scanned it again, he let his mouth follow his mind. "They checked out the Georgia site. They still don't know why the birds came early, but the growth rate on that site leads them to believe it might be a full year old –"

Jillian's sigh interrupted him. "Thank God no one lives out there."

This time he read word for word, "The animals in McCann are showing unusual, new activity, actually phasing back to – Dammit."

Jillian looked at Jordan, who was looking back at her. Neither of them spoke, and David did his level best to ignore them. The page had simply run out, and wouldn't you know it, just as he looked up, the fax machine spit out the next sheet, sending it floating right past his open hands.

"Son of a bitch."

"Is the 'dammit' another metamorphosis phase, like larva or pupa?"

David didn't even waste an eye roll on Jordan for that one. Straightening the new page, he started in again, "-phasing back to normal. Most recent amphib catches in McCann indicate normal development as best as can be determined by present tests."

Jillian practically climbed into his lap with excitement, and he sure as hell did nothing to stop her. "Did the site reverse?...I mean back to normal polarity?"

He looked the paper up and down. "Doesn't look like it."

She looked disappointed, which David took to mean she wasn't going to crawl into his lap. And letch that he was, he could admit that that fact disappointed him more than the site not returning to normal. He hadn't expected it to anyway. "We've never seen anything indicating that they reverse back. Well, not for about sixty million years anyway."

Jillian wandered over to admire Abellard's thumb-tacking job, and the next thing David knew the two of them were spouting off crap about white counts and B-U-Ns, which he figured had nothing to do with burgers, and David made the executive decision that this would be a good time to ignore them. He plucked up the super-teched CDC phone and called Greer.

"David!"

"Buddy."

He opened his mouth to speak again but Greer beat him to it, already rambling about the McCann egg clutch. "-full fetus in one of them. Unbelievable. I need to tell someone, I have muscle attachment sites that no one has seen before."

A deep pit formed in David's heart. He was starting to see himself as Chicken Little. Only he wasn't an idiot. He was just the only one who saw that the sky actually was falling. He wasn't sure how much he cared. But there was the distinct possibility that everyone was going to get sick from this. And with the fatality rate at a hundred percent, Greer might wind up having to limit sharing his joyous minutia to his wife.

David was certain that he should be having a crisis right now. Only he wasn't having it. "Listen Greer. I need to know something, and you can tell that snappy wife of yours, as she is the smarter half..." David pinched the bridge of his nose wishing he was elsewhere. Wishing he was siphoning off that trust fund he had broken into to start this whole crapload of a mess. He was ready for some straight-out baking on a beach somewhere, with girls in bikinis and beer and a sedate heart rate. If one of them in the hotel room suddenly spontaneously combusted, he wouldn't be surprised. "Greer, straighten me out on this: did your dinos die from lack of food or what?"

"No real telling. Just a good solid theory. Plants would have wilted in a matter of days given the dust cover–"

David interrupted. He'd been on the receiving end of Greer's theories before and he could qualify for a Ph.D. in paleontology long before they ended. "Yes, but that depends on the asteroid theory or the volcano theory. Go with this one for a minute and tell me if the evidence matches up: The dinosaurs got sick–"

"Wait, can I put you on speaker phone?" Greer was already doing it, if the clicking and the soft static were any indication.

"Hey," David turned to Jillian, "Does this thing do speaker phone?"

"Sure." She didn't stop her conversation with Jordan, just kept jabbering about qualifying diseases and healthy specimens, but her fingers flew over the secondary numeric keypad – the one she had punched link-up codes into the moment they had arrived. When she handed it back it was squawking at him at full volume. He told Greer and Leena to hang on a minute and looked over his shoulder. "You two might want to pay attention to this."

They jerked their heads apart.

"Who are we talking to?" Jordan frowned at him, which was fine, since David was certain that he was breaking several federal laws. But he didn't let that deter him. "Okay, Greer, we're all here."

"Who's 'we'?" Leena's voice was overeager, clearly way too stifled by her bed-rest.

David introduced everybody, then set about swearing the Larsons to secrecy, which he thought was hysterical, but did it anyway. "All right. Here's the question: is it possible all the dinosaurs got sick at the same time?"

"Yeah right. They all just came down with a deadly virus." Leena's voice was sweet, even shooting him down. "It was too global, too quick."

"You think what's going around now is what killed my dinos?" Greer hopped in.

Jordan shot David a death glare, but Jillian was already too wrapped up in the science to be concerned about treason, "I think what David's asking is if it's possible. Is there any evidence that they could have gotten sick?"

Greer and Leena talked over each other. "No." "I think it's more like there's no evidence against it." "We just have a sudden lack of fossils and we know they died." "Why? What does this have to do with that magnetic reversal we found?"

David sighed. Too damn many scientists in the kitchen. "The reversal is making people sick." There. He said it. Let Jordan call in the CDC police. "But only those in the hotspots. The die-outs seem to correlate to the last reversal. Is it possible that the volcanoes were an aftereffect?"

"Of course it is." Greer's voice amplified as though he were talking directly into the speaker box.

Jillian's face took on a look of horror that David had only seen once on a really bad actress in a schlock film featuring killer clowns. "Does that mean that we could face volcanoes along with the polarity reversal?!"

Leena ignored her. "I think the real question is whether or not the dinosaurs were warm-blooded. If they were, then they are more pertinent to your question, and if not, then they aren't. They relate less to humans and we might all react very differently." She sniffled at the end of the sentence and David felt his heart drop. There was nothing he feared more than a woman with tears. But Jordan voiced the question, and Leena answered. "Of course I'm crying. I'm pregnant. I cry at country music."

David steered the conversation back where he wanted it. "I know Greer thinks they were cold-blooded, do you agree?"

"Hell, no." And she launched into an explanation he had heard Greer shoot down a number of times, but it sounded a lot more plausible coming from her mouth. "There are too many channels in the bone, indicating a network of vessels. It's common to warm-blooded creatures. Some of them had necks so long that their heads would have frozen overnight if they didn't self-heat their blood. Greer's an idiot on that one."

Jordan smiled. "Well, I guess every marriage needs its spark."

"I don't think it's a warm-blooded/cold-blooded issue at all." Jillian had turned her focus from a distant spot on the wall to the speaker phone, as though it was the thing actually carrying on a conversation with her. "We have amphibian species showing effects of the reversals. And they aren't warm-blooded. We're all getting affected."

David heard pillows shuffle and Greer say something to Leena. He wasn't sure what he said, but by the tone and cadence of Leena's voice he got shot down. "Then, yes it is possible. No one's really looked at it, because it doesn't make sense for a virus to sweep like that. So no one has tried to find evidence for or against it."

There was a pause, no one wanting to fill in.

But apparently the gears had been turning in Leena's brain. "It does go with another problem I've been sorting through–"

Greer's voice walked on top of hers, "She's on bed-rest, all she does is lay around and think. It's dangerous, I'm telling you. She's decided all the dinosaur die-out theories are wrong."

"Really?" Jordan's voice jumped in, overlapped by Jillian's "Why?"

Leena picked her thread back up. "The issue is this: all the major extinction theories rely on the dust cover. There's argument as to what caused it, but no real argument as to the fact that it happened. And there's this problematic assumption that the debris cloud stopped photosynthesis in the plants, thus killing the dinosaurs…but somehow *not* the mammals."

Jordan shrugged. "The mammals were smaller."

Greer's voice answered. "No, not really, there were a huge number of dinosaur species that were a lot smaller than what we normally think of. Many of them were as small or much smaller than the average mammal. So it wasn't a size issue."

"The mammals were warm-blooded." Jordan threw out the next piece of evidence.

"No, so were the dinosaurs." Again Leena's voice was sweet, even in refusing him his basic beliefs. "And that actually is what gives the theory *real* trouble–"

It was Jillian who jumped in now, looking excited. The kind of excited David would be if she peeled off her clothes and straddled him. "Warm-blooded means faster metabolic rates. Which means that the mammals, the *smallest* mammals, should have been the *first* ones killed by the loss of plant life, not the survivors."

"Excuse me?" David cut in. Fuckin' biologists.

"Warm-blooded animals eat a lot more per ounce of body-weight than their cold-blooded counterparts. They have to: it takes a lot of energy to make that body heat. So the cold-blooded species would have lasted longer without food or even oxygen and been far more likely than any mammal to survive a month-or-more dust cover."

"So anyway," Leena's soft voice filtered through to them, "the dust cover doesn't work if the dinos were warm-or cold-blooded and I've decided we don't even have the real killer on our hands. The problem is that the killing factor is sorting who it takes and who it doesn't by some unknown mechanism. What we understand, or at least what we've put together, doesn't answer that question yet."

David finally stepped up. "What about the previous extinctions?"

That made Jordan's head pop up. "There were others?"

Greer answered, "Well, there was one about one hundred and thirty five million years ago. That wiped out a darn lot. And another about sixty million years before that… why?"

David sighed. "Just wanted to see if they matched up with the pole reversals." He sighed again.

"Guess they do." Jillian was staring at him.

"Son of a bitch." That was Jordan, followed closely by Greer, having chosen the exact same words.

"I'm sorry." Leena's ultrafeminine voice could have been the words of a woman at a cocktail party. "Are you all insinuating that we're headed for a mass extinction?"

David answered her in kind. "Yes, I believe that is what it sounds like."

"Do you have any guesses as to when?" She was one of the few women he knew who was capable of holding this conversation and not screaming, swearing, or breaking down.

"Any time between tomorrow and the next two thousand years."

Chapter 11

Head to toe in scrubs, Jillian walked through the prison as starched as she possibly could. For all her training, she had never provided care to inmates, and the way the men were looking at her was going to haunt her for more than a night or two. She would have felt more at home and less exposed walking through the middle of Atlanta in only a thong and red heels, in the dead of winter.

But the gauntlet turned out to only be the first half. Doors clanged. Metal scraped and moaned. Cinderblock only reflected the sounds; it didn't absorb or diminish them in any way. But when the doors slid closed behind them, Jillian's apprehension slid away as a deeper unease slipped in. Something was very wrong.

She had the feeling of being in the woods when the animals don't make noise. When you don't know what's coming, but you know that it is.

"He's down!" The cry was laced with a liberal dose of terror. Jillian knew then that these inmates knew something was taking them out.

Shoving through the nearly impenetrable wall Jordan and David had provided, she ran flat out until she reached the cell where the wail was coming from.

When he reached a hand through the bars at her, Jillian stepped back. She had compassion for the fear in his voice, "Help me doc!", but not enough to reach out and touch him.

An officer in shades of khaki green came up beside her and asked what she wanted to do.

"Get this man out of here. But put him on his own. Away from here."

The voice wailed again. This time the man with the straggling beard pressed himself to the cage bars directly in front of her.

As the warden approached and unlocked the gate, she stepped back, hoping to get out of reach of the prisoner, and smacked into a wall of muscle. She jumped, spinning, only to find that David had come up behind her. He was dressed in a spare pair of green scrubs from the prison infirmary, in hopes that he would blend in with the other doctors. It looked bad enough without having to answer why a geologist needed to be along.

Jillian turned to find Jordan further down the line, his arms laced through the bars, taking vitals from the prisoners who lined up. She saw the sense in what he did. If this cell had a bubble, they should check and see if it stretched down the row.

Looking back into the stall as the man was led away in cuffs, she took in the placement and order. This cell had two stacked beds attached to the wall, one higher, unoccupied, and the lower with the comatose body of the other inmate strewn across it facedown. She stepped over to kneel down and assess the man, but another officer put his hand in front of her, and without touching her, held her back, while he handcuffed each of the man's hands to the bedframe before letting Jillian near him.

Checking him over, she took his blood pressure and respiratory count, wondering even then why she was doing it. They all knew what he had, and they all knew what would happen.

The men down this row were quiet. They knew they were being stalked, only not in any rational way that any of these men of aggression could deal with. Sanity was slipping here, and Jillian could read it on the faces of the officers, too. How much longer before they realized they weren't getting paid enough? Before they jumped ship?

The CDC's ass would be in a sling then. There would be no stopping the news cameras. No way to hold back the wave of panic it would surely generate. So Jillian set about solving the problem the only way she knew how.

She stepped up to the warden and explained. "This man needs an ICU. He's comatose, and his ability to breathe on his own may be compromised soon." Then she turned away and went to the next patient, taking the charts handed to her by the prison physician and his assistant. Both the doctor and his young apprentice had the sense to not ask questions.

But Jillian asked questions. She asked every one in the book, and a few that weren't. Inside fifteen minutes time she knew that Landerly had been right to pull them out of Lake James and send them here. It's where he would have been if his arthritis hadn't effectively shut him down. The trip to McCann had been more than he could handle. She could tell in the way he walked, in his dry humor that waxed and waned with the amount of medication and rest he got. He would wish he was here, in the thick of it.

And while she was wishing that she wasn't here, she decided to make the best of it. What would Landerly do? She almost chuckled to herself. Then she decided that Landerly would get a history on every single one of them and start sorting the furthest gone. He would plot the locations, including the sleeping arrangements of the sickest patients.

And in another two hours, when she and Jordan pooled their data, she realized that Landerly would call the CDC mobile team, already stretched to its limit, and have them set up a temporary camp here. She called for quarantine.

Jordan led the three of them out of the head warden's office about fifteen minutes after they entered it. The man wanted a few minutes alone to call his wife and explain to her that there had been a 'serious situation' at work and that he may not be home for a week or more. Joshua Frank had taken some reassurance that they weren't all simply lining up and waiting to die.

It was David who seemed to know where he was headed, and he strode down the hall in front of both of them, this time with a purpose. The inmates were supposed to have been moved from all the cells where anyone had gotten sick, and David was already rummaging through his briefcase looking for his fancy compasses. He was ready to weigh and measure, and Jordan could see now that he had been from the moment they had set foot in this place.

So Jordan followed behind and took the opportunity to sneak a look at Jilly – she practically glowed. That was just damned annoying. She should be haggard; she hadn't slept enough; she was in the middle of a high pressure situation. And she *glowed*.

Calling the CDC in front of the inmates and the cops had been a truly stupid move, and even now Jordan couldn't figure out why Jillian hadn't thought just a little further ahead on that one. But he had glared at her, twice, mouthed the words to her to either shut-up or leave the room, and she either hadn't seen him at all or was putting in an Oscar-worthy performance of ignoring him. Since he was certain she wasn't that caliber of an actress, he truly believed she hadn't seen him. And here he was dealing with the flak, while she glowed. Bitch.

David was inside one of the cells, crawling around on his hands and knees and no longer looking anything like the physician he was dressed up as. His scrubs were blackened in long smears down the top, one knee was actually sporting a small tear, and both were ground deep with…well, Jordan couldn't identify the source of the dark stains and he wasn't sure he wanted to. He decided to catch up with Jillian and see if she had seen anything worthwhile yet.

She gave a brilliant smile, out of proportion to her surroundings, as he walked up. "What have you got?"

"Nothing." His files were tucked under his arm, as inactive as they were useless. "You?"

She shook her head, her ponytail moving from side to side as if to second what she was saying. "It's all here, but there's nothing new."

Jordan stretched his neck one way then the other, and left Jillian behind, not that she even noticed, as he went off to wind his way back to the warden's office. He found the warden with the framed photograph from his desk propped across his knees. "Sir, it's not that bad."

Frank grimaced. "I know it's not. You've done a good job of putting all our minds at ease. But I can't help think about them. You know...when something like this comes up..."

"Yeah, I do know." For just a moment he paused. Then, decision made, he plowed ahead. "My father is in the same situation. I do understand."

The warden simply sighed and asked what he could do to help. Jordan got to make his day by asking to use the phone, then booking the entire staff in the wing at the hotel they were staying in. The CDC could ride his ass for expenditures, if and when he survived this thing.

He left the office and wound through the long hallway yet again to find Jillian standing still in one of the cell rows watching David's backside as he crawled from corner to corner, measuring, mapping, and muttering the whole time. The arrogant bastard might have been happy to know Jillian was staring at his butt, but Jordan wasn't about to give him the pleasure. He touched her sleeve and she slowly pulled her gaze away from the ass molded in green cotton. "What?"

"Anything left to do?" *Besides stare at David?*

She shook her head. "I've got vitals on all of them, and blood draws. That's already boxed and waiting."

"Call for pickup?" He kept his voice low, but David wasn't listening anyway. He was lost in the world of his rocks. Jordan wondered if concrete and cinderblock qualified igneous or sedimentary, but he didn't dare ask.

"No pickup. The mobile lab will run it when they get here in 12 hours. Our one live patient is already at the hospital on a ventilator."

"Robert Willins?" The man she had rushed to as he was passed out on his bunk. Jordan already knew that was the man's name, and maybe he felt just a little facetious because he knew Jillian wouldn't.

Jillian simply ignored the question. It passed like light through glass, and left no feeling of satisfaction for having asked it. As though he had never spoken she changed the subject, "Shall we head back to the hotel and sleep? We're going to be neck deep when the crew arrives."

He felt the yawn coming only well after it was too late to stop it, and even before he managed to close his mouth Jillian was biting off her own yawn.

"David said not to wait for him. He'll catch a ride later."

"Sweet." He turned away from her face at her last glance back to David. Allowing her to make their goodbyes to Carter, he simply headed down the long hallway toward the exit, only barely cataloguing a muttered response and wondering if the blond geologist might look up later and wonder where they were. Well, he'd figure it out fast enough.

The adrenaline that had been fueling him barely held while he drove back to the hotel. When they arrived, she shuffled along behind him until he slid the magnetic key card into his door and was surprised when she followed him in.

There was only the one king-sized bed, and Jilly bee-lined for it.

The foolish words were out of his mouth before he could stop them. "This is my room."

"Haven't you noticed? I always sleep in with you."

"All right." He didn't want to change things, but his mouth again got ahead of his brain. *Why? When she was ogling David's ass? Whispering with him on the flights?* "Why?"

"Can't you tell?"

He was almost afraid of the answer. A small part of him sprung with hope, but the rest of him tamped that part down, and Jordan just shook his head.

"Ever since McCann, I've been afraid to sleep alone."

He nodded. It was the best he was going to get. Although that had to have been the last answer he would have expected. "Climb in."

David almost grinned. The prison was swarming with them. The bubbles were here, they were all growing, and they were all over. This was a hot spot among hot spots. And, in a new phenomena that hadn't let him get any sleep, they were growing fast enough that he could come back to one end of the hall and start all over getting new reads on almost every one. Previous growth rates had been on the order of a few feet a week. These guys were showing growth in a matter of hours.

As he came back down the hall, he couldn't suppress a grin. Some of the reversals were fusing. And damn if that wasn't the hot news of the millennium. His Dad would sit back in his chair and have a heart attack. In fact he just might call the old man and personally deliver a little comeuppance to Mister Superiority.

Just then a person, man or woman he couldn't tell, fully decked in the yellow hazmat suit, walked in at the far end of the hall. It waved, but whether or not it smiled was lost in the slight reflection off the surface of the protective face shield it wore. David made what he estimated was a friendly face and waved back before turning and rolling his eyes. Those suits wouldn't protect against magnetic fields. Anyone who wore them was just kidding themselves.

So here he was in his torn green scrubs, crawling the dirty floors and ignoring the human smell that was here, and about to be overrun by the highly trained idiots in the yellow suits.

The suit approached him and the face shield's technology finally made itself useful, the glare disappearing as the man got closer. "You Dr. Carter the second?"

"Yup." *The second, of course, as always.* He was certain that his getting out of their way was exactly what the suits wanted, since this one even pointed to where one of the guys had volunteered to drive him back to the hotel.

David nodded and began the arduous task of gathering all his equipment together. Another suit, this one female, and beautiful – a shame he was too exhausted to care – offered to help him. He didn't want anyone touching his things, even without the clumsy thick gloves.

Almost thirty minutes later, he had gathered all the stuff he needed and left the meters that would continue to record in his absence. But they had been roped off with the CDC's own *stand back* tape, and signs, hand printed *Touch Me and Die* on sheets of yellow legal paper. They swung just a little in air currents that they could feel even though he couldn't.

He pushed a weary and very dirty hand through his hair, noticing again that there was just a little less of it than last month.

Flipping open his cell phone, he saw the hour for the first time that morning. Already nine thirty. Damn. He dialed his father – The First's personal cell, the number that only David and every important scientist in the world had. His father had told him point blank once that David didn't have the number because he was a good scientist, but because he was the senior Carter's nearest blood relation. With a sour smile, he decided that this call could only feel better if he had actually roused the bastard from sleep. And while he waited for the ringing to stop, he suffered the brief moment of weight in his chest like he always did before his father's voice said, "Hello, David." He never said the words, but the tone clearly begged the question of why he was being bothered.

"Dad." He didn't say anything more, knowing that the term was bothersome in itself and knowing that his father knew he couldn't escape it. Of course, the great irony being that no one had ever been farther from being a 'dad' than this world-renowned scientist.

"What do you want, David?"

And he just started speaking, letting all the events of the past few days spill out. He broke about fifteen federal and contract laws that the CDC had specifically reviewed with him, but he didn't care. He came awake to the sound of surprise in his old man's voice. Though even the fact that he was surprised by his son's success was irksome.

David held the conversation as he rode back to the hotel and wandered through the lobby. The elevator dinged but David walked in and just kept talking. Let the line get cut off. He arrived at his room and tried the key, but it didn't open. He tried again. Then, wrapped up in the conversation with his father, he tried a third time. This time the door opened, although not from his key. The door handle practically flew from his fingers, startling him just long enough to realize that Jordan had opened it from the other side. He looked like death warmed over and David said so.

"Thanks." Jordan ran a hand through his hair, although he only proceeded in making it stick up more than before. His face was as rumpled as his t-shirt and boxers, and he didn't seem to come fully awake.

"Guess I got the wrong room." David said, turning his key card over, already knowing that the answer wasn't there. His attention, at last, turned back to the phone conversation with his father. "No, I'm trying to get into my hotel room. Anyway, the reversals are melding. What do you think of that?" Not like he gave a crap in hell what the old man thought of it. He should have just said, *How do you like them apples?*

"What!" This time it was Jordan, looking more awake in his eyes if not the rest of his appearance. "Who are you talking to?"

"My father." He said, and then into the phone. "No, I'm talking to one of the doctors here."

"You can't talk to anyone about this!" Jordan shook his head, although he made no motion to grab the phone away from David.

He just covered the mouthpiece. "Trust me, my old man will be too livid that I found it first to tell anyone what he knows. He'll take it to the grave, and that ain't that far away."

The look on Jordan's face was the look of good little boys and girls who were not only taught to respect their elders, but actually did.

A soft voice came from back in the room. "Jordan?" It was feminine and groggy with sleep and David smiled, making a fist for a mock punch on the arm. The good doc had gotten himself some Nevada ass. The only question was, did he have to pay for it?

His father was speaking into the cell phone, the age in his voice telling of the distance the sound traveled, even though the phone itself told no such truths. "Yeah, Dad. I've got to go." And with that he hung up on his father, the sole purpose for the call already achieved.

With a smile, he turned to congratulate Jordan, but as he opened his mouth, the voice came again. "Who is it?" And this time, as she came more awake, he recognized the cadence.

Jillian.

Oh well, she'd tire of Abellard soon enough, right? "By the way, your team showed up in their yellow suits about an hour ago. 'Night." He went down the hall enjoying the brief sounds of "oh shit!" and "the pager!", before the door clicked closed on the cozy scene gone awry.

Jordan was very afraid of the gnawing in his gut. His father had mentioned that Lindsey and Kelly were ill, but changed the topic as soon as he knew that Jordan had already been notified. It was Sunday again, and Jordan had heard the hiss of the waffle iron in the background of the call, making the Nevada heat all that much more unbearable.

There were eight more prisoners sick this morning, even though they had removed everyone from the bubbles. Maybe they had just been in for too long. Maybe David's numbers, which Jordan had leaned his head across the tapes to read, were indicating that this was another phase.

A voice shouted from off to his right and Jordan began to jog to the zippered tent where the metallic voice was coming from.

When he arrived, a yellow suit was standing over a prisoner, the man's arm cuffed to the gurney he was on.

The voice came again, filtered through a microphone inside the head piece and a polarizing layer of fear. "He's down!"

"Back off!" Jordan shoved the nurse aside, wishing he could claw the suit off of her and make her be human, make her participate in this. But he couldn't and he knew he had no right. Even through the refraction of the plexi-paned face plate he could see her perturbed expression. But he didn't care.

His left hand grabbed for the wrist not cuffed to the bed, already feeling for a pulse, even as his right hand grabbed the stethoscope from around his neck and with nimble fingers spread the earpieces, popping them into his ears. By the time he had the bell of the scope on the prisoner's slow moving chest, he had found the pulse, and was counting it. Although far too slowly. In another second he had ascertained that the man's breath sounds were as weak as his pulse and he was slipping.

Another practiced action put the stethoscope back where it had begun, draped around his neck, and brought the flashlight from his right pocket. A quick move had the light snapped on and shining into dull green eyes held open only by his own fingers.

He sighed, knowing that it was too late. But he practiced his Jillian maneuver and shoved it to the furthest corner of his mind swearing it wouldn't bother him, and dove back into the task at hand.

He turned to check the other two sleeping patients in this tent, realizing that they, too, were barely responsive. They weren't categorized as comatose yet, but their pupils were slow to respond to his flashlight, their respirations depressed, their pulses slower, indicating a heart that was overburdened and giving up. *Son of a bitch.*

Ducking through the zippered entrance, opposite the one the nurse had left through, Jordan walked out away from the soft burr of the fans and into the light, feeling the heat start to suck at him again. But he gathered his voice and called for portable ventilators and oxygen tubing.

In just a few minutes, mechanics showed, his voice having carried easily in the still desert air, unencumbered by the electronics of a microphone. But they carried none of the equipment that was their job. "We got almost nothing."

"You're kidding." Jordan snapped, biting back the words that in a few weeks it might be their families that would need the ventilators and tubing. "I don't care what you have to do. There has to be a hospital or a company with the machinery. Find it. Appropriate it if you have to."

The two men managed to produce one ventilator, and within five minutes their big truck rolled out of the prison yard and cleared the gates without much in the way of a security check, kicking up desert dust on the way into town.

The nurse was called back to help hook up the slowly sinking patient to the last ventilator. All three of the men in the tent got oxygen tubing and prongs delivering the last tanks of O_2 to their lungs. They worked quickly and efficiently, without speaking. You didn't get to be on a CDCP field team without knowing your stuff. And you certainly didn't get snapped at by the doctor and not get pissed at him.

Jordan wanted to conjure up some regret. But he was flat out.

Jillian held the page out to Jordan. Her back ached and her shoulders couldn't bear the weight of the world any more. Jordan didn't reach out to take it, just gave a little shake of his head as he carelessly peeled first his green cotton scrubs top, then the t-shirt underneath. For a moment, her mother's voice popped into her head, warning her about casualness leading to sex. Somewhere inside Jillian laughed. She was a physician, and a naked male form was nothing other than a body, especially when she could see the bone deep weariness from the outside. Jordan tossed the shirts aside and met her eyes, a motion without words to read the fax page to him.

But Jillian shook her head. She was ready to cry, and losing ground every day. Only David seemed to still be enjoying plowing headlong into whatever hell awaited them. In the half hour she had napped while Jordan added to the charts in the room next door, she had been plagued and finally jolted awake in a cold sweat by the nightmares that found her whenever she slept alone.

Yet right now she wasn't asleep. And this nightmare in print wouldn't give up. But Jordan would have to read this with his own two eyes, and those eyes peered at her from above dark smudges, read her face, and saw her refusal with the stiffening of her arm again motioning the paper to him before finally he took it.

Jillian followed where his vision tracked on the page, saw his features contract on the first few smeared words from the archaic fax machine. Then she saw him twist, and she knew. His gaze didn't trace the rest of the paper, he just looked up, piercing her with his eyes.

"I'm sorry."

The words took the remaining starch from him, and he collapsed, doll-like, laid out on the bed. For a moment, she sat and watched the even movements of his chest, listening as the air passed through his mouth in a far too perfect rhythm to be anything but forced.

The minutes stretched, and the room was quiet enough to reveal the creaks and ticks of an older building as it shifted. All the sounds normally masked by human conversation and motion, none of which existed in this room. Finally, knowing it was the right thing to do, she stood and walked the five steps to the edge of the bed. His eyes stared at the ceiling and leaked tears from the corners. Though she looked him up and down, he never made eye contact with her, effectively shutting her out.

The aching bones turned to ice. Jordan was in a space she couldn't get into. Her own family was safe. She slid and crawled onto the bed next to him, sitting against the headboard, waiting. It was all of a second before he rotated to her, her arms automatically opening in a maternal gesture she didn't realize she knew.

Still without making any eye contact, he curled into her embrace like a hurt child. Her arms closed on smooth skin as his head sank to her shoulder. She felt his hair against her cheek, not realizing that she had cocooned around him until she found herself there. "I'm so sorry." The raw whispering sound of her voice started her own eyes watering. But she couldn't distinguish if she was crying for him or for herself or simply from the abrasions her eyes had taken from seven days of desert air.

It started in soft confessional tones with his unmistakable timbre, "I left them all behind for school."

She wanted to say that she understood, that she too had left her family, had left their ideals to pursue her dreams. But she didn't think she really did understand. And in a moment he explained. "No one else there went off to college. My Dad worked in the factory. My mother ran a daycare when she was alive. Eddie was the most successful, starting his own construction business. But I was educated and no one knew what to make of me. No one knew what to say or how to speak to me, so no one really did."

His breath sucked in, and as he shifted she felt the wetness that soaked so easily through the shoulder of her scrubs. It dawned that the awkwardness she felt was due to the fact that she herself had cried to no one since she was small and no one had come crying to her.

"Eddie was my best friend growing up...and we got so far apart. I feel like I'm trained to be the hero here and I'm failing." A soft intake of air was all that revealed the depth of his regret, the pain as he saw his family falling away from him. "I left so I could save people, and I can't save them."

As he turned his face back into her shoulder, she could feel the muscles of his cheeks and mouth, biting his lip or such, and her hands slowly moved down the hot expanse of his back. Wrapping themselves around her waist, his arms stood out in muscled, bronze relief against the green of her scrubs, but the fabric blended from fold to fold making their legs virtually indistinguishable where they were tangled on the covers.

She felt and heard the two deep breaths at the same time, the only harbinger before he stood and turned quickly away, hiding the streaks that marked his face. But he didn't bring his hands up to wipe them away. Jillian saw one more deep breath before he announced that he would be on the next flight to Minneapolis.

Her legs curled under her of their own will, perhaps her body unconsciously seeking a more protected position before she told him what she knew. "You didn't read the whole thing." Jordan slowly turned to face her, no longer ashamed of the tracks on his face, his hands on his hips and his eyes steady.

"Landerly forbade you to go back. He wants you to stay here." She felt the cringe before she realized she was doing it.

But he didn't flinch at the news at all, and she knew before she heard it what his decision was. "Then I quit. I'm going back." He calmly walked into the bathroom where she heard the water running for a few moments before it shut off and was replaced by the sounds of zippers and the small clunks of things thrown into bags.

That galvanized her, and she sprang from the bed to find him in the bathroom doing exactly what she had expected. "Wait!" That stopped him. Cold as stone he turned to her, "Do you want me to not go?"

"No. That's not what I'm saying." Jillian felt the desperation rising inside her in a tidal panic she hadn't felt before this. "You should go. Let me make the arrangements through the CDC–"

"Maybe you didn't hear me: I'm quitting."

With a ferocity she hadn't applied in way too long, she stood up to both Jordan and the encroaching hysteria. "No you're not. I'm getting on the phone and talking Landerly into this. He'll pay for it out of his own pocket by the time I'm through. Keep packing."

She didn't wait for an answer because she didn't want to hear it. Too afraid he would disagree, she fled to the phone and began pushing buttons, unsure what she was going to say to change Landerly's mind and send them to Lake James. Her fingers dialed of their own accord, her brain having long ago memorized all five of Landerly's numbers, and while she got her thoughts together, Landerly answered. "Hello, Dr. Brookwood."

It would have been nice, to have such a distinguished colleague address her so formally, if he hadn't followed the first phrase with "I figured it would be you to call. So did you talk Abellard out of quitting or are you talking me into sending you both to Lake James?"

Surprised, she choked on the words, "The latter, sir."

"Well, this had better be a good argument." He sounded a trifle annoyed, and she would have shot something rude back, except that she was about to launch into an argument that had 'better be good' and she had no idea what that argument was.

"It is, sir."

Ten minutes later she hung up and finally turned to face Jordan who had moved from the bathroom into the main room and was gathering his shoes, stuffing them into the bottom of the barely serviceable duffle he always carried. "Anne will call in less than fifteen minutes with your arrangements."

"*My* arrangements?"

"Yeah, just you." She smiled the turned-in grin that confessed she was at the end of her rope, too.

He crossed the six feet of space between them, relief showing on every plane of his face, and embraced her, breathing out in one long sigh that let her know he was glad he didn't have to quit. Her face was inextricably buried in the white t-shirt he had thrown on, and the fake-fresh smell of laundry detergent assailed her, as did the fear of going it alone.

Chapter 12

Lake James wasn't what she expected. In the coffee shop, the waitress had answered her question with a 'ya' then laughed hysterically at 'y'all'. Becky was used to feeling backwoods, but this made her feel like a big city girl. And that was just uncomfortable.

The people looked like they stepped from a book she had read. It reminded her too much of McCann: small stores, no chains, and everyone knew everyone else's business. And just like in McCann, they greeted her and John with a "you guys aren't from round here." In their weird clipped, partially swallowed accent. It was never a question, just a statement of fact.

Unable to speak in public about their work, she and John quietly sipped coffee that came only in regular and decaf, at a table with blue vinyl seats ripped in a handful of places, stuffing slowly escaping where it could. They both refused the breakfast menus and drank in a noisy silence as the diner swirled around them.

John got a call halfway through the awkward breakfast, and the entire diner turned as one to see who was answering a cell phone in the middle of their pastiche. He ignored the looks and snapped the phone shut. "Dr. Abellard is on his way, he's already in the air."

Becky only nodded and drained the last slightly darker bits from the bottom of her cup. She already knew that Jordan's cousin Lindsay had slipped into a coma yesterday. From the fax John had pulled from the machine before they left this morning, they knew that her mother Kelly had slipped under just hours ago – a fact even Dr. Abellard was unaware of as he flew in from Vegas.

"Are you two ready? We are." Leon Peppersmith approached them from the booth behind where she and John sat in clear distinction between the animal handlers and the PhDs.

Becky and John both nodded and got up together, in tandem reaching for their wallets and dropping a few bills on the table. Silently, Becky tucked herself at the end of the line behind the four animal wranglers. Leon had his team: his brother as large and lean as himself; his sister, midsized but everything about her said she was determined to keep up with the big boys, including her brown ponytail; and a good friend of theirs who had worked for the first Peppersmith, when he had started in the animal wrangling business.

They were after medium-to-big sized game, and while the Peppersmith operation did a lot of for-hire work, they were contracted with the CDCP as needed. And John wanted good sized mammals. He wanted to see what was happening in other populations they hadn't happened to stumble across yet.

Though the coffee was warming her from the inside out, Becky turned up the neck on her jacket against the chill in the air. There were rumors that blizzards sometimes happened this early in the season up here. With a small shiver, Becky became a believer. She reached up to grab the handle at the back of the truck bed, but Leon stretched down to clasp her wrist and lift her in as though she was no more than a housecat.

He didn't speak, but motioned her to sit next to John, and moving his index finger in a circle in the air, signaled Linda in the driver's seat to start up. Two smaller pickups with wide, tricked-out flatbeds followed close behind, and Becky wondered if it was legal to be sitting in the back of a truck like this. They were strapped into small seats that had been bolted in, her and John. But Leon was free within the confines of the bouncing bed of the quadcab, and he moved like the panthers he was known to catch. He ran a brief lesson, showing them modern lassoes and tranquilizer guns and cages while they rumbled along. When he asked if they knew how to shoot a rifle, he barely suppressed his surprise that it was Becky who said yes. It was the only emotion that had flitted across his face in the whole five hours she had known him.

His dark blond hair was pulled back in a low ponytail that looked to be held by a classic red office rubberband, and his ball cap, emblazoned with the letters "P.A.W.", was well worn and molded to him, as did the PAW coveralls he wore. He quickly went through his efficient explanations and demonstrations, and before Becky realized it they had pulled off the back road they had wandered onto.

They passed a road block that looked like anything the city might erect, even with the city name painted across the scrap-board barricades. It was a trick Becky had learned recently that the CDC did when they really didn't want anyone to know of their presence. They made it look like they weren't even there, not until you were well within the borders, and by then you'd have had to pass some sort of security check. It all seemed very 'Area 51' to her, but she was becoming accustomed to it, a fact that scared her more than just a little.

They stopped in a small clearing next to a wide expanse of trees, and like back home, the trees seemed to go on forever. Mountains loomed up beyond the vast forest, and who knew what lived back there where homes and people hadn't encroached and destroyed?

Fish and fowl. Amphibs by the thousands. Insects she was sure she had never seen before. But John had brought them here for bigger catches. Cougar. Wolves. Bears.

And Peppersmith Animal Wrangling had a cage for anything they caught, on trucks whose beds unfolded to act as trailers to carry it all back. With disturbing efficiency and a disconcerting lack of language, each of them was outfitted with a food pack and water bottle, a thinsulate blanket, and flare gun, and Becky was handed a rifle on a plain brown strap and several boxes of ammo-tranquilizers of many shapes and sizes. Becky slung the rifle over her shoulder in the lithe motion of someone who had done this a hundred times before, but unease gripped her that they expected her to size up and mentally weigh her prey before loading and taking it out. She was certain that if things went down she would shoot first, and second, and third, before stopping to check dosages and weights.

The yellow suits had been here before, leaving droppings of little Day-Glo flags, indicating areas where they had found reversals. These animals had been exposed, and they would all be, too. But they wouldn't be able to stalk game in hazmat suits. Becky didn't even know if the Peppersmith operation had been informed of what they were walking into.

Their quiet became infinitely reasonable as she was engulfed by the deep stillness of the forest broken only by the obnoxiously human sounds of her and John's boots crunching through the undergrowth. The Peppersmiths moved like the animals they hunted: quietly, stealthily, in a pack.

They kept their rifles firmly in hand, and so Becky decided that she would follow their lead and, as silently as she could, un-slung the firearm from her shoulder. They had walked for half an hour, Becky bringing up the rear, when the line abruptly stopped. Leon's left hand was held up in a fist and he turned to look at John. With his two fingers in a V, he motioned for John to look beyond his left shoulder.

Looking back at all of them was a female cougar, showing her grace and stability across a fallen tree.

With hushed tones that didn't seem to disturb the cat anywhere near as much as John staring at her, the wranglers divvied them-selves up. Lincoln and Linda taking John off to try to follow the cougar hopefully to her cubs. Becky was motioned to trail behind Leon and his friend, whose embroidery read 'Jess'.

They hooked wide around the cat and hiked further, while Becky spent her time gazing around her and making feeble attempts to categorize the birdcalls she heard. What a crazy place to think of the overzealous Marshall Harfield, but what a help he would be right now.

They asked her about three white-tailed deer, all of whom she refused to have captured, even though it made the Peppersmiths shake their heads like kids told to clean their rooms. But the deer were juveniles. And Becky wasn't going to take them, not while she was making the decisions.

Her eyes spotted several species of frogs and lizards. And why were all the deer juveniles? Had something happened to the adults?

The frogs looked fairly normal. But she stopped and went to get a closer look, twice plunging her hand into water that made the icy creek back home feel like a hot spring. The cold was enough that it altered her physiology, keeping her fingers from grasping at their normal speed, letting these ice-adapted frogs get away from her. Knowing what was happening to the neural connections and muscular responses in her hands only bothered her. It sure didn't stop her from trying again and again until she finally came up with a salamander.

She counted all its toes and checked its eyes, before popping it into a plastic container she pulled from her backpack. She was pulling the pack back on when she spotted the two men staring at her.

It was Leon who opened his mouth and demanded a response. "What was that?"

"Salamander." She looked at them through narrowed eyes. She was the doctor; she was supposed to be making the decisions about what to catch and they were looking at her like she had a cracked head.

"Well, I hope you learn a damn lot from that guy." Jess had a southern drawl as long as the day, and a scowl to match.

Leon had his pack off and was pulling random things out of it: a spare pair of socks, a roll of thick blue tape. A wicked looking pair of scissors came from their own sheath on his leg.

He pointed them at her, scaring the wits out of her for a brief moment. Her mind flooded with horror movie scenes and she momentarily considered fleeing, back through the woods she didn't know, chased by a madman with his scissors and an uncanny awareness of the wilderness.

"Your sleeve's wet."

She jerked her arm back. "You going to cut it off?"

"I should, but I suspect you like that jacket." He pulled one long tube sock, emblazoned with the letter P, and snipped the toe end off. He unceremoniously yanked her sleeve up, allowing her to feel for the first time the frigid water that had seeped in even though she had been certain she had pushed it far enough back. Yanking the dry sleeve of her turtleneck down, he pulled his glove off in one smooth motion with his teeth and ran his hand over her arm in a reverent and nearly sexual way. She wanted her skin back. She wanted the crazy guy with the scissors and tranq gun to step beck. But she didn't quite have it in her to look him in the eyes and say so.

He pulled the sock over her arm, over her sleeve, and began wrapping the tape around and around. Allowing only the letter P to peek out near her elbow. "What is this? Some kind of scarlet letter?" As soon as the words were out she regretted the reference, wondering if two men who'd spent their lives 'rassling 'gators' would have heard of Hester Prynne.

"No," He cocked a look that was almost a smile. "This is a P, not an A. Your arm is now waterproof and will not freeze from where you dipped your sleeve in the pond. And maybe your jacket will dry out." He pulled the sleeve down over the tape, where it could no longer chill her wrist nor soak into any of her other clothing. She turned her hand over, thinking it looked a bit odd, but was fairly ingenious.

"Thank you." It was the least she could say to a man she had considered a possible serial killer just a few moments before.

Without a word, he slipped the items back into their various sheaths and pockets and pulled his pack on even as he started walking away. Becky followed, flexing her hand to re-warm the muscles, grateful that the sleeve wasn't wet against her wrist. Cataloging everything she saw, she wished that she had Melanie's memory and wished Mel could be here now to see these things.

It was then that she noticed Leon and Jess looking at each other and making faces even as she felt the odd odor trickle past her senses. She knew it was familiar, but not like this. Consciously keeping her voice low she asked without slowing her pace, "What is that?"

"Blood." Both men replied simultaneously.

Wanting to ask more, but knowing that they were headed straight for the smell, Becky held her tongue. It took fifteen more minutes to get there. In that time she felt the smell change from weak to pungent with a mild overlay of rotting flesh, a smell she hadn't detected ten minutes further back on the trail.

They made their way off the paths, finally coming to a clearing, silent as mice, until Becky gasped. A whole herd of moose lay dead, the river rushing by them as though nothing were wrong, even though a member of the heard had fallen in and gotten tangled in a fallen tree. Water rushed around it on all sides, the animal bobbing like a swollen cork. The bulk of the herd lay along the shores, feet curled under them like they were asleep.

But they weren't asleep. Wolves and cougars, even some Canada Lynx, chewed greedily on the haunches of the fallen animals. The closest ones looked up and growled in response to the gasp that had escaped Becky's mouth. Cubs and pups were there as well, there was no infighting over pieces. There was enough moose for all.

The stench assailed her now that she had a visual to go with it. Bloody muzzles came up and chewed before burying themselves deep in the torn open sides of the larger hooved animals. Juveniles tugged at loose flesh, trying to rip pieces free, unconcerned about their human visitors.

It was Jess who spoke first. "Damnedest thing. Usually they won't eat something that dies of its own accord."

Becky nodded. "What do they know that we don't?"

The water bubbled around her, the chlorine churning into a smell that was certainly unpleasant, but her brain ignored it in order to appreciate the joys of the foaming water and heat. She had a coke with a big red straw sitting on the edge of the tub.

The season being what it was, they were the only ones out here. A few of the prison officers had been in the casino, gambling at blackjack or playing nickel slots. Something pretty much all of them had sworn at one time or another they never did.

"You look sad."

David's voice broke through the shell she had locked herself in since Jordan's call. His cousin had joined her daughter in a coma, and his father had complained of a stomach ache. Jordan was staying with his Dad at the house, as his father's exposure to the reversals had come at the factory where he worked, which had since been shut down by the CDC. And that had prompted the news crews to come out. Jordan had explained how they'd held a small press conference and stalled, stating that they didn't know what it was yet. Which was true.

"I am sad." She just took a sip of the coke, enjoying it, even though she knew it was full of caffeine and would act in conjunction with the hot tub to dehydrate her even faster than the desert air could. But she figured dehydration was the least of her worries.

David pulled his arms out of the water, stretching them across the tiles and leaning his head back like she did. Her own arms felt cool from the contact with the tile, in the dark it had finally lost much of the heat it had retained from the day. The night sky was big and black and disappointingly empty. There were no stars visible above her; they were all blocked out by the pinprick of blinding light that was the state line.

"Do you miss him? Abellard?"

"Yeah." She said it with a force she didn't know she felt, the words falling out of her mouth. "None of these people will talk to me like they talk to him. They're getting worse by the day, and there's nothing medical to do. I may have something, but it isn't statistically significant yet–"

"What do you think you have?" David was leaning forward, carefully holding his brown longneck bottle out of the water.

"The glycosylated hemoglobin spikes ever so slightly before a person goes under. And I wouldn't have found it if I didn't have a whole pond of sitting ducks and nothing better to do than run blood draws on everyone all day long."

David nodded and so the words kept falling out of her mouth in useless rivers. "I swear I had a patient take a step back when I came to him. He looked like he had a heroin problem, we'd taken his blood so many times." She sighed, more to herself than to him, more out of exasperation than weariness.

Her bones were rubber, and her coke was gone, and suddenly she was tired. Dead tired.

Jillian bent her elbows and, flattening her hands against the tiles, lifted herself out of the tub, dripping water across the ceramic squares, and she made a brief note to watch where she stepped. She could see the headlines: CDC doctor kills herself in deadly cola/hot tub/water-slick incident. She'd already warned David about the alcohol he was drinking, but he was a big boy and he could call his own shots.

He followed her up, sitting for a moment on the edge of the rim, rubbing his hand up and down his face. "Wow. That beer does affect you more in the hot tub."

David didn't say much more, just followed her silent bare feet down the hall with his less than silent large ones. He waited while she got her door open, standing back and not crowding her, but being gentlemanly. "Need any help getting ready for bed?"

She mentally rescinded the *gentlemanly* idea. "No thanks." With a small smile meant to say goodnight and nothing more, she stepped past and into the frigid room.

She had hoped it would be warm, or at least not sub-artic. Given the time she had been here and her high IQ, she had thought she would have figured out what to leave the AC set at so that the room would be the right temperature when she returned. But, no.

Inside of five minutes, she was ready for bed, having swallowed eight giant pills for the third time today. She dreaded the short walk to the king sized bed; it had gotten just a little larger since Jordan had left. With a deep breath, she walked over and pushed herself beneath the covers, flicking off the last bedside lamp, letting darkness infest the room.

Feeling her eyelids pull closed, Jillian waited for sleep to overtake her, but her fear held it at bay. She'd been hopeful that she would climb into the bed and smell him on the sheets. But the maids had changed the sheets and it had all been destroyed with one easy stroke of efficiency.

Eventually she got bored with lying in bed and not sleeping, so she threw back the covers and began turning on lights. The room was boring in its simplicity, too neat, too dull, and she decided to make use of her time by checking out the charts in the other room; she could at least update the hemoglobin numbers she was getting.

As she pulled the conjoining door open to total darkness, her brows knit together. The light behind her didn't penetrate, and a deep unease walked through her. She tucked her hand around the wall feeling for the switch, to no avail. She tested with her foot, sneaking it across as it was almost swallowed by the darkness, but no floor rose up to meet her toes. Flailing wildly, her hands grasped at the door frame, stopping her just in time from plunging into the abyss beyond the door.

The darkness breathed.

The deep space at the door pulsed in a slow, even rhythm. Jillian considered reaching out to catch the doorknob so she could close off the menace, but even as she leaned out over the yawning gap beneath her into the darkness, hanging only by her left hand firmly grasped on the frame, she heard something.

Something familiar.

So she pulled back, clung to the door frame, and waited.

She wasn't sure how long it was before the sound came again.

"Jilly?" This time it came from behind her. Whirling into the sound of him, she knew everything would be all right.

"Jordan!"

But he didn't hug her. She didn't even see his face, just his strong hands coming up to plant across her collarbone and shove her backwards until she fell into the endless space beyond the doorway.

With a deep gasp, Jillian jerked herself from the clutches of the black, coming awake and gulping air in the hotel room. She lay alone, twisted in the covers, in the middle of her own bed.

Yesterday, Jillian had finally given him the keys to the car. He had needed it and she hadn't. And David simply hadn't handed them back over. He figured the car practically went from the hotel to the prison and back by itself at this point.

This morning, Jillian didn't even make a motion for the driver side door, just slipped limply into the passenger seat and buckled up without a word.

"Is everything all right?" He wasn't normally one to pry but the girl looked like someone had showed up last night and decked her, blacking both eyes. He knew that wasn't the case, since he'd seen the color forming for several days now. "You miss your boyfriend?"

That, at least, startled her. "He's not my boyfriend."

"Friend with benefits?" If you dug with a little trowel you could get pretty deep before anyone noticed what you were doing. Or decided they didn't want to answer your question.

She laughed. "Yeah, benefits. Like I can sleep."

"Huh?" Digging with his little trowel only worked when he was prepared.

"Since McCann, I have nightmares when I sleep alone."

"Jesus, Jillian, all you had to do was knock. You know you can stay with me."

Her eyebrows went up, making the fatigue look almost delicate across her fine features. All of it was clear across her face, left unhindered by the deep mahogany hair pulled up into her ponytail. He could easily read the distrust and the laughter.

"I don't think I would get any more sleep with you than I do by myself."

"Hey. I'd let you sleep." *What the hell? Was he defending his own honor?* Even he knew he didn't have any.

"Right."

Twenty minutes of silence later, they arrived at the penitentiary. He pulled the tires onto the soft sand lot where they parked with a slew of other cars, but Jillian was out of the car before he flipped the key. She almost closed the door, but then was across the lot like a streak of green, her hair flying behind her.

David looked beyond her fleeing form to see what she was running to. The only thing his brain processed at first was that something was wrong. He wanted to yell, to tell her to come back, but she was gone before he could call out. And all he knew was that something was dreadfully not right.

Canvas fluttered in the air. Fans and machinery could be heard. Yet nothing human moved.

Except for Jillian, who disappeared between the tents, running toward whatever was so wrong.

Grabbing his briefcase, David took off after her. Even as he ran, he tucked one hand down in the side pocket to pull out a small electronic compass. He clicked the power button and was rewarded with a screen full of dashes followed by a blinking **ERROR** light.

The reversal. That was the only explanation. He pulled out an old needle compass his father had given him back in his days as a boy scout. Even now, the feel of his hand around the metal case brought back the warning that he had better not lose it. But he slipped it out to watch the classic red arrow sway like a drunken sailor.

"Jillian!"

His heart was ready to pound its way out of his chest, and his breathing seared his lungs it was so deep and ragged. Jesus, had he just been talking about sex? And now…

"Past the computer tent!"

Or, at least, that's what he thought he heard. The wind ate portions of her words like a staticky broadcast. So he ran to his best guess, stopping short when he did finally see her.

Jillian was on her knees, working the hood off of a fallen suit. Another lay behind her, his head lolled to the side, mouth open, his helmet lying a foot away in the sand.

He heard the precious compass hit the dirt, and instantly his knees bent, his body's immediate reaction to protect its treasure. Her face turned up to his, her stethoscope hung from her ears, her penlight clung to her fingertips. "They're all under." Her eyes tracked wildly to either side of him.

"Jillian–" He grabbed her arm to pull her to her feet, thinking to embrace her in a hug, to comfort her. But she jerked her arm out of his reach.

Before he snapped out of it, Jillian was on her feet, racing away. Her standard uniform of running shoes carrying her well from one tent to another. He raked his fingers through the sandy earth, sifting out the round silver compass and he followed, watching as she lifted flaps and peered inside each one. He checked the needle periodically, noting where it went from the wild swinging to pointing due south.

This whole shanty town the CDC had erected was now in the reversal.

Jillian dove into one tent and David ran the distance to join her. Not knowing what he could do, but that he would do whatever was needed. They were in a maximum security prison made of loose canvas. There was no telling when or how the prisoners would get loose. Or what they would do to the cute little doctor if they did.

The tent was darker than he expected and his eyes took several seconds more than he felt was reasonable to adjust. When he finally was able to focus on Jillian, she was kneeling on the floor where a CDC employee, not in a hazmat suit, had curled up between the patient gurneys.

Jillian put her stethoscope on the woman's chest, rolling her from her side onto her back even as she checked the prone woman. The badge hanging around her neck flashed as the woman rolled over, revealing that she was an RN.

He didn't really want to know, but he asked anyway. "The others?"

She made eye contact finally, but he almost wished she hadn't. Her vivid blue eyes were bright with a gloss of unshed tears. "All the same."

He reached down for her with his right hand, having shifted the compass to his pocket and the briefcase into his left. "Jillian, we're standing in a reversal. We have to get out."

"What?" She focused on him. *In* him, somewhere inside his soul.

"We're deep in the reversal right now. Everywhere you ran is backwards." He tugged her to her feet, whether she wanted it or not. All of it made him uncomfortable: her gaze, the polarity. "And judging by what's happened, it's pretty powerful. We have to get out."

He simply turned and yanked her along, brooking no protests. He kept going until they had arrived at an untouched cluster of cactus, well beyond the tents, opposite the parking lot where they had come in. It had been the fastest way out. Finally, when it seemed she wouldn't protest, or just dash back in to save some chart or blood sample, he dropped her hand and plucked the compass from his shirt pocket.

North.

True north.

He breathed out.

But while he gathered himself together, Jillian fell apart. Her legs gave way and she sank onto the sand beneath her, gathering her knees in her arms and burying her face in the space between.

It took a few moments with him standing there, looking out over the desert while she cried at his feet before she spoke. "Why didn't they call?"

He shook his head, but mentally he flipped through image after image of what he'd just emerged from. "You know, it looked like people just fell wherever they stood."

She started to uncurl. And David knew he'd handed her something for that brain of hers to chew on. She'd come back around for that.

"No." She looked up into the sky and he waited for what she'd reveal. "They didn't fall. There were no broken bones or bumps to the head. It was like they curled up or lay down where they were. They had at least a few moments."

He nodded for her to continue.

"That would mean they got sick very quickly... even the RN didn't get out of the tent to tell anyone. But she didn't fall. Not the way she was lying." He thought he saw a ghost of a smile pass her lips. "That nurse was smart. She even thought it through and lay down on her side. In case she vomited. So she wouldn't choke on it."

Pleasant, he thought to himself. But he'd have to remember that, in case he came to needing it.

"Help!"

It cut through the air. A human voice that wasn't theirs, calling from the other side of the camp.

Jillian was on her feet in an instant, dashing back in towards the tents, until David caught her arm and hauled her off her feet, nearly yanking her shoulder from its socket. "You can't go back through there. We have to go around."

So she pulled him at a breakneck speed. He wouldn't let go and she wouldn't slow down. David wouldn't abandon his briefcase, so it slapped against his leg a few times until he learned to hold it out of the way. He ran with the compass in front of him, watching for the shift and pulling Jillian off to the side more than once as the needle jerked too much for his taste.

It wasn't reliable, this running and reading. The compass was meant to be used by a camper who had a moment to stop and let the needle settle, not running at high speeds around fatal pole reversals.

Just then, Jillian stopped short and, without any warning, he crashed into her back, eliciting a grunt from her and a quick save as she managed to keep them both on their feet.

Five county cars were sitting in the lot where they hadn't been before.

"Shift change."

Her voice caused a swell of nausea to rise in him. Twenty officers had just arrived to relieve their friends, only to find them comatose, scattered across the ground like forgotten toys. The sound came again, from off to their right. But this time it wasn't a cry for help. It was a muffled noise, a grunt, a groan, or somewhere in between.

And she was just too fast for him to catch. Jillian jumped into the fray, dashing between two tents and disappearing from his view. *What the hell, he was going to die anyway. He might as well go out chasing a hot doctor.*

When he arrived, she was leaning over an officer who was curled on the ground with his arms wrapped tight around his stomach. "Ahhhhh." It was soft. Not so much in pain as it was a release. And even as David stood there dumbfounded, the arms slackened. The officer's face lost its tension and his head eased to the ground.

The officer looked like he had suddenly gone to sleep.

Jillian looked over her shoulders at another man who was standing over a fallen colleague. A quick sweep revealed that almost all of the officers were already down. Only a few remained, clutching their stomachs, and one had his hands clasped over his ears, as though the eerie desert silence was the loudest feedback.

As David watched, Jillian rushed, helpless, from one man to another. Not able to help any of them without sacrificing the others. Not able to help any of them anyway. And one by one they dropped. Creating a pattern of fallen bodies in grey-green uniforms, aligned in small clusters, attesting to how they had tried to help each other.

The whole shift down.

"Jillian!" He paced up to her in several hard steps, again grabbing her behind the elbow and dragging her along. "We have to get out of here. Look at what it's doing to people."

He thought of nothing else but reaching the edge of this freak of nature and walking beyond it. He hauled her with him, completely unconcerned for her well-being. Mostly he figured he should take the only other standing person out of the reversal with him.

When he felt he was far enough beyond, probably way further than necessary, he pulled out the old boy scout compass again. This time he was able to use it in its intended style, standing still. Although his hand shook like Richter seven.

North.

Again the needle direction freed his lungs of their breath.

Jillian just stood next to him, a statue in kelly green, her eyes blinking on and off azure blue. He wanted to lean over and put his hands on his knees and breathe like he had just finished wind sprints. Feeling his lungs contract so rapidly and painfully was almost a relief.

"Why are we still standing? Why did they collapse and we didn't?"

He looked up to see her eyes connect with his. He felt it like a hit, square in the chest, as the words absorbed.

Those officers hadn't been inside anywhere near as long as they had, and yet the wardens had all fallen, most even before they could ask for help. They were rapidly affected by the reversal, the symptoms showing instantaneous onset to a man.

As his own eyes focused on Jillian, he saw the thought pattern in her head change. Her eyes averted and she grabbed for her stomach. Tumbling to her knees, Jillian lost the contents of her breakfast in the hot sand.

Chapter 13

His father's hand was slack and lifeless. Not warm, not cold. Not dead, but not the house of a living soul. Mr. Abellard's eyes didn't open, didn't show the telltale movements of tracking a dream. Nor would they. Jordan knew that, and felt the sharp stab somewhere untouched.

Eddie's death had been tough. Hearing about Lindsay and Kelly slipping away had hurt. Opened old wounds. Rubbed areas already raw. But when his father took one last look at him, before his eyes pulled closed and his breathing pattern changed, Jordan felt the world undergo some subtle shift.

In that moment, Lake James had ceased to be his home. It was simply a cluster of people he knew, or knew of, and a house that he had grown up in. The promise of pancakes on Sunday was forever rescinded. The smile his father would get when thinking of his mother. The last person who remembered her as Jordan did. All of it was gone.

Now he waited. Until his father took his last breath and died. Or until Landerly called his number and drafted him into service again. But now he would only fight for others. So they wouldn't lose like he had.

Another man lay comatose in the second bed against the window. Jordan didn't know him, but his Dad had once referred to him as Albert, and Jordan got the feeling that the two men had worked together.

As he often did, he squeezed his father's hand. Just enough to send pressure signals to the dormant brain, in hopes that Jackson Abellard was only sleeping, that his son's hand would get even the slightest squeeze back. But it didn't. Not any of the tries before, and not this time either.

The smell blanketed the room, not just with the odor of 'hospital' but of death. The whole room was waiting – the chairs, the window, the light that didn't quite filter in. Why should it bother? It was all just a matter of time.

Jordan stood and stretched, needing to get out where things lived and breathed, even if they didn't really connect with him. The cafeteria seemed like a logical choice – the eating of food being the road to sustaining a body. He put his feet in a rhythmic pattern on the floor, moving himself out the door and down the hallway, even though it required far too much thought. He was halfway there when his cell phone went off. Tugging it from the waistband of his blue scrubs, he checked the caller ID.

Landerly.

Well, that didn't take long. He flipped the phone open. "Yes?"

"We have two new cities near McCann that are losing people, and very rapidly. I want you there."

Jordan blinked twice. Thinking through….nothing. He would leave his father here, because there was nothing more he could do. And did he need to sit here for the two more days it would take, and simply wait? No. He could be helpful.

"Abellard? Anne will call you back with your arrangements." With a few more short sentences, Landerly conveyed the seriousness of the issue. These were *cities*. They were on the maps and had populations in the tens of thousands. Huge compared to what they had seen in McCann or even Lake James. Jillian and David had seen everyone at the prison go under, and they would meet him in Nashville and fly into Knoxville together on a small charter.

With only a click and no real closing words, Jordan was left holding the cell phone – staring at it like an alien in his grasp as the staff in the hall flowed around him in a sea of blues and greens.

He turned and headed back to his father's room. He hadn't really been hungry anyway, and in a minute he had re-perched himself at the side of the mechanical gurney. Again he held his father's hand, but this time he spoke. With gentle words, he explained that he'd be back after he packed, but only briefly, before he was off again to East Tennessee to pursue his place as a physician. Something he had only in the past few days understood that his father admired him for.

"I'll be back in a bit, Dad." Taking a deep breath, he forced himself to stand and let go of the shell that had housed his father.

On lead feet, he made the turns down the corridor, waited at the elevator, and walked through the chill air to the physician's parking lot. His father's beat-up Ford Falcon took the turns like a steamer, slow and wide, heavy and solid feeling. Like his father, the car was from a different era, and with a slight smile he decided he would come back to claim the antique as his own.

Within minutes, he was pulling up to the house where his father had spent his whole adult life. The house was emptier than it had ever been. The souls had vacated it a while ago it seemed. In quick leaps, Jordan took the stairs two at a time and raided his drawers for what he had brought – so much for settling in and staying a while.

The duffle was packed and slung over his shoulder without a second thought. He was, by now, too used to picking up and fleeing with only his bag to let sentimentality rule him. Key in hand, he bolted the front door behind him and sank into the driver's seat of the car.

He pulled out, driving in the exact reverse order to get back to the clinic where his Dad lay. He managed to get another fifteen minutes of time with his father. Not that that time made any difference to either of them. Jordan didn't speak, didn't think, didn't cast silent wishes. When the cell finally rang again, he took the call where he sat, Anne's dulcet tones telling him that his flight was leaving in just barely enough time to get himself to the airport, and maybe not even that. She mentioned the charter terminal in Nashville and how to get to it.

He hung up and waved the phone at his Dad, thinking to make a little joke. "Stop me now Dad, or I'm off to Tennessee."

His father made no response. No shift or hitch in his breathing, no twitch of a finger. Jordan watched for all of it and saw none of it. So he stood, stretched, and after a brief hesitation he leaned over and gently pressed a kiss to his father's forehead. "I love you, Dad. I'll see you on the other side."

"What!?" Becky shouted into the cell phone. John had called her three times while she was out trekking with Leon and Jess. Not that her super CDC phone had picked up anything in the back wilds of Minnesota.

"Clinton, Oak Ridge–" *static.* She wanted to throw the phone, but upon recognizing towns just beyond her parents' land, she knew she couldn't lose it over a cell phone. There were far better things to lose it for these days.

Like Leon and Jess making angry faces at her. Here she was yelling on a cell phone in the middle of their pristine wilderness. Well they could stuff it.

"Come…back…in…w…eeed…talk."

"I'm coming." She practically shouted it, again knowing it was useless. Louder only worked when you were yelling to a person far away, but Becky was beginning to wonder if maybe that wouldn't be a better method of communication. John said something else, even more indistinguishable than the previous sentences, so she yelled "Good-bye!" and hung up, only to turn and face the Peppersmith guys and their angry glares.

With a sigh, she ignored their expressions, just as she had learned to ignore the menacing way they held their tranq guns. That was for her protection, she had found out the other day when a wolf had come too close. "We have to go in, guys. John called me back. Something about other towns."

"Other towns?" That from Leon, his deep voice and blue eyes not hiding his surprise or concern.

Crap. She had no idea what kind of clearance these guys held. But she also knew her place – and her place was not to give information out. So she weaseled. Another *great* skill she had learned since hiring on at the CDC. Telling the truth to lie. "I don't know what it is. I really couldn't hear much of anything except that I had to come back in."

But she had heard a whole lot more. John sounded not scared exactly, but disturbed. Oak Ridge and Clinton were just beyond the boundaries of the little acreage her folks held. And she knew what the reversals were doing. More than she wanted to know.

She was under contract to *not* tell her family anything, even though death might be at their doorstep. Literally.

That thought set an ulcer to forming. She could feel the hydrochloric acid in her stomach pinching and wearing away at the delicate tissue even as she hiked back toward their base. The trucks stood ready, cages open and waiting for animals stupid or unlucky enough to get in their way, or to catch John's eye. It seemed that John, who had never held a gun in his life, who had always excelled at science and never sports, enjoyed having the raw power of the Peppersmiths at his command. Becky on the other hand felt guilty every time she gave the word to bring a creature down, to haul it in. She kept telling herself it was a necessary evil.

The hike seemed much longer this way, even though she knew for certain that they were taking a more direct route and walking at a faster pace. Pines passed by with a speed that was likely to have her wind up with a twisted ankle. But she was fueled by adrenaline, her brain not acknowledging the sounds of birds, even though it categorized that the aviary itself was changing here, day by day.

The Nevada prison scared the living daylights out of her. According to what she read, it was very lucky that Jillian and David were alive. They had actually run into the reversal, several times. Dr. Abellard was supposed to be monitoring them for signs of turning to the worse. That was enough to give her the willies.

From what she and John had gleaned that morning, it sounded like the suits were standing at the edge of the reversal and jumping back as it got bigger. They were using ultrasound and heat sensors to detect who was still alive. It seemed most of them were. They were looking to see who was moving. At last count, that was no one.

Becky chewed her lip. The sharp retort of the rifle just behind her made her jump and nearly bite through it. She turned to glare at Leon who was holding his gun still aimed and practically smoking. But it was Jess who pointed just a few feet to her left where a lynx was teetering on its feet and falling with a soft thud to the forest floor. Becky closed her eyes, wondering whether she should thank Leon or yell at John for this crazy adventure.

As casually as if it was a discarded towel on his living room floor, Leon picked up the lynx and slung it over his shoulder. He motioned for Becky to keep trudging forward. Her ankles were sore from three days of this. Her nerves were stretched. And the ground was giving way beneath her feet. But she slid down the small incline, touching her hand to various branches to stay upright, sending small rocks skittering in front of her. Leon and Jesse brought up a tight watch behind her as she picked her way back with very little grace. At least compared to the two men whose big booted feet were no more than cat's paws in the thick pine wilderness. But she tried to breathe clean air and pretend it was all okay.

Becky knew it wouldn't last long. If she ran, the clean smell would give way to the bloody scene they had twice visited at the riverside. The deer would be only juveniles, and unless she could turn her brain off, she would worry that thought in her head forever. Then there was also the promise of the maniacal gleam that would light John's eyes when he sent the Peppersmiths off after her to bring her down with their tranq guns. She, too, could come back to camp unconscious and slung across Leon's wide shoulder, arms hanging limp, flapping with the rhythm of his gait.

Her two low ponytails stirred in the wind that reached them as they neared the edge of the clearing. John approached, carelessly picking his way through the brush, branches snapping back behind him. "Oak Ridge is losing people and so is Clinton."

He held up a map in front of her asking what she knew. All Becky could think was that the whole of Anderson County was going under and the two Peppersmiths behind her were getting a serious education in what was happening. She could feel Leon approach, even though she couldn't see or hear him. Her instincts were the best detection for him, probably the only one.

John circled the map area, pointing with his pen. "People are going down fast! One hundred since our update this morning."

She watched as the tip of his capped red pen passed right through her parents' property as he made generous circles around the affected area.

She simply nodded, and waited.

"I want you on the next plane back down there." He turned at last to acknowledge Leon. "Can you drive her?"

Becky's mouth almost hung slack. Like a dog with a bone, John's manners had gotten just as canine. She was turning to apologize for her boss when John spoke again. "I'd like you to fly down there with her. See what you can check out. Catch what you can. I just have to stay here. It's way too interesting."

He half handed, half shoved a page at Becky. She recognized it as a species list, just as John spoke. "It's a list of all the species we're losing." His eyes were almost bright with anticipation. As though it were just a game – that the paper she held in her hand listed imaginary armies from a too serious game of 'Risk', not Bengal Tigers and Canada Moose and Elk and, of course, Georgia Warblers.

Jordan took in the scene before him. They had come in on the promised charter. Only this was no Lear jet, it was a wobbly Cessna that had wound its way down to a field in the open space between Clinton and Oak Ridge. After a touchdown that had felt as though the earth had risen up to them and the plane had stayed stationary, they cranked open the doors and tumbled out.

He let Jillian go first, being gentlemanly, and instantly regretted it. She stumbled a little as her feet hit ground, her soft blue scrubs showing the buckling of her knees, her hands tucking into her stomach as she folded over. He felt the raw stab of fear that knifed him in the gut every time she wavered. Again he came up with an excuse: it was just the plane ride. He was nauseous, too. *She didn't have* 'it'.

With an ungraceful thump, he landed beside her and took her elbow, seeing David come out the other side, compasses already in hand, briefcase and leather bag hanging from his arms. He looked ready to walk into the hotel and spend his workweek. Jordan's gaze naturally pulled back to Jillian, his hands encircling her upper arms, his eyes finding hers. "Are you all right?"

Even as he asked it, he told himself the pain was just because he had already lost everyone. Not because anything was so special about *her*.

She pushed at his chest. "I'm okay. Just need to get my feet under me." With that, she straightened. Shoved her hair out of her face. The dark strands, for once loose, had bothered her on the whole flight over. Wet and hanging limp when they entered the plane, they had a gentle wave to them now that rubbed beneath his fingers as he let her stand on her own.

He felt and heard her take a deep breath, and he grabbed both their bags as had become his custom. David had already planted himself behind the wheel of the midsized, mid-aged gold sedan. Why they didn't have grey or even a black hearse was beyond him. For the thousandth time, Jordan felt like they were walking blind. Only this time they were walking into a serious tragedy.

Holding the passenger door for Jillian, he waited while she situated herself, most of the green color having faded from her features. Then he let himself into the backseat while David gunned the engine, testing the feel of the car and his own level of testosterone.

With the map Anne had provided, they wound an uncertain way through the countryside. It looked much like the area outside McCann. The Appalachian Mountains cradled the sides of the small road, only this time they nestled ATV shops, car dealerships, and the occasional small windowless strip joint up along the sides of the two lane highway.

The shops gave way to churches, hillsides dotted with houses, and at last a storage unit of long gray buildings fronted by rows of garage doors. The chain link fence was a good fifteen feet high, winding its way around the property and then across the road in front of them. That made Jordan frown.

A uniformed security guard stood sentry at the gate that spanned the street at the edge of town, and David pulled up even as the guard approached them. But David was already whipping out his compass, and making Jordan wish someone else had driven.

The rent-a-cop tipped his hat and spoke to all of them through David's open window. "Sorry folks. City's closed."

The City is CLOSED? How does one even close a city? But Jordan could see the answer to his question looming fifteen feet in front of him. The chain link was old and looked unused, but the razor wire gleamed in the afternoon light, obviously a fresh addition to the precautions.

David pulled out his temporary badge, flashing it as though he were the president's guard. "We're with the CDCP." He didn't add that they needed to get inside, nor that they had clearance. He didn't need to. His confidence, that may have already passed well into arrogance, spoke all that for him.

The guard stepped back slowly, nodded again, and spoke into the police style walkie-talkie tacked to his shoulder. His movements all yielded to the slow drawl of the south. And Jordan could see where it was often perceived as laziness, but could also see that it clearly wasn't. It was bred into these people who hadn't seen a Minnesota blizzard, or had to do more to keep the cold at bay than turn up the collar on their coats.

But they also were possessed of a certainty that speeding up wasn't critical – a belief that clearly didn't run in Jillian's blood, southern cheerleader that she may be. She fidgeted in the seat, squirming this way and that, trying to look calm but not quite pulling it off. Jordan would have bet his life savings her right foot was crossed over the other, keeping to a silent rhythm.

The guard sauntered back to them, gave a brief nod and told them it'd be just a minute.

It was more like four, Jordan realized as Jillian fidgeted away the time and David sat calmly beside her, pulling instrument after instrument from the briefcase, recalibrating it or something, and then quietly putting it back. Jordan leaned back, trying to stay relaxed. He thought he was achieving it well. He kept the hyperventilation and the terror at bay, tucking his hands behind his head, and leaning back as though he were on the beach and not sitting in the back of a government car about to gain security clearance through the gates of hell.

The guard stood stationary at the side of the fence, looking exactly as he had long before they were parked there, engine idling. Jordan wondered what the guard would do to get the gates open, or if he was waiting for a code or such.

It turned out the guard would do nothing.

A black sedan, filled with men in identical suits and haircuts, pulled up on the inside of the gate, looking like something out of an FBI movie. But then again, this was *The Town That Built The Bomb*, Jordan thought as the four men undid a thick padlock and wheeled the gate back by hand. They threw their weight at the task, creaking it back foot by foot, before waving the car through. David pulled in and kept on driving, but Jordan turned around to see that they men in suits never acknowledged the guard outside and that they secured the gate with the large padlock set with something that looked like a magnetic key. Jordan fought off thoughts of having to climb the gate and throw himself over the razor wire with thousands of citizens when the lock failed.

David pushed the small map at Jillian and set her to navigating. She instantaneously spouted off directions.

"My god," Jillian shook her head and she spoke again before Jordan could finish the thought of wondering what pattern her brain had found within two minutes of entering the city. "The streets are alphabetized." She looked from side to side, and while David seemed to have his eyes on both the road and his compasses, Jordan followed her gaze to see that it certainly appeared that she was right.

"Good lord, who are these people?" He heard it from his mouth before he realized he had let it slip. This was Jillian's South and he didn't want to offend.

But she supplied an answer with a quirk of her mouth. "The government."

"That's right…" The town had only become public after world war two when the government had opened the city to the families of the scientists who were working on the top-secret Hiroshima project. The place was fuckin' nuts. As best as he could see, the gates encircled the entire city. Whether that was to keep people out or secrets in, he was unsure. The streets were not only alphabetized, they stacked the road signs. So drivers could turn down a side street that bore four perfectly ambiguous street names.

There were a few people on the streets. Of course all the activity was on the outside of the sawhorse barricades. The people who had lived inside the reversal's radius had already been moved to temporary housing. But the people who were out looked fairly normal in spite of the presence of the men in big dark suits, with small sharp haircuts.

The townspeople put gas in their cars and drove through the McDonalds. The Home Depot lot was empty, and Jordan hazarded a guess that food and gas ranked higher than repairs. Maybe this town full of scientists was smart enough to realize that barricading their doors would only trap them inside and keep nothing out.

"Shit!" David's voice cut through the air.

"What?" Jillian turned to him, and from her color, just that quick motion was enough to make her green. Or maybe it was the same thought that Jordan was having. David swore all the time, but not in a surprised way, and if something here had surprised him it would have to be bad. Really bad.

"We're either on the fuzzy edge of a very large reversal and we're going to hit it any second, or we've been riding the edge since three lights back."

"But the road is straight. It's not following an arc at all." Jordan didn't understand any of the magnetics of it. He knew just enough to pass the physics section of the MCAT years ago when he went into med school. Beyond that, he was a slave to what David chose to share with him. But he knew that what they had been finding was that the bubbles were circular. Probably how they had gotten dubbed that way in the first place.

"Exactly, Sherlock."

Jordan almost popped him upside the head, which would have been really easy to do from the back seat. Instead, he fought the urge while David began explaining, "Which makes me think it's a really big bubble…shiiiiiiiit."

Jordan didn't put voice to it. David would tell him or not and there wasn't much he could do about it. Jillian however seemed to believe she could hold some sort of sway over David. Jordan's first thought was that she was lying to herself. Then he realized there was every good chance it was him lying to himself. She might very well hold sway with David. Who knew what had been going on between them while he was in Lake James watching his family slip away one by one?

He tamped down the images, thinking that the news David had preceded with *shhiiiiiiit* was going to be happier thoughts than the ones he was having.

"We're in."

Jordan's back snapped straight. "Well then, get out!"

But David kept driving, not noticing Jillian turning green with fear or illness on the seat next to him. Neither option was acceptable to Jordan.

"Jillian," At the sound of his voice she turned to face him, and Jordan was unable to read all the emotions running stampede across her features. "Find another path on the map. Take us far left or right…or…"

David set down the black palm-pilot-looking-thing that was a serious navigational compass as best as Jordan could tell, and picked up the old boy scout version, complete with red needle and N E S W markings. "David, which way is out?"

"We'll just drive straight through." The blond head never really glanced up from the small hammered silver fob in front of him. He would have caused a serious pile-up if anyone had been on the road. But these people were organized.

"Get out of the bubble." Jordan didn't realize that he was unbuckled and hanging over the front seat. "You and Jillian have already been exposed to these for too long." He didn't add that he was giving less and less of a crap if David fell into a serious coma right this instant. Except that he'd prefer the asshole put the car in 'park' first.

David said nothing, just kept driving, occasionally glancing up to check the flow of traffic against the whispered directions Jillian was giving him. It seemed he was taking them into the heart of the reversal. The man had no concern for his own safety. Jordan couldn't care less. David had no concern for Jordan's safety. That was because he was a son of a bitch. But having no concern for Jillian's was beyond Jordan's limits. If he'd had a gun, he would have pulled it and tucked it right at the base of David's head, right up the foramen magnum. The hole there would make certain that a bullet couldn't glance off that thick head. Guaranteed death.

"We're fuzzy." The words came after long minutes waiting for a response. The minutes were deceptive – leisurely driving down a small town turnpike with the sun overhead and greenery that made both the Nevada desert and Lake James look like they were constructed from brown bags.

Jillian started to take deeper breaths and with shaky motions pointed out the cross street they were looking for, then the white tents gently breathing with the breeze. It was a high school soccer field from the looks of the sign posted just under the snarling wildcat. In running red light letters it read 'no school until further notice'.

David made a hard right into the lot and stopped the car at the edge. With a quick look at his compass, he shoved it into his pocket and pulled the black high-tech contraption from his brief-case and started to unfold himself from the car.

Jordan threw himself out the backseat and hustled up to one of the suits who was approaching with a manila envelope. With the way the past three days had been going, if he was lucky, it would be full of anthrax and he could inhale deeply and die a slow and painful death. Which would, of course, be far more humane than what he was suffering now.

What he was suffering was only compounded by David walking around the front of the car and offering Jillian his arm, "Baby, are you okay?"

Thoughts warred in Jordan's brain. *Now he asks how she's doing?* And *Baby?*

But the man was saying the envelope was from Landerly. And Jordan saw his own hands in front of him, only now aware that he was shaking far worse than he could detect through his own senses, even now that he knew he was doing it.

The pages came out neat and crisp, far better looking than anything they had pulled off the little traveling fax machine. He scanned the notes taking in the news: the churnings of Landerly's brain, gathered into understandable English by some tech or junior MD now that he and Jillian weren't there to do the job.

"David!" He yelled but didn't look up. Didn't want to see what was going on, didn't care. "Landerly says the magnetics of the reversals are getting stronger in the centers. There's a graph here, almost like regular concentric rings."

David approached and snapped the pages from his hands. It wasn't even an asshole move, just the unthoughtfulness of a man who had always gotten what he wanted. But Jordan continued. "The Nevada site maps like a target. But it's even stronger than here or McCann. Landerly thinks that's why it took everyone out. McCann's getting stronger, too."

Jillian peeked over David's shoulder. "That doesn't make sense. The wildlife is returning to normal. Becky Sorenson said the frogs were looking more normal, as were the insects and the other animals she tagged." Her brows knit together in frustration and there was almost a chugging sound as her brain ratcheted up a notch.

Jordan shrugged, simply grateful that the churning of her mental gears was a good indicator that she hadn't suffered permanently from David driving them straight through the last reversal. He felt his temper abate, even if the anger didn't.

Still David frowned, flipping one page and then the next. He rotated the papers and Jordan almost chuckled at the sight. As though this whole stinking pile of crap would look better upside down. But he didn't laugh. He couldn't fault the geologist for trying.

It wasn't like he had any better ideas.

Chapter 14

Jillian sat on the edge of the cold cot. It was green army issue fabric slung and stitched to a metal frame, and it had either seen better days or had recently been the recipient of a very large occupant. It hadn't held her heat, and she hadn't been smart enough to line the bed with the blanket before she lay down, so she had lost temperature while she slept.

And slept fitfully at that. There was no way to get Jordan onto that thing with her without it looking like something more and she wasn't anywhere near brave enough to climb into a bed with David, not that either man would really fit on a cot with her. And she certainly wasn't stupid enough to climb into any bed with David when what she wanted was *sleep*.

Jordan was still out cold, his arm hanging peacefully out from under the covers he had partially kicked off. His fingers were mere inches from the ground but they didn't seem to notice. His face was soft in sleep; clearly he wasn't having her problems. The only thing that betrayed his state was the dark circles under his eyes and the two day growth of beard that aged him considerably, making him look more like the man he was and not just the friend she considered him.

With a sigh, she just gave up, sinking bare toes into the rough dark carpet of the classroom they were staying in. Desks had been pushed back and stacked against the walls. The whiteboard left clean for the scientists to use. They hadn't. She felt like all the churning in her stomach had prevented all the churning in her skull from producing a single useful thought for quite a while now.

Her head felt like it was swaying at the top of a tall post, and so she nixed her original idea of wandering down to find the cafeteria. The CDC was supposed to have set up its own food supply there, but she was too shaky to go it alone.

Jillian turned back to the bed; if she was already out of it, then at least she was going to do this right this time. She deluded herself into thinking that maybe if she could retain her body heat she could sleep. With her mind focused on that singular thought, she rearranged the blanket and crawled back in. Pulling the free half of the blanket tightly across her, she squeezed her eyes shut and tried to fight the bright gray light streaming through the fairly useless blinds.

She relaxed her entire body, muscle by muscle. When she was a resident, she'd been able to pass out at the drop of a hat, anywhere, anytime. But now sleep eluded her in the most painful of ways.

After a while she gave up, thankful that she was at least starting to get warm, and opened her eyes.

Jordan was watching her. "Morning."

"It's not morning." Her voice creaked like old hinges. "Morning implies that there was a night. I don't recall one."

"Still not sleeping?"

"What do you think?" She regretted it as soon as the words left her mouth.

But she sank into a solid portion of shame when Jordan asked her if she wanted to join him. Completely spoken with sympathy and none of the venom she had thrown at him.

"That can't be comfortable."

"What will you care? You'll be asleep."

Jillian almost laughed and almost wondered how she could in the middle of all this. "But you won't be."

His mouth quirked behind the chestnut stubble that was a full shade darker than the sun-lightened length on his head. "Trust me, I'll fall back asleep quickly enough."

She couldn't very well say yes – there was no way they'd both fit unless she just climbed right on top of him, so she changed the subject. "Do you think the reversal has gotten this far since yesterday? They grow pretty fast now, and it was really close when we drove in. We could be in it right now."

"Don't change the subject on me." He lifted the blanket and made every attempt to scoot back to one side of the cot. But he was thwarted at every motion, sliding back into the center of the sling. Jillian raised one eyebrow at him, never making even the first motion to leave the confines of her finally warm cocoon.

"Fine."

He didn't say anything more than just the one word. He simply stood to full length, stretching his tall form and revealing sun-brown skin where his t-shirt lifted from the edge of his boxers for just a moment. His eyes scanned the room and settled in the corner on a pile of two spare blankets. He turned his cot on its side and motioned for Jillian to do the same.

With great reluctance she stood up, her bare feet draining their heat into the cold carpet again. She pushed the cot out of the way as she saw that he was layering the blankets on the floor. He put his own blanket as the top layer then kneeled down on it. "Come on."

It was only slightly softer than a rock slab, but she sank onto it willingly, letting Jordan pull the blanket from her shoulders and trusting that she'd be heated again within moments.

Stretching out along the rough blankets, Jillian had only long enough to shove her hair back out of her face, before Jordan was there and the covers were pulled over them. Lord, the man was better than a space heater. Suddenly she understood why women married men they didn't even love. God, the sleep!

"Jordan?"

"Shh."

Her stomach rolled and her jaw clamped to stop the sensation, but she didn't even get that far. She was falling backward into the black abyss.

David walked the hallway, lined with ugly green lockers, looking like the fresh paint hid layers of abuse. The worn linoleum on the floor had not yet been replaced, the black scuffs still marking time. His own high school had been so much more pristine than this. The lockers and carpeting replaced if they had worn even slightly. Even the children had been removed if they were too frayed, not quite up to snuff. He wondered what other differences his father's money had bought him.

Jordan and Jillian were sleeping in a classroom further down this hall. He didn't know which one, but relied on the hand-written pages taped beside each door, designating the CDC's purpose for each.

He almost walked past the one that read: Abellard, Brookwood, Carter. For a moment, he smirked at the irony, that even in print Jillian was caught between the two of them, but then he turned the knob, pushing open the heavy door, the wired glass lined with a shade so he couldn't see in.

As the dim room slowly came into focus, he was caught up in the cozy scene – Jillian snuggled into the grasp of Abellard's arms. Both of them sleeping like babies.

Son of a bitch.

The thought took him by surprise in its vehemence. He'd been telling himself that it didn't matter.

But maybe it did.

He knelt on her side of the makeshift lover's nest and reached out, taking just a moment to be sure that he only touched her.

"Jillian. Baby. Time to wake up." He nudged her shoulder a little, thinking that this was a first even for him. He'd slept with married women. He'd broken up more than one couple along the way, but he'd never, until just now, called a woman 'baby' while she was literally in another man's arms.

His thoughts stopped as she stirred, rolling away from Abellard to face him. "Whhaaat?" The word was soft and low.

"We're wanted out front."

He could see her chest move with a long sigh as she blinked and carelessly shoved the hair from her face. She rolled back into the space she had vacated, and for a moment David was certain he'd been given the ultimate brush off. But instead she gave Jordan's shoulder a gentle shake. "Jordan. Wake up. We have to go."

David cut her off. "No. Let him sleep. They want you and me."

"Huh?" She rolled again to look at him, but her job had already been accomplished. And Jordan was looking at him, too, through clear eyes.

"They want you two? Why?"

"We're going to go in."

Abellard shot upright, revealing a t-shirt, and letting David's brain breathe a sigh of relief that it wasn't as cozy as it had looked. "No."

David rocked back on his heels. Why was Jordan fighting back? He slung what he had. "Not your decision."

Abellard's eyes turned to ice. "Then whose?"

David wanted to smile. Jordan and Jillian were Landerly's babies, lackeys, peons, whatever, but the word had wound up in his hands, and that felt good. "Landerly's."

David watched while Jordan put a hand on Jillian's shoulder, gently holding her back. "Don't go. We'll talk to Landerly first. I'm not sure I believe this." He rolled up and off the floor on the other side, diving into his pants pocket for the cell phone.

Surprisingly it was Jillian who came to David's rescue. She sat with a slight shake to remove the last of the sleep from her head. "Jordan, Landerly ordered it."

David wanted to grin, but schooled his features the way he always did. Better to give away nothing. It hadn't been any great importance to him. But David knew himself well enough to know that he was a Carter through and through. If the challenge was issued, it was always answered. As his father had said, *it had damned well better be won, too.*

Abellard had thrown down the gauntlet. And in David's mind that meant it was just a matter of time before Jillian was his.

He watched while Jillian did his work for him and he bottled the pleasure at it.

"What do you mean Landerly ordered it?"

She sighed, leaning out to Jordan. But bless him, Abellard wasn't having it. "When we were in Nevada, all the wardens and officers walked right into the reversal and fell under. But not us. We had been in for longer than any of them and had no effects. We're fairly certain that we're immune."

"You're *what*?"

Jillian shook her head again, but continued, while David sat back and enjoyed watching the distance between them grow. "Immune."

Abellard's eyes narrowed and Jillian warily slid back at the menace. "You're willing to risk your lives because you did it once before and were okay?!?"

She was on her heels by now, too, and fighting back.

That's it Jillian, give him hell.

"No, I'm *not*. But we have to stop this or we'll all die from it. Landerly ordered it. And I have to admit that I don't know what else to do."

Jordan raked a hand through his hair, thinking hard and fast for a few seconds. "Then I'm going, too. Whatever immunity you got, it's likely I got it, too. It's probably because of the way we've been exposed to the reversals."

David thought that was a reasonable argument and was cursing himself for not foreseeing it, when Jillian again solved his problems.

"No, you have to stay out here. David and I were together the whole time. We know we got the same exposure. We don't know that for certain about you."

Abellard's jaw clenched. David wasn't even sure if the good Dr. Brookwood noticed, but he sure did. She just kept talking. "We need you out here, in case…in case anything happens."

"What!?" He was on his feet, furious at her and adding distance. *Bless the powers that be.* "I'm supposed to sit out here and wait by the sidelines in case you slip into a coma and die? While I watch?"

"Jordan–"

But he cut her off before she could begin. "Do you know what I did in Minnesota?…" He didn't wait long enough, just barreled ahead, "I watched every last member of my family go under. And I'm supposed to sit here and watch you purposefully throw yourself into it? No way in hell!"

With an angry snap of his arms, he whipped the pants off the floor, stepping into them and buttoning the fly as he stalked out the door.

Jillian's mouth hung open, but that was okay. David stepped up to fill in the void. "He'll get over it. He'll have to. We don't even know if he can survive going in."

She turned slowly to him. "We don't know if *we* can."

"But who else can go?"

God, he had never been one to play the hero. But hey, there was always a first time, right? The way he figured it, they were all radiated toast anyway. He might as well get the girl before he bit the big one. It wouldn't matter. If there was a hell, it likely already had a parking spot with an engraved nameplate for him.

She didn't answer. So he smiled. "Well, then let's get ready to go."

Two hours later, they had swallowed a complement of horse pills. And Abellard was still nowhere to be seen. Good.

David was in full gear, compasses and magnetic field readers strapped to and stuffed in a toolbelt around his waist. He'd never felt so working-class before. Jillian had cell phones, and paper and pencils, a stethoscope hung around her neck. David wasn't sure if that was because she thought she might need it, or if it was just as much a part of her as the scrubs. He peeled his eyes away from her and looked out at the town in front of him. It looked enough like any other. But he knew it wasn't.

They stood at the new edge of the reversal, twenty feet closer than it had been last evening. The fuzzy edges were wide and getting wider. They shouldn't encounter any people in here. Everyone should have been evacuated. And if they did find anyone, well, then, that would be Jillian's problem.

Jillian took deep breaths, as though she were preparing to walk underwater. It was all he could do not to do the same, but his job here was to be a calming rock for her, let her think he was unaffected.

"Ready?" He asked it nonchalantly. Or he tried to, not that Jillian even left her mental space to notice.

"As I'll ever be." She sucked in a lungful of air. "But I'm warning you, I'm not that ready."

He stepped in, waiting, as he always did, for the feeling of getting kicked in the gut. Of having all the air sucked out of him. Or maybe tingling in his fingers. But his stomach didn't even roll.

But he was past the yellow flags delineating the new boundaries. He was in the wide edge. Without looking back for Jillian, he took another few tentative steps, then started walking. Jillian skipped to catch up, like a swimmer who knows that the water is cold and it's better to just dive right in.

She slipped a small street map from the back of her notebook, showing him the highlighted line. He took the page from her and frowned at it. "How far is this?"

"About three miles." He could see her throat work, but resisted the urge to ask if she was okay. "They recalculated the center this morning. The edges keep shifting."

"Hm." Not really in the mood for conversation, he felt around the things at his waist. The weights hanging from his belt took him back to his digs, back to fist-sized rock chips in tough Ziploc baggies and midnight runs down the grid to see if the idiots had fucked up another orientation. That's what had started this whole mess, too.

He picked out the old school compass, shaking off fantasies of the days when he could swear at everyone around him. When they were all associate faculty, not physicians. Or better yet, students – students whose degrees depended on his good graces. David looked at the houses they were wandering past, just a few blocks beyond the high school. Some with pretty flowers in pots and window boxes. Some with peeling paint. And some with both. It was eerie with the absence of people.

He feared seeing the faces of the dead peering at him, as transparent as the windowpanes of the empty houses. He pulled his gaze to the needle which had stopped jumping, although he wasn't sure when. With a snort at himself for forgetting, he tossed a flag back a handful of yards. Close enough.

"You know, the paperwork this morning showed another bubble." Jillian didn't look at him, so he simply grunted, staying focused on his compass.

"It's up toward the north side of town. And it's growing pretty quickly."

He grunted again, then decided that if he was going to shut her up, interrupting was really the way to go. He didn't need chitchat. "What street are we on?"

She looked up, not pointing out that he could easily have tilted his own head and read the sign his damn self. "Pomona."

He made her write it down, pulled out another meter and read the strength of the field off to her, but it didn't shut her up.

"The bubble at the edge of town is really near the fence." Her mouth moved as fast as the pencil recording everything he spouted at her. "They're afraid it won't respect the city's boundaries. That it will cross the gate. We're not sure what to do then."

"Hm." He tried to leave it at that.

"There were fifty people reported down this morning. New since last night. And another hundred with stomach upset." She paused to inhale and let it out, and it still didn't sound like natural breathing to his ears, but he decided not to mention that. The compass needle in front of him jumped a little. He checked the field strength. Stepped into a front yard and popped a meter that looked remarkably like a meat thermometer into the ground.

He didn't even get to read it before Jillian started babbling again. "You know, our numbers have shown that of those hundred down, ninety to ninety-five percent of them will actually have it. The other five plus percent are just your standard G I trouble with a dose of panic."

David flattened the sigh before it escaped him. His eyes narrowed on the meter, but Jillian's voice cut through again. "David?"

Becky didn't even look at the greenery around her, just jumped ship off the tiny Cessna and ignored the pilot as he pointed the way to Oak Ridge. The blue sedan waited, parked casually just off to the left of the three mid-sized hangars that made up the Clinton Airport – if it could be called that. Trees scraped the bottoms of the planes at each end of the runway. Grass grew up through cracks in the barely paved 'landing strip', and nothing bigger than a tour plane had ever come through to the best of her knowledge.

But Becky just smiled and waved a thank-you to the pilot and waited barely long enough for Leon to close the sedan's passenger door behind himself. From the looks of him, he had been hoping to drive, but she ignored that and hit the gas before he even had the seat adjusted. With a grunt, he pulled his seatbelt across him and slapped it into the buckle. Becky wasn't sure if that was meant as an insult, but she didn't care.

Since they were driving to her house, she didn't see where she needed to sit in the passenger seat and give directions and be polite about missed turn-offs and do that squinting and head-shaking thing people always did when driving in an unfamiliar area. She was through with being polite and worrying about other people's feelings.

She ran two stop signs, ignoring Leon's outstretched finger both times. There weren't even police out this way, just the County Sheriff Office. And the deputies would just smile at her and nod if they wound up pulling her over. She knew them all.

Finally she came to a complete stop at a red light that was collecting cars waiting on the empty crosslane. Her fingers tapped impatiently on the wheel. Her foot hovered, barely holding the brake down, itching to ride the non-existent clutch. Her right hand grabbed for the gearshift hoping to slam it into second, but she consciously pulled her fingers away, knowing that throwing an automatic into low gear wouldn't help her one bit.

Her lip took some abuse from her teeth, and just as she squealed the tires out into the crossing she heard the distinctive synthetic music of her cell phone. Grabbing for it at the clip on her belt, she tossed it to Leon. "Check the ID, would you?"

With one hand making a graceful pass, he swiped the phone from the air before it arced in the careless direction it had been sent and saved it from colliding with the dash. Nimble fingers he oriented the slick silver thing and he read off the name, "Dr. Overton."

"Don't answer." She took a hard left at the next light, and out of the corner of her eye Becky saw Leon's fingers reach for purchase then tuck themselves away out of sight. She didn't say anything and he didn't either. He simply sat, huge and silent, and looking very uncomfortable, never mentioning that he was surely aware that they were going the opposite direction from where they were supposed to be. Or that they were going the wrong way like a bat out of hell.

She was grateful when, at last, she hit the old road that led to her parent's house. But it was too narrow and full of cracks from winter and grass from summer. She was forced to slow down too many times. But Becky couldn't really get mad. She knew all the people going by. They waved and she waved and drove on before they could get the windows down and tell her how nice it was to see her back from school.

The barbed wire fences gave way at last to the old sagging split rail that lined her yard. Melanie was out front with a spoon digging under the old tire swing, the first thing that had brought a smile to Becky's face this whole day. She was probably digging up worms or such to dissect. The little geek.

"That your–" Leon started the question then cut himself off.

"What?" Becky finally looked him in the face, taking in his long blond hair, again pulled back away from his sharp jaw, somehow always bearing about two days worth of stubble. His blue eyes matched the early winter sky in understanding and bleakness.

"Nothing." He looked the house up and down. "I'm sure this is a required stop on our way to Oak Ridge." He finished his sentence and sealed his lips, not once making eye contact.

Becky nodded. "I'll just be a few minutes."

Melanie was already running toward the car, having recognized her sister only after raising her hand to her red bangs to see who was driving the strange car that had pulled so boldly onto the gravel driveway. Becky caught the imp in her arms and swung her around a few times. She sucked in the air, knowing full well that it might already be in the reversal. Even though, by her own calculations, it shouldn't have come this far. Not yet anyway. But she knew she had to stop and take deep breaths. To smell her yard and the air, and really look at it, because it may very well be the last time.

In a practiced move, she swung Mel with a quick change of grasp that both sisters were familiar with. Melanie was riding piggyback by the time they passed through the front door, spoon and worms forgotten momentarily. She yelled right next to Becky's ear. "Mom! Look who I found!"

Her mother rounded the corner from the laundry room. "Hey, Baby." Her face lit up at seeing her oldest daughter so unexpectedly.

She slid Mel down her back until her sister's small sneakered feet hit the hard wood floor and Becky rushed to hug her mother.

Her mother hugged back just as fiercely before pulling away and looking Becky in the eyes. "What's wrong?"

With a deep breath that took in the pine cleaner and open country, and a quick look at the old furniture, covered with throws and battered pillows, she turned to deliver the news. "I can't tell you what's happening – only that it's bigger than me."

Her mother's brows knit together. "Are you in some sort of trouble?"

Becky shook her head. "But I am with the CDC now, so you figure it out." Another frown from her mother and another deep breath of the smell that was her home. "I can tell you this: you need to pack up the kids and Dad and go visit Aaron for at least a week. Call me before you return."

Her mother leaned back, a hand absently reaching for the washer to steady herself. "Is Aaron in trouble?"

"No. But *you* need to go visit him." Becky stared at her mother, hoping she would take the message and quit.

"Is something happening here?" Her mother's voice shook, just a little, but she straightened up, standing firm on her own two feet.

Becky did the only thing she could do: she nodded her head while speaking. "I can't tell you that. All I can say is that this would be a great time to go visit Aaron. Maybe get out of the house by tomorrow morning at the latest."

Her mother leaned forward looking for one last out. "Are you sure?"

"Absolutely." She reached forward, giving her mother a hug. "I'm not supposed to be here. I have to go."

Turning, she spied Melanie wide-eyed behind her, having heard the whole conversation. She scooped her sister up even as the words began flowing out of that little mouth. "This is about those frogs, isn't it?"

So Becky did it again. She nodded, contradicting her voice. "I don't know."

"Something is wrong there." Melanie paused, leaning back, "and it's coming here."

"I always knew you were a very smart girl. And Mom's going to listen to whatever ideas you have. Because you're probably right!" She yelled for Brandon, hoping he would make his way out to see her. She could hear the time ticking away in heartbeats.

With a last thought, she turned back. "You don't tell *anyone* about this. Do you both understand me? If you start a panic, there's no telling what will happen."

Both the Sorenson women nodded back at her and she turned to go. "I love you."

Brandon showed his face in the hall right as she reached the front door. She tried to scoop him up but he was too heavy, and from the looks of it, three inches taller than the last time she had seen him. Blinking back tears, she kissed his cheek and went out the front door.

The wood planks of the porch showed wear at the front door and down the steps. The grass had disappeared in a trail to the end of the drive, where the CDC sedan sat – with one very nonchalant Leon squeezed into the passenger side seat, looking anywhere but at her.

Becky walked up to his side and tapped on the window, startling him from his glazed over look. He opened the door to her. She smiled, holding out the keys, and asked, "Do you want to drive?"

"Hell, yes." He didn't look at her mother or her sister in the front doorway. He didn't acknowledge her brother's whoops that they were going to go visit Aaron. Just calmly walked around and situated himself in the driver's side, lifting the lever and sliding the seat back as far as it would go, which to Becky still looked a little shy of comfortable. He threw the car in gear and backed out of the driveway as though he had never been there.

Without needing directions, he took them back the way they had come, leaving Becky to her thoughts in the passenger seat, until he startled her by asking what she wanted.

Only then did she look up to realize that it wasn't a philosophical query, but they were about three feet from the Burger King drive thru. She rattled off an order, cringing as she realized that she was way too familiar with Burger King's menu, and listened while Leon ordered himself two large-sized value meals.

As they pulled away Leon pointedly looked at his watch. "Gee," even to her ears it sounded odd coming from him, "That sure did take a long time. And I'm sorry I got us lost back there."

Becky smiled, letting out the breath she had kept in. "Thank you."

Leon smiled, still looking straight at the long, bare, two lane road ahead of them. "Don't know what you're talking about. Now, am I headed toward Oak Ridge this time?"

"Yes, you are."

Jordan paced the edge of the bubble.

Three hours since they had left. And nothing.

He had heard phone contact, crackles of the walkie-talkies Jillian and David had carried in, spurts of conversation between them and the suits in the tent behind him. He stuffed down the wry thought that they would have to move the tent another twenty feet further before tomorrow morning.

The air bit at his legs through the blue scrub pants that didn't keep out the chill. He zipped his jacket a little higher up under his chin, not wanting to take the time to go back to the room put on heavier pants or lose the instant recognition the blue cotton afforded him. The others all knew exactly what to look for when they needed him. Right now that was very important.

He shoved his hands deep in his pockets, looking up at tall pines and oaks. Hills crowded up on either side of him. The city had purposefully been laid out in a hard-to-reach area. The roads had been contoured to the Appalachians, making it hard to predict where and when to turn. One of the local scientists had said something about making the city difficult to invade, as he had pointed on the map to crossing roads, circles off of circles, and even avenues that continued but changed names, the original name taking off at a ninety degree angle on a different street.

Jordan breathed in, the cold air chilling his lungs. In front of him, the place was a ghost town. Everyone evacuated from neat homes. The landscape looked like a handful of miniature houses had been tossed across the hills and rooted wherever they landed. Behind him, the city went on as normal. The library and town Civic Center had plenty of traffic. The gymnasium housed some of the displaced families. They held activities for the out-of-school kids while their parents continued to go to work, many at the nuclear labs further down the turnpike. Jordan shuddered to himself at the thought of the magnetics reaching the power plants.

"Dr. Abellard!"

He turned to see a young tech, complete with acne, old jeans, and Converse sneakers under the labcoat, come running up to him. "Dr. Sorenson is here. She wants to see you."

With a nod, he turned and followed the kid back into the tents, the grass growing strong beneath his feet and the smell of trees and green the only real distinguishing factors between here and Nevada. They wound their way through tent after tent, gathering papers as they went. Jordan was handed lab results on the people who had gone down this morning. He had read each individual report earlier, but now held compiled statistics on the group, on how many were down, who had died from the alpha group and who still clung to life and maybe even hope.

Lucy Whitman, one of the techs, approached with another handful of papers and a broad smile, her blond curls bouncing and looking overdone for a scientific endeavor of this magnitude and tragedy. Jordan couldn't abide the twinkle in her eyes or the makeup that was always perfect, even as the pieces of the world fell down around her. He faked a smile back at her, only earning her shoulder pressed to his as she held out the pages to him. "I know I'm not supposed to read these, but there was no cover sheet, and *look*!"

He did, but saw only black type on white pages. Until her perfectly polished red nail skimmed across some of the words. "Fifteen of the Nevada patients have woken up!"

His head slammed hard to the right to look at her.

"What!?"

But she was serious. The grin was genuine, and the sparkle contagious.

He jumped at the simultaneous digital ring and buzz of his phone going off. He simply opened the phone and answered it without thinking. "Hello?"

"Abellard!" Landerly's voice had a smile in it. "We've caught a break, boy! I trust you're holding the pages I just faxed?"

"Yes, sir. But I haven't read them all yet." He shoved the pages back at Lucy and turned away from her, putting his fingers over his left ear to block any noises. Perhaps the pounding of his heartbeat in his fingertips was louder than what was around him.

"Fifteen Nevada patients are out of the coma. There are a few stats in there, but not enough. The docs there are helping them and taking vital signs. I want you sitting near the fax machine. I've got a tech there assigned to record and fax everything they get to you and me simultaneously. This is the break and we have to be on it."

"Yessir." His heart pounded and he spit out the thing that sprang immediately to his mind. "What about Lake James?"

Landerly paused for just a moment, and Jordan knew what was coming. "I haven't heard anything, but I already put in an inquiry."

"Of course." His breathing had sped up there for a moment and now his shoulders and chest sank, heavy as granite. The murderers and rapists would wake up, but not the good people of a small Minnesota town.

Landerly's voice sliced through his self pity, bringing back the senses of reality with it: the phone pressed against his ear, the taste of metal in his mouth where he had bit down, the throbbing in his tongue further evidence. "Remember, the Nevada site fell first. So on this time scale we should know something within two days about Lake James."

"Of course." And just like that his heart rate accelerated again. His breathing went shallow and he would become hypoxic and pass out if he didn't get a grip.

"I hear Dr. Sorenson and one of the animal wranglers arrived. They're going after some local wildlife. You need to read their Minnesota data and report in to me what you can make of it."

"Of course sir, but Jillian's in the reversal now. We'll get back to you when–"

"Here's an idea: try thinking for yourself, Abellard. Or I *will* name this shit after you."

Jordan would have laughed if not for the three successive digital notes signaling that Landerly had already hung up on him. He stared at the phone for a moment before he realized that Lucy was watching his every move, and the tech in the converse sneakers was watching hers, even though he was way too young for Lucy to be anything but a farfetched fantasy. Jordan sympathized. *We all need our pipe dreams.*

He took the papers out of Lucy's outstretched and manicured hand as Becky Sorenson approached and clasped his hand in a warm grip. "Good to see you again, Jordan." She motioned to the blond giant behind her, "This is Leon Peppersmith. He's a CDC wrangler."

"Pleased to meet you." Peppersmith's voice was modulated if not cultured. Contrary to fears, he didn't grind Jordan's bones to meal with his handshake, even though the man would easily make Jillian look like she belonged in Oz.

Becky pulled the haversack she was wearing a little higher on her shoulders. "We're heading to the edges to capture what we can."

Jordan took a step back. "Don't go in. Not until we know what we're dealing with." He shook his head, waiting for a piece of the sky to break free and crash in flames inches from his feet. But it didn't happen.

"How will we know what we're dealing with if we don't go in?" Becky, too, shook her head, shrugging, at a loss for the words to express what was happening around them. Like Jillian, she saw no alternative. "It's the right thing to do."

But Jordan plowed on ahead, giving his best effort at stopping them. "Some of them are waking up at the Nevada site."

"Really?!" Becky's face lit up. "That's great! How many?"

"Fifteen. So far." It was so hopeful and yet such a small number. He clung to the belief that he could get Becky and Peppersmith to change their minds before he cracked from it all. "And you have data from Minnesota, so why–"

Becky shrugged him off again. "Just more questions. We need to find the links."

Jordan motioned them into a tent that was being used as one of the lab stations. There was only one tech in there, and both Jordan and Peppersmith gave him a look that did more than just request privacy. The tech shrugged as he pocketed his wrench and a small meter. He spoke over his shoulder as he exited, "Damned UV-vis is down. All of them are. Don't use it."

Then they were alone, except for the centrifuges, whirring and stopping, settling the contents in the blood samples everyone had been collecting. Lowering himself into a chair, Jordan motioned for Becky and Leon to do the same, and set about stalling them. "What did you find?"

"Moose." It was Peppersmith. "Canada Moose. A whole herd – looks like they all just laid down and died. Wolves and Lynx side by side, tearing at the carcasses."

Laid down and died?

Becky chimed in as Jordan felt his face pull further and further into a knot. "The white tailed dear there were only juveniles. There wasn't an adult to be found. Nothing over three point."

He felt the back of the chair support him before he realized he had slid back. He had started to open his mouth again, but Becky pulled a list from her pocket. "Photocopy this." She held it up to Lucy, who Jordan only then realized was hovering at the open tent flap. But Becky pulled it back, away from Lucy's reaching grasp, shoving it at Jordan, "Here, look at it first."

Species were listed to halfway down the page, and Becky's voice derailed his train of thought. "They're all missing or dead."

"Whole species?" He handed the page up to Lucy who fled from sight, hopefully for the nearest copier.

Becky and Peppersmith both nodded.

"Holy shit." Jordan blinked, wondering if the day could get any more surreal.

Peppersmith shrugged. "We have to go in. The animals' survival depends on it."

Before Jordan could argue, Lucy had returned with Becky's weathered original and a crisp copy for him, and the biologists were out of the tent, following a new tech who was showing them the way to the west side of the reversal.

With deep, even breaths that he had to count out, he stumbled his way to the fax machine, already piling high with printed pages. His butt smacked the chair and he began scanning the documents, quickly realizing there was an individual chart on each of the men who had woken from coma.

Men. Every last one of them, because it was a men's facility with male guards.

"Paper!" He shouted it to whomever would listen, grateful when two different techs showed, one with blank white pages and the other holding out a legal pad and retractable pen. "Thank you." He took the yellow-lined paper but didn't look up.

In seconds, the pad was spread across his knees and his hand went automatically to the pen in his breast pocket, carefully engraved with the words *Jordan Abellard, M.D.* It had been a graduation gift, unaccompanied by a tag or even words, from his father. He began writing furiously.

Men.

All prisoners. No guards.

White counts. Prior: normal. In coma: Low. Awake: high

All wing 3

Down date: 12, 14, 12, 11, 12, 12, 13, 14, 13, 12, 12, 12, 12, 14, 14.

All 12s down in pm, all 14s down in am.

He grabbed at his cell phone and hit Landerly on speed dial.

"What do you have boy?"

"There's a 53 hour window from when the first of these men fell to the last one. The down times correlate loosely to the waking times."

"What else?"

Landerly was seeing the same things he was, he knew. "There are no guards. Just prisoners. All from the same wing. These are the guys who went down before the reversal swept the CDC set-up. So it makes sense that there aren't any guards awake… Yet." He rattled off what he saw about the white counts, probably still not giving Landerly anything new.

"Abellard!" It came from far off. In that instant Jordan recognized the voice. David.

"Gotta go." He closed the phone, left the pages where they were and took off at a run, not realizing that it was the first time he had hung up on Landerly.

He arrived at the flag line marking the edge of the reversal as David pulled into view. The figure sagging at his side was Jillian. Her left arm was slung over David's shoulder which was far too high to be comfortable, and her right arm wrapped ominously across her stomach.

Once he recognized what he was seeing, he moved without thinking, crossing the unseen boundary into the reversal. He ran toward the two figures who came into sharper focus as he approached. "Jillian!"

"I'm fine!" Her voice snapped, but lacked true conviction. David's face appeared grim, although if he was suffering any nausea it didn't show. Jordan didn't care.

With one hand, he lifted Jillian's arm from where it clung fiercely to David's jacket, and in the same motion pulled her feet from the ground, lifting her to settle in his arms. His only thought was getting her the hell out of the reversal, even as she curled both arms around her stomach and rolled even tighter into a ball within his grip.

It was David's voice that cut through to him. "Don't run with her. I tried it, it just makes her worse."

Jordan clenched his jaw with the effort it took to maintain a reasonable pace. The whole time he wondered if it was better to let her get more nauseated and get her out faster, or keep her feeling better, even though the yellow flag line didn't approach as quickly as he'd like.

He bit down on his tongue to keep from flinging out insults, to not yell at David. *This is what you get for taking her into the heart of darkness.*

Her brows pulled tighter, and he could see the pain even though half her face was obscured by the neck of her jacket zipped all the way up and over her mouth. "Come on, Jilly, hang in there."

At last he made it, and even though he couldn't detect it with any of his usual senses, he felt his whole body react the moment he crossed the boundary. He got her to the nearest triage tent and laid her out on a gurney. Still, Jillian was sitting up before he had his stethoscope in his ears, her palm out to him.

"My heart rate is eighty-eight. My resps are twenty-two, and I need a GI cocktail, *now*."

It would have made him smile at any other time. But the stethoscope was folded back around his neck in one fluid movement as he pulled a plastic cup from a makeshift shelf next to him. All the ingredients were there, and he felt like a bartender, measuring out Donnatal, then peeling back the foil lid on the dose of viscous lidocaine, revealing the eerily green goo. He poured it into the cup, not watching it sink under the Donnatal, his hands already grabbing for the Mylanta bottle. He added the antacid, almost topping off the cup and ignoring a century of medical procedure as he stirred quickly with his finger. He handed her the concoction, licking his finger clean as he watched her toss her head and shoot it back.

It would numb her stomach and settle what she was feeling. At least at this stage in the game she didn't have to play guinea pig, suffering through all of it because they didn't know how to treat it, or if what they did would make her worse. He could at least offer a little relief.

His hand found her hair; she'd worn it down to give warmth from the wind, and his chest eased a little feeling her solid within his grasp. He prayed out loud, "It's just something you ate."

But she denied him. "I have ear pain."

Son of a bitch.

Chapter 15

Jordan heard David walk into the tent behind him, a little out of breath. That fact revealing that he must have carried, or helped haul Jillian, a good long way. "We didn't make it to the center."

Jordan almost exploded with *who gives a flying fuck?!* But he held it in check by the barest of glimmers.

Jillian started speaking. "No one was in there. We found a few bodies, though. The smell was enough to explain the nausea." She almost smiled. "The field is stronger as we got closer in."

Leave it to Jillian to be in mortal danger and worry about rattling off statistics.

Ignoring David, he put his forehead against hers, easy enough to do since she was still sitting on the gurney, hunched over, guarded against the pain that pulled her down. "They're waking from the comas in Nevada."

"What!" She sat upright, almost forgetting her own discomfort. He nodded. Not mentioning that they were all men. All prisoners. That there were only fifteen of them. Less than a percent.

Lucy Whitman appeared at the doorway just then, nudging David further inside in the process. "I just got off the phone with Dr. Landerly at the CDC. He said to give you these." She held out a sheaf of papers, still slightly warm from the fax machine.

It was Jillian who reached out for them, taking the folder from the perfect hand, "Are these the stats on the prisoners who woke up?"

Lucy shrugged. "Oh, I don't know. I just gather the papers."

Jordan almost called her on her lie, but Jillian was already reading. Sitting straighter, looking like the lidocaine had numbed her from the inside out. "They're all men. All prisoners. The white counts are high when they wake." She thumbed through a little further. Noting how long they'd been under, when they'd fallen, asking how many had fallen in that time, and what percentage of those men did these represent. She asked all the same questions, noticed all the same things in minutes that he and Landerly had spent the morning working through.

Her fingers shuffled quickly through the papers. "Murder, murder,…murder,…arson and murder…"

"What?"

"They're all murderers." She looked up finally. "Is that because they're all from the same wing?"

Jordan pulled out the cell and called Landerly even as she was talking.

"No, the wing that fell first wasn't this one. It wasn't maximum security." She paused and looked blankly at the canvas top of the tent, seeing something far beyond it. "But none of these are maximum security prisoners." She read again. "Single murders. Wife's boyfriend. Boss. Father…"

"Landerly, listen to this…" Jordan held the phone up to catch her thinking out loud, even though she didn't realize he was doing it.

"All one time murders.…Other prisoners fell at the same time. But they aren't awake." She paused long enough for Jordan to hear Landerly swear in the space she left.

"Oh, shit."

Holding the phone to his ear, Jordan initiated the conversation again. "Sir?"

"We have three more awake, since two hours ago." He heard the shuffling of paper through the line as Landerly looked to connect Jilly's ideas. "All murderers. No first degree. No longer considered a threat to society."

Jillian tilted her head. "Who's dead?"

Another question he and Landerly hadn't posed, so hung up on their break that they hadn't stopped to look. He passed the question on to his boss, even as he heard his name hollered out from somewhere out in the tents.

"Bye." Again, he hung up on Landerly. Not telling him that the brilliant idea of sending Jillian and David into the reversal had backfired. David had emerged unscathed with Jillian at death's door. Landerly could call Jillian directly if he wanted. Surely she would fill him in on all the stats she had collected, along with her own vitals.

Jordan figured she had a few more hours at the least – maybe a day at most – before she slipped away. If he was going to help her he had to gather what information he could. So, without a word, he turned and ran from the tent, leaving her to her musings and the paperwork on the prisoners in Nevada. He followed the voice that was calling out to him.

He didn't recognize it, although whoever it was knew him enough to boom his name at decibels high enough to shake the tents. He paused a few times, at last emerging on the north side of the field.

No one was there. Just the school stood silent in front of him, the long staircase off to his right was busy with scientists climbing up and down the four story flight that hugged the hillside. The classrooms had been put to use for containment and as dormitories. The chem lab was probably seeing the best action it had since its inception.

The voice called again, this time coming from his right. As his head turned, he realized the windows were open down the enclosed stairs. He recognized the figures before the voice.

Peppersmith and Becky Sorenson traipsed down the stairs, arms linked, neither of them looking up at him. Until Leon opened his mouth to shout out Jordan's name again.

"Here!" He yelled back.

His pace picked up as he realized the two were not in a friendly embrace after all, but that Becky was supported on Leon's arm. Her right hand snaked up to rub her ear.

Shit!

He raced back and slammed through the doors just as Peppersmith hit the bottom of the stairs, bellowing as he came. "What's wrong with her?"

Jordan ignored the man. Whipping off his stethoscope, he unsnapped the front of Becky's heavy jacket and placed the bell at the top right side of her sternum. Her heart raced. "Becky, what's wrong?" But he already knew.

"My ears hurt. It started after we found this dead cat...I–" She didn't finish. She just rolled a little, curling into a ball while Leon fought to keep her upright.

He didn't ask – didn't bother to look in her throat or her ears. The answers were in her eyes. She had *it*, and she knew it.

Lacking the will to lift her himself, Jordan looked to Leon, "Just pick her up, would you? I have a spare gurney in the triage tent if you can carry her that far."

Becky protested, and it looked like it wasn't for the first time, but this time Leon quoted doctor's orders and hauled her up. She didn't appear to have it in her to fight her way down, and Peppersmith looked like he could carry a sleeping hippo through the jungle without breaking a sweat. Becky wouldn't be any trouble for him.

Inside three minutes, they were back at the tent where he'd left Jillian and David.

Even before he saw her, Jordan knew she was on the phone with Landerly. He could hear her side of the conversation, the short spurts when she rattled off whatever her brain was clicking together. She sounded more alert and as he rounded the tent flap, she came into view, proving him entirely right. "Feeling better?"

Even as she answered, "Yup," he set about making the next GI cocktail. Leon laid Becky out on the bed, and Jillian interrupted her own conversation to say nothing other than, "you'll feel better in about five minutes," then launched back into it with Landerly.

Handing Becky the mix, Jordan waited while she eyed it. He didn't blame the biologist. He wouldn't drink it either if he hadn't known what was in it. It was a milky, lime colored substance with a faint sharp odor, and the lidocaine lent it some sort of almost-glow, even after it was mixed in. But she tipped it back, her face contorting at the texture if not the taste, and her mouth working even after she had finished swallowing it.

They stood there, the five of them, looking at each other, and wondering. The two women sitting on the gurneys, Becky starting to perk back up. None of them deluded themselves, and none of them talked. Except Jillian, who chattered to Landerly, making little sense to anyone around her.

Jordan wasn't sure how long it lasted – the wild silence in the tent, punctuated by people passing by outside, Jillian updating Landerly on what was happening.

He heard someone's name being shouted. He didn't think much of it, until he heard another name, then in rapid succession a third and a fourth. He was poking his head out of the flap when Lucy appeared there in front of him.

She was the last person he really wanted to see, but she was there in his face. Her own expression was less than chipper for the first time he had ever seen. He was about to comment on it when she spoke.

"Jordan, I feel weird." Her hands went to the sides of her face, tracing the flush as it spread up her skin. Her mouth worked like she had a bad taste in it, and her shoulders hunched forward as her eyes squeezed shut.

Oh, crap.

He touched her hands, pulling them away from her face, just as her eyes went wide. Only because he was looking at her so intently did he realize that she had focused over his shoulder.

With a snap, he turned to see Becky as she swayed from her sitting position, her eyes rolling back into her head, eyelids fluttering. She sank forward, a victim of gravity, and missed hitting the ground only because Leon had exhibited some lightning reflexes.

The giant man laid her back down on the gurney, lifting her eyelids, but finding nothing. Jordan was about to help, all else aside, except that Lucy pulled at his arm, turning him away from the shocked expression on Jillian's face. The intern looked markedly worse than she had just a few seconds ago, her color changing rapidly from the pink flush to a creeping gray tone. Her eyes lost focus and she grabbed her stomach.

With a quick step, Jordan moved closer to keep her from collapsing into the ground just feet in front of him. As he grabbed her, he realized that he had cleared the entrance of the tent and he could see in several directions down the evenly placed rows. Doctors, techs, and suits were stumbling out of the tents, reaching to others. Covering their ears. Opening mouths. Holding stomachs.

And his brain clicked.

They were all women.

Still holding Lucy partially upright with one arm, he turned to face Jillian as his adrenaline kicked in and the world began to slow on its axis. But Jillian just looked at him, having figured out some portion of what he had seen from the expression on his face.

Before he could tell her what was happening, a voice cleared its way through the pandemonium. Jordan couldn't see him, but heard his words as the man ran past. "It moved! The edge moved! We're in it!"

But Jordan and Jillian had both guessed that for themselves already. He turned to see that David and Leon had, too.

The voice was joined by others, or maybe his brain just cleared to hear them all. Urging everyone who was upright to run. To get out. To clear the edge.

Within their tent, it was Leon who took action. He grabbed the limp Becky, lifting her into his arms. Jordan's brain cranked overtime, realizing even as he watched it, that Leon had chosen Becky because she was limp and he had the most experience hauling dead weight. Peppersmith motioned to Jordan and David to grab the other two women, and even as Jordan yelled at him not to, Leon was out the door with Becky hanging from his arms.

Jordan watched as he followed the exodus, some of the men stopping to attempt to scoop up their fallen colleagues, none of them as agile as Leon with the spare weight. As Jordan watched, some of them gave up trying and simply stepped over whomever they crossed.

It was David who yelled out the open doorway. "Don't run! You can't outrun it. The whole world's going to snap any day now!" His fatalistic cries falling on deaf or disbelieving ears.

As Jordan watched, Lucy slipped from his grasp, her eyes going blank as she gave up her last hold on consciousness. Jordan bent to lift her, thinking to put her on the gurney that Leon had vacated when he left with Becky, when a second set of hands slid under her from the other side to help him lift.

He looked up into the face of a local physician whom he had seen a few times drawing blood and helping out with the people whose homes had been in the early parts of the reversals. With a slight tip of his head, he gestured to David, "Is that true what he said, about the whole world 'snapping'?"

Jordan didn't know what to make of it. The pace was slowing, but the adrenaline was still ringing in his ears, still bringing the false endorphin high. He shrugged. "Probably."

The other doctor bore Lucy's weight and Jordan let him. In silence, the doctor wandered off with the limp woman, her feet dangling, one red leather shoe missing, her nails sparkling at the ends of loose hands.

"Jordan?" Jillian's voice broke through to him.

He'd have known if she'd fallen. But he hadn't quite catalogued that she'd stayed upright.

But why?

She thought it, too, and her thoughts came in fragments. "I thought I was immune....then I didn't...now?..."

But he shook his head, unable to answer.

It was David who said, "I guess maybe it is something you ate." His face contorted in a weird, what-about-that kind of way. But as he finished the sentence, Jillian squinted her eyes, rocking her head from side to side as though fighting off a bad memory.

Jordan saw the flush creeping up her neck even as she felt it, her facial expression changing. He could see her stomach roll. "Jordan?"

It was her last word, and as she looked at him, her eyes went heavenward. In slow motion, she slumped backward and started to slide off the gurney.

While David watched, Abellard sprung forward barely catching Jillian's weight. Well, he didn't so much catch her as take the fall for her, cushioning her limp limbs from the hard ground she sped toward. He struggled to right her, and somewhere in the back of his brain David heard Jordan's voice asking for help. But he ignored it.

In a moment, the doctor had her spread out on the gurney, looking like she had simply had too rough of a day and decided that now was as good a time as any for a balls-to-the-wall nap.

David knew his brain wasn't processing correctly. That she might be dead. That she looked like a doll, reposed on the bed, because he couldn't handle the truth. But that was okay, because Abellard was here to handle both Jillian and the truth.

Creeping to the back corner of the tent, David molded himself to the canvas wall. Still it didn't allow him to escape the serious gaze Jordan pinned him with. "You stay here with her. *Don't move.* I'll be right back."

David's brain inserted a sleek "*I'm Batman*" as the tent flap shifted in the wake of Jordan's path. But he didn't laugh. He bit his cheek to keep the sound from overflowing. Because he knew if he did that the laugh would evolve into hysterics, and when Jordan returned he would haul back and deliver a stinging slap.

David did not want to be on the receiving end of Jordan's wrath. Certainly not when it was disguised as medical care.

Sliding into a chair, he waited the long minutes for Abellard to return. His eyes wandering to Jillian, one leg dangling precariously off the edge of the gurney. His thoughts turning to his father and wondering when the old man's place would experience the 'snap'. It was all David had been able to think while Jillian had been explaining to him what indicated who would fall and who wouldn't. If his father would bite it right away, as his vital signs indicated he would. Or maybe it would turn out he was just a son of a bitch, and instead of slipping neatly into a coma, he'd hang out and fuck up all of Jillian's numbers. Put a cog in that gear head she had.

Abellard interrupted his morbidly fun thoughts, returning with his hands overflowing. A clear jellyfish thing dangled from his fingertips, until David realized it was a fluid bag for an IV and the remaining hermetically sealed pouches were all the fixings to run it. Jordan didn't say 'hello' or anything, just let his gatherings roll across the countertop, and he searched them through, peeling back layers and lining them up.

In fluid movements, he pulled off one of Jillian's jacket sleeves, then rocked her from side to side, passing the jacket behind her before tossing it on the ground. Deft fingers raised a metal pigtail on a pole, tied Jillian's arm in a white rubber band, and began pressing at the back of her hand. In the doctor's actions, David could see the practiced swing of a chipping pick, the glance to assess for layer and slope. Abellard was in his element, and out of a grudging respect David didn't want to disturb him.

Before he could have said anything, the IV bag was hanging from the pigtail, dripping faithfully into Jillian's veins.

Another doctor came by and waited patiently for a moment before finding a break in the rhythm and asking Jordan what to do with the big box of IV jellyfish in front of him. "How do we triage them?"

Jordan just grabbed three extra bags, speaking only when the other doctor raised his eyebrows. "She discovered this – we make sure she has enough saline. You can triage the rest of the patients as you see fit." He turned away, essentially ending the conversation.

David, too, turned to check out Jillian, and was startled by Peppersmith's voice coming from behind them. "Is it true what you said? That we can't outrun the edge?"

The man looked weary, like Paul Bunyon about to fall, but David nodded. "All the previous data shows that the whole earth will reverse, and if this is what happens when it does, then no, there's no outrunning it."

The thought passed briefly before it cleared enough for David to ask it. "Where's Sorenson?"

Jordan snapped around at that, but before he could put in his pissed-off two cents, Peppersmith spoke up. "All the women were dropping. I tried to help, and I just finally laid her down on a gurney in one of the tents....she's alive."

Abellard nodded, pulling one of the clear IV bags from the pile he had carefully hoarded for Jillian. He slapped it into Leon's palm, surprising the giant, but following it with a sleek plastic sealed kit. "Take these back to her and find somebody to run a line."

"I can." Leon looked at the items now dwarfed in his thick hands, and disappeared from the tent on little cat's feet, far too quiet for the size he was forced to wield.

Abellard went back to doctoring his patient. As though he could help Jillian by taking her pulse and blood pressure. Like sticking her with a needle and sucking a vial of her blood would help her live through this shit.

David wanted to ignore the whole problem. Walking from the tent, he felt the ground beneath his feet. Below the grass and dark soil were layers of limestone and shale with stories to tell. There were oil pockets here. Not the size of the ones in Texas or Alaska, but enough to put a pump in your back yard and food on your family's table for all your years to come. David wanted to be under his own feet, down with the rocks and the strata.

So why was he here? Stuck with the CDC and sick people falling around him everywhere? Oh, and not just sick people, sick *women*. Just as a final insult, it was Abellard's pretty mug he was stuck looking at.

He shook his head, trying to look beyond the tent city. The mountains pushed up around him on every side. Caves were back there. Exposed surfaces, waiting for a man with a pick, a plan, and something to prove. Strip mining had ruined the beauty of the hills, but beauty was for crap. The exposed layers and angles were far more interesting than any damn trees could be.

His fingers itched to pick at something, to clip himself to a rope and slide down a rock face stealing little pieces of it as he went. All this compass and magnetic field stuff was interesting, but he wanted to break something. Instead, people were pushing by him, *talking* to him.

He didn't answer. They looked sick, and he had had just about enough of this vomit-and-fall-down-half-dead crap. Their faces looked uncomfortable, so he turned away. Only to be confronted by men, everywhere, coming out of tents, walking the straight lines between, all rubbing at their bellies, the sides of their faces, their ears.

Son of a bitch.

For the briefest of moments, David wondered if he was getting it too, and just wasn't medical enough to know it was happening. But when he checked his stomach the only thing he felt was hungry. Suddenly ravenous. He hadn't eaten since before he and Jillian had tried that hike to the center of God's green beyond. And he'd had to haul her sick ass out of there, too.

He grabbed the arm of a passing physician, "Hey, where can I get food down here? Or do I have to go back into the school?"

The man's facial expression questioned David's intelligence even as his finger was pointing at the double doors at the bottom of the staircase. The doctor greened up another shade before turning away. David ambled off toward the low building – better get some before all the damn cafeteria staff fell ill.

"David!"

Shit.

It was Abellard. "I need you!"

With a sigh as heavy as granite, he turned to help out the doctor. There was a knot of people at the front of the tent. At least David was pretty sure it was the right tent – they were all identical: four poles, white canvas, the only differences being where the flaps were open and how.

Pushing through the men clustered at the door, he found Abellard inside, tending bar, and making the Day-Glo shots he had fed to Jillian and Sorenson. Peppersmith stood by his side, looking green around the gills, but his hands were full of whatever Jordan was handing him. Leon handed them out, one by one, then turned back to the makeshift counter, "My turn." And he sucked down the next lime green mixer.

Men walked away from the tent flaps, slamming back the shots even as they pushed beyond the crowd.

Jordan turned around and pinned him with a glare. "So show me this immunity that got Jillian in trouble."

David shook his head. "I'm fine."

"Good."

Some of the others looked at him in surprise, or awe. A few even glared, but it only took one, grabbing his arm and asking "Immunity?" to start the ripple of murmurs through the crowd. David shrugged him off.

Jordan, too, ignored it and sent David with a list and a box, bare except for empty bottles so David would know when he found the right stuff. He hit the supply tent and pillaged it, haphazardly piling in what looked like individual lunchbox applesauce containers. He added industrial sized bottles of Mylanta, and carefully read the vial labels searching for Donnatal.

With his box full and his brain in pissed-off mode, he made his way back to the tent, still crowded with sick men. Hadn't he gone to college and even grad school to avoid being a manual labor peon? With less than no ceremony, he plopped the box on the counter beside Abellard who looked relieved at the quantities David had discovered.

He looked even more haggard than most of the men outside, and Peppersmith held one of the cups out to him, but Abellard waved it away. He motioned for it to be handed to one of those who were waiting, always the hero.

David hung back, then eventually began pulling cups off the end of the assembly line and passing them out to the crowd. He wasn't human and he knew it. His helping was just a matter of not having all the doctors glare at him.

The clusterfuck at the door thinned and David looked beyond the canvas walls to see that they were falling where they stood. A lot of good the medicine was doing if you asked him.

"I have no idea, but the bastard does seem to be immune." Jordan spoke to the wall, having finally lost his mind completely.

Or so David thought until he saw the cell phone propped open on the countertop, the name "Landerly" in bold letters across the face.

When the last hand had snaked in for a dose of GI cocktail, Jordan downed one himself. His color had turned gray as steel and he worked his mouth without speaking. Finally, he produced sound. But it wasn't for David, or even Leon Peppersmith, it was to the cell phone. "Bye Landerly. Thanks for the–"

His eyes rolled and with his last shred of consciousness he made sure he fell forward, cradling his head even as all his limbs went perfectly slack.

"Oh, shit!" It was the only real surprise David had ever heard from the wrangler.

But Peppersmith acted. From the looks of it, Jordan was just a big catch to him. He unceremoniously draped the doctor over his shoulder, turning until he spotted the empty gurney. He slapped Jordan down on it hard enough to make David think it was a good thing the doc wasn't awake to experience the humiliation of being hauled around by another man like a sack of flour.

"Abellard!" It was just a sound through some static.

David looked around for the source. But since it wasn't Leon, and it was inside the tent–

"Dr. Landerly?" Picking up the cell phone, he got a good look at the face plate. The time read 20:24. That was a long call. "It's Dr. David Carter."

"I know. Abellard's down?"

"Yup." He held the phone at a distance, eyeing it as though it might bite him.

"Is Peppersmith still standing?"

"Yup. He's fine, too."

Leon Peppersmith nodded and gave David the thumbs up, just before his eyes rolled into his head and he dropped like a stone. He went over straight backward, cracking his head on the gurney railing and jostling Jillian, loosening one of her arms so it slipped over the edge of the bed and hung like dead weight.

"Let me take that back, we just lost him."

Landerly's voice growled through the line at him. "Just like that? No warning?"

"Yup."

With a quick glance down at Leon, he turned back to the phone to concentrate on something Landerly was saying. As he turned away from the downed giant, his brain processed what he had seen.

A crimson pool was spreading in the grass beneath Leon's head.

"Shit!"

"What?" Landerly's voice crackled from the ground where David had automatically tossed the phone.

"He cracked his head!" He knelt beside the big man, thinking that he should touch the wound to know what to do. His hand pressed through the blond hair, to where he could feel the tiny fluctuations in pressure signaling that something important had been hit. Using his fingers to follow the flow backward, David was shocked to find the cut wide and gaping.

Jerking his hand back and not even noting the blood, he leaned into the shove, rolling the big man over. As he did it he suffered a thought about spinal cord injuries and paralysis. Leaving bloody handprints as he went, he checked the hair, and felt the inward dent in the skull.

With an unconscious jerk, David sprang back, landing on his butt, watching in fear as the wound fountained and fell, fountained and fell. Peppersmith lay unconscious, still as rock, while both the timing and size of the rhythm slid off to nothing.

With dry blinking eyes, David stood, leaving the fallen giant facedown on the ground inside the tent. Unaware of where he was stepping, he crushed the phone beneath the heel of his shoe as he left, silencing Landerly's voice while it hissed through the bad connection.

He needed a sink to wash his hands. It was just beyond the cafeteria. He *was* still hungry. David didn't worry about the stains on his shirt. Just washed up and headed up the long flight of stairs to change into something clean.

He found his doorway in the eerie stillness; the lack of noise breaking through his protective denial. He looked around, and nothing moved.

A laugh almost bubbled out of him. Of course *nothing moved*. He was in a hallway in an empty high school. But there was something else – a lack of any human sound that was far more powerful than any lie his brain could concoct. For the first time, his stomach rolled over in fear.

He unbuttoned his shirt, avoiding the bloody smears and prints, and threw it in the trash. He climbed into fresh everything: boxers, socks, pants, t-shirt.

His stomach rolled again.

He was tired. With a hand in his hair he decided that the cot was the way to go. The food would still be there when he woke up. Then he'd pack up and get the hell out of town.

David stretched out, not comfortable even though the cot was long enough.

All the energy left his limbs.

Only at the last minute did he understand what was happening.

He tried to open his eyes, and wasn't sure if he accomplished it.

The black was bringing the sparkles with it at the borders of his vision. It crept in, closer and closer, taking over his brain.

Oh shit.

Chapter 16

Jillian blinked. White showed above her and all around. Clouds.

Heaven.

The pounding in her head drove out thoughts of any such luck. She blinked with eyelids made of sandpaper. Her brain knew she was awake, but she didn't know where.

And why couldn't she move?

Another grainy blink revealed shadows in the endless white, lines coming to a crosspoint just up and to her right.

The metal structure draped in the white canvas that formed the gazebo top came into focus.

As she lifted her arm she felt a tug at the skin covering her hand, and figured it out just before she waved her arm into her line of sight.

An IV meant someone was here.

The memories swept quickly through her mind. Jordan putting her up on the gurney, after David hauled her out of the reversal. Becky being laid on the gurney next to hers.

With a shove and a groan, Jillian brought herself to her elbows. Only now beginning to catalog and question the eerie silence.

Extreme effort brought her to sitting, only to slump down quickly as she realized that she would pass right back out again. If not from lack of blood to her brain, then from the hideous pounding inside her skull. She recognized it as the cadence of her heart and for a few moments she counted, stopping only when she was confident she was at a nice stable seventy-two beats per minute.

She yanked her arm, forgetting why she had moved the moment the IV tugged at the back of her left hand, painfully taking tape and a little bit of precious skin. But the needle stayed put. Whoever had done it had done a good job.

While she took deep breaths and waited for her equilibrium to be restored, Jillian held the taped-up hand into her visual field.

Jordan had done it.

It was the first smile that cracked her face. She could feel the unused muscles as she stretched them, grinning as she recognized the careful pattern he always made securing IVs. Wide white paper tape. With three pieces neatly laid in rows holding the whole thing down. So you couldn't rip it out. So it wouldn't hurt so much.

She had to find Jordan.

Turning onto her stomach, Jillian paid careful attention to the tubing that fed her normal saline from the looks of it. But it wasn't Becky Sorenson on the gurney that shared the corner with hers.

It was Jordan. Flat on his back. For a few heart-stopping moments she waited, seeing if his chest would rise of its own accord. And when it did, her unfettered right hand snaked out to rest on his sternum, to buy reassurance that the one breath wasn't a fluke. After riding several swells and troughs of his breathing, Jillian tried to jostle him awake.

"Jordan?"

It was nothing but a movement of her mouth; no sound escaped her vocal cords. Not even the whisper of a voice. It took three tries before she produced something akin to the hiss of a steampipe. And several more before she could recognize her own voice.

"Jordan?"

But he still didn't respond. His chest kept rising and falling, but nothing else about him showed life. Her hand went to her front scrubs pocket out of habit, without her brain even being aware that it was there, until it grasped her penlight.

Jillian turned herself to the single-minded task of lifting his lids and watching the pupils focus automatically before the she allowed herself the sigh of relief that let out the tension and allowed a flood of thoughts of so many things that were not comforting.

Like the throb in her leg.

Like, where had Becky Sorenson gone? Was she awake?

How long had she been out?

Four days, like the guys in Nevada?

Her lips pressed a thin line. She had no idea.

But she was smart enough to put together the facts. Jordan was out cold beside her. There were no human sounds beyond the tent that she could distinguish. She had a slow dripping IV but Jordan didn't even have a line. Surely he would have run one on himself if he could have. There were two plastic IV drip bags, lying like dead urchins on the counter. So he had enough saline, but maybe not enough time. But he was on the gurney. So he had enough time to get there, or someone had put him up there. But why hadn't they run a line? Unless they couldn't.

David!

"David!"

It was meant to be a yell, but it sounded like steam being released from a pan. With a deep breath she tried again, her eyes still square on Jordan's face, waiting for any flicker of movement.

Her voice was loud enough the second time.

But David wasn't around.

And apparently neither was anyone else. *Someone* should have answered that call. As inhuman as it might have sounded.

She tried a third and even fourth time before deciding that she was just wasting her throat. And that she needed a drink and clearly no one was going to show up and hand her one.

Long slow moments passed before she positioned herself to sitting, feeling her muscles stretch and react from their silent time on the gurney. She was guessing she'd been out well more than a day.

Her sneakered feet dangled over the side, swishing in time to the rhythmic pounding of her heart. The desire to find something positive was enough incentive. With eyes staring ahead she took deep breaths, getting her blood flowing again, her heart working a little harder to feed fluid to all the corners of a body that was no longer stationary but becoming fully mobilized.

Jillian inhaled deeply and thanked God that she had survived this…whatever it was. She knew already that many hadn't, and many more wouldn't.

She also gathered strength for the jump to the ground. Her legs would need to hold her when she hit bottom, and it wasn't standard operating procedure at all to try this completely alone first time out of a coma. But she had no options. No one had come when she called.

Which meant they were all under.

Or dead.

Or incapacitated to the point where they couldn't answer back.

It was a shame that the last thought was about the most cheerful.

Jillian gathered the IV tubing, draping it to let out enough line in case her legs failed and she slipped all the way to the ground. Without looking down she moved her butt off the edge, feeling for the ground with her toe, but she didn't find it. When her arms got too tired, she fell, her legs taking the brunt of the impact, and not well because she hadn't been sure when it was coming. She crumpled, her feet slipping easily through the grass to splay out in front of her. Leaving her sitting with a sore butt, growing wet from the dew on the cold ground.

But she smelled something. Her eyes registered it before her brain matched the smell, her hand flying to her mouth.

Leon Peppersmith lay beside her, facedown and unmoving, with flies swarming in small patches. Her hand automatically made a brushing motion through the air, scattering them from their prey. And her fingers settled at his neck just under his jaw.

He was cold. He didn't move, didn't breathe. And the flies.

All of it told her he was dead, but her brain wouldn't believe until she checked for herself.

But after a full minute of not finding a pulse she resigned to defeat, if not tears.

And her brain turned over.

The flies weren't hatching on him. But there were plenty there, settling on him again from the moment she had abandoned her task of shooing them. She registered the handprints on him, marked in blood, the splay of long thick fingers.

Not Jordan's.

Jordan had artist's hands. He also would never have handled a man that way. The pattern suggested Leon was rolled and checked by a complete amateur; the handprints violated even the basics of any Red Cross first aid training.

The size, shape, and carelessness were David's. Which meant he'd survived beyond Leon's fall, long enough to roll him and check him. If David was truly immune, then where was he?

Jillian realized that she couldn't just wait here gleaning tiny fragments of data from Peppersmith, that she had sat long enough to gather her legs and push herself to the standing position she had aimed for in the first place.

She rolled to her knees, using her hands splayed out on the grass to stabilize herself, and only as she grabbed the railing did she realize that it wasn't just dew on the ground. The moisture had combined with Leon's blood and congealed to a thick red mess that she was leaving all over the side of the gurney as she hauled herself up. A task made much more difficult by the fact that her hands were covered in the slimy sludge that had once fed Leon's heart.

She wiped long red smears on her scrub pants, knowing without looking that the wetness on her butt wasn't clear dew, but more of the same. With steady hands she lowered the IV pole and unwound the flattened bag from its holder at the top. Briefly she noted the masking tape and markings indicating the dose of Raglan that had been added for nausea. Jordan had thought ahead to when she would wake up. Carrying it with her, she went in search of a clean pair of scrubs.

As she cleared the front flap of the tent, she left its man-made heat and was smacked by the chill of the air, and the smears of white across the ground. Upon closer inspection they were what she had known all along, fallen doctors, techs, lab assistants.

Harder to see, but visible when her eyes cleared, were the black slashes – the suits.

There was no rank or privilege here. No one was spared. Unless maybe you counted the absent David.

Her feet began to work, her heart racing. There was no telling how many of them were alive, but they had been left out in the cold overnight. Probably over two nights. Maybe even three. In their comatose state, they might survive. Especially with IVs.

With the clarity afforded by a fresh rush of adrenaline, Jillian headed back into the tent. Her eyes scanning, taking in the IV bags and her jacket tossed over the back of a chair.

She slipped into the jacket, knowing every second she was on her feet would be helpful to those outside. Unfortunately the IV tubing traced neatly up her sleeve and out the back of the jacket, at the base. At the neck it would receive the gravitational tug necessary to keep it dripping.

After a rapid search she found a safety pin and stared at it a second before shedding her jacket and pulling the tubing apart, shoving in the connection to a new, fuller, heavier bag. She pushed the pin through the wide hole at the top and attached it to the base of her jacket collar. Shrugging back into it, she felt the IV bag tugging slightly at the neckline, but it wasn't much of a bother, knowing what it would help her accomplish. She loaded her pockets with supplies and went to work, Leon's blood already crusting on her pants, forgotten.

Expanding her ribcage, she sucked in as much air as she could. Certain that the same place that had been so toxic to everyone no longer was to her.

Jordan was her first order of business. In short work, she propped him on his side, using the pillows from her bed and his. She used the same rubber tourniquet that he had used on her, and popped open a sterile needle and tubing. It had been months since she had run a line, she'd been so busy taking notes and trying to figure out botulism cases. But she had a motor memory, and once she got started her hands remembered even if her brain didn't.

The pattern worked its whole way through. So Jordan's IV bag was hung before she realized that he deserved the same dose of Raglan she'd been fed. And she carefully drew up the dose, injected it into the bag, and quickly slapped on a piece of tape jotted with the medication, time, and her initials.

Jillian shook her head even as she did it. Who the hell was she writing it for? It wasn't like there was another soul around here. And she wouldn't forget when she gave Jordan the dose.

But it was procedure, and hopefully someone would turn up.

She was halfway out the door before realizing there was another problem in the tent. Leon.

With a grim set to her mouth, and knowing full well that she didn't have the strength required to do it, she did it anyway. Slowly and surely. Grabbing at his ankles, she pulled him through the opening. Leaving a smear of his blood behind, his hands trailing, she wished that she had the means and supplies to treat his body in accordance with the laws of God and civilized man. But she had to clear the tent. She and Jordan had already been in there for several days with a rotting corpse.

She wondered why he didn't smell more, before coming to the conclusion that he must not have died right away. But he didn't have an IV either, so that would mean that Jordan couldn't get to him before he fell.

When she cleared the tent, she stopped. Breathing too heavily, Jillian leaned over, her hands pressed to her bent knees. She couldn't walk, didn't have the energy to start IVs for those who needed them. But she could survey.

There were two techs nearby who appeared to have run IVs on each other. They got just inside a tent but didn't get the flap closed. They were losing heat, but they were easy to fix.

Plastic cups adorned the ground, looking like there had been a party. Some crumpled, some just tossed – the GI cocktails. It would seem Jordan had been handing them out like Halloween candy. The fallen men and women were scattered like the cups. They looked tossed and forgotten. The only pattern was that they seemed to have collapsed on the west side of the campus, indicating that perhaps they had deluded themselves into thinking they could outrun the symptoms.

A few deep breaths tugged at the muscles in her ribs, stopping her and forcing her to do nothing more than look around for a few more moments. This time she saw brown dots beyond the tent lines and turned to look more closely. Chipmunks. Unlike the people, they had flies. She blinked as she realized one of the slashes of white was much smaller than the others.

Her brain was caught in the question, and her feet moved slowly until she stood over what was clearly a fluffy white housecat. Its mouth hung open and all four legs stretched straight out in front of it. Her breath caught, jerking at her ribs again. Unused for quite a while, the extended movement hurt them. But Jillian tamped down the thought and the vision of the cat. She couldn't help it. She had to get these people into the tents. And although Leon was by far the biggest of any of them, she didn't possess the strength to drag them all, even just the few feet required in most cases.

She glanced up at the clear sky for the first time. It was morning. So she had a good portion of the day to work. And the people she left out would be getting warmer, at least for a while.

She needed a rolling gurney system.

There was a dolly and some rope in the supply tent.

A wheelchair would be nice but was too high – she'd spend too much time lifting people, *if* she even could.

She picked her way around, making promises to do something as quickly as possible as she stepped over the fallen. In the tent entry, she contemplated the scene in front of her. Then began loading the pieces she needed. Rope, several roll boards, Velcro straps, IVs, needles, tape…a box to haul the little pieces in.

She wound her way to the next patient tent, stealing the first empty gurney she could find and leaving the mattress propped against the support pole. She wheeled the frame back to the supply tent and went after her first…*victim,* she thought to herself.

She encountered him not twelve feet beyond the opening, lying on the ground, head back. She systematically checked his pulse, felt for broken bones, and shined her penlight in his eyes. She wasn't moving him if he wasn't worth moving, she thought grimly. And more time had passed gathering stuff than she had planned. But she would save as many as she could, and that meant staying upright, not wasting effort.

After a few moments she decided he was worth it. She rolled him, before realizing she'd never been taught how to do this procedure by herself. And with good cause, *Who could have predicted this?* She stared at the bodies all around her.

This time she put the board in place first, then rocked her patient, quickly shoving the it behind him. She propped the two spare roll boards like ramps up the eight inches to the collapsed, mattressless gurney. With rope, she leaned back and dragged him up the slope, by far the most exerting of the activities.

But he was there, unaware of the abuse she had caused him and herself in the process. She popped him up and wheeled him to the nearest free patient space. Trying so hard to be careful, but having neither the time nor the strength to do much more than plop him onto the bed, she got her breath while she ran a line on him.

She injected a dose of Raglan for him, too. Then took a moment to gather her thoughts and her energy. Trying to be useful while she waited for her oxygen to catch up to her, she wrote the dosing repeatedly across the tape and stuck the tabs methodically up her jacket sleeve. Ready to grab when she needed them. The only question was, would her strength find her or would she just get weaker?

Only one way to find out.

David woke from a solid sleep to the cadence of army boots on a wooden bridge. Or a woodpecker in slow motion, each peck echoing forever.

"Ehhhh." It was a sound carried on a breath that rang in the hollowness around him. And he remembered. Climbing up here. Going to sleep. Being certain that *it* had found him.

He blinked by force of will, the light blinding as he pried open his eyeballs. At last they focused on the floor near him, on the thing least painful to his vision. *Wouldn't you know it?* The things he saw first were the army blankets made into the love nest where Jillian had curled into Abellard that morning.

Or maybe it had been longer.

He had been hungry when he came, but now it seemed his stomach had turned almost inside out. He knew he needed to eat, but it didn't hurt, wasn't even a bother. He imagined this was the way that people starved to death, knowing they needed food, but knowing there wasn't much they could do about it.

He flexed his toes, his knees, his ankles, worked his stiff fingers, and elbows – all of it painful, but necessary.

Last, he remembered not a soul had been awake. And from the sound of it, or lack thereof, it remained the same.

He slowly pitched himself to sitting. The pounding lessened now, he pushed to his feet, swaying like the tall trees, a state he despised. Only then did he realize how much of his pride was embedded in his nature – that he was solid, unchanging, predictable – readable if you knew the signs. A David Carter the Second who wavered on his feet was none of those things and he fought for balance.

But he didn't really find all of it. He lurched toward the door, throwing it open, not admitting to himself how much weight the doorknob bore while he turned it and swung it back.

He walked the few steps forward, unaided, until his shoulder banged into a locker he hadn't realized he was so close to. With a grunt, he massaged his muscles, and walked again, this time trailing his fingers along the cool paint, the texture changing as lockers passed by under his fingerpads. The wall told him which way was up, and he stayed vertical this time.

His brain didn't know what to do about it. Balance came naturally, it was like farting, you just did it. Conscious thought about walking was virtually impossible to a man who had left that up to his brainstem for decades.

The hallway down to the field was in front of him. There were windows lining each side, and from this height he would be able to see the white tops of the tents looking like Arlington Cemetery as they made neat rows across the soccer field. If he could get to the other side of the damn hall.

A deep breath.

Another.

And he started putting one foot in front of the other, stunned by knowledge that this was what it felt like to be an astronaut in space – no bearings, just sightlines. How did it work so well most of the time? David knew then that he had caught a glimpse into Jillian's brain, her fascination with the human form and function.

At last his fingers caught the smooth surface of the windows. Cold to the touch, he realized that the school had kept functioning even without its people, the heater making a huge difference.

Under the guise of making a visual sweep of the tent town, he rested his forehead against the window, enjoying the temperature difference that felt almost like wetness. While he breathed, he scanned.

Nothing.

He sighed, realizing he wasn't quite ready to move yet. And told himself that he should look a little longer. But the people where down there, and the food was down there. He would only get weaker while he waited.

Why the hell had he come back up here in the first place?

The cot didn't seem like such a bargain now.

His feet followed a line, one arm stayed out from his side, at ninety degrees, trailing fingertips across the cool windows as he walked, leaving fingerprints he didn't care about. The stairs got closer and closer, and David admitted to himself that he needed the railing. *Son of a bitch.* He wished this on his old man as he aged – this feeling of helplessness. And he wasn't sure if it was worse that there was no one around to help, or better.

With slow even steps he took on the first flight. It seemed, as he looked down, that it had gotten steeper. Every time his foot hit flat against the concrete step, the impact rang through his leg bones. His going was slow and he had to stop at the landing, his hand pressed flat against the cool window, supporting his weight. And for the first time he began to wonder what it would be like when he hit the bottom.

Would anyone be alive?

Clearly no one was awake yet.

His stomach pinched, the tiny reminder that he should be on a mission for food. It wasn't like the people were going to go anywhere while he ate.

He walked the level part between flights, one hand pressing against the small stitch in his side, a dogged reminder of his weakness. Then he faced the next set of stairs.

Again, he slapped his way down, lacking the control necessary for a smooth gait. Thinking that food would help, but knowing there wasn't likely to be a fruit basket waiting for him at the next landing, he just kept going.

Breathing heavier, he paused again at the level section, his ribs heaving, his harsh intakes and expulsions the only sound in the hollow stairwell. This time both hands rested on the window. His leg stretched out behind him in a mock calf stretch, as though a good warm-up would cure him.

When he got halfway down, the tent town came into clearer view. He could see down a few of the paths, not just skim across the tops. Now he could see the fallen doctors and nurses, in their white jackets and blue scrubs. Suits were down too, their black making them look sinister compared the angelic coloring of the medical staff.

"Holy shit!"

He heard his own voice before he absorbed the movement he had seen. A team of people had grabbed one of the doctors in the aisleway and was rolling him onto a board and a gurney.

He could only see one active person because the tents blocked his view but there appeared to be more than one. He could see better if he went down a few steps, all the way to the end of the row...

Taking it sideways and never peeling his eyes from the scene, he spent excruciating minutes gaining a few steps. And his view got clearer if not his brain.

There was only one doctor, and it was Jillian. Out there hauling some hapless med onto a metal bed. She popped it up and pushed it into the nearest tent disappearing from view.

David took a few more steps. Feeling his way, hands plastered to the windows that trailed the staircase. He was about to lose the sightline, the tents on the left would obscure the view. And he had to get Jillian's attention.

He waited where he stood, contemplating the fact that it was possibly just the two of them awake. Maybe there really had been something to that immunity theory.

She reemerged, oblivious to him standing there in the staircase.

"Jillian!" His lungs burned from the effort and she didn't glance up.

"Jillian!"

Again nothing.

He took two more steps down, to where a window was pushed an inch open to ventilate the place, keeping her in his sights the whole time. She was out there, rocking and strapping up another fallen doc, looking like one of the seven dwarves had gotten lost and decided to go it alone. He wouldn't have been surprised to find her whistling.

But he put his mouth to the space and yelled her name again.

She started, as though she had heard something, but shook off the sound. No doubt having no idea what the Herculean effort was costing him.

But he yelled again.

This time she looked up before turning back.

And he yelled yet again.

His ribs ached. His throat burned. His legs were weak.

But she was looking around for the source of the noise she had heard. With no more voice to spare, he did the only thing he could think of. He made a fist and banged on the window.

He would have cursed out loud if he'd had the voice to do it. The damned plexiglass absorbed his tender fist and released only a gentle thud. The noise nowhere near worthy of the pain it had inflicted.

But he had nothing else to hit it with.

He was wearing borrowed scrubs or he would have had a belt buckle. He was soft, and he was weak, and it was a bad combination. But he banged again and screamed her name one last time. "Jillian!"

This time he moved to the left, plopping down a step, and waved frantically, feeling like a lost child watching the search party go by.

Finally she saw him and waved.

From here it was hard to tell, but he thought she smiled.

Then she went back to her patient, finished hauling him onto the gurney, popped the bed up, and disappeared into the tent.

That bitch!

David took a few more steps. Still traveling sideways, watching the tent town for other signs of life. But there were none. None at all now that Jillian was out of view.

He hit the next landing, his line of sight down the tents gone, obscured by the first row, he was barely above them, and this last flight would bring his feet even with the ground outside.

His heart hitched, his breath released, when he saw her coming out at a near jog. Hell, she was in much better shape than he was. But he'd never been so happy to see her, to see anyone.

He faced the last steps. His energy renewed in a surge of hope, and he squared up to the flight, thinking to take it head on.

His eyes lifted as he saw the door swing open and heard her voice, breathless, "David!"

He felt the concrete corner of the first step bite into his arch, barely grabbing the treads on his expensive sneakers. The tenuous balance he registered in his fingers fled, and he tilted to the right, taking the hard metal rail in his lower ribs. His hands flailed, but the rapid bloom of adrenaline only made him think faster, not act faster, and in horrifying slow motion he watched his hands miss their grip, and the cold gray stairs come straight for his face.

Chapter 17

Jillian had no time to react, she had no more called his name and registered the rare smile that lit up his whole face, than he was at her feet in an inhuman crumple.

Stifling a scream, she compartmentalized that this was her friend, and let her brain go into ER mode. He was unconscious, so without moving him or speaking, she checked for a pulse, and found it, going strong if erratic. She pulled her stethoscope free of her neck and listened to his breath sounds. Again, no fluid, no hissing, just normal sounds sped up a little by the fall and the adrenaline.

Carefully she felt along several of his limbs. His right leg she didn't touch, it was already swelling and bent at such an angle that she didn't have to feel it to know that it was broken, a tib-fib for sure. His hip also wasn't placed right, and his pelvic girdle was wrong, although what the problem was she couldn't tell just by looking. His right arm flayed out to his side where it had been thrown by the fall. But it was facing the wrong way. Dislocated. A few touches and palpations confirmed her suspicion.

He was starting to come around, and she debated what to do. No one else had woken up in the time she had been awake. And it would figure that the one person who did would pitch down the steps to her feet the moment she discovered him. There was nothing she wanted to do less than spend her time setting a broken bone, by herself mind you, and taking care of the person who should have been helping her.

With a self-deriding shake of her head, Jillian put that thought away. She opened the compartment doors; this was David. And he was seriously hurt. But he was coming to.

"Jillian?" It was a harsh whisper, and he tried to turn his head from where she held it firm in her hands. She couldn't risk him moving his neck, not until she knew he checked out.

"David, don't move."

He did just that, trying to lift his dislocated arm and letting out a hoarse scream in the process. He seemed to hear himself, and she could almost see the testosterone working its way through his system. David bucked up and, blinking at her, finally made contact "Good to see you."

She ignored his attempt at humor and told him to stay still, she was going to get the gurney.

Her IV bag flopped inside the back of her jacket as she ran, although she could already tell it weighed less than before, a good half of it had dripped into her veins in the time she had worked today. But for all she had accomplished, there were plenty of people left to move and she could feel the temperature dropping in the late afternoon.

Her energy had improved as she worked, although she could find no scientific explanation for it. Now she wrapped her hands around the gurney bar and, with all the speed she could afford, she raced back into the hallway. Grateful when she could stop fighting the cart for a path over the grass and enjoy the slick feel and easy glide of the wheels moving on the polished floor they were intended for.

She was beside David in a moment, although in the short time she had been gone his eyes had changed from bewildered to wary. He knew he was in bad shape. But Jillian just started to work. She ran the IV with a newfound efficiency, leaving off the Raglan dose, but adding in some morphine sulfate to dull the pain.

She put a neck collar on him next, even though he protested and looked at her with wide eyes. She rocked him onto the roll-board with strong hands and the methods learned from thirty limp patients this afternoon. She had gotten better with every patient and was grateful now. David would be too, as she was uncertain if he had sustained any spinal injuries.

She had him up on the gurney and sprung the bed upward to a workable height before she made eye contact with him. His left hand shot out and grabbed her arm, startling her and keeping her from rolling him out to the lobby area in front of the cafeteria where the light was better.

"David?"

"Jillian, tell me–"

She knew what he wanted to hear. But everything wasn't going to be all right. He'd gone headfirst down concrete steps. He was messed up. His right leg had swollen even more since her initial assessment and she was certain there was internal bleeding. Of course Jordan would have followed all the protocol and briefed David on his condition and options and let David make those decisions.

She wasn't Jordan.

But she tried.

With an awkward motion she took his face in her hands, hindered by the thick plastic neck collar immobilizing him and looked him in the eyes. "You have at least a broken right leg and a dislocated right shoulder. I think something is wrong with your hip as well. I'm going to check you for spinal cord injuries first. Then I'm going to take you out to the tent and fix you up. It's going to hurt. Because I'm the only one awake. But ninety-nine percent says you're going to be okay." She paused, added, "Later."

With her penlight she checked his pupils. She was going to pray every night never to have to watch for 'equal and reactive' again. Then she prodded him repeatedly. It was a medical test, but Jillian admitted that it was just systematic poking to see if the patient could feel things. She undid the Velcro holding the collar in place before reaching both hands around his neck and feeling the vertebrae. Nothing felt damaged to her trained fingers. So she left the collar off and began what would be a bumpy and excruciating ride for David out to the tent.

He was clenching his jaw by the time they arrived. Wheeling him inside, her eyes darted to Jordan, lying right where she'd left him, not bothered by any of this. Leaving David on the metal gurney, she went about setting up.

Jillian stole bedsheets and cut them into strips. She lined up shots of pain medications and muscle relaxants. She administered the doses and braided sheets while she waited for them to take effect. She ignored all the protocol about asking David what he wanted. She would fix him as best she could.

He could sue her later. Besides there were surely sunshine laws to cover malpractice during mass human extinctions.

When the dosing had done its job, Jillian shifted him to the mattressed bed pushed into the corner by Jordan's, and warned David what she was doing just moments before she tied him to the frame. She palpated his hip and wished for an x-ray. But with a deep breath of acceptance she diagnosed that the pelvic girdle was broken. Without a team and an anesthesiologist, all she could do was bind it, and they'd have to re-break and re-set it later.

With great care Jillian bound his hip as best she could and she went so far as to tie his knee to the bed, thinking she could stabilize it and still be able to reset the tib-fib. She explained as she went. And David was a good soldier, stoic and cooperative, following all her suggestions no matter how bizarre. So she looped a sheet carefully around his foot and ankle and pulled with all her small might, and accomplished nothing.

"What did you do?"

With lips pressed together in disappointment and thought, she turned back to her patient. "In your language I believe it would be expressed as 'jack shit'." She turned away to think. Then tried again. The third time she applied pressure by hanging back on the sheet, the weight of her borne completely by his lower leg, hoping to stretch it far enough that she could settle the snapped bones back into their rightful places. Her feet climbed, both leaving the floor, and she wasn't sure if she'd be able to set his bones before she dislocated her own shoulders from the effort. But at last she managed enough pull and she felt her strength overcome the tension of his muscles and let the bones slide.

The hard part was in letting his leg slip back together gently. She couldn't afford to have them snap back into place and splinter or jam or, god forbid, miss and slide past each other again, causing more muscle tearing and tissue damage as they went. So her strength drained as she fought for control, and with a last sigh she realized the muscles were no longer fighting her. The bones had found each other again. She could let go.

Stopping to breathe for a few minutes, she make a quick makeshift splint then set about replacing Jordan's IV bag. It was non-exerting work. David's shoulder would have to wait, she didn't have even that simple procedure in her right now. Plus he was so doped up, it wasn't like he would know.

Jillian stayed clinical. She went to the cafeteria and fetched a few bananas, bottles of juice, sandwiches, and even a few cookies. With arms full, she wound her way through the slumbering tents back to David and Jordan.

David asked how the penguins were doing.

"Fine." She didn't look up. From the penguins question and the slightly slurred quality of speech the man was either seeing the birds or believed he was at the north pole.

Jordan didn't say anything. Just quietly submitted to the hand she laid palm down across his chest to be sure that he continued breathing.

Turning back to David, she rolled him, taking advantage of the muscle relaxants. With careful explanations that he ignored, Jillian educated him about the procedure. But the medications were working better than she had expected. He was of no help whatsoever. He agreed to everything, but couldn't even sit still. Worse, he tried to help – insisting on turning, sitting, and generally being a nuisance.

She promised him a cookie if he stayed still, and that, of all things seemed to work. But it didn't stop him from mooning at her like a lovesick calf.

"You know you're beautiful."

What do you say to that? If you say 'no' he'll just go on. "Yes."

"Can I touch you?"

"You have no idea what you're saying." After she popped his shoulder into place she fitted him with a sling and proceeded to adjust it. Leaning over him, she added an extra Velcro strap, thinking that goofboy might just do something stupid if he wasn't tied down.

"I know exsactly what I'm sssaying. This medissine just took away my concerns about sssaying it." *That was interesting.* "What were those concerns, David?"

"That jou would slllap me." His tongue sounded thick, but that would pass as he sobered up. As would this.

"You know, I think that was a good concern. – Hey!" She smacked his hand away from her butt, thinking that maybe a good slap was warranted. If she didn't leave a mark he'd never know better.

"I feel this way about you all the time." A conspiratorial look on his face, he leaned far enough forward to risk falling off the gurney, which was the last thing she needed. God, the man was a danger to himself.

"Yeah, well why don't you talk it over with the penguins?"

Confusion. Blessed confusion. He tried to gesture with his disabled arm, and seemed even more perturbed that it didn't move. "Where did they go?"

"They're visiting the back of your eyelids, David. You have to lie down and close your eyes for a long time. The penguins will…" *This had to be good…* "peck you when it's time to open your eyes."

"Yeah." He nodded, in complete agreement before slowly laying himself back. Closing his eyes carefully, he waited for the penguins.

If he hadn't been the last man on earth, she would have laughed. Instead she went outside looking for another gurney, and hauled it in. Keeping her gaze close to the ground, Jillian ignored the suits and med staff that were still visible in white and black against the grass. Those she hadn't moved yet. They would have to survive another night. She was exhausted.

It was the interrogation room of nightmares. Borne of too many cop movies. The light shone in his eyes obscuring everything else in the world.

He didn't even remember the world. Just that there were questions.

Voices were asking him things he couldn't answer. He pushed his arm up to shield his face, but it wouldn't come. He was rewarded with a sharp pain every time he tried to lift it. And he couldn't distinguish who was holding him down, who was speaking. Just the glare flooding his vision to the point of pain.

Jordan squeezed sore eyes tight to stop it, but the red glow permeated his eyelids, and snuck between every time he moved. The voice wouldn't shut up. He made a noise, the sound was painful to his own ears but it reoriented him.

Gravity was down, behind him. He was on his back, in bed.

With each time he squinted, he recognized more and more in the blobs around him. The light was sunlight, not artificial. The voice was to his left. The pain was in his left hand.

He moved it, snapping it painfully against something metal.

The bedrail.

He moaned.

"Jordan!"

Her voice pierced the haze.

Jillian.

It was all he got to think before he felt her hands, soft and cool, on his arm. Her voice was asking for his open eyes. He tried to say her name, and was quite certain that he didn't achieve it. But she responded like he had. "That's right, I'm here. It's good to see you awake. I was getting worried."

Don't worry about me.

But he couldn't form single words, let alone the whole thought.

It.

He'd had *it.*

And he'd woken up. The realization expanded his lungs to full capacity, to gasp in surprise at his own survival. With the dawning came the idea that he had to get his eyes open no matter the cost. He fought the burning and the low, shallow sound that accompanied the forced vision. But he waited. And the first blob came into focus.

It was David, on the gurney beside him who had provided the interrogation, and was still at it. "Abellard! You are about the last one up. Don't worry, I kept our girl here company."

Jillian's voice cut through the haze, clearer than anything else around him. "Yeah, you weren't much good as anything else."

"Ooh, baby, that hurts."

As did the banter that they shared when he couldn't even see. But Jordan forced his eyelids wide, waiting while she became visible. Still a little fuzzy, Jillian's smile was obvious.

Rapid blinks brought the world into sharp relief one painful frame at a time. The white of the canvas, bleeding in sunlight. The silver of the bed bars, used for children and the elderly. Or the comatose.

He considered asking to have them put down so he could feel human again, but the face that came into view was David's and in a blink Jordan realized what was wrong. It looked like David had gotten in bad with the mob. "David?"

"Yeah?" David shrugged, with only one shoulder. "In your professional opinion I am fucked-up, huh?"

"What happened?"

Jordan missed the first part of the explanation, simply because he was shocked he had spoken and David had answered. Despite the feeling that his mouth was stuffed with moldy gauze, he was articulate.

"-down the stairs. The rest is pretty obvious."

"Stairs?" He tried to lift his head, and it took a moment to realize the blue that had settled beside him was Jillian in her scrubs, her palm flat against his forehead holding him immobile.

"Don't try to sit up yet."

But he wanted to hear about these mythical stairs that had started wailing on David while he himself had slumbered on.

David pointed with his unslung arm, still dressed in doctors scrubs, although by now Jordan was sure that everyone knew he wasn't a physician. "The last flight. I'd just woken up and was weak. I was trying to get to Jillian. And I slipped." His finger gestured beyond the tents and Jordan recalled the long, tall stairwell that led up to the classrooms on top of the hill.

"You fell down the stairs?"

The world was undergoing a phenomenal change, the likes of which had not been witnessed by humans of any kind before. And David *fell down the stairs?*

Jillian's voice added in. "He was basically useless. Which sucked because he and I were the only ones awake for two days. We came right out of it."

His gut twisted, although in relief or fear, he was uncertain. "You *were* immune."

"Well, we went under. I don't know that I'd call it immunity." Again she pressed her hand flat to him, this time across his chest, and it was embarrassingly easy for her to push him back down. He hadn't even realized that he'd been trying to sit up. "I did blood tests out the wazoo… we've got nothing that I can find."

The way Jordan figured it, if she couldn't find the pattern, it didn't exist.

Licking the roof of his mouth, he tried to ready it to speak again. But Jillian saw him and went into action. Propping the head of his bed slightly she pushed his pillow into place and handed him a small cup of juice.

Positively heavenly, it made up for the abrasion of the invalid treatment. If he'd been strong enough he would have told her to quit. But, well, that was the point wasn't it?

After a second cup, he found his voice and spoke over the questions David was still asking. "Who else?"

Her chest moved visibly. "Well…"

He could see the gears. She needed to find a place to start and that meant there was a lot.

"I can't get Landerly on the phone. I think he's under." She busied her hands, drawing a dose of something and injecting it into David's IV. "In fact, we've set a couple of people to calling different places and recording what they report."

"Are we Central Headquarters now? That doesn't make sense."

"No, it doesn't. But we put ourselves in the path of the swap. So we were one of the first places under, and one of the first to come out. I'll be glad to hand all the data to Atlanta as soon as they come around."

"Nothing from them?" Jordan shook his head. His blood pumping stronger at the mention that Landerly was down. That all of Atlanta was.

"Not yet."

"Here?" He was sitting, having left horizontal behind, his legs dangling over the side down where the baby rail ended. His head would have been swimming from being upright if it hadn't been swimming from the news he was getting.

"We've kept just over a third." Jillian's sigh echoed in the still air.

And Jordan noticed the absence of the sound. "What happened to David?" The geologist's head was back and he'd passed out. A bolt of fear went through Jordan, that David had fallen under again. But Jillian's reaction was nothing if not nonchalant.

"His pain medications knock him out. He gets real chatty when he hurts."

Jordan eyed the blond man, who even in sleep, and looking like he'd seen the hard end of a big stick, maintained his aura of superiority. It covered him like a blanket, and clung to him like his last name.

Jordan turned back to Jillian; she looked fatigued, but stoic. "When did he fall?"

"Two days ago. Within an hour of waking up. Just down the last flight. Worst of it is the cracked hip girdle."

Jordan winced at the thought. But Jillian just continued with the list. "He also has a tib-fib, dislocated right shoulder, bruised collarbone, two ribs with hairline fractures, and three bruised. And a nasty cut on his head, stitches compliments of me. And a strained ankle."

"Damn." Jordan blinked. It sucked to be David right now.

"Yeah. I was the only one up. I didn't get everyone inside because of him…" Her eyes went to the ground, her breath in uneven expansions.

Jordan waited for her to lift whatever had weighed her down.

"I think some of them went hypothermic….When I saw him I thought he was going to help me. But then…he fell…he just needed so much care."

"Jilly. It's okay." He wasn't sure what else to say. It wasn't like he had been here to help. "You did the best you could. And you saved David." That fact was clearly important to her, so Jordan tamped down the fiendish little thoughts rising inside him at the idea of David heading to the great beyond and dozens of other lives being saved. But he didn't share those with Jillian.

He also knew there was nothing more he could do for her guilt. Not now. So he tried the fine art of distraction. "Who else is up?"

"I can tell you better who is down. We're waiting for more to wake." She rattled off some of the names of techs they had been working with. Some she just described: Steven, one of the guards; the two brothers in the cafeteria, the Sanders'; Mr. Miles and Mr. Moore the two high school science teachers who had helped out. "That cute blonde girl who liked you so much," Jillian tilted her head, her mouth pulled back on one side, conveying the sorrow she just couldn't quite hold in. "Lucy?"

He snapped up, "Lucy Whitman?" Not that he knew her well enough to miss her, but…he sighed.

Jillian's face turned even more grim, and he knew what was coming. "The ones you didn't mention."

She shook her head, but her voice left a little room for hope. "There are a few still under, but…Dr. Sorenson's animal wrangler friend hit his head when he fell and died fairly quickly. Maybe it was nicer that way. Fast."

"Leon Peppersmith. What about Becky?"

"Holding on, but faint." Her hands waved uselessly, sharing with him the knot inside her. That the simple technicalities of life were still beyond her skills. "We've learned to recognize the signs that someone is coming out–"

He smiled. Jillian. "Of course you have."

"-but she doesn't have any of them. Her breathing is getting weaker and weaker."

"Ventilator?"

"We don't have enough to spare….But I got her one anyway…not that it's doing her any good. You know, it's just like the beginning. It's always ahead of us. We can read the signs but we can't prevent or counteract any of it." Again the useless gestures. The breaths in.

Then a spark. Her head snapped up, she smiled, making full eye contact and beaming in a way he hadn't seen before. Good. Something good was coming.

"I got you this." She pulled several pages from her pocket. He saw the list of names, marching in precise columns.

He blinked. Pages of names. A list of what?

He started to ask but he caught sight of *James Linder Carvell* and *LeAnn Jessica Lee*. The back of his brain tickled. He should know–

They were from his high school.

Lake James.

"Survivors?"

She smiled and nodded. "In the order they woke up, not alphabetical. Kelly and Lindsey aren't there. But I found ten

Abellards. Jackson is your father, right?" Her eyes were wide wondering, waiting.

He nodded, trying to stop the tears that formed.

His Dad.

He flipped two pages, seeing the occasional name highlighted. Jillian had done it. The lines were too precise to be anything other than machine or Jilly. All the highlights were Abellards.

Jackson Stellman Abellard.

It stared up at him in black and white, painting a truth he hadn't even felt in his heart. Releasing the tears down his face. *Thank you, God.*

Jillian didn't give him any space, just beamed up at him. "I knew you'd want to see that."

He nodded, biting his lip. Trying to be more together, less hindered by babyrails and emotions. He used the backs of his hands to wipe at his face.

"Ow!" He had raked the IV needle down his cheek. It hurt enough to make him wonder if he had drawn blood.

But Jillian reached up and wiped his face, her fingers were soft and warm – and demeaning. He brushed her away. "Thank you." The mumble was all he could muster.

He started again, trying to learn what he had missed. "All of Lake James went under?"

She nodded, forgetting that he had pushed her aside, "Everyone. The whole US, the world. As best as we can tell the poles swapped. That was it. The shift."

"Really?"

She gestured to the prone form on the gurney next to him. "You'll have to ask David. But that's what he believes."

Jordan couldn't help but look around the ten-by-ten tent that had been his world for four days. Even the town of Oak Ridge was nothing in the global sense, "How did we learn all this?"

Jilly's smile was crooked. "Not by me." She punctuated with a sigh. "I think I'm not human really. It would explain a lot."

The frown pulled his features central, her phrasing was so strange. *Not human?*

But she stopped him before he could begin. "The women all went under first. Even with me and David, I went first. So, logically, the women started waking up first.

"Apparently when a real woman wakes from a coma the first thing she does is call everyone she knows. Three women woke up first. Within the hour they had made contact with forty different states and seven other countries. That doesn't even include the ones that didn't answer." She looked incredulous for a moment, before that slid away to reveal guilt. "I had been awake a full day and a half by then, and hadn't even thought to try to contact my own family."

Her eyes slipped to the ground. Never revealing what, if anything, she had found out about her sisters and parents. Not that he was surprised. That was just Jillian.

The gears slipped into place. Maybe she and David did have a lot in common.

But he didn't have time to dwell on it.

"Dr. Brookwood!" A tech ran into the tent, clearly out of breath, but pushing the words through anyway. "You said you wanted to be notified if anything happened to Dr. Sorenson." Jordan could hear her breathing from eight feet away. "She's slipping."

Jillian threw one last look at him before darting from the tent, stethoscope and penlight in hand. Looking like an ER doc in full mode. But she must be these days, he reasoned. He still hadn't figured out how she had taken care of David's breaks and dislocations all by herself.

He motioned for the tech to come give him a hand. And she caught her breath before reaching out and steadying him so he could slide down to shaky legs. But he stood firm after the first attempt. The IV remained attached, and he began to scratch off the tape at the back of his left hand, but the tech stilled him. "We've been leaving them on."

But then he'd be stuck, tethered to the bed. And he told her so.

She lowered the pole and handed him the half-full bag to hang onto, before turning him around and taking a safety pin to his clothing. Within moments he was strung up with his IV attached at the back of his collar. When he glanced up he saw that the tech was wearing one the same way. "So this is the latest fashion rage?"

"Dr. Brookwood thought it up." She smiled. *Of course they all loved Jillian. She was brilliant, she saved their lives probably. While he slept.* "She's very smart you know."

"Yes, I know." But he left the tech there to share her remaining praise of Jilly with the sleeping Dr. Carter. Taking off, he followed the little blue streak, full of energy that he didn't yet have, and brains that he never would. Her dark hair flying loose behind her a beacon he followed through the tents.

Becky Sorenson looked like an angel. At least the kind Jillian had always imagined as a kid – rosy lips, pale skin in peaches and cream, with a cinnamon dusting of freckles. Vibrant hair in shades of red reserved only for the very lucky. Colors she herself would never possess.

Jillian looked at the doctor lying there. She certainly didn't look like a world class biologist. She looked like another version of Snow White. They ought to get her a bouquet and glass case and let her wait for Prince Charming. In Jillian's estimation that part should be played by Leon Peppersmith. He was huge and handsome and sharp as a tack. And since Becky wasn't awake to say what her preferences were, Jillian would decide for her. Although she couldn't even force a mental image of Leon prancing a horse through the forest, looking for a princess. Possibly wearing tights.

She almost laughed.

And the thought disintegrated. Becky's knight wouldn't show. He had died of a blow to the head. Something any one of the handful of CDC docs could have fixed had they been anything other than comatose. Leon had been one of a few who had died, not due to the reversal, but to 'other' causes.

At least Becky wouldn't know that he hadn't survived.

Jordan nearly plowed into her as he entered the tent. She didn't have to turn and look. The labored breathing was all his.

It was only then that the nurse hovering over Dr. Sorenson looked up, stethoscope still in hand. "Her blood pressure is still dropping. Her pulse is uneven and fading." She shook her head, brown curls unruly from all the work. She stepped aside, revealing that the bed next to Becky had the sheet pulled up over the face.

"When did we lose him?" Jillian pointed.

"About two hours ago." The nurse looked over her shoulder at the body, her distress turning to compassion. "The crew hasn't found a place to put him, and we need to tag him so his family can find him."

Jillian's head spun. Again. Another thing her one track mind had never even been concerned with. She had been trained to do these things. Her checklist included 'notify family' and 'label patient,' but it just didn't spring naturally into her mind the way it had for everyone else.

The wedge that had always existed between her and society slipped a little further into the widening crack. With a nod, she checked Dr. Sorenson over for herself. Jordan slipped in beside her, remarkably steady on his feet for having just come around.

With wide eyes Jillian faced him. "It seems the longer they stay under the harder it is to pull out. At first people were waking up left and right. Then it petered off. When you woke up... well, no one else has since." Her shoulders hunched in abject misery. "I'm afraid no one else will." *And I can't tell you how glad I am that you did.*

The ventilator provided a steady rhythm and forced the rise and fall of Becky's chest while Jillian and Jordan worked silently. They ran extra fluid into her.

Becky's heart still beat, only missing the rhythm occasionally. Mostly it was just slowing down. The powerstroke of the left ventricle had reduced to little more than a squish of fluid. The peach tones of her skin, already lacking their usual vibrance, were slipping to grays. Jillian pushed medication after medication, until Jordan's hand on her arm stilled her.

She listened to the infrequent *lub-dub* of Becky's heart fade to just a single sound. Her head snapped up as the ventilator gave one last hiss, then stilled. Jordan stood with his hand draped over the switches he had turned to stop the machinery. The heart monitor gave one last beep, and Jordan turned it off too, before it could go into its synthetic whine, letting everyone within earshot know its patient had died.

She felt her shirt get wet before she realized that she was crying. And threw herself at Jordan, the only remaining human being that she *knew*. His arms wrapped around her. "Jillian, you saved so many."

"But all I can do is watch. I can't change anything."

His hand stroked her hair, following it all the way down to the middle of her back. Her eyes squeezed against the visions in her head, and focused where she had buried her face in the front of Jordan's jacket. "I didn't *save* any of them."

"Yes, you did."

"Before they fell, some of the men called their friends, they told them what was coming. Told them to get inside and lie down at the first signs of nausea. They saved people all over the world." She shook her head against his chest, leaving smears of tears darkening the fabric. "Even here, so many were inside, on gurneys, lying on the ground. Some even had IVs run on each other...." A hiccup forced its way up her throat, escaping in an embarrassing giveaway. "But I couldn't get them all inside..."

"You saved David."

Her breath let out. That she had done.

His voice flowed over her again like a wave. "I *told* them all to get inside – to lie down."

She sniffed. "*You* saved them."

"But the ones who didn't... well, that's what they *chose*. You shouldn't feel guilty about that."

She hadn't saved anyone, really.

She chewed at her lower lip, still not looking up at him. Taking deep breaths, she fought the feeling of being out of control.

Something that she hadn't known was so very frightening until just this moment when she admitted it.

And her brain started ticking. Fifty three hours she had been awake. And slept only six. In small shifts, too. She'd eaten only five small meals in that time. Thank God for the IV she had worn up until this morning.

No wonder she was so tired. The world had slipped away, and she was powerless against the changes that had come…that were still coming.

So she wasn't surprised to realize that Jordan was carrying her out of the tent, even though she didn't know when she had passed from standing on her own feet to having her weight entirely borne by him. As she looked over his shoulder she saw the curly haired nurse tug at the sheet to Becky Sorenson's bed, and pull it up over her face.

Jillian squeezed her eyes to block the image, but it followed her.

As if in reaction to the unwanted sight, she felt her brain just shut off.

Chapter 18

She had been trying to wake up for a long time. Maybe two or three hours. It wasn't her usual sleep. She heard sounds around her. Another person, several maybe.

And the thread snapped – the one that had held her back from consciousness. Even though her eyes wouldn't obey and open, and her fingers wouldn't quite respond to her commands. She was finally truly alert. Inside her own body.

The person next to her spoke in deep tones, but not to her. "How are you feeling?"

"Ehhh." Just a moan from the second voice – whoever the first person was talking to.

"We're glad to see you're awake." Becky could sense or smell the man. She knew that he had shifted, that he was looking down at her. "From this twitching, it looks like your friend will wake up here really soon, too."

Becky tried again to make her fingers move, her toes flex, her eyelids spring open. None of it worked as she intended. But she must have accomplished something, because smooth warm fingers glided into place, holding her hand. The deep voice spoke again. "I know you're coming around. Just relax, it'll come. I remember."

She breathed deeply, then fought pain as sharp light penetrated her vision. Her face pulled tight to counteract the intrusion.

"That's my girl." The hand continued to hold hers, to squeeze occasionally with human contact, but he spoke to the blurry voice. "Would you like some juice?"

A bell rang, and reverberated around her skull. "Aauuuhhh." She was shocked that the sound had been her own voice.

Another voice joined in, "What can I bring?"

"Juice. Several cups."

"Are these the last of them?"

She felt the vibrations of his body movement through his hand. He had nodded. "Probably."

Becky worked her mouth, the feeling of age-old cotton making her wish she was still under. "Mmmmhhhh."

"Dr. Sorenson, can you squeeze my hand?" The voice was close, she could feel his heat and detect that he was blocking part of the light that was causing her so much pain. She pushed aside the smell of the onions he had eaten recently.

She thought about squeezing. She could feel his fingers, but was unsure if she had actually accomplished the motion until he spoke. "All right, then." Pause. She waited for him to flip up her eyelids and shine a penlight in them. But he didn't. "Can you say your name?"

"Becky." It croaked out of her mouth like frogs escaping flashlights in the night.

"Perfect."

It had been far from it, she knew. Maybe the man was a dentist – that's how he could understand what surely was nothing more than a mumble.

"What are you giggling about?" His voice shook revealing that he, too, was laughing.

"You understand me."

He smiled. A kind, round face, with uneven teeth, and brown eyes.

She blinked slowly, immediately blurring her vision.

"If I sit you up will you drink this for me?"

The cup he held up looked like...urine.

She must have cringed. He spoke again. "It's apple juice. It's what we've got."

So she nodded. Her neck releasing loud moose noises within her skull as she moved it.

"I'm Jack. Your RN." He didn't hold out his hand, and Becky figured they'd already done their handshake. In efficient movements she was sitting, the gurney creaking louder than her own bones, and he had pushed her hands around the cup, helping her bring it to her lips.

Heaven.

She hadn't believed apple juice could be so good. She'd hated it since her mother had poured it down her throat day after day as a kid. But now...now it was sweet and clear and took her home.

To the living room with the old couches. The wear on the front carpet leading a path out the front door and continuing onto the paint and down the porch steps. The sagging split rail fence that greeted a person as they entered the yard, and asked them to return when they left.

Why had she memorized it so intently when she was there last?

Sitting bolt upright, Becky whacked her head on something.

No.

That wasn't right. Sitting had simply caused a headache the proportions of which matched a good whack upside the head. "My family!"

Did they know about her?

Becky knew the Nevada site had been under for four days before people started waking up. Were they worried about her?

The voice interrupted her worrying. "The lists are coming in as we find things out."

"Lists?" The light was still too bright and she shielded her face from it.

"Survivors. Who's passed."

Looking at her expression, the RN continued with his explanation, "The reversal hit everyone, right after it hit here. It was a few hours behind in some places, in others a whole day. But pretty much everywhere is waking up now."

Becky inhaled. *Pretty much everyone was waking up.* "So the lists of the dead are short?"

His kind smile faltered. "No."

"What?" How could that be? Nevada had lost some, but…

"We've lost over half."

"What?!" Again the pain of a baseball bat hitting her head. "Ahhhhh." She leaned herself back, squeezing her eyes against the light and the fire of tears. Again she said the two most important words. "My family?"

"I'll bring you the books."

Books? They had been 'lists' but now they were 'books'?

He squeezed her hand again, this time in sympathy and not as a medical check. And then Jack disappeared out the tent door into the bright world beyond.

When she opened her eyes, Becky found her tent mate staring at her in deep sympathy. She tried to change the subject from her tears. "Do you know what day it is?"

"It's Tuesday…I'd like to look at the lists, too. I have family all around here. Aunts, uncles, cousins. I already know my friend, Peter Wilson, he was a tech, didn't make it." Tears welled in his own eyes, and he showed no manly concern about hiding them from her, a total stranger. "He ran my IV for me, and made me get in and lie down." She saw and heard the intake of air, "He saved me."

But her sympathy was running low. Still she gave it her best shot, even though to her own ears it sounded hollow and vague. "Then he accomplished what he wanted, I'm sure. We're all going to lose someone in this."

Her words only served to wind herself up tighter. To make the outer edges of the world go fuzzy. Her family wasn't small. If they'd lost just over half…

She didn't want to think about it. So she checked out her IV, noted that vitamins had been added. Just when she had forced her breathing back to a shallow imitation of normal, Jack sauntered in carry reams of printed pages.

Becky sat herself upright. Ignoring the pounding in her head, she held her hands out. But Jack wouldn't give it to her, "Now, what city do you need?"

"Knoxville." Jack started to hand her the blue covered book. But Becky remembered. She had sent them to Aaron. "No! Charlotte!"

"North Carolina?"

She nodded frantically, barely able to wait while Jack thumbed through the books looking for that county. "They were visiting, so that's where they'd be listed, right?" *Right*?

"Your guess is as good as mine." But with two hands he held out a gray bound volume, green and white striped computer paper was compiled and clipped inside, looking like an ancient corporate budget.

She set it carefully across her lap, barely registering that the man in the next bed had asked to see the local book. Lifting the front cover she saw only the word LIVING at the top of the page, and immediately with no fanfare it listed names, social security numbers and addresses on some. A few were just descriptions. In the order they'd been found. No real rhyme or reason.

Names sounded familiar to her, but not familiar enough to pause and think back. She was searching frantically for her family. She found her father. Her breath escaping. She had one.

Three pages later she found Brandon. Both listed at Aaron's address.

Twenty pages later she had found no one else. Just a half unfinished page, and the top of the next page reading DECEASED, as casually as LIVING had been labeled at the top of the first page.

Breath held, Becky read on. She knew what she would find. Her mother, her brother Aaron, and baby Mel. But she had to know for certain.

She found her brother on the second *deceased* page. Melanie was less than half a page later. Becky felt her lower lip curl, her teeth biting into it in a rabid attempt to stop the tears even if she couldn't stop the knife cutting through her heart.

She blinked it away, telling herself she would let go when she found her mother.

But nineteen pages later she still hadn't.

Jack had stood by patiently, helping Wilson, as his name seemed to be, locate people he knew.

She interrupted, not caring about the manners her mother had drilled into her. Not when she didn't know where her mother was. "What about the people not listed? In either place?"

Jack shook his head. "It usually means they're unknown. Not found. Still comatose." He shrugged. "Like we just put the word out on you two, and a couple others from the past hour. But there's still a good handful of people here who haven't either come around nor given up the ghost yet." He shrugged again, looking like the whole world had gone crazy and he just wanted to be a nurse. *Well,* Becky thought wryly, *the world is now populated with patients.* "Other towns fell after us, so they're coming around later as well. They have even more undecideds."

Undecideds?

That was what you were in college if you didn't know your major. It seemed a remarkably callous label for people who had not yet died.

Her mother was 'undecided'. "When do we find out about them?" She couldn't lose her mother.

"We're getting wires and phone calls and faxes all the time. If you want to give a few names the hub will keep an eye out for them. I think there's a form to fill out. Would you like one?"

A form to fill out?

But Becky held it together enough to nod.

Jack swept away the juice cups and de-cluttered the tiny tent in efficient motions as he made his way off to retrieve the offensive forms. But Becky stopped him short. "Do you have the local lists?"

She had to do something to keep from breaking down. She couldn't turn into Jell-o now. She forced herself to breathe deeply and evenly. She chewed her lips. And graciously accepted the green bound forms.

She found no one on the LIVING list. A few techs, a few nurses. But of the small handful she really knew, there were no names.

The DECEASED list held just as much mystery as answers. Only two names were on the list. Early on, Leon Peppersmith. His even had an asterisk by it. The small star took her to the ends of the row where it was listed: *blow to the head*. She had to flip back to the first page to discover that the notation meant he had died of something other than the reversal.

Blow to the head.

Had he fallen while he carried her? What? God forbid, murdered?

Becky shuddered, and shoved it out of her mind. There wasn't a damn thing she could accomplish from this hospital bed.

Jillian Brookwood and David Carter II were missing. But on a fresh page, labeled DECEASED and obviously quite recently added, were ten names. Dr. Jordan Abellard appeared near the end.

Jordan hauled Jillian back to their tent, her weight getting heavier every minute. He'd barely come out of a coma himself. But he wasn't about to complain, everyone was making superhuman efforts. Trying to keep as many alive as possible didn't allow for relaxation and recuperation. Unless you were Doctor David Carter the second.

The geologist sat propped up on the gurney that Jordan had initially put Jillian on several days earlier, toying with his IV and drinking a soda. Jordan resisted the urge to tell him that both actions were bad for his health. But then again, if you were willing to pitch yourself down the stairs to get out of helping, then Jordan didn't have a real vested interest in making things rosy.

He pressed his lips together, forcing the thought aside. David certainly hadn't thrown himself down the stairs. The man was no idiot. It was just circumstance. So he forced a smile. "Hi David. Are you feeling better?"

Dr. Carter nodded, then motioned with his chin – probably everything else hurt – to Jillian lying limp in Jordan's arms. "Is she okay?"

Again a nod was sufficient. Jordan spoke coolly as he arranged her on the bed he had vacated only hours before. "She's either sound asleep or passed out. Too much work in too little time with too little to eat."

"So what will you do?"

Jordan shrugged. "Let her sleep. Maybe run an IV if it looks like she's dehydrated." Out of habit and the necessity to do something, he checked all her vital signs. Of course they all checked out. Jillian probably wouldn't suffer her pulse or blood pressure to be anything less than textbook. He asked David if there was anything he needed. Without coming right out and saying that quiet was necessary for Jillian to sleep, he suggested reading materials, or a headset.

But David shook his head, and rolled away, making like sleep wasn't far off the horizon for him either, and Jordan was grateful for that small thing. He closed the flaps to the tent, hoping to create a false darkness in the room, but only succeeding in marginally dimming it. The tent leaked sunlight like a sieve.

He considered letting himself back out, thinking he should go and be useful. But David's chest was already rising and falling in steady cadence. And just the short time watching the two of them sleep was enough to lull Jordan into a chair. Painfully uncomfortable, he leaned back, lolled his head to one side until it contacted the pole of the tent.

He watched Jillian lie still on the gurney for…

Well he wasn't sure. Only that he dreamed Landerly had shown up and was shaking his shoulder.

Then the tent pole thunked his head as Landerly tried a little harder.

With a purposeful wrenching of his eyes, Jordan got them open to see that Dr. Landerly was, in fact, standing beside him, a cane clutched in his hand. As Jordan looked, he became more convinced that he had woken within his sleep state.

The left side of the older doctor's face had a bit of slack to it. His left arm seemed a little less rigid than usual. But Landerly looked just as formidable as ever. And now in his right hand he grasped the cane, either as a walking implement or a weapon.

Jordan had no doubts that Landerly would never use the cane on anyone. He could simply point out faults and weaknesses until you admitted you were lower than worms, and begged to be beaten instead of fired. "Sir?"

The dream vision answered back. "Abellard. Good to see you awake. How long has our girl been under?"

He looked at his watch. 5pm. It was getting dusky outside and that translated to a portion of the dark he had strived for inside the tent. "Five hours. I figure she has another ten before she even begins to catch up on what she's missing."

"What the hell are you talking about?" Landerly lifted the cane from the ground as he gestured.

Jordan sniffed away the last clinging vines of sleep and told Landerly. "I think she only slept about six hours over more than two days." He sighed. "And about worked herself to death."

"You've been asleep."

It was just a statement. But from Landerly's mouth it was a bit more of an accusation. Why wasn't Jillian awake to talk to the boss? The two of them would be laughing like old pals in a heartbeat. But no, he got Landerly all to himself. He decided if things got tough, he'd just sic David on the old man. He nodded his acquiescence – yes, he'd been sleeping, God forbid.

Landerly leaned down. "She's not asleep."

"What?"

"She's comatose." Landerly walked over to her and lifted her hand. She showed no response, neither to the invasion of another person moving her limbs, nor to the drop her arm endured flaccidly back to the mattress when Landerly let it go. "I checked her. She's showing nothing."

Jordan was on his feet and wide awake. But this time he was desperately trying to talk himself into the fact that it was a dream. "She was asleep when I brought her in here." He paused, thinking back. "She almost passed out, but she showed movement. She murmured or something…"

"Well, not now." Jordan heard Landerly drop himself into the chair he had just vacated. But he kept his back turned. He blinked. He breathed deeply. Did everything he could think of to wake himself up from this. He did everything he could think of to wake Jillian up.

But she didn't rouse. Not to pressure or pain. Not to her name or his. And he realized that she hadn't moved from where he had laid her when he brought her in.

Through tightly clenched teeth, he turned back to Landerly and asked, "Well, what do we do now?"

But he saw his anger was misplaced. Landerly's cane sat off to one side, his head rested in his right hand, and that elbow rested on the arm of the chair, as though the effort to hold any part of him upright was just too much.

Jordan didn't ask. He suspected that Landerly's own coma hadn't been too kind to him. He hadn't been sure the old man would make it out. Especially when, with the final sweep of the reversal, so many young, vibrant, and perfectly healthy people were succumbing.

But the poles had swapped. David had predicted it and, as usual, he'd been right. Everyone had fallen under for at least some period of time. The world had lost billions as best he could figure. The whole population reduced by slightly more than half.

No more China's Only Child Policy. Property values would be reasonable again in New York and LA. There was clean-up to do – everywhere. The earth was shattered as far as he was concerned. And fallout was going to last for decades, minimum. At no point in his memory could he pinpoint a worldwide disaster like this since the dinosaurs had died out.

But at least, he had thought, they were finished.

Now was the time to pick themselves up and move on.

But Jillian…

How was she under again?

What the hell did she have?

He threw all these questions at Landerly and then some. But Landerly shrugged, said he didn't know.

Jordan shook her again. But, of course, there was no response.

His eyes blazed holes in the top of Landerly's head, the only part the old man was showing. "How the hell are we supposed to figure this out? She's the brains of this operation!" He gestured back at the prone form in her blue scrubs.

That, at least, made Landerly look up at him. Finally some strength in his eyes. "This took my wife and daughter away from me….and I don't mean to sound horribly trite and cliché, but I *did* spend too much time at the office. And I *do* regret it." He stood to his full height, able to look down on Jordan if only by half an inch. "But I will not let you tell me that we're useless without her. You and I have more brains in our heads than ninety-nine-point-nine percent of the population, and we are trained for this. So let's get a move on."

He began walking out of the tent. "Draw her blood and meet me in the lab. We have profiles to review and phone calls to make."

Her eyes hurt. Her fingers twitched randomly. And there didn't seem to be anything she could do about it. With effort Jillian pried her eyes open. The tent top came into view again along with a weird sort of déjà vu.

She remembered she had practically passed out after Becky had died. And Jordan carried her back and laid her on the gurney.

She looked around, the dim light in the tent telling of evening.

But something was wrong.

It took her a moment to place it.

She'd been moved. The gurney where Jordan had laid her down, the last thing she remembered, was at a ninety degree angle to the one she was on. She could see that it was vacant when she bent her neck back and looked. The empty bed was military sharp, the sheets drawn up quarter-bounce tight.

She breathed in, thinking that she felt well rested. And wondered why they had left her alone. *Well, I needed sleep, that's for sure.* But it had only been about five hours according to her watch.

Or…twenty-nine hours.

That was a distinct possibility. That would explain the well-rested feeling. Much better than five hours.

David!

She was in his bed. So where was he? And why hadn't she woken up when they moved her?

With an audible groan and severe pressure in her head, she swung her legs over the side. Stopping there to take a rest and wait for the little man with the ball-peen hammer in her head to stop whacking her, she squeezed her eyes. And heard the muscles move in what sounded like a mid-pitch thunder roll.

She must have sat there for about five minutes by her musing. Brain churning despite the pain.

Twenty-nine hours. Definitely.

That was the only explanation for her muscles feeling so unused. She forced her breathing to deepen, her ribs feeling the stretch again.

A normal life would be so appreciated. Waking up in her apartment. Going in to work to fill out forms about botulism. Or salmonella. Maybe a pet dog to keep her company. Or a cat.

With sadness she wondered if both species still existed. That was a bizarre thought. A world without cats. Mushu. A portrait of her beloved childhood kitty, the first and only fuzzy pet she'd ever had, popped into her head.

She pushed off from the gurney, landing on shaky legs and, using the bed frame, stabilized herself. Another minute. Time to walk.

Just then she heard a voice. Her reaction time being slow, she was barely able to shield her eyes as the tent flap was thrown in. Because she was facing west, the sunset poured through the open side, illuminating the silhouette of a woman holding back the heavy fabric.

"Oh my God, Doctor Brookwood! You're up!"

"Of course I'm up." Why wouldn't she be? Again something niggled at the back of her brain. She knew that voice.

As the woman approached into the darker portions of the tent, she developed eyes and features. Lucy. Jillian sniffed. She blinked. Hadn't Lucy died? Well, whoever was keeping the records had done a crappy job. She wondered who else was mis-recorded. Her own family. Jordan's. She shuddered.

"Is something wrong?" Lucy tilted her head as if trying to see her more clearly.

"No. It's nothing." But Jillian wondered. She held her tongue, figuring Lucy wouldn't want to know she'd made the 'dead' list. Or maybe she would. "It's just...I thought I saw your name on the 'deceased' list. You might want to call your family." Lucy raised her eyebrows disbelievingly, and turned to a physician who was standing right beside her. The young man shrugged and Lucy turned back to Jillian. "Dr. Brookwood, I'll check that right out. But if you'll just sit back, Dr. Lee will take all your vital signs."

"Vital signs?" Jillian almost laughed. "Wow. Are y'all getting paranoid?" But she knew what it was like to have a non-compliant patient, so she shrugged out of the left sleeve of her jacket, being careful not to drag the cuff along the IV insertion site on the back of her hand. But she didn't even scrape it, just continued to question the doctor.

Her first thought was that he was very intent on listening to her pulse as he took her BP. He didn't even make eye contact. As though he had never done this before. Her second thought was that he was young. Which was disturbing, because *she* was considered young to be a practicing physician.

He stood upright and nodded at her. "It's all textbook."

She smiled, feeling a little condescending, even though she wished it would go away. "I'm always 120 over 80." He wrote in her chart, having had it thrust out to him by Lucy. And Jillian startled. She hadn't remembered to pull a single chart this whole time. It was the right protocol but it hadn't even crossed her mind. And clearly the record keeping was getting screwed up if Lucy Whitman had made the 'dead' list.

But she shook it off. "What's with the complete set of vitals after a nap? Did it concern you that I slept so long?"

"Well, it was a *long* nap." Lucy looked at her young physician in some side glance that Jillian couldn't decipher. But she didn't want to. She hadn't ever been able to make hide nor hair of Lucy. So she let it be.

She started out of the tent. "I'm going to go now." She had to find Jordan, and David. And the more she thought about it, they needed to be in charge of notifying Becky Sorenson's family, whichever of them had survived. And Leon Peppersmith's, too. She'd let the person in charge handle the rest. But she felt she owed it to those two families. And she knew Jordan would agree. But as she passed the front entry of the tent the young doctor's hand shot out and grabbed her upper arm. The grip wasn't harsh, but she also wasn't going to go anywhere until he decided to release her.

And that pissed her off. Trying to stay as level-headed as she could, she ground the words out between her teeth. "Would you mind explaining to me why you're restraining me?"

She felt the heat flare under her skin as he had the balls to look sheepish. "Oh, I'm not restraining you, doctor."

"Then remove your hand."

He did, but stepped in front of her. And just as she was about to yell at him, he spoke. Again sounding trite. "I just think it's important that you understand that you just woke from the coma that you saw so many patients go into."

Her muscles relaxed. "Well now, there's the problem. I was actually out of this coma before any of you were. I woke up first." She continued even though they were clearly questioning her. Sharing furtive looks as if she were a child. "I went back to sleep because I was exhausted. I had spent so much time hauling people inside and checking them out that I practically passed out."

She could see that they didn't believe her, but she had really ceased to care. They had been busy sleeping their time away, while she had worked herself to the bone. Then the little smartass in the white jacket tried again to stop her from leaving the tent. "Dr. Brookwood…"

"Dr…" She read the name on the front of his jacket, since she had forgotten it precisely the moment after Lucy had told her. "Lee." She'd had enough. "I'm leaving."

"I don't think that's wise."

Her teeth clenched again. As if it wasn't bad enough that the world had dropped dead one by one around her. That Landerly was threatening to name the damn thing after them. This little…whatever he was, was trying to restrain her. "I understand that you don't think that. I don't care."

"As your physician–"

She didn't let him get any further than that. "You aren't my physician. You'll do well to remember that I am a physician."

He opened his mouth and she didn't let him start, just gave him something to chew on. "I am also your superior."

With that he huffed out his breath and turned to Lucy Whitman. "Well, I guess we've done what we can."

"All right then." Lucy handed him the chart. "We did the right thing. If she won't listen then that's her own fault." The two of them strolled out of the tent looking like old chums. Like there hadn't been a fully charged atmosphere just a second before.

But Jillian took it as a breath of relief. The air was clear now. They were gone.

And, as usual since this whole thing had started, she had plenty to do.

She had to find Jordan, and see where he had moved David. And…

Jillian blinked.

She had just realized that she never found out what had happened to Dr. Landerly.

Her chest constricted a little at the thought that he was probably gone. She'd seen his labs, and he had all the hallmarks of the ones who had failed early.

David's stare had gone blank.

Jordan had witnessed the blow to pride the man had taken just to ask for morphine, and he had happily pushed the drug into David's IV. It took only a second away from the paperwork that he was pouring over with Landerly. And for a moment it took his mind off Jillian.

It was all insane.

Jillian and David had seemed immune. But she had slipped back under – for no apparent reason. Why hadn't David gone back under? It had to have something to do with the pattern of exposure. Jordan's hands clicked through the rhythms of capping the needle and flicking it into the sharps container while his brain wandered through problems.

He had identical exposure to Jilly, up to a point. When he had gone to Lake James he had continued going in and out of the weaker bubbles. Jillian and David had stayed in Nevada, and had wandered into the path of that sweep – which felled everyone in its path, healthy, old, young. And now they were showing different symptoms than everyone else.

His theory was Swiss cheese it had so many holes. The problem was that they weren't just different *now* – they had been different even as far back as Nevada. When that reversal had swept, Jillian and David had walked out. And the way Jilly had told it, they had stood within the bubble and watched others walk in and fall at their feet. So they had to have been mutated, or different, *before* that.

If only Jillian would wake up and tie the loose ends.

Landerly hadn't come into the tent to check on her. The old man was too much like Jillian. If it was scientifically interesting he would be able to stand for hours and watch a patient breathe. After about two minutes of that he would be able to point out that every seventh breath was some micro-seconds shorter than the others and why that was significant. Then he'd check the chart for the patient's name. But if there was nothing new about this patient, someone else could make the effort.

So Jordan had called his father, leaving Landerly alone with the reams of lists. Glad to hear Jackson's voice, and no longer startled by the fact that his Dad would cry over the phone. Jordan didn't know what had connected them again, finally, but he wasn't about fight it or hinder it in any way.

Now he watched as David passed through the initial phases of morphine intoxication. David's musculature relaxed, his face no longer quite so tense. The glazed look wasn't uncommon either. But David hadn't been really talkative since they had brought Jillian back in.

When Jordan explained that she was under again, Carter had wrenched himself around trying to get a look at her, even though she was directly behind his head, and the shoulder harness prevented him from doing anything of the sort.

What Jordan hadn't been able to get the geologist to say what he was feeling. Jordan had two good guesses. The first was that he was actually concerned for Jillian, which normally Jordan would have dismissed. But Dr. Carter seemed to have developed an attraction to the little dark spitfire and Jordan certainly couldn't fault that. The second option was that he and Jillian had gone step by step together. Immune in Nevada. Falling under here just after everyone else. Waking early. It was a logical progression that David was watching her to see what was coming next, if he might fall back under as well.

But he just stared at the white walls of the tent. He said he was writing his paper in his head while he waited for his laptop. Someone had confiscated it for medical use, while he'd been recuperating from his fall, and the staff had yet to locate it. David wasn't happy about that either. His theories were floating out there in the ether, he had said.

Jordan watched while David sank into a peaceful slumber, then woke the man, just for a second. Just to be sure.

Then he steeled himself, knowing he had no more cause to avoid Landerly, which he knew in his heart of hearts was exactly what he was doing. And he marched himself right back into the records tent.

Landerly didn't look up, or acknowledge his return in any way other than to begin speaking. Jordan briefly wondered if Landerly had simply continued the conversation all along, not even realizing he was gone. He suppressed the smile that fought to be free and tried to pay attention.

"We don't have an age bias. Or a race bias. Nor seemingly a continental bias."

"Why 'seemingly'?" Jordan seated himself and picked up one of the tomes.

"Many continents aren't fully reporting – like Africa. There's an interesting case. With their numbers of AIDS infected I'm curious how they'll fare. But they're barely reporting at all. The towns that are look like they match our numbers here and Europe."

"What about India?"

"Same. Their reporting is better, but not great." He removed his glasses, aging himself ten years in the process, and rubbed at his eyes. But his voice continued. "There's some issue with the Australian Outback as well. There are a lot of people, some aboriginal, that may never have been accounted for. And we don't know what happened to them."

Jordan thought for a minute. They had been frantically writing everything down as they thought of it and discounted it. Although he hadn't been sure what it mattered until Jillian had slipped back under. But now there was a goal – they had to see if there was any way to pull her out. And help anyone who went back under like her.

"What about gender bias?"

"What?" Dr. Landerly had already engrossed himself in the next long list, jotting on it in slashes of pencil, with no regard for the fact that the book would be looked over by anyone with family in that area. That they might not want to see Landerly's number counting or comments on age and race in their family member's margins.

Jordan spoke, knowing he was rehashing, but thinking that it might trigger something important. "The women went under first, pretty much everywhere. So this thing does have some sort of gender distinction. The only person who's slipped back under is female."

"Hmmmmm." He flipped through several pages. "I haven't seen it in the survival rates."

Jordan just set down his pencil and began flipping pages looking for anything unusual. But after several hours his butt hurt. He hadn't found anything that stood out. And he needed to check on David.

And Jillian.

Without a word, he got up and walked out. He couldn't go into the tent though. And without even a hesitation stalked past, going through the dark of night, under glaring overhead field lights creating enough light between the tents to see by. Stepping carefully on the cold dark grass, he made his way into the now functioning cafeteria and got himself a soda. Which he'd gotten hooked on again after having practically given them up when he graduated med school. Oh well. He wasn't dead. He'd survived a disease worse than the plague. What was a soda going to do him really?

With his soda in hand, he forced himself back to the tent that Jillian and David shared. Afraid of what he would find when he checked Jillian, he tried to rouse David first. And had no success.

Tamping down the frisson of fear that escaped up through his senses, he set down the drink and went about it the right way. But he got no response. "David!" He tapped on the man. Pinched him. Yelled again.

Nothing. The geologist didn't even sputter when Jordan yanked up his eyelids and shone his penlight directly in. Damn the man.

"Landerly!" He used all his lungpower. "Somebody get me Dr. Landerly from the records tent!"

A tech popped his face in and asked Jordan to repeat the instruction. Jordan thanked him and went through with the rest of a vital signs check. After he'd been through everything he knew to do, twice, he gave up and turned to Jillian. Landerly walked in just as Jordan finished taking her vitals.

"Landerly." He heard the shaking in his voice, and there wasn't much he could do about it. "Her respirations are at sixteen."

"So? That's within normal."

He shook his head. "Jillian's always textbook. She's always eighteen. Right when she went under the first time and this time, too. When she's asleep…she's eighteen."

Landerly cocked his head.

But Jordan kept going. "She's slipping."

Chapter 19

With her lower lip between her teeth, Jillian walked out into the dark beyond her tent. People scuttled here and there, each seemingly with a purpose. Many of them held charts, and most of the tents were lit like Jack-o-lanterns, a soft glow perfusing through the canvas and pouring blindingly out of the openings. In one of the open tents doctors in white coats were passing papers around in a lively debate while a mechanic in the background took a wrench to one of the UV-and-visible-light machines. It looked like a Christmas card for the scientific community.

It was organized. Purposeful.

What a difference a day could make.

Jillian took a deep breath and found her own purpose. She was starving. All the family notifications could wait, but she'd pass right back out if she didn't eat something. With determination, she headed toward the building, passing square white tents, the flaps ruffling in the breeze, and she pulled her jacket a little tighter.

With luck, she'd find Jordan in the cafeteria. Maybe even David – if she'd been asleep for twenty-seven hours and woke up in his bed then his hip must have been well enough to get into a wheelchair. He could be anywhere, as long as he had someone to keep an eye on him. She figured he'd be downgraded from morphine to Percocet by now.

And if they weren't there, then at least someone she knew would be. Throwing open the door she was assaulted by the smells of cheap Italian food. The pasta wouldn't be quite al dente, and the sauce would be thin. And the bread would be steamy, meaning not crusty.

And it would be heavenly.

She followed her nose, not even bothering to look around for anyone she knew. If they wanted her, they would have to yell. Loud.

She grabbed a thick Corian tray and piled it high with food as she moved down the line. The bread was in her mouth before she even began ladling up soggy looking green beans.

But in minutes she was sitting alone at a table, methodically moving the fork from plate to mouth, eating as fast as she could, breathing deeply and inhaling the smells until she had finished every bite.

After sitting for a moment, she hauled herself up and stacked her tray on top of the trashcan as she exited into the cold night air. The sky had gone from trailing reds, that she remembered as fact and not as feeling, to dark navy set with bright stars.

For the first time in her life it gave a deep feeling of belonging, of being a tiny part of something else. Jillian stood silently. Digesting. Breathing. Staring. Wondering if the world would shift again beneath her feet. If she'd get sick, pass out, fall under again. But she was fairly confident that it would stay steady now. That her deep inhales wouldn't draw in anything dangerous.

It was all broken by the revving of an engine as the car pulled into the drop-off lane, reminding her that they had hijacked a high-school.

Her brows pulled together.

If the car was pulling up, that meant it had been somewhere, even if it was just around town.

The reports told that the whole world had switched. That everyone had gone under and either woken up or died. But that meant as soon as they cleared things up here, they could go home.

Suddenly the air wasn't so inviting. She didn't feel so safe.

She longed for the streets of Atlanta. Not even Signal Mountain where she'd grown up. Georgia was the home she had chosen. She could go back to her job, maybe even get in a few days of nine-to-five, write some reports. Jillian snorted to herself, likely she would spend the rest of her career writing *this* report.

Turning away from the parking lot, she heard another car turning over and pulling out, more evidence of freedom seeping in through the closed gates of the city. She headed back into the tents to find Jordan and David. A smile played across her lips. At least David wouldn't be able to move very fast, and that ought to make it easier to catch up to him.

In her own tent again, she was shocked to see that all evidence of Jordan was gone. Jillian frowned before realizing that he had probably moved back upstairs.

Without thought, she turned and pounded her way up the four flights. Thinking that signs of David had been removed from the tent, too, and he certainly wouldn't have moved back up stairs he couldn't climb. But she continued. Empty of life and sound, the dim hallways were lit only at every fourth fluorescent, to give you a way to see, but saving energy as well.

Jillian started to laugh out loud at that, but stopped herself when she heard the noise start a macabre echo down the length of the hallway. Energy conservation would be a whole different ballgame with less than half of last week's occupants now on earth.

Reaching the top, she saw that the room signs, the plain hand-printed taped-up notes, had all been pulled down. But she found 204, and turned the knob.

The room was lit only by the light peeking in from the hallway, and that was low at best. She flipped the switch, squinting against the instantaneous full glare. And blinking at the...lack...of everything.

The cots were stacked in the corner. No duffles or briefcases were anywhere. The maps, where Jordan had plotted the growth of the bubbles and the sites where people had gone under, were gone. As well as the flow charts and the grids of lab values, all pulled from the walls and absent.

With a sigh, Jillian switched off the light, leaving the hallway a dim shade of gray as her eyes adjusted. She took off at a jog, back the way she had come. Rushing through the halls at a ground eating pace, she only slowed when she hit the tops of the stairs, thinking of David's fall. Tightly holding the railing, she forced herself to slow down, finally reaching the bottom after what felt like an eternity.

As she shoved open the double doors out onto the field of tents she was greeted by the sounds of humanity – busy people wandering in the glow of the corner floodlights, just not very many of them. The wind shifted and caught a faint odor, carried in from beyond the tent city. Her nose twitched at the decaying flesh that was more a slight burning sensation than any real odor. But then the wind must have changed direction again, and it was gone.

Making her way into the maze, she said hellos to those she recognized and those she didn't. Finally arriving at the records tent, she pushed back the canvas and startled the person inside. "Can I help you?" He sat by a bank of phones, his hands cradling a yellow legal pad filled with lists. People to call. Places to hear from. Faxes to send.

"Please." She smiled even though she was frustrated that her own search had turned up fruitless. "Where can I find Dr. Abellard and Dr. Carter?"

The man blinked. His brows drew together, but not in thought. He looked concerned. For the life of her, Jillian couldn't figure out why, and she was too tired to work at it. So she simply leveled a look at him that she wasn't going to wait very long. And he got to work. Pushed his glasses up his nose and began thumbing through a list of names and tent numbers. *Damn, everyone had gotten organized while she'd been asleep.*

"Dr. Carter is in tent forty-three."

"And where is that?"

He smiled again, a fake look that mean nothing but that she was being placated. "There are fifteen tents per column. Starting on the left, from the cafeteria. They number front to back and then snake back to front and so on."

She nodded. David was near the back of the third row. "And Dr. Abellard?"

The man tilted his head. "Dr. Abellard passed away a good number of days ago. I'm surprised no one told you."

Jillian sighed and shook her head.

For having all their charting done, and numbering the tents, they had only achieved the look of organization.

Because their lists were fucked-up.

David bit back a low moan. He ached everywhere. They hadn't woken him up for his Percocet. And he needed his Percocet. Every muscle protested as he moved it. Each piece of him creaked and pulled.

It was deep into night inside the tent. Even though he could tell that there was an overhead light just outside. The top of the tent gave an unearthly glow that didn't go further than a foot or two, leaving a fog of black huddling in all the corners and thick along the grass floor.

He breathed deeply, waiting for any monsters within to jump out at him, but after a minute nothing had moved, so he went about pushing himself up on his elbows.

David tilted his head from side to side waiting for the pain to stop his movement. When it came, it was softer than he had expected, a stretching rather than tearing feeling. His head was able to turn further. He could look directly over his right shoulder. Although what that gained him he couldn't say as the tent was nothing but dark.

He breathed again, a little deeper each time, wishing he was repelling along the side of a sheer cliff. Layers of rock and time passing up as he slid down. Each telling of a different age. A few feet of color denoting millions of years of life and death and silts. In pure silence.

Instead, he was dealing with a dry throat. So he couldn't call out to the people who were invariably making the shuffling noises outside his tent, couldn't ask for the medication. Unlike the morphine, it wouldn't make him drowsy. But he would be able to sleep, pain free.

So he worked up a good breath to shout out.

But just as he started to hiss out a noise, the tent flap pulled back, allowing in light and a dark figure he recognized instantly.

"Jillian." He croaked.

"Hey, David." But she didn't look up. Just scratched at the back of her hand, and turned to examine it in the light of the opening.

"What's wrong?" Again it was barely more than a hiss with some voice behind it. But she understood.

"I just…" She turned back to him, then reached up and flipped on the overhead light, drowning him in the harsh glare that receded as his eyes adjusted.

After he stopped squinting he saw that she was holding the back of her hand up to him for inspection. But he didn't see anything. And he shook his head at her. He wasn't a damn doctor so he didn't know what the hell she wanted him to see.

"No mark." She stated the obvious. "There should be a mark."

"Because?"

"Because I wore an IV for four days! It just came out yesterday. But it's gone! There's not even tape residue, that's the weird thing."

"Bully for you." He laid his head back down and found some air. "Can you get me a–"

"Your leg!" She practically screamed, like she had completely lost it. He was getting ready to say so when she yelled it again. "Your leg!"

So he looked, to see the black widow or rattlesnake that was going to end it all.

He'd be grateful if the death went quickly.

But there was nothing there.

Ah, good to know I've discovered the final phase. Utter insanity.

Jillian still stared, and he sighed. She wasn't going to listen about the Percocet.

Her voice was tinny, and frightened sounding. "Where's your cast? I worked really hard putting that thing on you! And your shoulder sling?" Her hands were on him, testing him for injuries and her face was frowning. Not at all the image he had harbored of Jillian feeling him up.

But he looked, and the cast was gone.

With a sharp frown he bent the leg.

"No! Don't re-injure it!" She grabbed for him, trying to stop him, but wasn't fast enough.

His leg bent – and it didn't feel that bad.

So he shrugged. "You must be really good, Doc." He smiled. "Someone must have taken it off. Do you think you can get me a–"

"They wouldn't take it off while you sleep! That's medically contraindicated." She started to walk a tight circle. Thinking and worrying a trail into the grass beneath her feet.

What it seemed was that Jillian was contraindicated with his getting his damned Percocet.

"Where are your x-rays?" Her hands flew across the practically spotless countertop. "Are they in the other tent? When did they move you?"

"I don't know." Juice. Juice would be good, too. Or maybe some liquor. Hysterical woman always went down smoother with a good Jack and Coke.

Jillian planted her fists on her hips and her glare on his face. "How did you not wake up when they moved you? Or cut off your cast?"

Like he would know! He shrugged. "The morphine?"

"We didn't give you that much!" She turned away from him, taking her scrunched up face and his hopes of getting a Percocet. She stepped just outside the tent and grabbed the next tech she could find.

He heard her ask about his x-rays before he decided to close his eyes and wait it out. There were some raised voices, akin to yelling, but not quite a fight. It was clear that Jillian disagreed with the tech and the tech was a bit afraid of the angry doc. Then again, Jillian wasn't just any doctor. She had found this thing. She was hot shit in her little blue scrubs and ponytail, seeming no older than twenty until she opened that way-too-intelligent little mouth of hers.

David smiled. It *was* a hot little mouth, and oh, what it would do to him–

"David! Tell him you fell down the steps!"

Good, just the thing he wanted to rehash. Maybe she'd ask him to tell about the time his Grandfather had walked in on him masturbating, too. That'd be some nice icing on the humiliation cake. So he closed his eyes and mumbled to the tech. "I fell down the steps."

"No you didn't."

David blinked. And stared at the kid. The little prick sounded awfully sure of himself. "Yes, I did. When I walked down. I broke my leg and bruised my ribs."

The tech laughed then, as though he had finally caught on to the joke. "Must have been a bad dream then."

Jillian's mouth hung open for a second. And the tech turned to leave, his white jacket puffing a little in the night breeze. "Wait!"

He turned back, a question in his eyes.

"Bring the portable x-ray, please. I need films on him."

David sighed. Then he popped up. "And Percocet!"

But the tech had already cleared the open space of the tent flap, and Jillian was worrying her circle in the grass again. *Son of a bitch.*

Becky pushed herself off the gurney. She'd fallen back asleep almost instantly. Even as she had been sucked under into dreams she had wondered how a person got so tired in a coma.

But she'd woken back up. The covers mussed and tangled around her. Sleep had been a light wrap that had been easy to throw off this time. And she yawned and stretched and faced a new day.

For a brief moment.

Until she remembered that she had lost Aaron. And Baby Mel.

And maybe her mother had been moved from the 'undecided' list. Either woken up, or died. The heaviness wrapped and suffocated, but Becky shrugged it off. There was nothing she could do. And this wasn't her personal tragedy, either. It was everyone's. She had to go out and help. And maybe that would help her, too.

She leaned out and worked the safety rails. Popping the side down and slipping onto the ground, testing out legs that were barely sturdy enough to stand on. But that made sense.

After a moment she stabilized herself. When the world stopped swirling around her, she cursed her fuzzy mouth. She'd sell her soul for a toothbrush. With a languid blink she realized that she didn't have to.

Her duffle was stuffed under the gurney, all things organized and neat. So she squatted down and rifled through the bag until her fingers brushed against heavy steel. Closing around the barrel, Becky brought the gun out of its hiding place. Clearly no one had searched her bag. With raised eyebrows she rummaged, and triumphantly held up her overnight pack.

A few minutes later she dried and repacked her face soap and toothbrush. For a moment she fingered the bottle of sunscreen, then thought that one day's exposure wouldn't kill her. She needed the feel of pure sunshine on her face.

She needed to walk.

To get away.

She'd have research to do for the rest of her days, trying to prove or disprove what had happened to various species and why. There'd be a whole new field- 'Post pole – reversal biology'. So, for now, she didn't need to do much. It would still be there tomorrow. Right?

But she didn't much care.

There was a civic-center across the street. She could walk over, and get away from the scientists and the bustle and the worry.

Tucking her toiletries bag away, she felt her fingers brush the gun again. She could hear cars on the road. But she didn't really know how it was out there now. With a pause, she grasped the gun and tucked it into the back of her jeans, then rummaged again until she came up with the clear snap case that held three extra tranquilizer darts.

She wouldn't use it unless she had to, and it wouldn't kill anyone.

Becky set out of the tent. Quickly making her way to the edge of the field, she gave one last look over her shoulder then bee-lined for the sidewalk that paced the turnpike. With a startled glance, she saw that the traffic lights were working. But of course they were. This was Oak Ridge – the town of physicists – if they couldn't get things up and running no one would.

The few cars on the road obediently followed the signals, stopping patiently and waiting, even though the road was completely clear. Her brows lifted in shock. And she decided against crossing straight for the civic center, instead going down to the light where she wouldn't have to jaywalk.

Becky was grateful for her decision when a cop pulled into the intersection and sat patiently while she got all the way across the street. The convenience store on the corner called to her.

She walked up the pavement and pulled back the door, startled by the loudness of the bell. Maybe it was just that the bell sounded so much louder now that the world lacked its usual turbulent background noise. She looked about, "Hello?"

But no one answered. She went to ring the old-fashioned ding-bell on the counter but saw the hand-lettered sign instead. *Leave money. Make change. Honor system. Thank you.*

Honor System!?

But there was already a pile of money. Pennies and quarters strewn amongst bills. Just waiting for whoever would take it. Becky could have. She *wouldn't* have. But she *could*.

She contemplated it as long as it took her to decide that she needed two packs of Cheetos and a large fountain cherry coke. She was eating while she added up her purchases and looked up the total on the tax-finder card that had been left on the counter. She took coins in exchange and made her way back out into the strange day.

The civic center loomed ahead, and she crossed through the damp grass, wetting her sneakers and not much caring. There was a crowd gathered in front of a tiny stage; they cheered periodically but she didn't know what at. A few steps further and she began to hear the voice.

"-we have almost all the police force!"

A cheer rose up.

"-and the FBI!"

Another cheer.

"Most of the thieves and murderers gone!" Cheers again. But Becky waited to hear what was coming.

"The CIA gone, too." This time the cheers were punctuated with laughter.

The woman on stage raised her fist high into the air. "I tell you, it is The Ascension!"

The roar of the crowd continued for several minutes this time, while Becky stood on the frayed edges. Her eyebrows knit together, while she contemplated the deaths of Aaron and Melanie. The Ascension?

But the voice broke her thoughts again. "This is God's world. And we are God's chosen. And we are to re-build Eden. Here!"

Becky turned her back to the thunder of cheers. Hadn't these people lost loved ones, too? Or did they just believe that those they had lost weren't worthy?

With a heavy heart, she turned to go back to the safe little village of tents. Back to the place she had so recently sought to escape. This time she had to seriously fight the urge to jaywalk. But God forbid, any of the ascension-ites saw her and deemed her unworthy of Eden.

It was hard to be upset with people who wanted to make heaven on earth, who thought this was a chance to make a better place for everyone. But where did they get off thinking they were the ones God had chosen? Her mother had always told her that those who died were closer to God. So that would make this crowd a composition of the un-chosen by that standard.

Becky almost chuckled.

Jillian woke with a start. The gurney was uncomfortable, although not in any way she could pinpoint. It was also heart-stoppingly high. From up here she could see the large brown envelope that held David's processed x-rays.

She hopped off the bed, the icy dew from the grass seeping instantly through her socks. "Shit." She tried to keep it under her breath. A quick look revealed she hadn't woken David. And the damage was done. She'd change her socks in a minute. First she wanted to see those x-rays.

She had kept several techs up half the night worrying over x-rays and demanding that the films be returned as soon as humanly possible. Every one was making weird faces at her and Jordan hadn't stopped by at all. With a sigh, she held the x-ray up to the light and wondered where he was. No wonder these people all thought he was dead.

Her face pulled into a fierce frown.

There were no marks of a tib-fib fracture at all. She pressed her face closer, looking for details, but still found nothing.

Wanting desperately to believe it was the light, she moved to the opening of the tent, her socks squishing with each step. She frowned, turned the large stiff picture, and frowned again.

Nothing.

Even years-old fractures showed on x-rays. Bones bore the marks of past sins long after they had healed. But David's showed nothing.

Not on the chest x-ray. The tiny fissures she had seen on his earlier films were gone.

And so were the films.

She shook her head.

There was suddenly this veneer of organization. Protocol was being followed to the letter. Yet too much was messed up. David's films had disappeared. Jordan was 'dead'. Lucy was supposed to be dead, but was walking around.

And then the healing thing…

Her IV puncture was minor. But David's tib-fib…that was huge. What if the reversal had sped up the healing process? It was hypothesized that the dinosaurs were so large because the magnetic field had been stronger seventy million years ago – the bigger field supported larger life. Would it also heal faster?

Her heart started racing beyond her standard seventy-two beats per minute. It was enough to make her want to run to the cafeteria and steal a good serrated knife and cut herself, to watch how long it took for the scar to close.

But there had to be a faster way. A better way. Just in case she was wrong.

With her lower lip between her teeth, Jillian thought for a moment, then smiled.

Feeling every step upon the cold grass, she pushed through the flap into bright day. People milled everywhere, and she grabbed a tech as he walked by. "Did you ever break a major bone?"

He shook his head.

Damn.

But she tried again.

And again, until one guy laughed. "I used to skateboard. You'd be hard pressed to find a bone I didn't break!"

"Excellent." She didn't bother to explain much beyond the fact that she wanted to x-ray all of him.

He grinned and handed his tray of urine samples off to another tech passing by, glad to give up the mundane in exchange for being a guinea pig. Jillian wended her way through the tents, the tech in tow behind her. Without much ado, and throwing all of her authority around, she shoved the operator aside and shot every inch of the kid, using up film like there was no tomorrow. Handing each one off in turn, she demanded that it be processed immediately.

The first film came back as she was finishing his jaw, having saved his head for last. And knowing that she'd radiated this kid, top to toe, in the name of science.

She held the film up to the light, with the tech looking over her shoulder. There were two breaks. One clean, the other not so much. "Did you break this twice?"

He nodded, pointing. "Six years ago, and ten years ago."

Jillian frowned, then accepted a second film as it was delivered from the tent next door where two techs were developing the x-rays as fast as they could. He had broken his left femur. It had pins, and bone scarring. She could see the old collarbone break. He even admitted to having cracked it twice in the same place, which was perfectly consistent with the level of damage.

This kid was a mess.

And it was all still there, in black and white and foggy gray.

She asked him questions, pinpointing break after break. And about to give up as she slid the last film into the envelope. "Did you ever break anything else? Anything we didn't look at?"

He shook his head. "I think you caught them all."

Her breath sighed out of her, she'd been so certain that she'd find something. "Well, if you think of anything, come get me. I think I'll be in tent 43."

With a shrug and a sad smile, he went off to find more work to do. And Jillian went back to the tent to find David, and shoes.

Now that she'd proven nothing, the cold had seeped into her feet, and through the bone up her shins. She needed to soak them in a hot bath, or at least wrap them in a foot warmer.

Was it just her and David that healed rapidly?

She slogged around the last corner, looking into the tent at the back of the person standing by the gurney and laughing with David. Memory tugged at her brain, until the woman turned around. And Jillian screamed.

Becky Sorenson was smiling, until the bloodcurdling noise came out of Jillian's mouth.

Techs and physicians rushed through the still open tent flap, dragging in biting air that she didn't – couldn't – feel.

Becky Sorenson was staring at her, questioning the scream that Jillian only just managed to shut down.

"Are you all right?" The physician had shoved everyone else out of the way, and had his fingers on her neck, already checking her pulse. Although why he would check that, when she was clearly alive and upright, was beyond her.

Jillian pushed at him, only wanting him to go away, and beginning to believe she was truly crazy. "I'm fine. I was just startled. Becky reminded me of someone who had died, and I thought...well I had a shock. But I'm good, so you can go..."

She knew she was prattling, but she couldn't stop.

Where was Jordan? He'd make her a flow chart and explain some of this. Or at least offer something. Was she really going insane?

At last when the extra people crowding the tent had been shoved out, Becky pushed her down into a chair. "Do you care to explain what that was really all about?"

Jillian shook her head, knowing she had held Becky's hand while she died, just two days ago. The healing power of the reversals must be even stronger than she had thought. That was the only viable explanation she could come up with. But it was hardly a reasonable one.

She just looked up at her colleague, into Becky's blue eyes, and asked, "Did you ever break any bones?"

"Just my finger. A long time ago." Becky gave her that *are-you-losing-your-mind?* look. "What does that have to do with anything?"

Jillian buried her face in her hands and fought back tears. She couldn't go mad. She just couldn't. She wouldn't survive it. The only thing she always knew to be true was that she could put pieces together. But someone had dumped her puzzle, and nothing fit.

She started with what she knew. "David fell down the steps. About four days ago. Right after he woke up. He broke his leg. But it doesn't show on the x-ray. In fact, someone took off the cast I put on him."

Jillian looked up just long enough to see Becky nod. She continued telling how his shoulder had healed, and how her IV mark was gone.

"Wow. You two were immune for a while, and now you super-heal?" Becky's hands found homes on her hips and she stared at the tent ceiling, making sure the view in her retinas was nothing that would interfere with the cranking of her brain.

But Jillian had no qualms about interrupting Becky's thinking. "No. There's more."

"What?"

"You're the best."

Becky's brows raised.

With a sigh, Jillian let it slip out. "I held your hand two days ago while you died."

"I'm not dead."

"Thanks." Her tongue was laced with dry wit, good to know she'd still have that when they locked her up. "I'm a physician, I already diagnosed that."

"I woke up yesterday at four." Becky shrugged. "I never died."

Jillian felt the old familiar cold steel of a gear click in place in her head. "What day is it?"

"Thursday."

She gulped air. It was a day earlier than she had thought. "But that's it. You *died* yesterday. At…just before four."

"No, I woke up."

Jillian stood, ready to fight. "I checked your pulse. Jordan declared you dead. I watched them pull the sheet over you."

"But I didn't die."

Again, *click,* another gear shifting. "Do you have a twin?"

Becky shook her head and looked at Jillian like she would a small child. "Did you dream it?"

The cold seeped up Jillian's socks into her feet, this time going straight from there to her heart. Becky's voice interrupted her thoughts again, "Because Dr. Abellard died several days ago according to the lists."

Jillian shook her head. "The lists are messed up. Lucy Whitman is listed 'deceased' and she's not. Jordan isn't either. And David fell down the steps." She looked to David, beseeching, knowing that if he didn't corroborate she'd have to check herself in to the loony bin.

Becky looked over at him, too. And much to Jillian's relief, he nodded. "I fell down the last flight of stairs. Broke my hip and leg, dislocated my shoulder, and cracked ribs. I don't feel any of it now. But I remember Jillian pulling on bedsheets and stuffing my shoulder back into place."

It sure wasn't how she'd describe it, but he did get the job done. And he smiled showing even white teeth. A smile just for her, that reached to his eyes. He knew she wasn't nuts. And that was enough, for now.

He explained how he didn't remember getting moved here, or the cast coming off. And Becky took the quandary upon herself, leaving the tent, and asking the people passing by how Dr. Carter had come to be in this tent.

Jillian stood and listened just behind the tent flap. Three techs told the same story. They had found David in the room upstairs, and carried him down to this tent. Down all four flights of stairs. He'd been comatose the whole time.

Becky came back in and looked from Jillian to David.

David sat fully upright for the first time. "So I never broke my leg?"

She smiled, while Jillian watched in abject horror, but unable to do anything, as her body virtually refused to listen to any of her commands.

David slid off the gurney and stood on wobbly feet. In a few minutes he let go of the gurney and walked on his own. Another fact flying in the face of all her memories. Even David remembered the fall.

Had they simply shared a dream?

Becky walked back in the tent, even though Jillian didn't remember her stepping out again. Her face conveying that she had bad news even before she spoke the words. "They said that Jordan is at the mortuary. A few of the bodies were transported waiting for someone to sign off on them."

Jillian shook her head. Jordan was alive yesterday.

Because she'd only slept for four hours yesterday if it was Thursday. That meant she'd seen him less than twenty-four hours ago.

Becky nodded at her. "We need to go. I'm headed there to get Leon Peppersmith's belongings. They should go to the CDC or to his family."

Silently Jillian agreed to the trip. Her brain telling her that if Jordan was at the mortuary he would be there working, making decisions or taking samples.

Becky waited while Jillian changed her socks and put on shoes. Then told them she already arranged a car to go see about Leon's things. Softly she asked. "If he's alive, then where is he?"

At the mortuary! But Jillian fought down anger, accompanied with fear and bile pressing at the back of her throat. Without a further word, she followed David and Becky to the car.

David walked with an easy swing to his stride. He clearly hadn't broken the bones. Not four days ago. He chatted with the biologist. Somehow able to make meaningless small talk, even though he said he remembered the same things she did.

Sliding into the backseat, she listened quietly while Becky told of the woman rousing the crowd about The Ascension.

When they arrived, her feet stepped out onto the gray of the blacktop, the morgue and coroner's office located under the small police station that served the entire town. A steel door let them inside, where they passed down a long hall and through a walk-in refrigerator door.

The air changed texture, to a created, and probably expensive, climate, that was, ironically, nearly the exact temperature as the air outside.

Jillian still couldn't find her tongue when the coroner told Becky that they had Dr. Abellard. The fuzzy noise behind her eyes worsened. There was no way that Jordan was here. She hadn't dreamed him alive.

Yet the coroner pulled open a door and slid out a tray.

He peeled back the sheet, revealing Jordan. Sleeping in shades of gray. Lacking the small movements that betrayed life.

Still not believing, she reached out, felt his hair. It didn't feel right. It felt dead. He didn't respond, as her brain told her he wouldn't. He looked like someone had cast Jordan in wax, and laid him out here, a la Tussaud's. But her brain knew it was deceiving itself. Even as she refused to accept, it was her own voice telling her the truth. He was gone.

Jillian felt the pressure at the edges of her vision. She saw the sparkles, right before the roaring worsened, and everything went black.

Chapter 20

Jordan stood at the edge of the gurney, just on the other side of the baby rails. Jillian slept. Just caddy corner, David, too, slept the sleep of the dead. There was no eye movement, no motion whatsoever from either of them.

He had allowed himself five minutes every hour to come and check in on them. *Her* – if he was being honest. He had slept here in the chair last night, in case either of them came around. But he had barely roused himself each time the alarm on his watch had gone off. He had forced himself to set it for two hours, thinking that he might get into a much needed deep sleep cycle if he could stay asleep for long enough.

But from the way he had creaked this morning, and felt like he was moving through sludge all day, Jordan was sure he hadn't had any REM.

He had talked to his Dad on the phone this morning for an hour.

Jackson Abellard had joined up with the work crew, hauling bodies, demolishing houses where people had been left to rot, and getting Lake James up and functioning again. He'd said it was sad what had happened. But that he felt truly alive for the first time since Jordan's mother had died.

Jordan had told about his own woes: that there was no pattern to the deaths, that he was ready to give up, but Landerly felt there had to be something. So they'd been pushing, and analyzing, and finding jack.

Jackson had laughed. "It does seem random as hell. We lost the vast majority of our electricians. But for some reason we've got lawyers out the yin yang."

Jordan had laughed, too. Wishing Landerly would stop beating the dead horse. Or the billions of dead horses. Wishing Becky Sorenson had lived, to go check out the frogs and report something of use to distract Landerly.

His watch beeped at him. Signaling that his brain had wandered and he'd lost track of his five minutes.

Not surprising.

He looked down at Jillian again, seeing her hand hanging loose within his own grasp. He told himself that fingers twitched first a lot of the time. That he touched her so he could feel what he might not see, not because he wanted to.

Turning to go, he reluctantly let her hand slip free of his, almost missing the finger jerking as it slid from his grasp.

Without covering the space between, he was over her bed, hovering, watching.

Waiting.

And seeing nothing.

It must have been nothing.

But still he picked up her lifeless hand, holding her fingers sandwiched between his own. Rubbing them. Hoping for a response.

And finally his breath hitched, when he felt it again.

Just a twitch.

His breath gushed out. "Jillian! Jillian!" He chided himself for calling out to her. She would come around as she chose. Not because he said something. Something she probably still couldn't hear, or even process as her own name. Then he did it again. "Jillian, can you hear me?"

Another twitch. This time it was her whole hand, quickly grasping his, before slackening again.

He patted the side of her face. Tapped the back of her hand. Listened to her breathing. Counted eighteen breaths per minute.

She groaned.

"Have you been standing here looking at your girlfriend this whole time!?" Landerly yelled like a man half his age, even if he hobbled along with a cane at his side.

Jordan's jaw clenched and he didn't turn to address the man yelling at his back. "She's not my girlfriend. She's my partner."

"Then why are you standing here making lovesick puppy eyes?"

Yup, the old man couldn't be bothered to notice a person he was speaking directly to, but he seemed to have pegged Jordan without a sideways glance. Son of a bitch. He ground his teeth and focused on the tiny quivers of Jillian's lips. "She's coming around."

"Really?"

He heard the uneven footsteps. The grass was cold enough to crunch with the punctuation of his cane as Landerly made his way beside Jordan. With quick, agile fingers Landerly took her pulse, watched her eyelids as they began to show REM signs, and pulled out his stethoscope to hear her breath sounds.

Jordan spotted the cane hooked over the baby rail, looking for all the world completely unnecessary. Landerly's feet planted apart, as though the earth might tremble beneath him and he'd need his balance. After a moment, he nodded.

Another few minutes later she began to mumble. And Jordan started speaking again. "Jillian. We're here. Jordan and Dr. Landerly. Open your eyes. Come on—" *Baby.* He bit off the endearment before it slipped out.

In the space his slip provided she mumbled again.

Then again.

Jordan leaned over, smiling as her eyes slowly opened and closed. Opened and closed. They rolled, denying her the focus she was trying to achieve. And he remembered forcing back the darkness and crawling out only a few days ago himself.

Finally her eyes opened fully and stayed that way, they found him, latched on to his grin, and he watched, smiling, while recognition dawned.

Until her scream shattered his eardrums.

She looked at him like he was Satan incarnate.

And screamed again.

Then he watched in abject horror as her eyes rolled back in her head and she passed out.

"What the hell?" Landerly shoved him out of the way, the strength in his arms surprising but unnecessary. Jordan was as stable as a wet noodle and shuffled easily to the side, sliding into the chair, barely looking up as Landerly's voice cut through him again. "What did you do to her?"

Glad to know you're so certain that I did it, old man. But he didn't speak, only shrugged and wondered if Landerly was right.

This time it was Landerly tapping her hand and her face. None too gently from Jordan's viewpoint, but maybe she wouldn't scream and pass out when she saw him. He could see the twitches as she came around again. And he sent up a silent prayer of thanks, to a God he was no longer sure was there, that she hadn't slipped right back under.

He heard her voice as though it came from under glass, "Doctor Landerly?"

"We're here." Landerly motioned behind him for Jordan to get up and join him at the bedside.

Again the soft lilt of confusion, "But you're dead."

Landerly thumped his chest, and Jordan would have laughed had he had it in him. "Nope, alive and hale."

"Jordan?"

He stepped up. "I'm here."

Her breath whooshed out of her, "Oh thank God," as she launched herself into his arms. Her face pressed into his neck, the scent of her permeating his senses, her soft breasts pressed to him as she wrapped herself around him.

His hand stroked at her hair. Even as he realized he was giving himself away to Landerly there was nothing he could do to stop it. But he ruined it anyway. "Why did you scream?"

She pulled back, untangling herself from him, taking the warmth with her. "You were dead."

"Hmm?" He heard Landerly's voice on top of his own.

"You were both on the 'deceased' list." Her face looked so earnest. "From several days ago."

"You must have dreamed it. We both woke up several days ago."

Her head shook, in the stilted manner of someone denying, not to the world but to themselves. "I didn't dream it." Her eyes bored into him, and he felt as though they could see straight through to whatever was behind him. "Becky Sorenson took me to the mortuary."

He started to point out that Becky had died, that Jillian had been there, but she spoke again, cutting off his thoughts, again chilling him to the bone. "I saw your body."

"Pinch me!" Jillian held her arm out. She looked to Landerly, "that *does* work, right? If I feel the pain I'm not dreaming?"

Landerly actually reached out and took what felt like a good bite out of her arm. "Ow!"

Jordan looked at the two of them like they'd gone mad, and Jillian felt the chill wrap around her heart again. Her voice was barely a whisper as she pushed it out. "Don't look at me like that. I can't be crazy. You were dead."

"But I'm not." He shrugged. "I woke up the day after you did... the first time."

Click. Another gear snapped into place.

"Oh shit!"

Landerly's eyes snapped to her. He'd probably never heard her swear before, but she didn't care. It was falling into place. "That's it!"

Both men raised their eyebrows, identical expressions on very different faces. Her tongue fluttered in her mouth, trying to form words for the abstracts in her brain. "That's what Becky said. She said she woke up at the same time we saw her die."

"Okay. But she's really dead." Jordan squeezed her fingers.

Only just then realizing that he had been holding her hand, Jillian yanked it away as though it burned. In essence it did. This man, who had become her best friend, maybe by default, clearly didn't believe her.

"None of them are dead!" She wanted to shake them, make them believe. But her brain rolled over and took charge. She had to tell them first.

"Sit!"

Both men scrambled to obey the authority in her voice. Jordan politely gave Landerly the chair, and hoisted himself onto the counter. When she looked to the gurney, expecting to find it empty, she started.

David was laid out there, as still as the desert night, and trussed up like a turkey.

But after a thought it made sense.

David, comatose here, was still with Becky, wherever that was.

She smiled, because when he came around, he'd corroborate her story. And she started by telling the two men that.

"David will corroborate what?" It was Landerly, interrupting before she even started.

She pinned him with a glare. "Everything. No more questions until I finish."

She explained that she had seen people who were deceased here. That those that were alive here, were dead there. "Gary Winchell. He's a tech. He's dead, right?"

Jordan shrugged at her, still not putting together all the pieces she was feeding them.

She pointed to the open flap of the tent, at the white coats scurrying by. "Well, send a tech to check the 'deceased' list. Because I x-rayed him head to toe this morning."

Jordan hopped to his feet and obediently sent for the lists.

"I hadn't met him until this morning. But ask around. He was a skateboarder. He's broken every major bone in his body. Two tib-fibs on his right leg. Left collarbone, twice in the same spot…" Her voice failed her again. With her eyes she pleaded with Jordan. "How would I know that otherwise? You've been around me the whole time, how else did I learn that?"

His gaze was steady. "To be perfectly scientific, Jillian, I haven't been around you *all* the time. You were off with David a lot."

But just then, an out of breath tech arrived with the local binder. Jordan flipped through, stopping at Gary Winchell, and handing the book over to Landerly.

His voice was uncertain as he probed. "So everyone who's dead here, is alive…*there*?"

Her shoulders sagged. "No." The admission sounded small and hollow even to her own ears. She hated the holes in her story, wished that it all sewed up neatly and precisely. "They lost most of their elderly, too." Her head snapped up. "And Leon Peppersmith. He's dead there too."

Her jaw hurt, and she realized she was clenching it. "People are waking up there at precisely the times they die here, and dying there at precisely the times they wake up here." She was repeating herself and getting nowhere. "David was out the whole time. He was awake here, breaking his leg, while he was comatose there. He only woke up there about nine last night."

The two men looked to each other with a sharp movement.

"That's when he went under again, isn't it?" Her excitement sharpened in her bones.

It was Jordan who spoke, and she could tell he tempered his response, not wanting to give in, to validate her too much. "I discovered he had slipped under shortly after nine."

Her voice softened. "He didn't fall down the stairs there. Because he didn't wake up until yesterday. So his leg isn't broken, his shoulder never dislocated. I was trying- *we* were trying to figure out how he healed so quickly, but I realize now that he didn't. He was just never injured."

Click.

"Leon Peppersmith!"

They looked at her, waiting.

"He died in both places. But it's because he didn't die from the reversal. He hit his head. He lost blood, that's what killed him."

Jordan again stepped into the ring. "But he did that *here*. So why would he have that head injury *there*?"

"We were *all* here. But here isn't here."

Oh, hell. She wasn't making any sense now. But she plowed ahead and tried again to untangle what she was thinking and saying. "We were all here. We all went under, and things shifted. Making two parts. Some people woke up on one side and some on the other."

Jordan leaned toward her. "So there are two earths?"

"Yes!"

"Jillian, that all sounds very...*Hitchhiker's Guide to the Galaxy.*"

She let out a frustrated breath.

"Fine! Let me tell you who I met there. They'll all be in your little 'deceased' list." She jabbed her finger at it.

"Lucy Whitman." For a moment she pronounced the name, feeling triumphant, but then she shook her head. "That doesn't count, I saw her name on the list before I went under. I could have conjured her."

She thought again. "The coroner is a Dr. Whitman. He's Lucy's Dad right?"

Jordan nodded. Of course he would know that.

But she kept talking. "He's an older man with gray hair."

But who wasn't? She saw the question mirrored in Jordan's eyes, so she did a better job. "He had male pattern baldness, and piercing blue eyes. He has the same smile as Lucy's. He's about five feet six inches tall, short for a man. He's medium build, mild clubbing of his fingers, and has a thick gold wedding band on his left hand, no other jewelry... Oh, and silver glasses."

She sat there on the edge of her gurney, feet dangling, feeling very self-satisfied.

Jordan nodded. He looked to Landerly. "She did describe the man to a T."

Jillian looked over her shoulder. "And David is there...right now, he and Becky are probably wondering what happened to me, why I went back under."

Landerly steepled his fingers, not talking, not looking at her, letting his brain digest. It was Jordan who leaned forward and questioned her. "Do you really believe all this?"

She nodded slowly, turning her lips inward, as though that might hold back the tears that threatened. "If I don't believe it, then I have to accept that I'm crazy."

"You may have dreamed it all." He shrugged.

She nodded again, acceptance not coming easily. "Then I may very well be dreaming you now."

His smile was quick and steady, "I assure you I am quite alive." He stood, stretching, his movement proclaiming him finished with his part of the conversation. "You aren't dreaming this."

"That's what they told me, too." A small laugh burbled out of her, but she stopped it before it bloomed into hysteria. Tears pushed at the back of her eyes. "I don't think I'm dreaming."

Jordan nodded. "It's a shame we didn't put an EEG on you." His hands rested on his hips as he paced slowly.

Her eyes opened, wide and clear, as she looked up. "But we can put one on David right now."

Landerly nodded. "If he *is* dreaming…"

She shook her head vehemently, "It doesn't prove anything one way or the other. I know. But if he isn't…" She let out the sigh that had fought to escape. "When he wakes up he'll tell you all the same things I did, then you'll *know* he didn't dream it. I'll even leave the room so you can question him separately."

Landerly's voice was smooth and modulated. "You seem very sure of yourself."

"I am." Holding out her hands, palm up, she played her last card. "If he doesn't corroborate everything, then you can lock me up."

In unspoken agreement, Jordan left to fetch an EEG, and Landerly stood, putting too much weight on the cane to get out of the chair. His fingers quickly probed along her jawline. She almost laughed, thinking that a massive infection *would* explain some serious hallucinating on her part. But she could tell he didn't find any enlarged lymph nodes. He took her blood pressure, and listened to her heartbeat, and let out a tiny chuckle.

"What?" As she asked it, she noticed his eyes had changed from calculating and scientific to human and warm.

"Abellard was right. You are textbook."

She only nodded. Of course she was textbook. Humans varied, everyone deviated from the norm in some way or other. But not her, and this whole mess was just another convincing factor that she was less than human in some way.

"You pass all the physical inspections, so I'm going back to the records tent. You and Abellard get something to eat and bring me some when you finish. Maybe you can help us find the sorting factor."

"Sorting factor?"

He turned back. "Why those people died – or lived."

She couldn't raise her voice, couldn't find the energy to be loud and forceful to this man. But she just as much could not let him walk out uncorrected. "It's not just dead and alive. There are three categories. Alive here. Alive there. And dead in both."

His back to her, he nodded, and left. As he hobbled off, looking older than he ever had before, she wondered if he really wanted to study or just didn't want to trek the distance to the cafeteria.

Alone in the tent with David laid out on the other bed, Jillian moved her sore muscles. Her jaw had already gotten its workout, but her legs and arms could use some good range-of-motion exercises.

She stretched and twisted, feeling for the third time the strain of movement on long unused muscle. She began to wonder if she would feel this every time she awoke. If each time she fell asleep she would have to wonder where she would wake up.

Before the thought could depress her, Jordan wheeled in the cart containing the EEG set up. Wires hung in wrapped loops off the side of the cart, the ends little silver snaps waiting for the corresponding pads. Jordan had two pages of the thick foam stickers with the snap backs and small sponges in the center holding conducting gel.

When he turned his back to her she heaved herself off the bed, and grabbed the babyrail as her legs tried to buckle under her. Without seeing him move in behind her, Jillian only felt his arm slip around her waist and lift her fully upright, legs extended, and finally supporting herself. She batted his hands away and carefully walked the two feet to get to the head of David's bed. Without a sound she began pushing away his blond hair, snapping the wires to the pads and sticking them across his head. For a moment she pushed away her own concerns, and admired the pattern that the probes made – simple, mathematical, containing no fear, concern, or disbelief.

Within minutes the small screen was tracing a series of green lines across its face, showing the brainwave activity of a comatose David. The theta waves were low, indicating a non-dreaming state. But that didn't mean anything. Not until he passed at least three hours – overnight would be better to prove that he hadn't entered any REM sleep cycles, no dream phases.

They watched silently until the lines completed their first trek across the screen, then they turned to get dinner.

Jordan watched her while she ate. She consumed food like he had normally only seen her consume information. But he didn't judge. He hadn't been through what she had. Even in the simplest sense.

He hadn't walked the reversal long after it wasn't safe for anyone else. He didn't awaken before anyone else and toil to save lives. And he hadn't slipped back under. Never mind what she claimed she had seen.

She wasn't speaking to him. Not in the flat-out-refusal way that a child would mete out punishment, but he could sense her withdrawal, her pain that he didn't just blindly believe all that she said.

The one thing she had done was convince him that *she* believed it. But it didn't make sense, not the way she said. And she could have dreamed it. Hell, everyone had a dream or two that felt so real you bought into it, even after you woke up. His lips pressed together. The difference was that people who dreamed woke up. And, once confronted with some sort of evidence, they let go. He had once dreamed his puppy had died, but he woke up and was corrected by a single bark. A good lick on the face and the dream was banished.

Here, two full hours later, Jillian still believed. And she was trying to spread the news, at least to him and Landerly.

And she *could* have dreamed it. He had watched her thumb through the 'deceased' list when she'd been awake the first time. Jordan also knew that her brain was razor sharp. It could have memorized, somewhere in her vast subconscious, the entire list. Who knew what a brain like Jillian's was able to catalogue? If she had once passed by that tech's file, if it had been open, she could have absorbed every fracture, every nick on every bone.

He watched as she carefully cut the turkey slices on her plate with the dull cafeteria knife, slicing neat squares from the ovals before her. She dunked them in gravy then chewed them, her motions as uniform as her cuts, and she never made eye contact. She was angry.

Equivalently she'd had the answering bark. He'd talked to her, they'd touched. Landerly touched her. She had dreamed they were dead, but all the signs saying otherwise couldn't convince her.

And that theory. That was neat. She managed to sew it all together so it worked. One set here, one there. She could simply continue the dream when she went to sleep.

With new eyes, he looked at her, knowing that she felt it, and that she wouldn't return the gesture. Was she simply so smart that she could drive herself insane? His dream had dispersed, although the memory of the terror was still glass-clear in his adulthood. But he didn't-couldn't-make up ways for it to have truly happened. Jillian was smart enough that she could.

He waited while she methodically finished the food on her plate. Wordlessly, she stood and went back into the line. If her back hadn't been to him she would have seen his jaw unhinge.

Maybe she's pregnant.

David.

Like lightning, a bolt of deep jealousy traced a sharp path through him. He worked to push the thought back down inside, to shove it low and bury it deep. She was just eating a lot because of the stress on her system from being comatose for a good portion of the past week.

He saw her exiting the line and coming toward him. The cafeteria plate no longer in her hands, but replaced by a paper napkin roll of plasticware, and a black plastic plate piled high with food he couldn't identify through the steam inside the lid.

His breath let out. *Not pregnant.*

"Ready?" She looked at him, but only at the surface. And when he nodded she began walking away. Not waiting for him to get up. Not looking back to be sure he followed.

He trailed behind, mesmerized by the soft sway of her hips, the light blue scrubs hugging the curves that were partially obscured by the jacket she had slung on. Her sneakers cut even steps in the shortest path to the records tent. In the dimming light, it was one of the few lit up like a bulb. A faint shadow marked the spot where Landerly sat just inside.

Jillian lifted the flap and pushed her way in, the canvas falling back into place behind her so that Jordan had to open it for himself.

Landerly was taking the plate from her, looking more like her grandfather than her boss. For the old man she had smiles and easy conversation. They were already discussing the fact that Landerly still couldn't identify a sorting factor, other than the one that he and Jordan had already figured out. He lifted the lid from the plate and stabbed at the turkey with his fork, explaining while he cut the meat into neat, even squares. "The elderly and infirm died. The people who had any or all the markers you two found before the complete reversal hit. But a lot of young people died that I can't account for. There's no age or race bias..." His voice trailed off as he dunked the perfect cube of turkey into the little puddle of gravy Jillian had gotten him.

And Jordan almost turned tail and ran. Dear God, he was stuck in a small tent with two of them. Falling hopelessly head over heels for one of them, and she wasn't speaking to him. Instead of fleeing screaming, he opened his mouth. "There's a gender bias that the females fell under and woke up or died first. But beyond that, there's no statistically significant difference in who woke up and who died."

Jillian cocked her head. "Did you check for a religious difference?"

"Huh?" Jordan heard it come out of his own mouth. Years of education and student loans down the drain.

"The Jewish people are the only religion that's its own race, but there may be a religious bias in the sorting. I don't know anything about the physiology of religion, but something must exist."

Jordan resisted the urge to roll his eyes. Of course, he and Landerly had been wracking their brains, but Jillian in her first few minutes in the tent proposed something they hadn't thought of. She drove him nuts, so why the hell did he like her so much?

Without being asked, Jordan slipped out of the tent and went in search of Jason. Lucy was gone now, and she had been a fantastic go-to girl. He'd wondered if she'd had some sort of crush on him, or if she was just that efficient and willing to do whatever needed to be done. Jason was simply driven. He saw the opportunity afforded by the drastic shift in population, and he was going to come out on top.

Jason was in one of the other lit up tents. Of course. He would work well into the night, sleep a few hours and wake up early. He'd make sure he was indispensable. And certainly that's how Jordan found him, sitting at a desk, frowning at the yards of graphs in front of him. "What's the trouble?"

Jason looked up, a hint of startle showing on his face. "I must have messed it up, but…"

Jordan almost smiled. Messing up didn't seem like much of an option for someone like Jason. "What did you mess up?"

"Well, I figured that if compasses were acting up, maybe other things had, too. My first thought was the MRI. It's magnetic, so that made sense."

"Is it messed up?" Jordan stifled his inward sigh. The last thing anyone needed was more problems, but if they existed they needed to be checked out.

Jason shook his head, still looking confused. "No, it was fine. I guess the internal field is just too strong to be bothered by the earth's field. The NMR was next. Same issue. But both the IR and UV-vis are honked up."

"Honked up?" That was one he hadn't heard in a scientific sense before.

"I got nothing. So I tried to recalibrate it."

Jordan felt his fists hit his hipbones. "And…?" It felt like he was pulling teeth over messed up machinery when he needed Jason working on finding out what he could about Jillian's religious bias theory.

"I recalibrated the UV-vis."

"Oh." Well, that certainly hadn't been what he expected, not given the look on Jason's face. So he launched into what he needed. "We–"

"No. I recalibrated it. But our visual red recalibrated in the UV scale. The whole thing's off by a frequency of 300 hertz."

"Hmmmm." So the machine was fucked. He tried again to speak.

But Jason wasn't having any of it. "I got my Dad to check the ones out at the labs. They all recalibrate the same. I even called U Mass and UCLA. They're the same."

Jordan nodded. "Good, I'm glad you got that solved." And he shifted mental gears. After explaining what they needed, Jordan headed back, pushing aside thoughts of the future. If Jason reacted by over-working and over-thinking, others would react by shutting down. Suicides were a highly likely outcome. Some had lost their entire families. And it was inherent in the human species that some people just didn't survive that.

He shook his head, trying to make out the two voices as he approached. Jillian's soft lilt, her laugh, and Landerly's response, for the first time Jordan detected a scratch in the old man's voice and wondered how many years of his younger life the man had spent smoking. He pushed through the canvas flap, enjoying the feeling of the heat enveloping him. Lord knows, the two of them had probably solved all the earth's problems while he was out.

Jillian was at a desk, her seat turned to face Landerly's, while she sifted through reams of printouts, talking as she went, and Dr. Landerly was polishing off the last bites of the dinner she had put together for him.

"Jordan," It was the first time this evening she had spoken directly to him, since he had dared to indicate that he wasn't completely on the dual-earth bandwagon. Landerly wasn't either, but for some reason the old man remained in her good graces. Jordan looked at her, eyes up, waiting. "Didn't they say something about the wardens all dying in Nevada?"

He frowned. "They didn't all die."

"Yeah, but wasn't there a disproportionately large number? Far more than fifty percent?"

Landerly nodded, wondering where she was going. "All the first people who woke up were murderers. Single killings, passion killings. You found that."

But Jordan shook his head, for the first time since Jillian spouted off about her dreams, he and Landerly were on the same page. But Jillian wasn't and Jordan put voice to his concerns. "I don't think that murderer/non-murderer is going to be the sorting factor, I've looked at the list."

She brushed them both aside with her hand. "Of course not, but job description might. Oh–" Her eyes widened as she cut off her own thought.

Again he and Landerly waited.

"You weren't there…" He could see her getting excited. But even when she opened her mouth she still didn't make sense. "I wasn't there either!"

For a moment he wondered if they were really going to wind up putting her into a straight jacket. And he barely managed a sad sigh before she spoke again.

"Becky mentioned something on the way over to the coroner's. That she'd been over to the Civic Center across the street and they were having a rally."

"I didn't see a rally." He looked askance to Landerly and the old man just shrugged.

Jilly's eyes narrowed and her face took on the expression of a viper ready to strike. "Of course you didn't see it. *Becky* did.

It wasn't *here*." She gave a long suffering sigh. "So try this on for size: At the rally they believed the reversal was the Ascension because all the lawyers had died and…the police force had mostly lived. So had the FBI," she paused, her eyes rolling up skyward as she relived the memory, certainly in her brain she could hear Becky speaking. "But almost no CIA. Low survival among thieves and murderers."

She pinned him with a glare. "Check it."

"What?" He still wasn't quite up to speed on what the idea was, even though he'd understood what she said as plain English.

"Job descriptions. The lawyers and CIA and thieves and murderers are alive. *Here*. Because they're dead *there*. We'll also be short a good police force, and the FBI."

He frowned. He understood; he just wasn't buying what she was selling. "The FBI just all died?"

"I doubt it was *all* of them! But the FBI believes in good and evil. The CIA doesn't. It's by job description." She was as frustrated with him as he was with her. And from off to the side he could see Landerly watching the whole exchange with his eyebrows so high they almost popped off his head. Jordan was just too damn frustrated to laugh about it.

Jillian started in on him again. "Most of the FBI is dead. I'll bank on that just like I'll bank on David corroborating my story. Has anyone thought to check on him?"

Of course not, no one really likes him.

Jordan tried to squelch the thought. His mother had taught him better. And as a physician he had taken an oath to be better.

But it was Jillian who stomped out of the tent and went on her way to check on David.

He tried to take a moment to gather himself. But it was practically impossible with Landerly sitting there watching him. So he forced himself to don the appearance of *not* being wound into knots. He faced Landerly, "Now what?"

Landerly shrugged from the seat he had occupied the whole time. "I guess we get cracking on checking the job descriptions of everyone we can find."

"Dammit Leon." Becky muttered under her breath.

"What?"

"Nothing." She managed about half a smile and shook her head at David. She wasn't going to repeat it. Not the cursing of the dead. Not her anger at Leon for leaving her here to sort out the species by herself.

Of all the people who had died in the reversal, Leon was the one she had been sure would make it if anyone would. He radiated health. It was worse that he had died of a hit to the head – nothing more than a scratch to Leon. But there had been no one awake to lift him into a bed and stitch him up.

The only remaining Peppersmiths were still in Minnesota, faxing in fabulous data on some seriously unfabulous extinctions. Leon's sister had stepped up to fill the lead spot, the business running smoothly in the face of personal and global tragedy. John Overton had died as well. And Becky let out a breath when she thought of the gleam in his eyes when they talked about the downed moose. Overton hadn't been anywhere as useful as Leon had been. And it was wrong of her, but she couldn't muster up any real pain at the loss.

David went back to working on his hands and knees some five yards away. He was chipping at an exposed surface of granite, the tiny pickaxe making a rhythmic ping against the scar he was creating in the earth. He was making too much noise now to hear her if she muttered.

The crickets had stopped for a mile in every direction when he had started the nasty noise that signaled to the wildlife that they were not alone. The predators had gone into hiding, away from the now rotting feast that had been left out for them. Luckily they had eaten enough that the smell wasn't overwhelming and Becky had adjusted to it. David worked like he didn't notice anything, quiet except for his little axe and his breathing, in a circle of illuminated glare. One knee flat, the other up, with his elbow resting on it, his fit torso encased in a red L L Bean jacket that spoke of money and sport. He looked like an ad rather than a scientist. The only glimmer of truth in the whole bright image was that his hair was thinning on top.

Becky went back to unearthing the things that had taken great pains to earth themselves in the first place. They squirmed and fought, but only rarely did they escape. She apologized to the souls of each of them, and again wondered what God thought of what she did to his creatures.

Her minister when she'd been in high school had thought God wanted the people to use the creatures to help the people. She was certain there wasn't any real danger of being smote down by anyone organic or overly holistic in the East Tennessee Baptist Church. But nowhere in the bible was there any good solid reference to God's or Jesus' ideas about the worms and their scientific versus holy purposes.

So she dug them up.

"You about done?" David's voice was clear in the unearthly quiet.

"Yup!" She scrambled to gather the few containers she had brought with her. Her cell phone shoved deep into her pocket. She wasn't 'finished'; she hadn't really started. She was simply taking advantage of being out. David had said he was coming out here to check the rock formations, either with her or without her.

And after Jillian had gone back comatose, Becky didn't think any of them should be anywhere alone, and certainly not David. He was the one who seemed to function the most like Jillian. And he could simply pass out and slip under at any moment.

Granted, Jillian had been triggered. She had seen Jordan Abellard's body in the morgue and let out that soul shattering scream. The hideous noise had only ended when Jillian had passed out.

So Becky didn't find the brilliant Dr. Carter so all-knowing wise when he decided to come out to the back of beyond in the middle of the night to chip rock, even if it was her own back-yard. Her mother and father would be bringing Brandon back here. They had Melanie and Aaron buried in Charlotte where he had been working, where the reversal had hit them.

For a moment she had to scrunch up her face to keep the thoughts and therefore the tears at bay. The steady ringing of metal on rock had stopped. And with a sniff, she looked to her right, to the perfect size twelve tan hiking boots that bore just enough scuffs to show that they had been worn, once before, maybe. "Need a hand?"

The fitted black glove reached down into her view, and she was certain he was offering to tug her to her feet, but she couldn't face him yet. And David wasn't the kind of man you just threw yourself at when you needed a good cry. So she slapped a salamander in a clear container into his palm.

The palm lifted out of her vision and came back empty, so she held up another and another, until she had corralled her thoughts and was able to face the man.

And to think she had come out here believing she was pro-tecting him from going comatose out in the woods. Nope, he was far more stable than she. It was just Jillian with the issue.

She stepped pace behind him on the trail, only briefly musing at following *him* down trails she had walked since she was old enough to wander away from home. But before she realized that they had come that far, she was blinded by the sudden glare of the motion-sensor spotlight on the side of the empty house. Her hand flew up to shade her eyes and she caught a brief burning glimpse of David doing the same thing, just before she ran into his back.

"Umph."

Well, that was beautiful. With a deep breath in, she apologized.

"Don't worry." He pushed the button on the car key and the sleek black Mercedes in front of them blinked and made a few laser-like noises. Becky figured he'd gone out and bought it. But she wasn't sure when. Or why. There were tons of available cars these days. But it seemed that David just *needed* the black Mercedes. Or maybe *it* had needed a man that wore L L Bean and breathed money.

Again, she held out her gloved palm, waiting patiently until he relented and handed over the keys. She wasn't about to let him drive. No matter how sure she was that he wasn't going to slip into a coma.

A few minutes later the black leather, hand-stitched backseat was covered with pieces of rock, baggies of silt and soil, and plastic containers of water and writhing creatures. Definitely not what the Mercedes-Benz corporation had built this luxury-mobile for. Why couldn't the man just admit that he played in the dirt for a living and get a truck?

Becky turned the key, threw the car in gear and, when the gas pedal made the car start reversing out of the bumpy gravel drive, she figured the engine was running. The flood light snapped off as they pulled out of range, shutting down the still picture the house had made beyond the windshield.

But Becky put that thought out of her mind, too. At least her folks would be back in a couple of days and it wouldn't feel so eerie. She hadn't even brought herself to go inside this time. Even though the dust layer would have been microscopic, she would know it was there, feel that the house no longer had a family in it. That it knew it was unused.

So she pulled away, using the high-beams to illuminate a road she knew by heart.

David stared out the side window, although if he could see anything other than the green reflection of the dash lights, she wasn't certain.

Twenty-five minutes later she pulled into the lot at the high school. The tent town was ghostly white, moving slightly in the breeze. A few of the tents were lit up from the inside, like Japanese paper lanterns. But David didn't see any of it.

He had fallen sound asleep on the ride back, having reclined his seat and wedged his head against the door jamb.

"David." She kept her voice soft, as though maybe it weren't her intention to wake him.

But he didn't respond.

A seed of thought began forming at the back of her brain, and she decided that she didn't care if she startled the hell out of him. She grabbed his shoulder and shook him for all she could. "David! *David!*"

Chapter 21

"**D**avid! *David!*"

The voice seemed muffled, and at a distance. It was a wonder he could make out his own name it was so murky. And he was tired. Why couldn't Becky let him sleep? It seemed like he had just slid away. Finally, peacefully getting the rest he needed. The seat of the Mercedes was warm and soothing, because he'd turned on the ass-warmer.

The salesman had a better name for it than that, but David didn't care. It made everything else about the car worthwhile. Even the pricetag. So David wrote yet another check out of his trust fund. He'd sworn never to touch the account, but lately it seemed that was all he had done.

He started to roll sideways, away from the sound of her voice, but the sheets were cool, and her voice was receding. Good. She was going to let him sleep.

He slid away, letting the recesses of dreams come close and fold him into a place where he simply didn't care that he was in a car, sleeping in the parking lot. A thought about hubcaps slipped through his head and he could see the parking lot filled with rows of little black Mercedes.

"David."

Damn, her voice had gotten–

It was a man. A male voice. And he remembered that she had left, that he had heard her skittering out of the-…the car?

"David." A hand clasped his shoulder, the grip commanding rather than soothing. "I can see that you're coming around. Watch that arm."

Arm?

Son of a bitch. They weren't going to let him sleep. He sighed and rolled toward the sound, trying to force open his eyes, but it wasn't working. He rubbed at his face.

His arm was ripped from his body. For just a moment causing a blinding pain, then the feeling rescinded to a bright burn.

"Aaaaagggh!"

He barely registered that it was his own voice through the haze. Even though he didn't move it again, his shoulder punished him with a throbbing sear that onset with every heartbeat. He opened his eyes even as he chewed the inside of his lip in an effort to create a controllable pain that would overshadow the uncontrollable one.

Finally his vision settled on the man in front of him. Forcing his eyes to follow the clean lines of the scrubs, he looked up into Jordan Abellard's too-blue eyes.

He screamed again. And scrambled for the head of the bed, hoping to get away from the face he had seen cold on the slab just that morning. But again his shoulder punished him with a tearing feeling, followed by a sharp burn that permeated the whole area.

David would have let out another yell, but as the doctor leaned closer David pushed with his legs, and was rewarded by the hot certainty that the limb had been sawed off and left open about halfway down his calf. Something stabbed, swordlike, through his hip up into his abdomen.

His left arm held. His left leg didn't feel like it had been severed, and so he used those to right himself. Holding one hand in front of him, he warded off the dead hands reaching toward him. "Back off, you son of a bitch!"

Finally he was able to feel his throat, and it too was mad at him. Sandpaper rubbed on every exposed surface, creating an intense, raw, seeping pain that clouded his vision further.

"It's me, Dr. Abellard." The head tilted, the chocolate hair sliding and falling a little too long, as the eyes focused on his face.

"No shit. Get back." He held his palm out, as though the sight of the soft side of a hand would keep anything at bay besides a gnat.

But the Jordan-thing did as it was told.

"David?"

It was a kind, soothing voice. But that was all it said.

David started running at the mouth. Although he wasn't sure why. "You're dead! I saw you this morning dead-…cold-…at the coroner's."

"Huh?"

It wasn't Jordan. Jordan was more eloquent than that. Every bad zombie movie he had ever seen flashed through his brain. Becky was complaining about extinct species. The techs and doctors droned about all the deaths. There was no reason that the walking dead couldn't be a part of all this.

The Jordan-thing stared back at him; its mouth moved asking something about the morgue. But David ignored it. He was frowning at his arm, and a horror worse than the dead man standing and talking to him poured over him. The pain that had receded to a dull rhythmic ache was in his right arm. At the shoulder. The shoulder that was in a blue standard issue immobility sling. With the Velcro strap around his chest. Just where he had remembered it. "My shoulder was dislocated?"

"Yes." Jordan nodded.

"When I fell down the last flight of stairs?"

"Yes." His expression clearly telling that he thought David might have injured his brain in the fall as well.

"But I healed…my leg healed." Again the words stumbled out of his mouth, along with some weird belief that if he just explained, things would right themselves. "I was walking. Becky took us to the coroner's. Jillian can show you the x-rays. I—" He wasn't making any sense and he knew it.

Jordan pulled up a chair and a notebook, before pulling a sleek, expensive pen from the unassuming pocket stitched on the front of his scrubs. "I'm going to ask a few questions and take some notes, okay?"

David gritted his teeth and remembered from two days ago. "Can I have a Percocet?"

Jordan nodded, but his words didn't quite match. "When we finish, okay?"

Again his teeth ground – one of the few body parts he could work without instantaneous punishment in the form of rending pain.

Jordan dove into the thick of it. "I'm dead?"

"Well, you don't look very dead." He could feel the sarcasm flowing through his veins. "You got a twin?"

He shook his head. Looking far too like Jordan for David's stomach to stop clenching. "Well, there's a body at the morgue that had your name on the toe-tag, and your name on the 'deceased' list. And from the looks of it, I can see why they got you confused. You should check into having a brother you don't know about."

Jordan nodded.

"When did you see it?"

"This morning. Maybe eleven a.m." It felt like an interrogation, but he let the doc go. The sooner this crap was over, the sooner he got his Percocet.

"Who was there with you?"

"Jillian Brookwood, Dr. Rebecca Sorenson, and the coroner, Dr. Whitfield, Whitson, something." He stated each name clearly for the record, mentally pushing back the feeling of having his hip ripped open.

"Becky's dead." Jordan leaned forward trying to see how David would react.

Was this one of those horrid mental studies? "Hey doc, I thought they banned this type of psychological research years ago."

"What are you talking about?"

David shook his head. "You know, where you tell people their family is dead just to see how they react...this ain't right."

Jordan breathed deep and shook his head. "I'll explain it all as soon as I can, but Jillian's telling us some pretty weird tales, and she says you'll corroborate them. She ran to get me when she saw you coming around."

Jillian! She would get him Percocet. "Bring the doc around then."

"I can't. Not until we're finished."

Anger burst through him, washing past in a hot rush. "I'm in pain here. While you pussyfoot around. And I don't even know why the hell I'm re-injured. So get the hell on with it."

"Why don't you believe Becky Sorenson is dead?"

"Because I was just with her." He looked at his watch. The time and date matched. "I was in the car. My black Mercedes I bought this afternoon. I fell asleep. About twenty minutes ago maybe."

"You saw her twenty minutes ago?" Jordan leaned forward, his face a mask of incredulousness.

"That's what I just said." He forced his breathing to stay steady. Percocet was coming. Just ignore the pain and the fact that you are at the mercy of this sadistic doctor. He almost admired Jordan for having the balls to hold him hostage in his bed.

"And Jillian was there?"

"No. She passed out when she saw your body at the morgue. Screamed like a banshee and dropped like a stone. She went comatose. Becky and I brought her back. One of the docs had checked her out and said her heart rate was low and her breathing shallow." He watched while Abellard's face gave away everything he felt for the pretty little brunette. Whether he admitted it to himself or not, it was there in plain writing for all the rest of the world to read. But David kept talking. "They hooked her up to monitors and watched her. Becky and I went out to gather some data."

"You left her?"

"I wasn't going to sit around and watch her not move. Not much I can do to help anyway." Yup, Abellard was in a bad way.

"You walked?" He motioned with his pretty pen to all the breaks that would clearly prevent any of David's story. David ate a sigh. None of it made sense. And if Jillian was awake then where was she anyway?

"I healed. No marks on the x-rays that there ever was a break on any of the bones. Hip in the socket, girdle unfractured. I don't know what this is about," He gestured to all the casting and bindings he wore, "but it hurts like a mother-fucker."

Jordan muttered under his breath. David heard the words *son of a bitch*, but it was hard to believe that phrase had come from Jordan's mouth. David knew he must have simply heard the words he would have said. Abellard stood and stretched, long lean lines that made David ache with jealousy and wonder where the hell his good health had escaped to.

"I'll send Jillian in with that Percocet. You can talk to her."

He straightened where he sat, propped against the pillows, his hip burned, reminding him not to bend. His arm twitched, and his leg sent pulses of pain to every part of him. He ignored it. "When did Jillian wake up?"

"As of about noon."

"But she was still under when Becky and I left this evening, around six."

Jordan nodded, "She'll explain. She was awake here."

Jordan walked calmly from the tent, making certain he was well beyond the flap before he bent over and put his hands on his knees, finally allowing himself the deep gulping breaths that his body had been fighting for. Oxygen seeped into his system like a drug, reassuring him about everything in the world except the fact that Jillian had been right.

Whatever the hell she had seen, truth or not, David corroborated it.

She had seen him start to wake up, and bolted from his tent, fetching Jordan. Telling him to ask all his questions, her eyes gleaming with the promise of vindication.

Well, she had it.

Jordan had checked the EEG readings several times and found the only conclusive thing he could have found. David showed no markers of dreams at all – which meant that the creepy explanation that he and Jillian had shared a dream wasn't going to fly. Instead they had as conclusive of evidence as they would ever find that the even creepier explanation Jillian had proposed would hold.

The toes of small, very familiar sneakers entered his line of sight, and he fought to stand upright and look less shaken than he felt. Jillian's voice reached him before his eyes made it to her face. "It all matches."

She didn't ask. She didn't have to. Jordan knew it was obvious from how he was reeling from his interview with David. But he forced himself to stand erect and look her in the eyes. "He needs Percocet. Then come back and talk to me, please." He heard the begging quality in his tone. Recognized that it was in response to the instant her eyes had fled elsewhere worrying about David.

"He doesn't even know why he's in casts; why he isn't healed." It was a statement, in a faraway voice, deep concern about the only patient he hadn't seen Jillian treat as a scientific subject. He told himself the rolling in his gut was from the fact that David's story had smacked him around and upended his world.

Jillian scampered off, fetching meds for David and disappearing into the tent.

She had woken up on the other side, wherever the hell that was. And so had David. He had talked to Becky, less than an hour ago. He had chatted with Lucy Whitman's dad long after the man had died.

Jordan started. For a moment he didn't care about Jillian and David. Was his mother there? Eddie? Was it just the land of the dead? Had it always existed and Jillian and David had simply been thrown there by the reversal? His breathing picked up pace again and he sprinted into the tent, to ask her.

But he pulled up short when he saw her standing beside the bed. Talking. Telling David about the two parts, how they were passing back and forth. Jordan held himself in tight check waiting for a spot to interrupt, until Jillian shifted revealing her hand held softly in David's. His voice found itself, putting the setting to rights. He had no claim, and wondered where the hell all this was popping out from. He had sat across a desk from her, finding her cold and impersonal. And now…well, intense attraction was a normal outcome to a shared traumatic stress.

Armed with this explanation, his brain worked again, and he pushed out the words. "Was it just a place that has always existed? Were other people there? Grandparents who died a long time ago?"

He shook his head in frustration, wondering how to explain what he meant. But Jillian gave him a sympathetic 'no', needing no further background, knowing instantly what he was trying to ask. "There were still a whole slew of people who actually died in the reversal. Remember, Leon isn't anywhere. I didn't find any evidence of anyone's long departed ancestors, and no one seemed to think they were in heaven, which I'm sure would have come to mind if suddenly all your dead relatives were around."

Jordan nodded. And admitted to himself what he had only briefly hoped: his mother wasn't there.

Until that moment, he had simply accepted her loss. That a long round with cancer slowly ate her. That it had destroyed his father as well, even though it didn't kill him. Only in the glimmer of chance did he realize how much he missed her. But he re-packaged it into its small neat box and shoved it back into the recesses of his brain.

Jordan stepped out of the tent, knowing Jillian would follow, soon. And steeling himself to the reality of it all: that Jillian had wandered across unbreachable barriers and hadn't even known it.

With far more force than necessary, startling Landerly from his now almost permanent spot in the straight chair, he shoved his way into the records tent. Jordan made a note to get a recliner. He thought he'd seen one in the faculty lounge. Landerly's brows went up, silently asking what Jordan knew was coming.

He nodded. "It all matches. I–" He shrugged. "I guess it's all correct. Hers is now the only theory that makes sense."

"What about all the dead? People deceased from a long time ago?"

That creeped him out – the fact that it was now *his* brain working like Landerly's. "I already asked. And no."

Jillian came into the tent behind him, her sneakers so soft on the now worn grass that she didn't make a sound, but he felt the cool night air follow her, and he smelled her. "So, you two believe me now."

Both men turned to face her and nodded. Jordan knew what was coming next.

"There's not much option is there?"

The two men simply stared at her.

Jillian knew.

They wanted to believe she was crazy. That she simply *believed* it was true.

But it was.

"I'm right aren't I?" For some feminine reason, it wasn't enough to feel vindicated. They would actually have to say the words. Their acceptance meant everything.

Jordan looked at her through suddenly narrowed eyes. "Until we come up with a better explanation."

She felt her mouth form into a shocked 'o'. He would just keep looking until he found a way to discredit her. "What better explanation is there?"

"Well, maybe this one: you and David share a psychosis, nothing more."

"Psychosis!?" She could have thrown something at him, and wished she had something solid and heavy at hand. Something better than the stethoscope she had casually tossed around her neck upon standing upright. If her boss hadn't been watching, she just might have slugged him, then slugged him again for being right.

It was possible. The world didn't turn on her wishes.

She sniffed in and tried to put the pieces of a calm expression back into place. To let her clenched lips relax. It was much harder than it ought to be.

"Children?" Landerly's condescension made it happen much faster than her will did.

She looked over and saw that Jordan, too, had been distracted from their fight.

Dr. Landerly held up his cell phone, "I have a Doctor Melanie Sorenson on the line…"

Jillian felt her brows pull together. But it was Jordan who filled in the blanks. "That's Becky's sister's name, but I thought she was a child…"

Landerly smiled. "That explains a lot." He turned back to the conversation he had muted with a well placed thumb. "Yes, Dr. Sorenson, what do you have for us?"

While they stood there, hovering, he had a conversation with the small girl. Jillian could make out a high-pitched but well-modulated voice because Landerly had his volume up so loud. "notebooks, huh?…Becky's field notes….Thank you. We'll come and get them."

In a few more sentences he signed off and looked at the two of them. "You guys get a fetch job. I want those notebooks."

Jillian didn't object, but she was curious, "How did she get your cell number? No one has that."

Landerly grinned. "I think she talked her way through."

"She's seven!" Jordan looked incredulous.

Landerly laughed. "We'll have to keep her in the CDC's sights….Now go get a map and get out to Dr. Sorenson's house."

Jillian turned to go, her jacket still around her even in the warm tent, she really just hadn't thought to take it off. Jordan's hand on her shoulder stilled her, but it was Landerly he spoke to. "Jillian's not going."

Anger exploded through her in a wash. "Excuse me!?"

Still he didn't face her, simply made his case to the man sitting and watching with a bemused expression. "What if she slides back under?"

"I won't!"

When his eyes found hers, dark lights burned in his gaze. "You don't seem to have any control over it."

"I'm up and around!"

"Yeah, and we thought that last time, too!" His fingers gripped her arm, in that one sure way letting her know she wasn't calling the shots here.

"Well, you could slip back under at any time, too, you know."

"No! *I've* been out here doing research. There doesn't seem to be anyone else in the world that slipped back under. No other fantastical tales of the 'other side'. Just you and David."

"Fantastical!" He was still trying to undermine her. *Bastard.*

"She can go." Landerly's cool calm rode over them, radiated out from his seated position, where he clearly still commanded the respect he was due.

"But—"

Jillian resisted the urge to stick out her tongue when he cut Jordan off. "You'll be with her. She'll be fine even if she does go back under." With that said, he turned his attention away.

Jillian knew where her bread was buttered, and she started off toward the operations tent.

Jordan didn't follow her, just seemed inclined to stay behind and stew, so she let him. Five minutes later she emerged from the tent with the keys and quick printed map, thinking she'd just go by herself, until Jordan turned the corner and smacked into her. "Ready?"

His voice was tight and clipped, and he yanked the keys from her fingers even as he asked. "I don't trust you to drive. You might slip away and kill us both."

Her mouth hung open but she followed him out, through the rows of mostly stationary cars and trucks, until he seated himself in the driver's seat of one and expected her to slide into the passenger spot.

Fine. Two can play at that game.

And she managed to stay silent for about half the trip. Then finally it just burbled out of her. "Why are you so upset about me coming?"

His hands visibly clenched on the steering wheel, but he explained. "The last time you went under, your vital signs started dropping."

"That isn't uncommon."

"Yes, but yours kept slipping. That isn't uncommon either, in patients who die in their comas. So no, I'm not real comfortable having you in the car and driving you further away from medical care."

She kept her mouth shut and waited out the rest of the ride. They finally arrived at the old farmhouse, where the front door opened even before they put the car in park on the gravel driveway.

A small redhead with her hair flowing down past her shoulders came out the front door. She was in typical kid clothes, but no pigtails. And she walked with an air of intelligence and introduced herself in perfect little belle form before handing over a pile of black and white, well-worn composition books. "These were Becky's. She left them here, because she did a lot of the frog research here. Y'all should have them."

It was Jordan who thanked her by name, took the books and shook hands with the hunky blond older brother, took a few minutes to learn what they did.

Aaron was a lawyer. And Jillian resisted the urge to point out that fit the profiles of those who had survived. The lawyers were over here. Of course, one lawyer didn't prove anything.

Melanie sniffed and ignored her. That made sense. Jillian didn't think she'd ever had a way with kids. Even when she'd been one. But the little girl spoke a mile a minute to Jordan. *Didn't they all?*

"Becky told me to go to the magnet school in Knoxville. I didn't want to, but–"

"Why not?" He was down on one knee, just below Melanie's eye level, and Jillian watched, fascinated. She just wanted to see how it happened, because a real conversation with a child was so far out of her own scope.

"I didn't want to ride the short bus. I didn't want to be different." She sniffled again. "But now I think maybe that's okay."

"If you want."

Her little head nodded vigorously. "I can learn to be a biologist."

"From what I hear, you already are." His hand settled on the small red head, and he managed to do it without coming across as condescending.

They said a few good-byes and Jordan made it clear that he needed to get Jillian back right away, although that was a pile of crap as far as she was concerned. But on the way back she put her head on the windshield and curled into the car door.

Jordan's hand was rough on her shoulder. "Don't you dare go to sleep. Don't even think about it." His eyes looked out over the road but his attention was on her, she knew. "You are not going under on my watch."

Becky sat virtually still in the heated tent as she shuffled through the composition books she had dragged from home. The house hadn't felt quite so cold or lifeless when she had gone back this morning, and wound up having an hour and a half all to herself. Maybe it was because she and David had been through there. Maybe because she had accepted that the house no longer answered her back.

The notebooks, too, felt useless.

All the creatures in them had survived. The Warblers were thriving, and in the right place. The bees were still making the weird columns in Los Angeles. All her frogs were out and hopping: in her own backyard and in McCann. And she had to wonder what the hell it was all about. Why did they mutate? And would they ever know just what the effects were? And since the shifts only happened once every 60 million years or so, there was no real scientific need to find out.

But they did have to find out what the hell was happening to Jillian and David. Maybe there was a connection between what was happening to them and the frogs and other amphibs. The shift had taken a different toll on some species. Maybe it was doing the same to Jillian and David. And in the meantime it was taking its toll on Becky, too.

The mirror in tent 43 revealed the blue marks under her eyes. Initially only smudges, they had bloomed to full on bruise-like shades in the last twenty-four hours. Jillian passing out at the morgue had shocked a solid ten years onto Becky's age. Just when she thought everything had stabilized – hell, the frogs had righted themselves even – Jillian managed to scream herself into a coma.

Luckily David had caught her. Becky had her wonderings if it was because he felt something for the dark-haired doctor or if it was because he *didn't*. She couldn't read him. And wasn't sure she wanted to.

Then he had slipped away in the car on the ride home. That had put another ten years and two shades of pale on her face. If she added it all up she just might need to start smoking.

Dr. Jordan Abellard had died early.

David Carter was under, and so was Jillian Brookwood.

And she sat here, staring into space, because she had gotten tired of watching the clock move, sleeping in the straight-backed chairs, and fearing the ever-present slowing of the heart monitors.

The last two were slipping away, of the four who had initially discovered the reversal.

So she was here. The only survivor.

The day sent sun streaming in through the pores of the tent, making the desk lamp into a simple waste of electricity. The heater worked overtime, even though hot spots formed on her jeans clad legs where patches of sun filtered down to her. But she shivered.

Maybe when her folks showed up.

Maybe then she'd start to right herself.

"Becky?"

The voice was soft and familiar even if she didn't place it, and Becky turned to see who had approached through the open tent flap behind her, and let out the same ghastly sound that had come from Jillian's throat at the morgue.

Jillian Brookwood stood upright in the doorway, the straight-forward expression and blue scrubs not any sort of indicator of whether Becky was having a hallucination or seeing the real person. Jillian didn't respond. She couldn't. She was being jostled by the doctors and techs who came to check out the unearthly sounds emanating from tent 43. Becky closed her mouth, having developed a sudden fear that she, too, could scream herself into a coma.

Jillian's frown at being jostled around and shoved aside was all too appropriate, and Becky lost the fears. Shoving the techs out of the way, she engulfed Dr. Brookwood in a too-familiar hug. "When did you wake up? You seem fine! How are you feeling? Do you want to sit down?"

Jillian just waved away all the concerns and looked Becky in the eyes and smiled. Her grin revealing even teeth and a dimple. Her eyes nearly glowed and Becky wondered what was up.

She was baffled as Jillian shooed the others out of the tent, closing the flap behind them, before forcing Becky to sit.

"You're going to think I'm crazy–"

Becky had to interrupt. "Trust me. At this point there is no *crazy*."

"While I was under I figured it out." Jillian's eyes flashed: she knew something, and Becky knew that she would, too, in just a minute.

"You are the only person I know who could 'figure something out' while comatose. So what did you discover?"

Settling her hip on the desk, Jillian spoke and Becky absorbed. "During the time when everyone was under the earth shifted. It split. Not in half…" She gestured like slicing an orange, then waved a hand while she searched for words, which was significant in and of itself. Jillian was never at a loss for the right word. "There are two places now. Identical. Maybe two whole earths."

This time Jillian's hands found purpose. She wrapped them around an imaginary ball, fingers entwined, then pulled her hands apart, leaving her fingers in place. Her motions now showed her holding one of her imaginary earths in each hand. She shook her head at Becky, "I don't know where the other earth is, but I've been there. I think they're actually in the same place," her hands gestured as though the two little earths melded, "But in different...I don't know the word...'realms'?"

Becky followed and Jillian must have gauged something from her face, for her eyes scanned once then she continued. "So the people who died here, woke up there." She gestured as though she still held small planets in her hands. "And those who died there–"

"Woke up here."

"I don't have it all worked out, but I am certain people can't exist in both places at the same time."

"So in order to wake up here, they had to die there, and vice versa." That was the logical tail, Becky knew, and in confirmation, Jillian nodded. Her thoughts turned over, and for once Jillian waited for someone else to draw their own conclusions. Becky didn't stop to wonder why she had been granted this rare privilege. "So, on the other side there are otters? But no frogs? No honeybees?"

Jillian shrugged, her blue scrubs revealing the sharp curve of her shoulders, and Becky realized that the doctor had lost weight. But even as thin as she was, she had shucked her jacket first thing when she'd come into the tent. And only now did Becky reach out the short distance to turn down the heat. Only now did she feel a little less cold herself.

But Becky saw right away that Jillian wouldn't wait for her feelings to catch up, so she tuned into Jillian's voice, already in progress. "-don't know about the otters but we have all the animals that were having troubles before the reversal."

Becky felt one eyebrow rise, "And you know this how?"

"Because when we went back under, David and I woke up there."

Becky wanted to release the sigh she was holding back, but years of southern manners forced her to retain it. "Of course you did, otherwise how would you have figured that out? I bet David fell down the steps there, too, but what about–"

Becky gasped as the air was forced out of her by way of a merciless hug from Jillian. She had blinked and missed seeing it coming – only suffered the feeling of having the wind knocked out of her.

But Jillian didn't apologize; she shined. "You are so much smarter than the boys. Even after I explained the whole thing, they still didn't believe me!"

Becky shoved aside the sinking feeling that Jillian was serious, and ignored the dance of joy. "The boys?"

"Jordan. Landerly. David's there now." Jillian had answered straight up, but her brain wasn't engaged with Becky. It was on its own track and further into the conversation than Becky was. And for a brief moment she wondered how Jillian could do that.

But because it was Jillian, who would take the conversation and run, Becky pushed through another round of thoughts and tried to give credence to the theories. "If all the animals that were abnormal before the reversal survived both here and there, then maybe they were reacting to it. Preparing in some way." Jillian nodded, and Becky dove in with her objection. "But where did you get your list? I don't know if anyone had as comprehensive a list as I do."

Jillian's eyes twinkled again. "We have *your* list…well, on the other side they do. We got it yesterday. Seems a kid talked her way through to getting Landerly's cell number and called him up posing as a biologist–"

"Melanie?!" Becky felt her whole body lean forward, and even as the name tumbled from her mouth, she knew she'd be devastated when Jillian said 'no'.

But Jillian was nodding before the word was through. "She said she was Doctor Melanie Sorenson. Said she had your notebooks and that you would want the CDC to have them. That she'd found them in the house."

"In the house?" Everything had made sense up until that.

"They came back a day or two ago, and yesterday afternoon Jordan and I drove out to get them."

Becky's belly clenched. "Dr. Abellard? You two drove to my house? But I was there this morning!" She paused as it washed over her. She wouldn't see Melanie ever again. She wasn't going to slip into a coma and find the missing pieces of her family. "But I was *here*."

Again Jillian nodded, her head looking like the little bobble dogs everyone had in the back windows of their cars, what with the incessant nodding and the grin. The funny image kept Becky's tears at bay. It helped that Jillian didn't see how she felt and just kept talking. "We met her and your hunky older brother Aaron. They came back and he decided they should stay."

"Aaron." The name rolled off her tongue in some sort of homage, but she was too mentally busy to figure it out. "Of course he's not here, he's a lawyer."

Jillian almost cackled. "You know, it took me *hours* to convince Abellard and Landerly that people were sorted by their occupations. And they still didn't begin to get any of it until David woke up pissed off about being casted from hip to toe." With a sad smile she changed the topic with no segue, but Becky followed her. "Melanie said she was going to go to that magnet school you suggested, that it didn't matter if she had to ride the short bus."

With that the constriction in her chest expanded saturating every part of her. Creating pressure inside until it forced its way out in tears and sobs. But she didn't know what she cried for. Because she was happy they were alive. Or because, no matter where they were, they were still gone from *her* world.

Chapter 22

David pushed through the blackness. Struggling to find light. And knowing even as he came around just what was happening. He was coming out again. And from the feel of his twitches and jerky, involuntary hand-squeezes and such, he wasn't broken up.

Hal-a-fuckin'-loo-yah..

The other side wouldn't be so bad if he wasn't bashed all to hell.

He laid there, eyes still closed and lacking the control necessary to open. He didn't push much. It never seemed to help anyway. The darkness would recede on its own terms.

So he waited it out, feeling the air pull into his lungs a little deeper each time. His breathing and heart rate sped up bit by bit, while his consciousness rolled around in his head, waiting to solidify.

"David?"

The tone came through sweet and clear.

Jillian. "Are you coming around?"

No, honey, I thought it'd be best to hang out in the nether-world for a stretch.

He felt rather than commanded the exasperated sigh that fled his lungs.

And, pure as bells, Jillian laughed from somewhere over him.

"Well, we don't have to worry about any impostors."

He would have smiled, but was caught off guard by a second female voice coming from behind her. *Sorenson.* "With all the other problems we have, I'm glad we don't have that one."

But Becky's sarcasm was brushed aside by the slightly southern lilt of Jillian, so close. "We're glad you made it back to us, David."

Was there any question that he wouldn't?

He cringed at the raw scrape in his throat. He could live without this wrenching process of waking up. Sound forced its way out of his mouth, but he didn't have much time to process it, because light shined in through the miniscule slits his eyelids had formed and it burned like a mother-fucker.

Another sound emanated from him, and he turned slightly, wincing as he went. But in a moment of clarity his consciousness congealed. *No pain.* No breaks. Here he was as good as new.

David let his breath out and blinked his eyes a few times even though they felt like they were filled with sand. Jillian's gentle hands grasped his shoulders and applied soft pressure to wake him up. *Hold off on the shaking, honey, I'm coming around.*

"He's coming around." Her voice was a little muffled, and within the light he could make out a long, dark chocolate streak – her ponytail. She was talking over her shoulder to Becky. But the streak swung out of the glare and her face moved in closer to fill his vision. Her eyes burning like aquamarines and becoming clearer with each moment. "We weren't sure when you'd come out."

He nodded slightly, and opened his mouth to speak, but Jillian beat him to the punch. "Your vitals were getting concerning until about an hour ago. You were dropping well into the low end of normal and we were debating a few measures. But you're here now."

"You, too." He wasn't sure why those words were the ones that came out of his cotton-filled mouth. And from her frown neither was she. But he licked his lips and worked his tongue for a moment before he explained. "Abellard put you on an IV….for low heart rate. Something about your volume."

She nodded, absorbing and understanding what he relayed, even though he didn't. "My blood volume. Goes with low blood pressure. Over there?"

He nodded. Then with a few deep breaths he gathered the energy to prop himself on his elbows. He ignored Becky and Jillian while he sat up, piece by piece. They didn't seem to take much notice of him until he was fully upright and rotating his ankles and knees, the sensation of stretching muscles flowing through him in the sweetest of ways. This beat the hell out of living in casts and popping Percocet.

He wanted to get out and walk around. Hell, he'd have turned cartwheels if he could have. Well, maybe if it wasn't so gay.

"Hey, cowboy," Jillian's grasp wrapped around his upper arms and held him on the gurney, "don't go anywhere without a little help."

He thought about waking up with the searing pain in his shoulder and hip, and that, over there, he never got out of bed at all. "Well, I only have half the practice at it that you do."

"Touché." She had the grace to wince.

With a sigh of acceptance he let Becky and Jillian brace him on either side, and he actually enjoyed the sharp pains that shot up his legs when his feet hit the ground. He looked at the small women trying to hold him upright with Lilliputian efforts. Men might have done a better job, cushioned his landing a little more, but right now neither woman seemed to notice that she was plastered, full-length, down his side. David noticed. And smiled.

"I'm hungry."

They both looked up at him. Maybe wondering why such normal words had fallen out of his mouth in such an absurd situation.

Becky shook her head, and he could feel the movement where her chest was smushed against him, just under his ribcage. "I forget how fast you two come around once you do wake."

David stifled a perverted smile as Jillian shrugged and the movement drew her breast against him. She explained, "Once you come around, it's just like any other day... except the part where you're crazy."

David actually laughed at that. He didn't care to imagine the way that Abellard and Landerly must have grilled her. They had given him hell and they hardly knew him.

Her voice cut into his thoughts again. "So, let's head over to the cafeteria." She tugged on his arm, and he realized that even together, they couldn't budge him.

"No." He extricated himself from their grasp. "What I want is to drive my new Mercedes and go out somewhere and have someone cook me a nice big steak."

"That sounds heavenly."

They almost started drooling and he had a momentary vision of a bubbling hot tub, with the drooling faces inserted. Except he had once had Jillian in a bikini in a hot tub, and there had even been beer, and...nothing.

Becky's voice chimed in, "I'm game. But where would we get a steak now?"

Still they proceeded with full hope that it was possible, the women shrugging into their jackets and Jillian tossing him his brown suede bomber after her hands were through her own sleeves. They filed out the tent flap, his fingers encircling the ring of keys in his pocket. A brief burst of relief settling into him that they were really there. That he had actually bought the car. Here.

He pulled the keys out, letting the short frigid gust of wind steal heat from his fingers. But he didn't care. Looking up to see how far the chattering women had gotten ahead of him, he stopped dead.

No way in hell.

But it was.

In the flesh.

"David." The old man spoke through thin lips. His hair whiter and wispier than the last time they had seen each other. His chest a little more of a barrel, but in general he seemed the same. Certainly in great shape for a man of sixty-nine. And David knew, with the certainty that he knew himself, that if the weight was there, then the old man simply hadn't been able to get it off. "Dad."

His right hand shot out, years of reflex and training, and grasped the slightly wizened version that met it.

"How long has it been?" His father's voice was cultured and smooth. Of course. Naturally, everything about him spoke of wealth and power, just the way he planned. And David felt the added pressure of another disadvantage: David Carter The First also hadn't just awoken from a coma.

God, he hadn't even thought to check the lists to see if his old man was alive over here. And here he was – in Tennessee of all places.

David's chest settled into lead. *He came to see me.* He gathered himself and answered his father's question. "Two years."

"Too long."

Not long enough. But he mustered a weak smile.

Jillian and Becky stood in the background of the portrait his father made, behind the space the old man commanded. He wished they would go back to their female chatter, and stop watching this drama unfold, because David knew what happened every time he and the old man talked.

Damn, he had really thought he was done with the man when his name had turned up on the lists. But that was *there.* It would be best to just get it over with. "What are you doing here, Dad?"

He felt his body shrink back to adolescence, his maturity level drop several notches. And things he had carefully shoved to the back of his life begin a steady seep into the here and now.

"I came to see my son." He gestured with the brilliant mahogany cane David had only just realized he was carrying. "I hear you're the wizard who discovered all this."

Where the hell was the old man going? David waited for the knife to come out, the other shoe to drop. But he only nodded. Knowing, even as he did it, that Jillian and Becky were standing right there listening, and that they deserved their due. But he couldn't bring himself to give it, not when The First stood in front of him.

"Very impressive."

David heard, but didn't believe, the praise. Years of experience had taught him that the better the complement was, the harder the knife came from behind. So he waited, and the old man spoke again. "Did you use my hotspot theories?"

Ah, the joy of honesty. "I used a few. But in the end they didn't pan out." Again he fronted what he hoped looked like a genuine smile, and promptly changed the subject. "Dad, I'd like you to meet Dr. Jillian Brookwood and I believe you've met Dr. Rebecca Sorenson several years ago. They're both with the CDC."

Jillian nodded, of course she had already figured it out. His father scanned the two women, keeping his smile in place. But David knew. Dad wore a full business suit, and a small tic of the muscle along his jaw revealed what he thought of Jillian's scrubs and sneakers, and worse yet, Becky's faded old jeans and hiking boots. But his father just nodded in return, and acknowledged the two women in a polite way. Only David knew that it was less than his usual greeting. The one he reserved for esteemed colleagues and ornament women.

The invitation he extended was with his usual graciousness. "I was wondering if you would do me the honor of joining me for dinner."

David felt both stares swing his way. He warred between being grateful that the females deferred to him in front of his father, and frustrated knowing there was no polite way out.

Before he could answer, his father stepped up to the plate and steered the conversation. "I have my limo waiting."

Great. He felt his insides congeal and sink. Becky's jaw dropped open and Jillian tried to hide the lift of her eyebrows but didn't quite swing it.

David conceded defeat, a position he was used to when The First was around. And his father smiled, a big genuine grin that ate at David. Was it because he was happy that people would join him for dinner, or because he had succeeded in manipulating the situation?

The driver stepped over, decked in his full black suit, and held the door while Becky and Jillian slid in the back. They resembled puppies running loose in a mansion – young, out of place, and oblivious to all of it. He followed his father into the tight black confines of the car, wondering how the hell this had happened.

The earth had undergone a radical transformation. Over half the population had died. People were still trying to just get their lives back on track, to get institutions up and running. And his father had found a limousine, complete with a monkey-suited driver.

The voice, so like his own, broke through his thoughts. "Now, do you have a preference for dinner?"

Jillian and David looked to Becky, who shrugged as if to say, 'I don't live here either'. But her mouth opened and she spoke the words. "We were thinking about steak, but I'll be honest, we have no idea where to get one right now."

David bit down on the end of his tongue, wondering what his father would say. But the old man reached across the space between them, his hand clapping his son on the back. And for a brief moment David thanked the fates that his father had found him in this world and not the other one, that he hadn't been forced to have this conversation from a gurney, behind the safety of the babyrail. "I'm staying at the Garden Plaza Hotel."

"It's open?" Becky's voice cut the air with her shock. "The convenience store is still on the honor system. There are a few fast-food joints that are up and running, but–"

David watched while his father nodded at the plebes, unsurprised by their lack of understanding. The First always lived as though money could buy anything. "I had them open it. The driver will have called ahead to tell them how many to expect."

The old embarrassment crept over him. He had been raised this way, but for whatever reason, it hadn't stuck. His father considered it a huge shortcoming. And David was appalled that his father believed the world came running with the wave of a few bills. It was worse when The First believed that his son should, too.

He saw Becky and Jillian exchange glances. But whether it was awe over his father's abilities, or a good moral sense that disliked the buying and selling of everything, he didn't know.

It was clear that The First was through with their shock and he simply turned to David. "That was some very impressive work you did, son." His father's eyes caught his. The complement seemed genuine. "All the universities will be trying to grab you for next term."

His father actually seemed proud – like he was glad The Second was his son. He never really had been before. There had been moments like this where it had felt like the rift was closing, not healing, but getting narrower. And always before, David had reached out. Always before, when he had pulled his hand back it was bloody.

Still, he wondered.

Jordan stared at the inert form as he felt his chest caving in on itself.

Jillian lay still and quiet, spread across the gurney in front of him. At a perpendicular was David. They had watched him slip away about ten hours ago. The geologist's vital signs were dropping slowly but surely.

But it was Jillian who had already sunk into dangerously low numbers.

She was the one that worried him.

Jordan couldn't say he'd feel anything but professional failure if David completely slipped away. But if Jillian did…he didn't even want to examine that too closely.

They had initially covered her with a blanket, in a feeble attempt to retain some of the body heat she was so rapidly depleting. A few hours ago he had added an electric blanket, heating her from the outside. He and Landerly had made the call to run an IV into her just after David had slipped away.

But she'd been under now for sixteen hours.

A long time.

Her vitals were lower than he had ever seen them. And still slipping lower. The electric blanket made up for some of the cold leached into her system by the IV fluid. Her core temperature was ninety-seven-low, but close. He began tucking the blanket around her, under her feet, along her side. She made no response.

Not that he had thought she would. But he did keep hoping.

With a last look, he turned his ministrations to David, noting with professional detachment that his temperature was stable and very close to normal. Jordan pulled the hospital issue blanket up just under David's chin after taking a full round of vital signs and recording them in the chart left open on the desk at his side.

With a glance at Jillian, Jordan reached down and calmly turned up the space heater. He told himself that it was chilly in the tent, that any additional help maintaining her body temperature would be welcome. But there was nothing else he could do. Techs were looking in on the pair every five minutes. And her vitals signs were ebbing away in a flow that was too slow to actually watch.

He wandered to the cafeteria and ate a dinner he couldn't remember ten seconds after he swallowed the last bite, staring straight ahead the whole while.

Where was Jillian? If her theory was right, then she was somewhere with Becky and now David, too. And if there were two separate realms on top of each other, maybe she was here, in the cafeteria. His eyes darted from one spot to another. Thinking he might catch a shadow of Jillian, or, just maybe, see through to where she was.

He didn't want to believe it. Coma was a medical mystery of sorts. Unlike near-death-experience, it was believed and quantifiable, but with no true underlying explanation. No solid evidence about what happened to patients' conscious minds while they were under.

A black composition book sat unopened on the table beside him, and all around him real shadows existed, cast by other team members. They talked and waved like a hurricane around the silent eye, but they didn't interact with him, these straggling last CDC scientists.

The tent town was still up in its entirety, but in the past day or two the population had thinned out as the scientists had returned to jobs and families. There was even talk of needing to re-open the high-school.

His watch showed that he had been sitting there, eating his forgettable food, for nearly an hour. He'd been lost in the blank walls of the cafeteria, looking for Jillian, when according to her, the other side was just as populated as here. There would be shadows and hints of people everywhere if he could see them.

He turned to make his way back out into the cold night, through small but vicious gusts of wind, that wouldn't register with him at any level other than the most cursory. And he would begin again – go through his whole routine, checking on Jillian.

She looked exactly as she had when he left her. But when he counted, her heart rate was another beat per minute slower. She was another breath per minute slower, too. And that was very significant given the low rate she was already at.

He wandered off to get Landerly. "Her resps are slowing." He spewed it out as he pushed through the tent flaps, any 'hello' a wasted formality on the old scientist.

"We shouldn't interfere until she's in serious danger. We'll go back in an hour."

Jordan felt his heart clench. The old man had simply brushed it off. But then again, he was an MD, too. He knew his numbers and had seen far more than anyone's fair share of medical mysteries. So Jordan forced himself to sit. Then to open the notebook and pretend to do…something like working.

He felt Landerly's eyes on him before he heard the voice. "So what do you think of our girl's theory?"

Jordan shrugged. "She believes it."

Landerly nodded. "That puts a lot of weight behind it for you." It wasn't a question, so Jordan decided to neither acknowledge nor refute it. "She has all the right information. And I don't know how she could have gotten it any other way. Nor how she could have gotten such perfect corroboration from David…"

Again Landerly nodded. "Let's work from the assumption that she's right. How does this second earth work? Where is it?"

He almost laughed. That was exactly what had been ricocheting around his brain since Jillian had slipped under. The only thing that occupied his thoughts except Jillian's status. "It's right here. It's the same earth you and I are on."

"Then why don't we see them? Where are they?"

His brain focused. God bless the old man for the distraction. "It's like x-rays. It passes right through and we don't detect it."

Landerly scrunched his face.

So he continued. "There's more space between atoms than the atoms themselves take up." He tapped his hand on the table. "My flesh doesn't go through the table, not because there's too much *stuff* but because they vibrate in the same range. That means they bump into each other. Higher and lower vibrations pass through us. Like UV light. It's borderline, and it gets through the top layer of our skin. So if something was much higher or much lower, it wouldn't even be in our range. We'd pass right through it and never know it was there. Like x-rays.

"If we follow Jillian's theory, then at some point while everyone was under, the vibrations could have shifted into two distinct bands. And some people stayed with one and some with the other. Jason found that shift in the UV-vis scale. Jillian put a lot of stock in that. She's probably running a panel on the other side right now." Landerly didn't say anything, so after a few seconds Jordan continued, just to fill the empty space. "It might explain some of the shifting. In fact, that shifting may be why everyone got sick in the first place. We just didn't hold up well in the Earth's splitting vibrational level."

Landerly pondered it. Jordan could see it on his face. And saw that he, too, had found holes or gaps in the theory. It wasn't a perfect theory, but as usual, Jordan was stuck waiting for a better one to come along. Certainly Miss Jillian could come up with something.

Landerly tapped his thin lips with his pencil. "So how did it get decided who wound up on which side?"

"Jillian says there's a job description bias."

Landerly shrugged. "She's right. They've got most all the cops, we've got the lawyers. They've got preachers and we've got teachers. We got the CIA almost to a man. Now that's creepy."

Jordan almost laughed. But it *was* creepy. "Surely there's no God sitting up there saying 'lawyers this way, cops that way'. What I can't figure out is how it ended up that way. Geography would have made more sense, especially given that the root of the problem is a geological phenomenon."

"There is some geographical bias." Landerly leaned forward, the fact that he moved from his standard, laid back, steepled-fingers position indicated that he was interested in the topic. Very interested.

"Like what?"

"It's not obvious, but it is statistically significant. We have more Californians, less southerners, more east coast, less bread basket." He dragged a pencil across the map he had flipped open as he spoke.

"But there are greater and lesser populations in those areas. It just matches with the census."

Landerly shook his head, and Jordan knew he'd been chastised, "Beyond that. Based on percentage of the population those areas are higher and lower."

"Oh." Of course Landerly hadn't missed an obvious point like that. Jordan and Jillian had been hired to be the man's field hands – not his brain. "Maybe there's a meteorological factor, like humidity or cloud cover."

There was never a response to his idea. The older man simply bent back to his work, flipping pages, making spreadsheets with data from the deceased lists and survivor lists, adding in colored bands with Jillian's info.

It wasn't long before the requisite hour had passed, and Jordan popped up to check on Jillian.

He was back within a heartbeat. "She's too low."

He reported the fact to Landerly, but he didn't ask anything. He simply left, running through the tents, asking everyone where he could find a ventilator, wondering why he hadn't been better prepared when he had seen this coming. Maybe because he hadn't wanted to believe.

He called the hospital, who said they couldn't spare one. So he yelled until he was hoarse and a ventilator was on its way. Luckily the small local hospital was barely across the street. Within twenty minutes the techs were wheeling the thing his way, bumping it across the chewed up grass, while Jordan cringed, wondering if it would still function by the time it reached her.

He pulled her gurney out so he could stand at the head, and lowered her a notch, then drew a deep breath before beginning the process of intubating her. He was far more stressed than usual. Jordan had done a hundred intubations, but this one *counted*. As he finished and let out a shaky breath, the techs hooked up the machine and her lungs started expanding with the forced air at her normal eighteen respirations per minute.

The tent cleared out, leaving him alone with the two patients, and he wanted to feel relief. But he was closer to crying when Landerly showed up. "I figured you'd do it sooner or later."

Shock sent him staggering back a step. "You wouldn't have done it?"

A deep sigh, holding untold decisions, preceded the remark. "I don't know. I only knew that I didn't have to, that you would make that decision. I might still let her go." He shrugged, old bony shoulders making points beneath his white jacket.

"Why?!" Fury raged through him alongside the despair he had felt at his father's bedside. But this was worse. This time he felt he *should* be in control. He just wasn't.

"I—"

But he cut Landerly off. "Why did you hire me anyway? I thought I was this brilliant scientist and she would do all the nitpicky stuff. Then I realized *she's* the brilliant scientist *and* the perfectionist. So why the hell am I even here!?" God, he should have been in a pediatric office. He could have made a difference there.

Here, what had he done? Tagged along behind Jillian. Nodded acquiescence to her ideas. Charted her theories.

His breath rushed out, his volume shrinking.

But Landerly's voice caught him. There was a smile in it. "I thought you would have figured that out by now."

But Jordan only shook his head, pacing a small section of the grass while his eyes darted everywhere revealing the scattering of his thoughts.

This time it was Landerly who filled the space, compelled to talk to cover the harsh mechanical rhythm of the ventilator. "There were other doctors who were individually more qualified than either of you. More experience, et cetera."

Not helpful, old man.

"But I put you two together thinking you would be the best team."

"But Jillian is just like you. Why would you need me?"

Jordan's gaze went to the upper corners of the tent, the glazed focus an attempt to fight off the waves of emptiness. His fists perched on his hips, as though he might physically fend something off. So he was surprised when he felt the weight of Landerly's arm across his shoulder, the paternal gesture so out of character. "Jordan, Jillian is not just like me. She's smarter than I ever was or ever will be. I think she thinks in the same kinds of patterns, but she's faster and better at it than anyone I've ever seen."

Jordan nodded agreement, thinking that the one thing he wanted to know still wasn't answered.

"And you, son, are a fool if you don't see it."

Well, then, I guess I'm the fool. But he didn't say it out loud. Just waited while the ventilator clicked and grated its way through another two mechanical breaths.

"You're the heart. Jillian couldn't be what she is without you. I know *you* got those people in Florida talking. I'll bet you're the only reason that we have any data from Nevada that isn't just a jumble of numbers. I'll bet you've even listened to her think, then turned around and managed to interview everyone to find out if she was right or not. Jesus, five minutes into your interview you had me telling you things about my family and lifestyle that people who worked with me for years don't know."

Defeat. That's what was sagging in him. But he answered the absurd ideas Landerly laid out. "Sure, but anybody could do that. There's no effort or special skill, I just–"

"No, anybody can't. *I* can't. *Jillian* can't. Most good physicians can't. There must be special talent or someone as smart as Jillian would have figured out how to do it. Or at least fake it. And I'll tell you something else, if you asked Jillian how she does what she does, she'd tell you the same thing: she just does it. It's just the way her brain works."

That much was true. Jillian brushed off her gift as though it wasn't exceptional or unique.

Jordan pulled in a few sighs, finding it difficult to let his body just breathe when he was faced with the fact that Jillian just wasn't.

So he changed the topic, found a way to get out of the tent, if only for a few minutes. He probably would be compelled to come back after that long anyway. "Speaking of Jillian's brain, I want to hook her up to that EEG."

Landerly nodded, before slowly and painfully making his way out of the tent. Jordan followed, his gait a shuffling mimic of the old man in front of him. In a moment he returned with the EEG set-up, thinking he should have brought two back and hooked David up as well. But it wasn't like he was busy for the next ten hours or anything.

The gurney was still pulled out, so he stood at the head of the bed, where he didn't have to look at her motionless face. With gentle hands, he brushed her hair aside and placed the probes one after another in the appropriate spots. But as much as he wished it, there was no response from her.

So he stepped back and flipped the switch, watching as the green lines crawled across the screen. To anyone else, they could have been anything. Lie detectors, seismographs, heart beats. But he knew what he was seeing, and he stared. For how long, he didn't know.

The rustle of a person coming through the tent flap finally roused him back to himself. And while he hadn't been really 'in there', his brain had catalogued every passing line. He knew them all and he knew what they meant.

Landerly's voice cut through his thoughts. "Well?"

"She's almost brain dead."

Chapter 23

Jillian had been shivering beneath the covers of the gurney in tent 43, and finally it was getting warm. Becky, of course, had simply crawled under the blanket on the bed next to her and sunk into sleeping oblivion without a second thought.

For Jillian it wasn't so easy. Alone now with her thoughts, she was unable to find rest. The shifting plagued her. She had looked for answers for most of the day. Checking out that UV-vis problem that Jordan had brushed aside. And sure enough the scale was way low here. And getting lower.

That was concerning. She had checked out the machine earlier in the day and then come back later with another sample. The machine had been just a little off, and she'd had to recalibrate.

But if that was due to anything other than her own error, that could mean the vibrations were moving further apart. The earth wasn't finished separating, it still had further to go. And where would she get stuck?

When she admitted it to herself, the insomnia was a physical manifestation of her fear – of not knowing where she would wake up, or with whom.

She was the reason Becky had insisted they stay together. Even going so far as to sleep alongside each other on the plastic coated and damned uncomfortable gurneys. So Becky would know on waking if Jillian had gone under again during the night.

Not at this rate she wouldn't.

Becky had also insisted that David sleep in the tent next door and had drawn up a schedule for the techs on the night shift to check in every hour. It seemed like they were gremlins, breaking the seal that the tent flap had made against the light. Just as she would feel she was finally drifting off, resting, the light would shine right into her eyes.

She had asked – begged – them to stop checking. Even if she went under what could they do except say 'look, there she went'? But none of them would agree to leave her be. The second check had come just minutes ago, kickstarting her brain when it had finally begun to fall silent again.

She knew they were checking on David as well, although there was every possibility that he had managed to sleep like a baby. He seemed to be able to just turn himself off and on. But then again, maybe he wasn't doing so well tonight. He was facing bruised and broken ribs, fractures and learning to walk again on the other side. He'd rather wake up here.

And he'd been agitated all evening. While she could quantify it, Jillian was hard pressed to name the source. Even though the steak dinner had been great and his father had been nothing but proud. Once she added that thought in, she would bet her life savings that he wasn't sleeping either.

Jillian tucked that thought back under her bonnet as well. At dinner she'd said something about hating that Landerly didn't believe her, and the server had leaned over and quoted the Bible to her – warning her that her hateful thoughts went against the teachings of Jesus.

Becky hadn't said anything, she'd been familiar with the parable the woman had named, but David had commented on the high quantity of Jesus and God he'd seen around. More than one group thought they'd ascended. Jillian was just waiting for them to don their identical Nikes and drink the Kool-aid that would get them to the mothership. The way she figured it, Darwinian selection wasn't just about predators selecting you out of the herd. Self-selection was as good as any, and darn cheap in light of societal costs.

"Pssst."

Had someone just said 'pssst'? No way, no one said that! She ignored the sound.

But it came again. This time accompanied by a crack of light at the tent flap and a "Jillian, you awake?"

Even whispered, she recognized the voice. "Coming, David."

Part of her didn't want to wake Becky, the other part of her wanted to do it just to disturb the peaceful sleep she was so jealous of. But she slipped softly into her sneakers, and pulled on her jacket, before passing quietly through the tent flap to where David waited, rubbing his hands together for warmth.

"Couldn't sleep?" They both said it at the same time, then laughed, until they remembered to curb it. Aside from a few night shift techs, everyone else was asleep.

David grabbed her hand, and she was grateful that he'd kept his warm. "I was thinking we might take a walk to wear ourselves out, but it's really too cold." She nodded agreement, and didn't protest as he pulled her along to his tent, where he popped on the interior light at the end of the table.

She blinked a few times, then adjusted. Finally upright, and admitting she was awake, she could feel the exhaustion in her muscles. "So, we'll just sit up and keep each other company until we finally pass out?"

"That's my guess." He shrugged, "I don't want to go back. I'm bashed to hell over there."

She climbed up on the gurney, getting her feet out of the cold that pooled on the floors of the small tents, "But with physical therapy–"

He cut her off. "I've had three doctors over there tell me that I'm facing at least a year of rehab. And another surgery to re-break both my hip and leg so they can be re-set."

Jillian cringed, but he waved her discomfort and guilt away. "You did an amazing job. All by yourself. But I may never walk without a limp. And that's after all that therapy. Why do it?"

She nodded, understanding straightforward reasoning for a problem that was anything but. "And your Dad's here."

"Yeah, I don't know what to make of that."

She felt her head tilt, the outward manifestation of her natural curiosity.

"We've never gotten along. He never accepted me; I was always inferior…"

"But he was nothing but complimentary tonight. You're the best son in the whole world." She didn't mean for it to come out as sarcastic as it did, but David understood. He laughed.

"Yeah, that worries me." She could hear the resignation in his sigh, "We've been so far apart for so long that…I don't know."

"Do you want to patch things up with your Dad?"

His shoulders shrugged. His head shook 'no'. His mouth said "I guess." And his hands came out, palm up, to question all of it.

It was all she could do to stifle the laugh that bubbled low in her. And she was grateful for the lightness of it. It beat the hell out of the fear she'd been trying to sleep with. She was only sorry that her improvement had come at David's expense. "Oh well. True, your Dad is here, but so are the Jesus freaks. And it's not like there's much you can do about it anyway."

His head turned square on to hers, and their gazes locked. "So doctor, tell me what you think is going to happen to us."

Just like that, it was her turn to shrug, to shake her head. "Our vital signs keep dropping lower and lower every time we go under."

"Abellard said something to that effect when he looked in on you right before I popped over here."

Good. She knew where she'd wake up if she came to over there. "I figure we keep passing back and forth until we die on one side, then we'll be stuck on the other."

David didn't respond. How could he when she had just placed their mortality squarely in front of them? Her voice was low, in response to the difficulty she was having pushing it out. "With the way our stats have been dropping recently, I don't figure we'll go back and forth too much more. Maybe two times. Three or four at the most."

He nodded. "Do you think we'll feel it? Or we'll never know, just realize that we keep waking up in the same place over and over?"

Again her head shook. It was the only thing she could think of. She couldn't just shrug a response to every question. But the same ones had been tumbling through her own head all evening. "There's another possibility."

"Name it."

"It's worse." She couldn't look at him. Instead she studied the neat, even stitching on her once white sneakers, noting how the dirt had clung, clearly outlining the threads as they marched in efficient lines across her toes. "We could get caught between. Die both places." Again her shoulders went up, and she suppressed the thought that she would get some really buff deltoids from all this shrugging. "We have to acknowledge that we might not survive this at all."

Still she didn't look at him, just waited through a few well-placed breaths until he spoke. "Any ideas why we got caught between?"

She laughed, a short bark of disbelief. "I still can't figure out why people ended up on one side and not the other. There are a lot of Bible thumpers over here...but..."

"I think Becky had a good point that there was a lot of right and wrong over here. The Bible thumpers just seem to fall into that category."

Her brain wrapped around that for a moment, wondering whether there were a lot of shades of gray on Jordan's side.

In that moment, as she drew that breath in, she knew that this wasn't the place for her. That if she could choose, she'd be *there*. With her job. With Jordan and Landerly. The way David would chose to be with his family here. But she couldn't choose, so she ignored the thought, and started herself in another direction in hopes of shaking it. "I figure we got caught in between because of some weird pattern of early exposure. But I can't figure out why Becky or Jordan or anyone from McCann doesn't have it, too. Jordan says there are reports from about three other places in the world. Each with one person who keeps going back under."

"Have any of them actually died yet?"

She knew he was looking at her, but she wasn't ready for eye contact. "Not that I know of. But I haven't seen Jordan in a full day now." Maybe it would have been easier to stay in her own bed and toss and turn with her own thoughts rather than dealing with David's.

"What if there were another option? What if you could choose?"

Her head snapped up, to find his blue gaze boring into hers. For some reason she felt he saw deeper than the surface of her for the first time.

He broke the spell by speaking. "It works because we want to stay on opposite sides."

That was all he said, but she could see where he was going with it. "No." It was just a whisper. She couldn't do it. "We don't even know that it will work." Fear ran through her, icing her limbs, holding her still when what she wanted was to leap from the bed and flee back to the cold gurney waiting in tent 43.

"We may die if we do nothing."

"I can't!" She started to actually move away from him, but his hand shot out, grabbed her arm, jerked at her as her feet hit the ground, preventing her flight from progressing past that first leap.

"Then you go back and forth. But do it for me when you wake up over there."

"I can't." The anguish in her system burst forth in tears, "I can't."

He wanted her to...what?...hold a pillow over his face? Squeeze his throat? Medicate him? Any way to end his life. Over there.

"Then hire someone." He hadn't let go of her arm, and while he wasn't bruising her, neither was she going to wrench free. "I'll give you all my banking codes. You can draft yourself a check from my account and pay them."

"David..." She searched for any logical 'no'. "I'd go to jail."

His gaze was steady, and should have been ice cold for what he was suggesting, but it was warm as the blue center of a hot flame. "I can get the names of some people from my Dad, it won't be traced. You can just give them the banking codes. Let them get their own money. I'll be very rich over there because my father has died and I'll have more than I can spend."

She couldn't fault his logic. But neither could she agree.

Her head still shook back and forth. He slid off the bed, and stood looming over her, holding her upper arms firmly in both hands. Only then did she realize that streams of tears were pouring down her face. She couldn't do any of it. Not go back and forth anymore, nor could she end it. He looked her square in the eyes and asked again, "Please."

Again she shook her head, and started to refuse again, but he headed her off.

"What are you going to do? Go back and forth and maybe die? Wind up wherever you happen to be? Maybe in between, and who knows what the hell that is! I can release you over here, too...and stop this."

She heard the soft ripping of the Velcro on the tent flap behind her. A tech popped his head in, and she saw David's gaze connect over her shoulder with whoever it was. "I guess you two are both still awake."

David simply nodded and started to look back at her, a certain dismissal of the young tech, but the voice came again, "Are you two okay?"

Her nod and David's curt 'yes' must have sufficed, because the tent flap softly closed behind her, and the heat from the small orange-glowing heater at her feet seeped around to envelop her again, shutting out the cold that had reached in and tickled her from the open gap.

David's stare returned to her face. "I don't want to go back there. I live there on a gurney in a haze of pain and Percocet—"

"You'll get better!"

"I *am* better. Here." He was restraining himself from shaking her. But it wouldn't have mattered. She could feel her heart thundering in the empty cavern of her chest. But she forced even breaths, afraid that if she passed out, she'd only shuttle herself back and forth again. Her eyes burned. Her mouth was swollen from where she'd been chewing at her lip, and her vision was glazed with tears.

"It's simple. And it's what we both want."

She didn't try to respond. She couldn't have anyway, his mouth closed over hers, stopping all her protests.

Jillian simply surrendered. She needed this. Needed to feel his hands slip from her biceps to the back of her shoulders and pull her closer. His sweater was softer than she could have believed when her fingers passed over it, feeling the hard muscle beneath. She didn't even stop and make any quantifiable assessment of him. Just kissed him back.

She didn't protest as his fingers, tough and soft at the same time, pushed the tears away. "David…"

He pulled away just long enough to get her to open her eyes. And when she did he shook his head. So she closed them again, and raised her mouth, never once wondering if his would meet hers.

Jillian didn't realize when he had backed them the two steps to the gurney, only that he had followed her shoulder blades down her back, arching her body into contact with his, and finally arriving behind her thighs, where he lifted her astride him into the heat of him, and the unmistakable arousal.

He took one sharp look at her eyes. He knew what he was doing, and he wanted to know if she did. His hand snaked out to shut off the desk light that was now glaring in his face. With a blink they were bathed in the soft orange glow of the heater and the deep shadows that filled the spaces.

Later she remained there, naked in his arms, untied from her existence, until the pieces started gathering and settling back into place. There were no sweet words. She wouldn't have believed them anyway. Didn't have any of her own to speak in return even if he lied and said it. There was just the sound of two bodies, breathing heavily out of rhythm in the blackness of the tent.

He pulled the blankets over the both of them. Letting her drift with her own wayward thoughts while he settled in, his arms locked around her.

They hadn't used any sort of protection.

But it seeped slowly through her, not causing any real alarm. She wouldn't likely live long enough to be concerned about that. Her muscles were limp, and the darkness was saturating her thoughts. And she was grateful that she was finally going to get some sleep. Grateful that the pull of sleep was deeper than usual, not just because she was sated.

Because she knew she'd wake up on the other side.

His voice murmured to her while she sank away. But she made out the words. "I'm staying awake, Jillian. You go. And when you get there you can keep me here."

She couldn't gather the thoughts to fight him, nor the muscle to protest. Couldn't even really remember what her objections were. It was a simple solution to a simple problem, based on her own logical theories.

"Do you want me to leave you there?" His breath was humid against her cheek, letting her know how close he was. But she was too far gone to gather an answer.

She thought she said 'yes'.

Jordan felt Landerly's shoulder beside him. He didn't know if the older doctor was aware that they were touching or not. If maybe he was leaning for a little physical support, or if it was because they had been staring at Jillian's stats for too long now. Listening only to the machinery and the sounds of crickets beyond the tent. Looking at the lines on the computers that tracked her progress, or lack thereof, while the artificial light held the dark and the night at bay. Unable to make a decision about the lifeless looking body that Landerly had started referring to as 'Our girl' when he wasn't talking directly to her.

Jillian's hair was neat, untangled and lying behind her on the sheet. She was in blue scrubs. Jordan had talked a few of the techs out of changing her into a gown. The gowns were demeaning no matter who you were, but she was their superior, she was a doctor. She deserved the scrubs.

She was pale, beyond pale. She didn't look dead. Thank god. The oxygen that the machinery was forcing into her system kept her skin tone within the range of the living, if not exactly healthy-looking.

For a moment Jordan allowed the morbid thought that the mortuary make-up person wouldn't have to do a lot of work on her. But he squashed it as soon as it arose. They wouldn't have to do *any* makeup on her. He couldn't let it get that far.

Landerly shifted, finally bearing all of his own weight, or supporting himself on the cane so that he didn't lean on Jordan anymore. That probably signaled a decision.

"Our girl hasn't sparked a sign in hours. Her EEG looks almost brain dead. There's no real activity."

It was just a statement of fact, not a manifesto to unplug her, but Jordan reacted as though it was. "So? She *isn't* brain dead. Not quite. And we don't know anything about this. We can't make this decision. There's no precedence…"

"True."

Jordan felt the tension ease, seeping slowly from his system.

"But that doesn't mean we can justify the machinery, the cost, all of it. We may need to let her die."

The taught wire feeling returned, instantly solidifying in him. He had barely held back his protests about Landerly treating Jilly like a cost-benefit analysis. He shook now with the strain. "I know you care about her, so how can you think that? How can you say we should 'let her die'?"

"Because I do care about her. Because I see her as a person and not as…well, I don't have the feelings for her that you have."

Jordan finally admitted it to himself. His father had seen it, had even asked him point blank. And if Landerly saw it too…well, the only person less observant to human feelings than Landerly was Jillian.

And for a moment Jordan cursed her. If she could have looked at him and seen it, then she could have responded. Whatever her answer may have been. That she was crazy about him. That she lusted after him. Or maybe felt pity for him because he'd fallen in love with her and she didn't feel anything in return. At least he would have known.

Instead he had this – this unholy clinging to another person. She wasn't responding to anything that went on around her, much less his feelings. And he had to admit, in light of what was happening to her, his emotions were small potatoes.

"She's too low. Are you going to take her off?" The voice came from behind him somewhere and he didn't recognize it. And that was probably a good thing. He held himself back from smashing in the face of the tech who had walked in and made the remark about ending Jilly's life as casually as if he'd been updating them on baseball scores.

"No." He pushed it out through clenched teeth, turning to face the tech for a brief moment, hoping his expression meant that he was not to be asked again.

"Sorry," The young man was tall and skinny, just gaining some peach fuzz, and he began backing away. "I didn't realize…"

Jordan managed a nod. This was probably a high school kid who was volunteering and getting training. Jordan remembered how green he'd been back then. It had been easy for him, and interesting. And he remembered the first time he'd been scolded for saying how neat something was when a patient was suffering. He'd paid attention. Maybe this kid would, too.

"Well, are you?" Landerly's voice broke the roar of thoughts running through his head.

"No." He didn't look at the numbers. Didn't read the printouts. Didn't listen to the beeping of the heart monitor, as it slowly lost some of the steadiness that was the hallmark of a stable heart. And he didn't look because he knew what it would say.

If it had been anyone else, he would have turned it all off. He probably would have turned it off hours ago. It wasn't that she'd been gone for so long, it was that she was entirely sustained by machines. And he knew she didn't want that.

Chapter 24

Jillian might not want to be sustained by machines, Jordan thought, *but screw her.*

"There's no sign of brain activity. People don't come back from brain death." Landerly's voice was softer than usual. Jordan could hear where the sounds were tempered with his own sadness at the loss of Jillian. Or maybe at the loss of her brain.

Knowing that he had to come from a place of logic, and nothing else, he fell back on the one solid argument he had. "There's no precedence for this. So we can't take her off. We don't know what will happen."

"But–"

There wasn't a counterargument good enough as far as Jordan was concerned. And he had lost his fear of Landerly days ago.

So he plowed right over the old man. "The only thing we know is that they took the man in Sri Lanka off his mechanics and he died nearly instantly. So we can predict that if we take her off, we'll kill her. We need to leave her on for scientific purposes, if nothing else. So we can see what happens when one of these people gets the chance to come back through."

Landerly nodded, and Jordan saw his smile. "Good idea. But it would help if you could find some evidence here. Anything that justifies keeping them hooked up. I like the 'it's for science' angle. I'll have to see what the brass thinks. They get the final say."

Without anything further, Landerly turned and placed his weight against the cane that was constantly with him. Jordan felt the sweep of pride soak through him, it seemed the old man had been rooting for him, placing his faith in Jordan to find a good answer that would keep her alive.

So, with renewed energy, and the constant tension of one whose fate is decided by others, he turned back to the charts and beeps, this time listening with a purpose. For a moment he just stood and counted, hearing the synthesized blips interspersed with the techs outside the tent and the bugs that lived here where it was city, but not all concrete. He didn't have a musician's sense of rhythm and timing, but he could count. And so he rattled off a silent 'one-two-three-four-five-' before her heart triggered the machine to beep again. He counted to the next one and the next, getting four and six then six then five again. She was bradycardic – definitely too low, and not keeping good pacing.

He turned to the papers, the tiny strip of green grid with the single black line that represented all the functions of her heart tracing across it. It told that she had been this way for a while. Yards of it unfolded, showing that the rhythm had declined steadily and not stepwise

He next used the attached keypad to scroll back through the EEG stored on the computer screen. It didn't print out unless it was commanded to. So he scrolled back to the beginning of the reading, and watched as her theta and delta waves lost their height and depth. Nothing. It slowly transformed from a linear representation of the basic workings of a human mind to flat lines. He thumbed through, his eyes occasionally skipping back to looking at Jillian herself, and not just the computerized readouts of her.

But her chest rose and fell in an inhumanly steady beat. She didn't twitch or move.

And his eyes went back to where he was scrolling through the hours. The green lines passing in front of him as they had when they were recorded, only in super fast-forward.

He almost missed it. It was beyond the middle of the night and his eyes were tired. But there it was – brain activity – a cluster of bumps and ridges. Not the kind of upper consciousness activity he would have liked to see, not like when a person worked a math problem, but something deeper. It registered mostly in her theta waves. Just a few simple bumps. But Jordan quickly highlighted the section, and typed in a few comments about the time and duration, before sending it to the printer.

With a purpose, he got up and slapped at her hand. "Jillian, wake up, wake up."

But it was futile, as he had known it would be, even though he had hoped.

He almost grabbed the printout and ran to Landerly when he decided to look one more place.

With a few commands the computer shifted screens, to David's readout. Jordan hadn't been much concerned with David's vitals or EEG. And why should he be? *David* was holding up much better. His vitals were low, but he didn't yet need a respirator. They had only hooked him to an IV an hour ago.

The lines in front of him were the same as they had looked when they hooked him up the first time, in an effort to see if he was dreaming. Before he had corroborated Jillian's wild story.

Jordan realized that he didn't question her now. That she either made sense, or he was simply grateful that, while he might lose her, she wouldn't actually be dead. It was possible he had wrapped his brain around that and latched on so tight because he wished to believe. He had noticed that neither he nor Landerly had been out spreading the theory around. There was no talk of papers or panels or meetings, just the ongoing discussion between the three of them.

Holy shit.

David had it, too.

Jordan popped up and pulled the three pages from the printer, holding the first one next to the computer screen. The time was identical. And so were the bumps and ridges in the theta waves.

They ended at the same time as well. *What the hell was going on over there an hour ago?*

He highlighted and printed again, not bothering with typing this time. Jordan stood and waved at the printer. He told himself that three seconds wouldn't make a difference in whether or not Jillian made it, but he still swore at the cheap printer. Jerking the page free even before the machine released it, he darted out to find Landerly. Seconds later he ripped through the opening of the records tent, already explaining before he had even made eye contact. Landerly's head snapped up and Jordan knew he had read the hope there. But he also saw the cell phone pressed to the old man's ear, and he stopped mid-word.

He waited while Landerly waited, listening to what was being said on the other end of the line. Landerly nodded, though the listener wouldn't see it, and did what Jordan guessed was as close as he would get to actually rolling his eyes. So Jordan held up the printouts, knowing that Landerly could look while he disagreed with whoever was talking. He pointed out the blips and bumps.

But that only lasted a second before Landerly yanked the paper out of his hands and interrupted the person on the phone. "Listen, we have evidence of brain activity. We can't take her off. I'm faxing it over, and you're authorizing this."

Jordan smiled.

"Goodbye." It wasn't friendly, more curt and resigned than anything. And Jordan was glad that he only had to deal with 'the brass' through Landerly. Dealing with Landerly was tough enough.

Landerly held the pages back out. "Make copies and fax them back to Atlanta. Attention Brassard." He nodded to Jordan. "Good work."

But he didn't ask anything about what Jordan had found, didn't examine the lines any more closely. He had turned back to his books and charts before Jordan realized that he had been dismissed.

Feeling blank inside, he stepped away to photocopy his pages, walking softly, no longer at the breakneck speed he had used to get here. He was at the tent flap when Landerly's voice caught up with him. It was almost softer than the air, and held the loss of all Landerly's years. "Did you forge those?"

Jordan was stunned speechless. His mouth hinged open, but no sound came out. Finally, he found his voice. "No!–"

But he was too late and Landerly spoke over him, drowning out his protest. "Never mind. Those pages are keeping her alive. I don't want to know."

With utter disbelief he turned back to his boss. "They're real. I didn't *forge* them."

Landerly just smiled. "Don't act so insulted. You *do* have a history of it, you know. I just hope that you did a good job, so they won't discover it."

God, it was unpleasant to be a grown man and feel like a scolded kid. It was just the kind of kick in the pants he could do without these days. His voice was soft, not betraying his frustration. "They're real. I swear it."

Landerly nodded his head. "Good. Good. Plausible deniability and all."

Jordan simply left. He had found a way to keep Jillian alive, and right now it didn't matter if the doc believed him or not. Jillian had her funding.

In a slow daze that told of the middle of nights spent sleepless and tense, he wandered over to the communications tent and looked up the numbers. He pushed buttons and sent the pages through, thinking that Jillian would have had the Atlanta fax number memorized. He promised himself she'd be glad to rattle it off when she came around.

Without any of his previous impatience, he didn't pay much attention to the pages chugging through the fax. He simply blinked one moment and realized the machine had gone silent, and the pages had fluttered around his feet.

He made copies in the same daze, then shuffled back to the tent where Jillian and David slept. But as he pushed his way through the flaps he heard the moan.

His head snapped up. Hoping.

But he knew that hadn't been her voice. He knew the voice that moaned. And while he was anxious, and excited, he was also deeply disappointed.

Walking over to the bedside, he began talking before he even got there. "David?"

Fingers twitched. Eyeballs moved beneath the eyelids in a pattern similar to REM sleep, but now identifiable as coming out. The moan came again, sounding more like the creak of old hinges than anything human, and Jordan wondered briefly why their bodies weren't getting more used to this. Why it wasn't seeming just like a normal waking up.

As usual, a stray glance cast its way toward Jillian, but registered nothing.

David, however, was rapidly coming around. His eyes fluttered. His hand clenched in a full grasp, and his right arm twitched, eliciting a swift intake of breath that Jordan guessed was none other than pain from having pulled against that dislocated shoulder.

"Son of a bitch!"

Jordan almost laughed at the words. They weren't perfectly formed. But he could tell what David had said.

"Hey, David." He smiled at the man on the gurney. Maybe this meant Jillian would wake up, too. But then again she had gone under first.

Jordan pushed that thought away, it would do him no good, and he turned back.

David's eyes focused on him and he spoke again. "Son of a bitch."

"Thanks."

"I'm not supposed to be here." The words were thick but no longer slurred.

"What do you mean?"

A sigh of defeat escaped David, and for the first time that Jordan had ever seen, the regal bearing slipped away from him. "I was staying awake. I was…well, I guess I wasn't." He turned to look at the wall, and Jordan heard the whisper, "Shit."

So he distracted David, waved the EEG papers in front of him. "You want to tell me what happened about an hour ago?"

"What?" It worked. David was no longer swearing nor looking at the blank white canvas in front of him.

"About an hour ago both you and Jillian registered some brain activity."

"Really?" He reached for the papers with his left hand at the same time he asked, "What time is it now?"

"About two a.m."

David examined the readouts in front of him, and, as smart as he was, Jordan figured he had at least a rudimentary knowledge of what he was looking at. "So that's what it looks like."

"What *what* looks like?" Jordan held up the second set of papers. "Jillian's got it, too. What is it?"

David took a breath and gathered himself, looking at Jordan, really looking at him, for maybe the first time ever – not just sizing him up, but reading him. And maybe even reading correctly. Jordan couldn't say he liked it. David reading him made him damned nervous. But he needed to know. "What is it?"

"Jillian will have to tell you."

That was what happened when David read you. Nothing good could come of it. So Jordan nodded and tried again. "Maybe you can ask her next time you see her."

"Why don't you ask her yourself?"

His mouth opened for a rude comeback, but he noticed David pointing with his right finger. The hand wasn't good for much besides pointing to the left, but it did its job now.

And he heard it: a rustle of sheets.

Abandoning David, he flew the three steps to stand directly beside her. Eyelids quivered with the rapid movement beneath. Her fingers twitched again, and her chest moved like she would moan.

But she couldn't, because of the tube down her throat.

So Jordan stood over her, barely feeling the smile that spread unknowingly across his face, as her lids fluttered and fluttered again before opening. "Welcome back."

Her eyes burned. And all she could think was that this was the worst part, so she forced herself through a few rapid blinks.

Jordan stood over her, an idiot grin on his face. "Of course you came back, I just saved your life."

What the hell does that mean?

But she really couldn't give it much thought. She couldn't talk yet. She still felt rusty. But if she could have she would have started in. That was just like her and Jordan. She wakes up from a coma, and he starts sparring with her.

It felt good to be home.

The air was better over here, or something.

But she closed her eyes, letting the grit slide past. Because she remembered what David wanted her to do. What she was pretty sure she had agreed to do, just before she drifted off to sleep.

"No! Jilly!" Jordan's voice, frantic with worry, broke through her morbid thoughts. She felt his hands on hers, smacking at the back of them, touching her forehead, resting on her cheeks. But she couldn't much blame him for panicking when she closed up and shut out the world. She *did* keep slipping into a coma. So she opened her eyes to the relief on his face. And only then did she register the sounds around her.

Crickets chirped in the background, a few birds made calls in the middle of the night. It sounded like home. But overlaying all that was the bleep of a heart monitor, the hiss of a ventilator, and the feeling that she was wired to everything. Only then did she catch a glimpse at the edge of her vision, and managed to tie together what the dry feeling in her throat was.

She was intubated.

And Jordan would never have done that to her if he hadn't had to.

A moment of pure panic settled over her. Now that she knew what the tube was, she had to get it out. Her brain knew she shouldn't remove it herself, but her hands scrambled for purchase and her eyes watered. Her chest fought for the right to breathe, fighting the ventilator.

Warm strong hands closed over hers, and while she knew it was Jordan, and that she should have been comforted, the hands pushed hers away, stopping her from her goal. Before she could protest, his face was over hers, his eyes staring at her, making certain she understood. "Jilly. You have to wait. Let me listen, then we'll take it out."

He was lying. He wouldn't necessarily remove the tube. Only if the sounds were right. Only if she was going to breathe well enough for herself when he took it out. But she wanted to believe.

The urge to swallow was overwhelming. She wanted to fight, but she tamped it all down, knowing that Jordan was right. And she simply blinked a few tears back, as she felt his hand slide under her shirt. The plastic circle of the stethoscope touched her once, twice, waiting each time, while she forced patience upon herself. She counted.

"You're good."

The words brought a flood of relief, but no real comfort. She managed a slight nod, filled with panic and tension, when he asked her point blank if she was ready. Jordan walked her through coughing, while he steadily slipped the tube up her throat. She had to cough twice, even though she knew it took most patients only once.

Finally when she was able to breathe for herself, she felt like oxygen was flooding her, even though she was fairly certain she'd been getting more of it through the machine. Her lungs worked rapidly, reestablishing their dominance.

Again she felt the hands. They grabbed hers and pinned them at her side. Why? Why was he holding her down?

Again, teal eyes looked into hers. "Jilly, you're shaking, you were about to knock out your IV." His arms came up to hold her, one hand stroking her face, and only as he said the words, "Jilly, don't cry" did she realize that his fingers had come away wet.

So she squeezed her eyes shut, and leaned into him, while he pulled her into a sitting position, as she re-learned to breathe.

In and out. In and out. Finally settling into a semblance of her normal rhythm.

"You feeling better now?"

Her head jerked around. And her lungs began to shove all the air out. It should have been a scream, but she still didn't have much of a voice from being intubated. Instead, she pushed out a soft but shrill wail that seared her throat like nothing she could ever remember.

David nodded at her, not bothering to look happy, or surprised, or anything other than pissed off.

When her breathing returned to normal, she realized she was staring at him. Just as she was going to do something about it, a gentle pressure on the side of her face turned her back to where she was inches from Jordan's concern. "It's just David." But he looked at her a little deeper, wanting an explanation of why David would make her scream.

So she told him.

Only no sound came out.

And after a moment she realized it was a damn good thing that no sound came out. Because she had started to explain what had happened.

David was going to have to kill her over there. There was no way she could show her face again. No doubt the techs had already found their naked, comatose bodies entwined on the gurney. Oh yeah, that was one for the books.

She felt the heat flood her face, and she did her best to bury it in Jordan's chest.

At last she found a whisper, and, figuring it was the best she was going to get, she settled for it. "David's supposed to be asleep."

"Because?"

Her breathing was kicking up and she wanted to fan her face with her hand. To fight the flush, to work off some of the nervous energy, to cover for the fact that she was panicking again. She never did things like that – and certainly not where she was going to get found out.

She turned and looked David in the eye. "We made a deal."

"Good." His voice was like ice. "I was afraid you were going to back out."

"So you showed up here to check on me?" She shifted in Jordan's arms, but he didn't seem to want to let go of her. Jillian really gave it no thought, other than that it was comfortable, and it was working to stave off another panic attack. There was nothing she hated more than being a helpless female.

Word by word, her voice grew stronger, "Trust me, I'm not backing out after that wake up." Her eyes focused on the straps and casts that held David in the bed, if not by force then by inability. "Is that what it's like for you when you wake up over here?"

He didn't speak, but his eyes held hers as he nodded.

She shuddered a bit at the thought. "I don't want to do that again."

"No shit, Sherlock." He grinned, but it wasn't in humor. "So you'll do it?"

She couldn't look him in the eye, not with what she was agreeing to. But in the end, this would set her free, too. "Yes."

When she found some backbone, some of the flash of anger she had felt before returned. "So why are you here?"

He spoke plainly as though it wasn't his fault. "I fell asleep."

"Why?"

"I'm male, it's what we do!"

She couldn't help the flush that crept up her cheeks, and David laughed just a little, a real laugh, at her expense. She felt more than saw Jordan's bewilderment through his arms. Finally, he found a voice to add to the conversation. "What?"

"Nothing." She and David both said it at the same time, looking away, and she figured Jordan had to have figured it all out. But when she finally looked up again, he seemed just as confused.

Silence reigned for a while, but it was David who started up again. "So, do you want to tell him what we decided?"

Thoughts of conspiracy charges flitted through her head. It was bad enough that she would do the thing. "No."

But David surprised her by taking a stance. "I think we ought to. I don't want to take a chance that you'll back down."

"I won't—"

But he didn't allow her to finish. His eyes quickly darted from Jordan to her and he simply began talking over her. "I think the boy has a vested interest in setting this to rights. I think he'll be helpful."

"What the hell are you two talking about?" Jordan's voice cut through the argument, and Jillian knew there was nothing she could do to stop David from telling Jordan whatever he wanted. She also realized in that moment, that she didn't want Jordan to know what she had done. That she had been curious and frustrated and scared, and that she had turned into willing arms.

She couldn't really work up any good shame over it. She just didn't want the embarrassment of the explanation. And the way she figured it, in this world it didn't exist. But the men talked right by her thoughts, and Jillian needed to know what David was spilling.

But he wasn't spilling anything, he was performing a careful set-up worthy of a courtroom. His question was directed at Jordan, "What happened to Jillian while we were under?"

As Jillian waited for his response, she realized that at close range his jaw was squarer than she thought, his shadow had progressed well beyond five o'clock, but it wasn't enough to hide the clench of a tiny muscle in the side when David grilled him. "Her stats got so low we had to put her on IVs and intubate her to keep her breathing. Then the brass decided you two weren't worth the money to keep on the machinery."

Her breath pulled in, again burning her raw throat. "They were going to pull the plug on me?"

He nodded, "You looked brain dead."

"I woke up just in time, then." The pure chance of it didn't sit well with her, but it didn't have to, Jordan spoke up.

"No you didn't. I found enough evidence to mount a case and they decided to let us keep you on it."

Jillian felt her bones lose some of their starch, and she slumped down against him. "Thank you."

When he nodded, she felt it against the top of her head.

But David interrupted again, keeping the conversation on the track of his choice. "If we can work this out, then Jillian won't go under again."

"I'm listening." Jordan's voice was hard, and so were his arms. He clearly didn't think he was going to like what he heard, and Jillian knew he wasn't.

"When I get back over there, I'm going to pull her plug, or medicate her, or suffocate her if necessary."

The arms around her tightened with each gruesome description, until she couldn't draw in enough air. They let up only when she started the makings of another panic attack. But Jordan had only a quick apology for her before he lit into David.

But she watched David, and he may have been lying on his side, casted from stem to stern, but he spoke with authority and slowly chipped away at Jordan's resistance.

Jordan threw every what-if? at him. "What if she dies?"

"Then I die." Jillian jumped into the fray. She wanted Jordan's help, but she wasn't about to let him talk them out of this. "It's better than this going back and forth. That was the worst wake up ever. At the rate things are going I'm going to die soon anyway. At least this way I get a choice."

Jordan focused on her, effectively removing David from the conversation, and by his intensity, David might have not even been on the planet. "So if he kills you over there, then you stay here…"

She nodded.

"Are you sure that's what you want?"

Again, "Yes."

Jordan stared David down. "What do you get out of this?"

But David didn't give any ground. "You two do the same for me over here. So I can stay there."

"But why?" Jordan had leaned back away from her. He looked back and forth between the two of them, as though he saw what had happened, even though it hadn't been mentioned. As if to ask, 'why would two lovers want to go separate ways forever?'

Jillian stepped in before David could. "His father's over there. And over here he's facing massive amounts of therapy and at least a couple surgeries. There he's whole."

David looked embarrassed by that last bit, like he always was when the topic of his tumbling down the steps came up.

For the next half hour Jillian stood up and stretched, and traced a circle already worn in the grass, while Jordan grilled them both. He brought up every contingency he could think of. Threw out every way it could go wrong. Pointed out time and again that no one knew what could happen and that they just might really kill themselves in some very warped version of Romeo and Juliet.

Jillian pressed her voice into service. "I'm going to die soon anyway. If I'm lucky I'll get stuck on one side or the other – just wind up wherever I am when my vitals finally give out. This way I get to choose, I get to stay here."

His eyes looked through her. He saw so much more than anyone else. But he was thinking. And she knew he couldn't argue her logic.

Finally he spoke. "Potassium chloride."

She almost jumped with joy, she just didn't have quite enough energy.

"Will you please tell me what the hell he just said?" David's droll tone cut into her happiness, but she simply turned and gave an explanation.

"It will stop your heart, and then mostly break down. No autopsy would turn it up unless they were looking for it. And you already have an IV so there won't be any puncture marks."

David nodded. "Painless?"

Jordan shrugged. "You'll be comatose, you shouldn't feel a thing."

David rolled over and looked at Jillian, "And what about you?"

How did she answer that? How did she choose a method to die? Especially when what she really wanted was to live. But in order to do that, she had to kill off the Jillian on the other side. She shuddered before opening her mouth.

But the sounds she heard weren't from her voice. It was Jordan. Explaining that the potassium chloride was the best method, where to find it unless the tents had been rearranged, how to draw it up, and how to inject it.

"Good." David turned and rolled onto his back, staring at the ceiling, speaking to the air in general. "Now there's just one more problem. How do we get me back under so we can do all this?"

Chapter 25

Jordan had begun to question his own sanity. He was walking through the tents with a syringe of potassium chloride in his top pocket. It was hidden by the jacket he wore, and he was certain that no one would notice.

What he wasn't certain of was why he had done it. They should have plenty of time once David went under to get the medication and dose him. They should have hours. But he had seen the opportunity and drawn it up right there in the supply tent.

No one had been around and this way he didn't have to steal a whole bottle. Record keeping was still pretty poor, but a whole missing bottle would be pretty suspicious.

His heart tripped along at a faster rate. Jillian walked quietly at his side, having stood guard outside the tent while he drew up the liquid. She had spoken out loud, letting Jordan know that someone was there, and loudly repeated that the man was going to the cafeteria. It was a good job of relaying the information without letting on that she was speaking to be overheard or that Jordan was following the conversation from inside.

God, he had felt like a kid stealing a look at the files in the principal's office, and he couldn't remember the last time he had felt so guilty or so low. Jillian didn't speak as they traipsed quietly to the cafeteria, and he wondered if her thoughts were the same as his, if she ever questioned her theory. If she was wrong, and it was all a shared dream, then they were killing David. Just flat out murder.

He pushed that thought aside. If she was right, and they didn't do anything, she'd die if she fell under again. The trend that all five of the people going back and forth had established was to have their vital signs drop lower and lower the longer they were under. And to drop more rapidly each time they went back under. She had barely survived the last time, and Jordan was certain that she wouldn't survive the next one.

He saw his hand go out to the cafeteria door, swinging it wide and ushering Jillian through. She walked like nothing was wrong, like a normal human, not one who had nearly died two hours ago. Not one who had him arguing with the heads of his company, a *government* company nonetheless, to keep her on life support. People on ventilators shouldn't just get up and walk around.

And doctors shouldn't carry syringes of potassium chloride in their pockets in case the opportunity to kill a patient arose.

Jordan also doubted the quality of his decision making skills. He wanted Jillian here. No doubt about that. Having the threat of David removed didn't bother him any either. *Killing* David to get his way did.

He was halfway down the cafeteria line before Jillian tugged on his jacket sleeve and pointed out that he hadn't gotten anything. Shaking his head, he started choosing food from the other side of the line, not really caring that he didn't have anything but side dishes. He was simply here because he was hungry. His brain didn't care what he ate, just that he did it.

Jillian's plate was piled high, with carefully chosen and precariously balanced foods. A moment's surprise registered until he remembered she had eaten this much the last time she had come out.

Her enthusiasm for the rather inedible food relayed that she wasn't thinking what he was. How could they be certain that Jillian wouldn't go under first?

They had discussed the possibility of trying to medically induce coma in David. But that had problems. If they didn't get David through to the other side, then when they killed him they might actually *kill* him. And if he didn't wake up, he wouldn't be able to cut Jillian loose. Which meant she would slide under again, and most likely die, if not just here, then in both places.

And there was another critical problem with it: they had no idea what they were dealing with. So they had no idea if it would work. And there wasn't time to experiment.

So they would simply have to wait for David to go under.

And keep Jillian here.

And Jordan had no idea how to do that.

Eventually he realized that all of his food was gone from his tray except a spinach side dish. He must have disliked it, because he had eaten everything else. But he had no memory of that decision at all. And Jillian was looking at him weird.

"You ready?" His voice slipped out as his eyes finally made contact with hers, real contact in the here and now, and not in the missing world of his thoughts.

She nodded yes, a tiny gulp showing along her exposed neckline as she blinked. Too quickly his brain registered that her eyes didn't reopen and he forced himself to not reveal the hot rush of adrenaline he felt every time she closed her eyes for longer than a second. Every time, he was suddenly and certainly afraid that she was slipping. But she had opened her eyes wide each time before, and he waited until she did it this time, too.

He understood again the meaning of the phrase 'with heavy heart' as they walked silently back to the tent. He supposed his heart would sink through his abdominal cavity if this didn't resolve itself soon. But then again, there was a murder to commit, and the way he figured it, it was likely that Jillian would want to shed herself of him and any reminders of this night as soon as possible.

Jordan didn't like it. But he had to find a way to be okay with it. He'd be able to call her, or at least check up on her, and know she was all right. Killing David didn't lead him to any fantasy worlds where he could roll over at night and watch her sleeping. And he forced himself to re-examine all his decisions.

Was he doing this just to get Jillian? Or was there any real justification to break his Hippocratic Oath? He understood and believed in all that Kevorkian had fought for. That people had the right to die, to choose their own quality of life. And David had initiated this idea.

Grass crunched under his feet in the chill night air as he considered the geologist's sanity and his own ability to show proof that he had agreed to the wishes of a logical man when he came up before the judge and jury for this one. But he couldn't come up with anything. They were operating on a theory for which the only proof was in Jillian and David's heads. And half that proof would be dead shortly.

Jordan considered calling it all to a halt. But one glance at Jillian beside him changed his mind. There was no way to stop this for her if they didn't let David go back. He couldn't even imagine David's job on the other side, though for a brief moment he tried. Hopefully the potassium chloride would do the trick. But in the end David was a logical man to his very core. He would hold a pillow over Jillian's face and be sure he felt her slip away if it came to that. Jordan almost laughed out loud at how well he could place his trust in David's aberrant code of honor.

But as he pulled back the tent flap even the cynical laughter died in his throat. David was glaring at him.

"Yes, I'm still awake." His teeth gritted and Jordan noted the pale clench to his jaw, figuring it was pain even before David spoke it. "I need a Percocet to get anywhere near where I can sleep. And I really want to get some sleep."

Jordan nodded.

Again it was David who drove the conversation, but with him sitting on his gurney waiting to be killed by an overdose of KCl, Jordan wasn't as threatened by it as he usually was.

"Just give me enough to send me under."

"No!" Jillian's voice jumped, strained and brittle, into the edges of Jordan's brain.

David glared, his eyes issuing some very serious threats for a man in slings and casts. "It's what we all want. Are you afraid of autopsy reports or something?"

Jordan knew what Jillian was thinking, and, unfortunately for David, he agreed. His voice ground out low and conspiratorial. "We could send you into medical coma. But we have no idea what it would do to you, if it would be the same as slipping under on your own. So you can only have the same doses that we gave you before."

"Then give it to me."

Jillian darted away, as quick as one of Becky's lizards, and returned with a paper cup with two of the round blue pills in it. It was a large dose, but Jordan figured they were no longer concerned with addiction.

David swallowed them down with a jerk of his head, then instantly fixed his stare on the two of them. "Go! I won't go under with you two watching me. I'm hoping I'll pass out from boredom."

They turned, and Jordan watched as his hand went out to hold the tent flap for Jillian, a dying, useless piece of misplaced chivalry if ever there was one. The night air hit them like a slap in the face, and with it came the jarred thought that Landerly hadn't been by to check on David since he had awoken.

But Landerly was a pretty sharp tack and Jordan wondered if the old man hadn't figured out what they were up to. His absence wouldn't be a stamp of approval necessarily, but at least it meant he wouldn't interfere.

In the distance he could see sunlight behind the mountains. He'd never really been anyplace like the Appalachians before, where sunrise was visible in the distance while it was still pitch black where you stood. The irony wasn't lost on him, and in a desperate bid for sanity he tried changing the subject. "So what went on with you and David last night? Around midnight?"

He could see that he had startled her. She blinked a few times and made an attempt to gather up scattered thoughts, but she didn't do it all that well. "What?"

He shoved his fists deeper into the pockets of his jackets, keeping them warm and out of the way. "Both of you had EEG activity at the same time – the same activity – even though you were reading almost brain dead."

"I was almost brain dead?"

"Yeah, so I figured something major must have happened…"

Becky stared down at the human shape on the bed. It was so much easier to think in terms of frogs. When she distanced herself, she wasn't bothered by the fact that she had found the two of them entwined and naked. She had reached her hand into frog terrariums before and simply removed the amphibs from all kinds of compromising positions.

Never once had she felt she had violated the frogs' sacred privacy. But never had she been in the position of moving the frogs, and adjusting things so that the techs wouldn't see. Never had she had to threaten a cage cleaner so that he wouldn't report what he saw.

So she had nearly broken her back putting a gown on Jillian and pulling a spare pair of scrubs pants onto David. She had sweated bullets in the fear that one or the other would wake up while she was dressing them. She had even rehearsed a small come-uppance speech to level at them if they did wake.

But they didn't.

She had moved Jillian rather than David, simply because she was lighter. It was hard enough lifting any amount of dead weight.

But now she stepped back as the techs moved around the room like bees in a field – working, making rapid efficient movements, flitting from one body to the other. When she lost focus the machinery became the drone of the hive, and she could imagine she was elsewhere. Somewhere where she didn't have to stand over two friends and wait.

To hear vital signs that she barely understood for humans. She knew appropriate blood pressures and pulse rates for cheetahs and moose and amphibs of all types. But with humans she knew just enough to constantly ask the techs if it was time to worry.

And from the looks on their faces it was approaching time to worry.

She hadn't mentioned a damn thing to David Carter The First. Even if he didn't recognize her, she remembered him, and how upset he had gotten over being given partial information. If she kept him up to date, the man might worry about his son, and Becky wasn't about to go spreading rumors that she couldn't substantiate, not to Carter Senior. No, she would wait until she had all her numbers, then she would tell him the facts.

But she could see what wasn't being said. There were frowns, and stethoscopes, heads nodding, followed by electrodes being attached. While she stood silently, the river of activity flowed around her on all sides. Her breath heaved in when she saw one of the women return with fistfuls of supplies. Becky recognized the IV bags and needles even in their sterile plastic casings. She had seen enough of it over the past week to know what it was all about. She knew that it wasn't good. And she knew that she should help. She just wasn't sure how.

So she stepped back to the edge of the square tent and bent her head. It had been far too long since she had done anything like it. She had missed church for a month of Sundays, always neck deep in one project or another. But her mother had pointed out, that with what had happened and all, the churches were now full. It came as no surprise that people would turn to God. But for the first time, she felt the need for it herself.

The words rattled in her brain, rusty from misuse, but she felt her way around until they became clearer, cleaner.

Please God, help my friends. Guide me to help them. Show me how I can do your work. Help me to understand. Help them to understand. She didn't feel her hands clasp together in front of her. Didn't know her lips were moving. Didn't feel the activity in the tent slowly come to a standstill around her. But she felt the peace. *Help all of us here to help them. To come back healthy and whole, or to find your kingdom in heaven.*

Becky didn't worry too much about the sex the two had clearly engaged in. There was too much biology ingrained in her as deep as the Baptist teachings she'd grown up with. God wouldn't punish them for doing what he had evolved them for. This was about finding the way. Whichever way was right for each of them.

"Help me to be helpful."

"Amen."

"Amen."

The chorus of voices startled her head up, shaking her from the cocoon of prayer she had woven around herself. Her eyes shifted, focusing on the roomful of medical techs and nurses, splashes of color in varied shades of blues and greens against the white of the canvas tent.

But, to a person, every head looked up from where it had been bent. Eyes met hers. Nods were directed her way. And hands went back to work.

Jillian fought the yawn that escaped her mouth. She knew it would simply cause Jordan more worry. But she wasn't good enough to hide it from him. Hell, no one was.

"Stay awake, Jillian. Walk."

His fingers grasped her arm in a purely clinical manner and she had to wonder why that was. He was Jordan. And he'd never distanced himself from her before. Not when she'd thought he should. Nor when she'd wanted him to. He was always Jordan. But right now she'd have ground out the formal title "Dr. Abellard" if she could have found the energy. "Walking makes me tired!"

"You have to stay awake!" His breath washed over her face, he was so close. And for a moment she thought of the mint gum he had been chewing. That was Jordan, friendly even when he was hauling her around, trying to keep her awake even though it was late in the evening. The sun was setting and her nerves and brain were setting with it.

Her body pulled away from her thoughts, creating a sense memory of one of the better hotel beds where she had curled up next to Jordan's heat, and sunk into warm soft sheets, the covers velvety beneath her fingers and across her cheeks.

She almost drifted off there on her feet.

But Jordan yanked her arm nearly out of the socket, and she was catapulted back into the cold night and away from her reverie.

She sniffed in, her lungs and nose searing from the tiny icicles in the air. "Medicate me–"

"No." He didn't even look at her, just interrupted before the last sound was out, his mind made up.

"Then I'm going to bed."

That got his attention. And as he spun around and glared at her it dawned that that was exactly what she had intended to do – shake Dr. Abellard back into being Jordan. "If you go to sleep, you might die." His own breath was ragged, and for a moment she snapped fully alert, realizing that maybe the cold, clinical Jordan was easier to deal with, rather than this face of fear and pain. But what would she feel if it was the other way around? And in fact it *was* the other way around as well. If she slipped off, she would lose Jordan…

His voice cracked even as it cut a path through her thoughts. "We don't know what the medication will do to you."

"True, but we have a good idea what sleep will do, and it isn't pretty."

He started to walk away, conversation closed, but she held back, stopping him when her arm and body didn't follow his lead. "You know, I have slept and woken up on the same side before."

"But that was several times before. It hasn't happened recently, and I sure as hell don't trust it." He let go of her arm and it felt as though the night seeped under her skin, chilling her where the heat of him had comforted just a moment before. "I just wish David would go under." His hand, now without purpose, scrubbed aimlessly through his hair. As usual a few pieces stood up on end, leaving him looking as frazzled as she knew he felt. "I feel like fate is fighting us here. That your body is trying to get you back over there and his is trying its damnedest to stay here."

"Medicate me."

All his peripheral movement stopped. His gaze squared on hers. "And if I kill you?"

"I have to stay awake long enough for David to go under *and* to wake up *and* get the job done." She couldn't give explanation to David's *job*. "There's no way I'll make it now. Not that long. We have to try it. My brain is shutting down. I'm beginning to not care that I might not wake up. My body wants sleep."

He blinked, leaving his eyes sheened in a glaze, and then he blinked again and it was gone. She wasn't sure but that she might have imagined it or maybe she was just looking through her own frustration. Her muscles ached, and her eyelids fought for closure. She was ready to sit on the hard earth and simply cry at the injustice and frustration of it all. But the earth was too cold. Her butt would freeze. And while that might keep her good and well awake for a little while, it would quickly lead to hypothermia, and blissful, if deadly, sleep. Since that death wouldn't be due to the coma-state sleep induced she was pretty certain it would actually *kill* her.

Jillian made the best decision she was capable of, her shoulders slumping, and her head tipping forward to allow her hair to hide the tears brewing in her eyes. "Please." The word fell out of her mouth, with no force behind it.

But Jordan heard it. He always did. And as she started to drift away right there, she knew he was taking all of it in. The slumped shoulders, the exhaustion, the tears – he would know they were there even if he didn't see them.

She felt his hands, cold, on either side of her face. With all the energy she could muster, which wasn't much, she fought against him seeing into her when he lifted her face to look in her eyes. All she could do was glance away and pray that the tears didn't fall in fat, rolling drops and embarrass her.

"Okay. But you stay awake until we get to the medication tent." He stared right into her eyes, waiting for her to make visual contact and acknowledge what he'd said. But then he slapped her cheeks a little bit, jolting her. Jillian wanted to be mad about it, but knew that the startle had woken her up, just a little.

His hand encompassed hers and, without looking back, he pulled her one shuffling step at a time to the meds tent. Her butt immediately located a chair that was upholstered but still remarkably hard. *Government chair.* The words flitted through her brain as she slouched into the corner, waiting while he checked the meds. He kept up a steady stream of chatter, but she couldn't have said about what.

When her brain worked enough, she threw in an "uh-huh" or "mmmhmmm" and he didn't slap her again so she guessed she had him fooled. The poles of the tent came up slowly behind her, cradling her head and making the chair just the tiniest bit comfortable. Comfortable enough. Tension drifted from her shoulders as she thought of fluffy beds and hammocks on beaches. The ocean sounded so soothing, and she inhaled deeply, enjoying the scent and the heat of the sun rising in front of her.

Shit.

Someone was upset.

Jordan was upset.

But the sunrise was beautiful and the day was so warm. Her hammock swayed in the heat. All was orderly until a fly began to buzz in her face. She waved it away, swatting at it haphazardly, but thinking that it was surprisingly heavy when she did hit it.

Something landed on her arm, and in curiosity she turned her head down to see a large chameleon. It was purple and slow moving and made her smile.

Until it bit her.

"Ow!"

"Jillian!" Jordan's voice was in her face. As she blinked, she realized that his eyes were too.

A panic attack overtook her, her hands shaking, her breath pushing in and out far faster than her usual eighteen breaths per minute. Her eyes scrambled through the scene before her, searching for some sort of purchase, some reason for the growing dread.

But there was nothing of concern. The space heater sat directly in front of her, its warm glow heating her face and chest and leaving her back feeling chilly.

"Jillian." Again Jordan's face swam before her. "I gave you some adrenaline to snap you out of it."

That explained the panic attack. She would feel all the effects because of the medication, but her brain had back-figured that, if she felt it, she must also have been alarmed. She managed to slow her breathing for the most part, but couldn't stop the shaking in her hands. Then the damn chameleon bit her again.

As she looked down at the little fucker, she realized that Jordan had a second needle in her arm. It wasn't much more than a sting once she had identified it.

He quickly removed the needle and shelved the medications, letting her sit through the seeming eternity while he did all of it in close to slow motion.

Jillian knew that she was experiencing the adrenaline the same way people felt in the middle of a car accident, that time stretched and they could stop and think things through. She almost laughed as she realized that he had simply medicated her to *feel* like she was awake for a long time. In reality, the adrenaline would wear off soon and she would slip back asleep.

But he had given her something else, too…he had explained it while he shelved the medications. She could dig that much out of her memory, but she couldn't remember *what* he said he had given her. Truth be told, she didn't really think she cared, just as long as it worked.

The palm of his hand swung squarely into her field of vision, and it took her a moment to realize that he was offering it to her to grab. She latched onto it, and before she realized what was happening, he had used her own grip against her to pull her to her feet and haul her behind him.

"It's time we went to go check on David again."

Jillian agreed, but was too strung out to say so. She found herself able to perceive the cold, but not care. If her jacket had fallen off she would have simply shrugged and gone on walking through the frigid air, leaving it in the grass behind her.

"I'm not leaving you for a moment, Jillian. I don't trust you not to pass out like you did in that chair. You scared the shit out of me."

Again she nodded, even though she knew he couldn't see her. Not when he was walking at a brisk pace facing into the night, and away from her, while he kept up his steady stream of talk.

"I also need to be sure that the meds don't do anything to you. So you won't be able to shake me for a good while."

She almost laughed out loud.

And when he turned and looked at her strange she realized that she *had* laughed out loud. In fact, she still was. From the look on his face Jordan wondered what was so funny, or if she had finally cracked from all of it.

It took effort, against the drugs coursing through her bloodstream, but she formed the words. "Like I could shake you anyway."

He nodded, his face in an odd resigned expression, and went back to pulling her like a skier through the maze of tents. *Why had he made that face?* Her own face scrunched up in thought and she tripped over a...blade of grass or something. Would she ever be able to figure Jordan out? Probably not. Not completely.

She was just beginning to wonder if that was a good thing or a bad thing when she ran into his back. She felt her nose crunch against him. She registered that it hurt, and that her finger had bent, too. She just didn't care.

She laughed again when the words came out of her mouth. "I am so thankful that I never developed a cocaine habit."

"Great, you're high."

It was just a statement of fact. But Jordan's exasperated tone made it even funnier. He got into her face again, and she wondered briefly why the hell he kept doing that. When he shook her gently she figured it out for herself. Even in her face he couldn't quite get her attention. Whatever he had given her sure felt good.

"Jillian. Be quiet. I don't want you waking David if he's asleep."

She nodded. All gravely serious for the one instant that she could hold the straight face without laughing. He pulled her through the tent flap and she ran into the back of him again. With a quick jerk and movements that she couldn't catalog, Jordan yanked her around in front of him, so her back was pressed against his front, and got his hand clamped over her mouth. With all that restraint, her eyes focused and she saw what he saw.

David, passed out cold.

She shook off his arms, and walked forward, her focus entirely on the man lying on the gurney. He was reposed, looking peaceful in spite of the casts and slings. So she did the easiest test she could think of. She reached out to lift his arm.

If it fell, dead weight, back to the mattress that was as good a sign as possible.

But when she grabbed his hand his fingers curled against hers reflexively. Jillian heard that her voice was too loud only after the word had escaped her mouth. "Damnit!"

The touch that he felt on his fingers was enough of an anchor to pull him back. His eyes fought to open, and already he perceived the faint light from the other side of his eyelids. He smelled the tent, felt the sheets, and heard the voice. All his senses were functional, now he just had to gain control and get up.

Funny how the very act of waking up, which he had done every day of his life, was only now something that could be catalogued – something he could control. It seemed it had always just happened before, with alarm clocks or daylight making the decision for him.

As he fought to make his muscles obey, they came into play one piece at a time.

His fingers jerked against the hand that touched him.

"You're waking up, huh?"

His brain recognized the voice, it just didn't quite place it.

But with a few determined tries David forced his eyelids to flutter then open. They snapped immediately shut, squeezing against the dim orange light thrown by the space heater. He fluttered them again, allowing his pupils to adjust and at last, he managed to focus on the woman standing over him.

"Good evening."

Becky.

Thank-fucking-God.

He scrambled upright, checking the next most important thing. Jillian.

His brain registered that she wasn't in the bed with him, and that he had scrub pants on.

"I moved her, she's right behind you." But Becky's hands pushed him back down. She wouldn't let him up, and he fought against it, opening his mouth to protest only to realize that he was muzzled.

His hands scrambled to remove the thing that hindered his jaw, but again Becky just pushed his hands away. "Let me check."

Her face looked sincere, and it was Becky. He didn't think she could lie about slipping the family dog her broccoli. Deciding he'd have to be a fool not to trust her, David sat back and waited.

Becky kept talking. "The techs told me that if you woke up, I could take the oxygen mask off–" *ohhh.* "-if you were above 95. And you are. The numbers rose right up while you were waking. So give me a moment to untangle you." Her fingers worked at the elastic that held the mask onto his face, setting him free of the bindings. "You dropped off pretty fast once you went under. And you can't run off just yet. No big movements. I have to watch you for at least fifteen minutes to see that you hold that 95 percent."

Fifteen minutes?

"I can't have you crashing on me."

"Thank you." They were the first words he had pushed out, and as usual they were a little froggy sounding. But he figured that he needed to be nice to everyone, as he had some serious business to attend to. And he wondered if Jillian had already set him free back on the other side, or if he would feel it when it did happen.

"Don't move too much. You're still hooked up to IVs and electrodes and such. There's an EEG and an EKG and pulse oximeter."

He looked down at his body and saw what looked like a human circuit. Wires and tubes fed in and out of everywhere. And suddenly, his chest and head started itching. Surely it was just perceived sensation from knowing that there were stickers holding electrical contacts on him, but knowing that didn't make it itch any less.

With a deep breath he decided to do what was needed. He would have to find a way to turn around and look at Jillian, even if he couldn't do anything about her until the techs and doctor set him free. He could at least start assessing the situation.

Slowly, pulling and tugging wires, he twisted until she was in view.

Jillian was draped peacefully along the gurney. Her hair fanned out around pale skin, her eyes stayed closed and still in a way that could never be mistaken for real sleep. She wore a medical gown, and while he knew she would have hated it, it was far better than lying there naked. With a deep breath, a certainty hit him in the gut. She would die in that gown.

"I untangled you two." Becky's voice was soft over his shoulder, and he listened for, but thankfully didn't hear, any condemnation or rebuke.

"I moved her myself and dressed both of you before I let anyone else in. I figured it wasn't their business. Or mine for that matter, but…"

Her wariness bled through into her speech. And David looked back at her, taking in the soft, droopy red curls, the age that had layered itself onto her face, and the worry that made her look much more adult than the first time he had met her. He didn't think anyone would mistake her for a kid again.

"Thank you." He heard the words and the sincerity. And realized that she would get suspicious any moment now if he didn't get it together and stop being so polite. "So what's up with Jillian?"

"She's got lower vital signs than you do."

He could see the oxygen mask, the IV and all the brightly colored wires. She looked like the bride to his Frankenstein.

David scanned, looking for the rubber covered point along the IV line where nurses could inject medications. Jillian had pointed one out to him when she had explained what to do. His eyes stopped and rested when he found it, just a short ways up the tube coming from her left arm.

He needed to get to the supply tent and find the potassium chloride.

"I don't know if she'll be okay."

That jerked him back. Becky's face had a layer of worry, and her head shook slowly from side to side.

"Will she die?" Would it all be better if she just died? God, he prayed he didn't sound hopeful.

But Becky shrugged and didn't look at him like he was evil incarnate.

He sat, breathing, in and out. Silent while his mind chugged. Becky must have better things to do, but she didn't budge. Maybe she had promised not just to keep an eye on him but to actually watch his every movement *literally* until that fifteen minutes was up.

David needed to sort through his thoughts. And he didn't like her staring at him. Although it didn't seem there was much he could do about that.

For a brief moment he entertained the thought of bringing her into his confidence. But he squashed that quickly. Becky was too religious to help him kill Jillian. Even if it was what Jillian wished. Even if she would be set free to live elsewhere in the process. He was pretty certain that Becky believed they were getting shuttled back and forth, but he was certain that, if left to chose, Becky would let God handle things.

But God hadn't handled much in David's life to his satisfaction, and he wasn't about to let the big man have another go at it over something this important.

Besides, if he didn't succeed, Jillian would likely wake up over here, and he had no doubt that she'd have no qualms about killing *him* for failing. And if the thought of the promised eight surgeries and twenty-four months of physical therapy didn't terrify him, living with Jordan while Jillian was stranded here sounded even worse.

He sat with his thoughts while Becky sat with hers and watched him. He wasn't much for prayer, but he did ask that she not be able to read his face. Rebecca Sorenson was probably one of God's favorites, and *He* would use her to stop David if necessary.

The tent flap lifted and a physician walked in. David knew he had seen the man before, but couldn't recall the name.

Thank God doctors knew they weren't memorable and saved everybody time by stitching their names onto their jackets.

"He's up!" Dr. Lee exclaimed.

Becky nodded, "About ten minutes."

The doc frowned and both of them knew what he was about to say. Becky cut off the protest. "I was told not to leave him, and no one was nearby. Not to mention, as long as you guys are doing your job, someone will be by within fifteen minutes. Still want to yell at me?"

The snippiness registered with David, making him wonder when she'd grown a backbone. But come to think of it she'd been growing it all along, just like she'd been adding those years to her face.

The doctor shook his head at her. He couldn't yell. It was a southern thing, David saw, for the women to be able to lay you low and leave you with no good response.

But even if the doc couldn't give Becky the what for, he could torture David. Coming over he started in with his stethoscope. He listened to David's chest and back. He held his two fingers over David's wrist, counting the pulse and feeling for its strength in a way that always seemed vaguely sexual. He was glad when the doc nodded and said he was good enough to get up.

I could have told you that. How many times have you woken from a coma, huh?

The snide remarks churned in his head, and probably across his expression, until the doctor started yanking off the EKG attachments, taking tiny patches of hair with them. "Ow!"

The smile he got said *suck it up.*

Damn doctor.

After he yanked every last sticker, the doctor turned to Jillian, taking stats and jotting things in her chart. Which, of course, he just had tucked under his arm. They were way too technically precise around here. Which was odd, because here and there were really the same place, and he hadn't seen a single chart on the other side. And he sure had a hell of a lot more to chart over there. The doc scribbled a few things, and David tensed.

But the two fingers against Jillian's wrist didn't rouse her. Neither did the thumb raising her eyelid to reveal an unfocused lake of blue beneath. David couldn't hide his shudder as he wondered if the docs had been doing that to him. The doctor smiled and left. And aside from being unhooked, it was like the man had never been there.

"I guess you're cleared for take-off." Becky's voice interfered with his thoughts again. Bringing him back to the fact that he had to hide what he was going to do.

With his legs wobbling beneath him, she helped him down. He was getting better at it every time. But hopefully this would be the last.

A few precariously balanced steps later he shrugged Becky off and said 'seeya' to her startled face. But better that she be pissed than suspicious. He wandered into the cafeteria forcing himself to eat something, even though his stomach rebelled at what he was about to do. All he could even pick up was a bag of chips, and he forced himself to munch them slowly, one by one, while he wound his way back out into the cold day. The red glow of sun hit him where it had made it's final bid to creep over the tops of the mountains while he had been in the cafeteria.

He tried – *tried* – to be normal, knew he was an asshole, and tried to put that into his walk. He tried to find the meds tent. And found it exactly where Jillian had said it would be.

David just wasn't sure how to get potassium chloride out of it without looking furtive. So he headed in, thinking he'd play innocent and act all confused if someone caught him and kicked him out.

The light inside was a too-bright fluorescent, and he was glad. He would be able to read the names on the shelves and bottles clearly. His only concern was that he might be casting a shadow on the outside.

He wasn't sure if he'd find it filed under the scientific 'K' or English 'P'.

It jumped out at him in the 'P' section after he'd checked every 'K'. Pocketing the bottle he scrounged for a needle. Knowing that if they saw him now he'd have less of a chance of bluffing his way out.

He found the needles, and a syringe, and fumbled with thick fingers to plug the two together. He'd contaminated the injection all to hell, and he knew it, but since he was going to kill her with it, did a little bacteria really matter? He bit his lip at the thought of actually, purposefully killing another human being. And not just any human: Jillian.

He drew up the solution into the syringe, realizing only after he did it that he'd forgotten to wipe the top with alcohol, and he'd contaminated the whole bottle of clear solution, too.

Why hadn't he watched ER more often?

He couldn't steal the whole vial. They'd count that it was missing, and Jillian's death might get investigated. Being here wouldn't mean much if he was in jail. And for a brief moment he thought about Jillian incarcerated on the other side. She might not have figured it out yet, but Jordan would be the one pulling the trigger for her. David knew it.

He couldn't in good conscience put the contaminated bottle back. He'd hurt others.

He squelched the laugh that threatened to bubble up.

After a minute of frantic searching for a way to right the problem without stealing the bottle, he squirted the solution out of his needle, wetting the grass at his feet. But it was such a small amount that it disappeared before he could account for it. He drew up more, again squirting it at the ground. After about ten times, he drew up a full syringe, carefully twisting the needle to get the solution out when it was low in the neck of the upside down bottle.

A sound outside made his neck snap straight. And for a moment he held rabbit-still, quiet except for the volcanic rush of his breathing, waiting while footsteps passed by outside with voices laughing and chattering.

His stale breath let out, the steel in his shoulders dissolving. He had to finish, and quickly. He'd give himself a heart attack and die. Then Jillian wouldn't. And he'd be dead here. Then they'd kill him on the other side.

God what a cluster-fuck they were going to have if anything went wrong.

Chapter 26

David replaced the contaminated bottle exactly where he'd found it. It was there to be catalogued, but now too low for anyone to use. Someone would get pissed at whoever had left it, but no one would get hurt.

Except him!

He re-grabbed the bottle and wiped the fingerprints off it. *Stupid, stupid.* A clean bottle was a giveaway that someone had been intentional with the meds. He touched the glass to the backs of his fingers, thinking that would leave it not looking wiped, but not leading directly to his door.

Surely a DNA test would point to him, but they'd have to be pretty suspicious of him before they dragged out that artillery. Capping the needle and pocketing it, he listened at the tent flap, and, not hearing anything, stepped out into the still morning. With the syringe safely ferreted away, his brain wandered to what would happen after he killed Jillian.

His lab in Chicago waited for him.

The First had been kind and proud and supportive for twenty-seven hours in a row.

His body worked.

He could settle in there. Dig into his lab, and run core samples from the local oil wells for the rest of his life. David figured no one was going to come after him for a few rock plugs after the whole apocalypse thing.

The morning air bit at him as he walked back to the tent he and Jillian had shared only to find a tech pushing a medication into her IV, while she watched the numbers.

David stood quietly, wondering if he'd been beaten to the punch. Especially when Jillian's heart rate began to race, then slowly leveled and dropped off. The tech shook her pretty blond head, and turned away.

"Ack!" Her blues eyes jerked wide open at the sight of him, and her hand jumped up splaying perfectly manicured nails wide across her chest to slow her own racing heart. "I didn't see you there." Then the hand came out in a gesture halfway between a handshake and a request to have the back kissed. "Lucy Whitman."

David had to unclench his right hand from around the needle hidden in his jacket pocket and he grasped her fingers, making sure he didn't reveal anything. Just in case he had squeezed so hard he left an imprint of the syringe on his palm.

"What did you do to her?" He pointed at the still prone form, getting paler as she lay amidst the dark ribbons of her hair.

"We've been injecting potassium chloride into her every half hour." Lucy missed the shock that registered on his face and kept going. "Trying to raise her heart rate and maybe even jolt her out of it." The slim shoulders lifted in the shrug that seemed to be the new universal response. No one knew much of anything these days. At least the sun was still coming up regularly.

He schooled his voice to remain steady, grateful that he was standing behind Lucy, watching Jillian's lack of movement from over the tech's shoulder. "Won't that stuff kill her?"

She laughed, a soft airy sound that shot straight to his groin, as she turned to face him. Her red lips looked like they were good for more than just explaining medications, and David was grateful that he would stay here, where he was clearly functional.

"It won't hurt her in the concentrations we use. It's very dilute."

He focused on the words and their meanings, absorbing what she'd said and not just how she'd looked. By the time the oxygen was going to his brain again, she'd excused herself and left the tent to report on the patient.

David blinked a few times, searching for the way that this would help him. He wished he had Jillian's brain right now. But that would defeat the whole purpose. He didn't even realize that he was gravitating toward her until his hip was spiked by the slightly open drawer Miss Blonde must have left. *Son of a bitch!*

He stilled his hand just before he slammed it. Revenge never played well against inanimate objects, and he could see needles lying on a once sterile drape in the bottom of the drawer.

Dark marker, in very bad handwriting denoted that there were four KCl syringes and that the solution was very dilute compared to what he'd pulled straight from the bottle. There were also a few in varying concentrations of epinephrine. Although why the docs would want to give Jillian a 'fight or flight' response, he couldn't figure.

Pulling his own syringe from his pocket he compared the two. His was fatter and would never pass as one of those if he just laid it in the drawer. Plus it didn't have the bad handwriting on it. For some reason all the anal retentive people were over here. He might like that in his lab, he thought. But now he got himself back to the problem of making his syringe look like the ones in the drawer – the ready-made injections for Jillian.

Becky ducked her head in, and he quickly yanked his hand back behind him, hoping that he could hide the needle and that the second-grade maneuver had actually worked. But it seemed she didn't notice. "Lucy just came by and told me that it didn't work. Jillian's heart rate is dropping lower and lower." Becky's soft sigh came to him through the air that was suddenly too warm in the little tent with the tiny sun contained in the space heater. "Maybe next time."

"When is next time?"

His heart soared. And crashed. He might not figure it out in time.

"Maybe an hour. They're afraid they're losing her." Her lips pressed into a sad smile. But like everyone else, Becky had gotten used to the idea of losing people.

He tried a very un-David-like move, and hoped it would get filed under 'everything is weird these days'. "I think I'm just going to sit here with her."

He hoped that Becky understood that he'd like to do it *alone*. It worked too well. Doctor Sorenson's sweet smile held the belief that he was truly Jillian's lover, wanting to sit and hold her hand. And obligingly she ducked out while he held back the laughter that threatened from the irony of it all. And for a moment he just stared at the syringe in his hand.

He did sit vigil beside Jillian's bed for a while. At least it would have looked that way to anyone who stopped in. But his mind was churning, trying to figure out how to get his solution into one of those syringes.

Then he wouldn't have to pull the trigger himself. He could just wait until a tech picked up the right syringe and did the job for him.

He sat there staring at her, until he was startled by another tech beside him. He hadn't heard the kid enter, just jumped when the finger tapped his shoulder, and the young voice asked would he please scoot over so that Dr. Brookwood could be examined?

David blinked a few times and didn't say anything, just watched while the boy, who must have been no older than twenty, went through all the same motions of taking vital signs that the doctor had. He cranked up the oxygen, opened the flow on the IV a touch, scribbled notes in the chart and left.

David's own heartbeat set up a steady countdown. He had to do something quick, get that syringe traded out. He was reaching for the drawer when the tech burst back through the tent flaps again. The sun was up high enough that light filtered through all the pores in the tent, and the tent flaps let in just enough that a person who was paying a little attention would know that someone had come in.

David nearly jumped clean out of his skin, his senses hyper-alert with the work he was about to do. But the tech was paying no attention to him. As long as David was out of his way, the practiced movements came off like clockwork.

His eyes focused with fascination, David watched as the guy pulled the first syringe from the left of the row in the drawer. For a few brief moments he executed the precise rhythmic set up, yanking the needle cap with his teeth, he swabbed the rubber covered spot on the Y-tubing, and injected the full syringe. With his eyes transfixed on the machinery and the numbers it was blurping out, the tech's hands slid the used syringe into the red plastic biohazard box mounted behind the countertop.

Again David watched with perverse fascination while her heartrate spiked and then plummeted again.

The tech sighed in defeat and turned to leave.

David almost let him go, but blurted out at the last minute, stopping the tech. "Wasn't that fast? I thought it was going to be an hour before you tried again."

The tech nodded solemnly. "Her sats are too low. We've bumped it up."

David took a swallow, and tried his best to look like a heart-sick lover. He hadn't tried to act since high school theater. His father hadn't come to see him in that performance either, and for a brief moment he reminded himself that this Eden had a snake. Swinging his focus back to the job at hand he started to ask how long it would be before they came back, but he stopped himself, knowing it would be soon enough. "I'm not sure if I can watch this. If I leave, can I just come back and sit with her?"

The tech tilted his head, and gave a sad smile. "Of course you can, Dr. Carter. We don't mind."

David made short work of plucking the left-most syringe from the drawer and squirting the contents onto the ground before carefully pulling the plunger from his own fat vial. He stuck the needle in the back and drew up the pure stuff, trying to splurt out the air bubbles, then delicately aligning it with the level on the other syringes.

He replaced it at the left-hand side of the drawer and carefully shut it. His feet had almost made it the tent door when he spun and went back – switching the pure syringe to the second spot.

It would be soon enough.

And he would be nowhere near when it happened.

Home beckoned.

Jordan's hands had a fine tremor. He could read the same in Jillian's, but knew that hers was due to the medications. His was due to the fact that he was about to kill a man.

As they walked quietly back toward the tent where David lay, his brain was anything but silent. That was the tent where Jillian had spent so many hours, unmoving and unresponsive. She wouldn't go there again. Not after this. She wouldn't be reminded of it, and neither would he. They would pack everything up and head back to Atlanta.

Landerly had flown out this morning, leaving only a note. There were a few lines that made Jordan believe that the old man knew what they were up to and was heading out of town to get himself a little more of that 'plausible deniability' he liked so much.

Inside his jacket pocket, Jordan's gloved hand made a warm nest where it curled around the syringe. Outside of his pocket he tried to keep himself relaxed and looking less than suspicious.

But his lungs breathed in a little too deeply, and he forced his eyes to wander the landscape. Although the sky cut bright shades of blue above him the daytime hours were cold now, too. And the air smelled heavy with tiny shards of ice. Snow wasn't far away, and he wanted to be back in Atlanta before it fell.

He wouldn't be able to stand being trapped in this town when the ice came and made all the roads through the surrounding mountains impassable. It was the exact reason the government had built the town here, and the exact reason he had to get out. His heart hammered with it, and he wondered absently if he would suffer a major coronary at a relatively young age from all the stress he was enduring now.

The heat hit him first, signaling that he should pay attention. He had stepped through the tent flap Jillian held open for him, and he was assaulted again by the vision of this man lying on the gurney. When David was awake he was every inch holier-than-thou. Richer-than-thou. Better-than-thou. And funny and charming enough to be fairly likable anyway.

There was going to be a perverse satisfaction in pushing the plunger.

"Can we do it this time?" Her voice was the only organic sound in the tent. Barely loud enough to be distinguishable over the beeping and printing noises that provided a lush synthetic jungle.

Every time they had decided it was time to do it, they had talked themselves out of it. The last time, an hour and a half ago, they had talked themselves up to this. Their first concern had been that he was truly under. Not on some snap turnaround. When David had been out for just half an hour, they said he certainly wasn't awake on the other side yet. If they stopped his heart before he awoke over there they might truly kill him. At an hour and a half they gave him until three hours under, just to be sure.

David's vitals had taken the steady plunge they expected. He might well die on his own, they offered up all the possibilities, but Jordan knew that he and Jillian were just chickening out one way after another. And being smart, they were able to come up with really good arguments for allowing themselves to wait.

This was it though.

If they didn't do it this time, David might wake back up.

Jordan ignored thoughts that told him he might really be killing the man. And that the woman at his side was delusional. With his feelings for her he couldn't overlook his obvious bias. Yes, jail time was a definite option. Or perhaps he'd just suffer a simple lifetime of guilt.

He sighed as she pressed the Velcro on the tent flap together. "All right, keep watch." He pulled the syringe from his pocket, quickly clenching it between his teeth and swabbed the IV tubing.

"Don't you dare!"

He almost jumped, and nearly coughed out the syringe. "Wha?" It was all he could pronounce with the thing in his mouth.

"*I'm* doing it."

Removing the potassium chloride so he could speak, he braced his fists at his hips and stared her down. "Jillian, no."

"Jordan, *yes*." Her eyes were unrelenting, and matched her tone.

He felt his mouth open in protest. But as usual, Jillian's brain worked faster than his and she shot him down before he even got a good aim.

"It's *my* life I'm buying. I'll pay for it myself." Fire leapt in her gaze and she lunged for the needle in his hand.

Only then did he realize that he was stronger and taller than she was, and he could win this argument even if her little tongue was sharper. He jerked the needle over his head.

"Don't you *dare!*"

"Dare? It's done." He shrugged, keeping the needle high while she plastered herself to him and jumped, attempting to reach what was way over her head. While he controlled the needle, he could think at his own pace. "Let me do it. If anyone suspects anything, they won't suspect me."

"Bullshit! You two have been circling each other like caged tigers for weeks now. But I'll be damned if I know why. Anyone with a brain in their head would suspect you."

Circling each other? It was that obvious? Jesus. But the needle was still out of her reach, despite numerous jumps. So he had time to think.

"You're clearly mentally deranged. For God's sake, you think you're going back and forth to another planet!"

That stopped her in her tracks. "What?"

"That's what they'll say, Jillian. You're high up on the suspect list, too, you know." He kept his voice soft, but not soothing.

"Then even if they convict me they'll put me in the psych ward, I'll be out in no time. Give me the damned needle."

She jumped again. And Jordan fought for another argument, another hurdle to put in her path. But again she thought it through before he did. "I'll scale you like a tree."

"I'd like to see you try."

And try she did. He almost laughed, it felt like junior high all over again. Except the part where the argument was about who got to kill David. That sobered him up.

Again as he opened his mouth to argue, the words that filled the air were hers. "You do it. I'll just sit down," she stopped the useless jumping and lowered herself into the corner chair, tucking up her legs and letting loose a languid yawn, setting off coils of alarm in him, "and go to sleep." Her head drifted down against the pole, her soft lashes fluttering shut and then going still.

His heartbeat stopped with her eye movement. "Damnit, Jilly!" It was practically a yell. People would come from all around to see what was going on. They'd both get locked up and David would come back. All this arced through his thoughts as he grabbed her shoulders and violently shook her awake.

"Here!" He slapped the needle into her hand. She played dirty, but with that threat he had to let her win.

Even now she was blinking and re-orienting herself. Just like that, she had actually fallen asleep. And he couldn't let her. Not until they were sure.

As he watched, Jillian forced air into her lungs. She awoke by sheer willpower, and stood on less than solid legs. But then she mustered up the sweetest *I win* smile he'd ever seen and he bit back the word that appeared at the back of his tongue. *Bitch.*

He stood at the threshold of the tent, hoping to hear through the Velcro closures if anyone was coming. And grateful for the excuse not to watch her. He heard no one, and so after a few seconds he turned around expecting her to be done.

But no. She came square into his visual field, burning into his retinas an image that he would see for the rest of this life. Long after Jillian was gone, he would remember that he had watched her kill David. She injected slowly, counting to make sure she kept the pace.

Four-mississippi-five-mississippi-six-mississippi–

He thought the sound was simply in his head, but then realized he could hear her voice faintly, her lips moving across the texture of each sound while her eyes stared at the readout screen. Just as it should, David's heart slowly picked up speed, passing normal, and plateauing at 110 before finally starting to slow.

Jordan knew what that meant, and sure enough, when he looked, Jillian had depressed the plunger all they way to the end of the syringe. But she didn't withdraw, just stood there mesmerized by the numbers. Jordan softly crossed the room to her, but she didn't notice until his hands closed over hers, grasping the needle and IV line tight in her fingers and separating the two.

Still she stood, just staring, until he decided to pull the needle from her hand before she dropped it. Jordan busied his hands shoving the syringe down into the sharps box, the red plastic probably having swallowed the last evidence of their crime. The drugs would break down quickly inside David and, given his condition, hopefully no one would ever suspect anything other than that his heart gave out.

But looking at Jillian, Jordan suspected a lot more.

Tears swarmed her face, marring her cheeks and dripping unceremoniously from her chin out of time with the slowing heartbeeps. She didn't shake or sob, just swallowed her air in tiny gulps. He couldn't place his finger on it, but he could read it, something about the way she leaned in toward the man on the gurney, something in her eyes. She didn't feel guilty. She felt loss.

With the evidence gone, they could simply stay and watch. Jordan felt compelled to be certain it worked. He would never forgive himself if he came back and David was alive, or God forbid, awake.

He didn't control his hands so much as he felt them settle on Jillian's shoulders. Somehow that touch let loose what had only been the surface, and she began sobbing in earnest. Still, it took a moment before she turned and buried her face against him.

His arms went around her, a gesture of simple human kindness. He didn't really want to comfort her for the loss of a man he was glad had somewhere else to be. But the curiosity was too much. And the need to finalize it in his head was overwhelming. So he forced himself to get it out quickly. "You fell in love with him."

After the words came, he realized that he hadn't asked. He hadn't needed to. And he held her while she cried, and let himself kick his own ass for how he had fallen for her.

It was definitely time to go back to Atlanta. He realized now that he had a job waiting for him, with or without her. And that he couldn't simply pack her up and make her come with him. She had family to attend to. He had to get up to see his Dad more often. Call his father and tell him that the girl had made it, and that it hadn't all worked out in his favor but that he'd be okay in a while.

His skin itched in the restless way it did when he needed to act and hadn't for whatever reason. He hadn't itched going to Atlanta. The job offer had come through and he had simply thrown all his belongings in a few boxes and notified his student loans where he was moving and took off. There hadn't been time to *want* to go, simply the going. But now he needed to leave, and he was tied here, at least for a few more days.

He had to be sure that Jillian could sleep, and only sleep. Not slide into some brain-dead state and slip away. That she would wake up if she was roused, and make all those normal movements that she did while she was asleep.

"No."

The word startled him from his thoughts and, for a moment, from his restless urge to leave. "No, what?"

"No, I'm not in love with him." Her voice was soft and low, but solid. He knew when she lied, and this wasn't one of those times.

"Then why all the tears?"

At first she just sighed, and he could feel the movement against his chest. Her mahogany hair was loose and hanging heavy down her back, teasing him just under his nose. Reminding him that he had to pull away, that he needed to pack up and leave.

"I'll miss him." She jerked against him, and he thought it was a sob, but when she looked up the grin on her face was unmistakable. "I know he could be an ass, but I liked him."

Jordan shook his own head, "Yup, that's David. Too much money and too much charm." *But at least I still have all my hair.*

"*Was* David."

His body jerked as he realized the beeping had gone silent. The EEG showed no activity at all. The pulse-ox was slowly dwindling lower and lower and was already low enough that it was well below the amount of oxygen necessary for human life.

Jillian turned away and looked at the body for a moment before she began methodically removing all the electrodes and needles. She put a cottonball over the needle as she slid the IV out, but didn't seem surprised when no more than a dot of blood welled from the site.

There wouldn't be any CPR, no heroic measures. Not like if it had been Jillian that slipped away. For a moment the thought entered his head, wondering if he would have been able to push the medications into Jillian if she had asked him to.

Truth be told, he didn't know. And he shoved the thought to the back parts of his brain, refusing to let it go any further.

At last her hand rested softly over David's as she turned to look at Jordan, "It's time to go tell everyone." Tears still hovered at the edge of her eyes, and even though she had wiped them away, the tales of crying were all over her face.

No one will suspect her.

The thought was comforting even in its morbidity.

They left the tent side by side, and immediately ran into a tech headed their way, "How's he doing?"

The timing fused through Jordan, they could have easily been caught. But he quelled that with the thought that they *hadn't.* And that was all that was important now. It wasn't like he was going to make this a habit and needed to be better prepared the next time.

"He didn't make it." Jillian's voice hitched at the end of the sentence, giving credence to her sorrow.

The tech looked to Jordan and he offered a quick nod confirming what she'd said. "We unhooked him, he needs to be transported to the morgue. Would you set someone up to do that?"

"Of course." The young man started to duck into the tent, but stopped himself. "Are you headed over to fill out the death certificate?"

Jordan nodded, even as he saw Jillian stiffen beside him. Neither of them had thought of that apparently. Well, it was a good thing they were desk jockeys for the most part. And luckily they'd been headed that direction anyway.

Half an hour later the certificate had been signed. Landerly had been notified, and he asked Jordan how Jillian was doing. "She's awake sir. But I'm not sure how much longer she'll stay that way."

"Keep her up." Was all he said before he disconnected the line. Somehow, Jordan didn't even consider it rude. His mother would have killed him if he'd done anything like that. But Landerly was just that way. And Jillian could easily become that way.

She stood and stretched, letting loose a long yawn. "Okay, bedtime for Bonzo here."

"No!"

She frowned against the violence of his retort. "Why not?"

"What if he isn't finished?" Jordan couldn't stop the words, "He isn't us, he doesn't know where everything is. He'll be slower at getting it done. You haven't felt anything–"

"Who's to say I will?" She pushed against her back, calm despite his fluttering. "If that's our criteria I may never sleep. I'm already half nuts. Good night."

"No, Landerly told me to keep you up."

"Landerly can bite my ass. I'll be asleep so I won't even feel it." She shrugged her jacket back on, having shed it in the heat of the records tent. "Good night."

Jumping to give chase, Jordan tugged on his own jacket and followed her out. "Just a few hours more. I'll medicate you again."

"No." She stopped cold in the middle of the walkway and faced him, standing her tired ground. "That stuff felt like cocaine as best I could tell."

"Then eat. You need food."

Her eyes blinked, but slower than usual, causing panic to surge through him.

"I won't eat cafeteria food anymore. Good night."

"No. I'll get you something good." He waved a pointed finger in her face and watched as her eyes tracked it. "There's a Chic-Fil-A just over that hill." He pointed with one hand and grabbed her wrist with the other. "Let's go."

She resisted, but didn't have enough body weight to slow him down. "We're walking?"

"Yup. It'll keep you awake." He tugged and she stumbled along beside him, but he didn't slow the pace. His own feet were keeping beat with the jack-hammering of his heart. He hoped David had gotten the job done. But he didn't *know*. And the consequences were too severe if they were wrong. She would just have to keep up.

So she did. She didn't utter a single word all the way up and over the hill. Only placed her order at the counter and bordered on falling asleep in the booth when he went back to get the food.

The skeleton crew of the fast-food joint eyed her a bit. But her behavior wasn't that odd considering everything else that had gone on.

Jordan made her chose a soda with caffeine and forced her to drink all of it. But he didn't have to make her eat a single chicken nugget or waffle fry. Those went down all on their own. Her only comment the whole trip was, "I can't believe this was right here and I didn't know it." But he was grateful that at least she wouldn't be losing any more weight today.

He thought about weighing her when they returned to the tent town, but she was falling asleep on her feet, even as they paced their way back. Jordan recognized that she had led him back to the tent she and David had shared. But they both stopped cold at the sight of the draped body on the gurney.

Jillian did an about face and walked off in a different direction for a few steps, before realizing that she didn't know where she was going.

Jordan grabbed her elbow, "Come on, my tent's over this way. I need to keep an eye on you anyway." He pulled her through the white rows to another of the identical tents, and pushed her inside.

He saw it with new eyes as she scanned the tiny square of space: the single gurney, the orange light shed by one of the standard space heaters, his duffle bag tossed into the corner, open with scrubs and one pair of jeans flowing out of it and across the once neat line of shoes that sat beside the bag. The countertop covered with squared stacks of folders.

Jillian laughed. There wasn't much energy behind it but it was an honest sound. "I would have known this was yours, it looks just like your desk back home." With that final statement, she shed her jacket and crawled onto the gurney he had lowered to a normal bed height. For a few minutes they were quiet while he hooked her up to every available machine and set the alarms. When they were finished she adjusted covers while he grabbed folders and lowered himself into the uncomfortable chair in the corner.

He had been awake as long as she had, longer even, and his eyelids blinked in slow rhythm. The paperwork would keep him alert. But it was Jillian that kept him up. She rolled over, adjusted the covers, curled up in a fetal position, and rolled back. His own head lolled as he started to drift off, only to be pulled back by the soft rustle of Jillian's feet touching the ground. "I have to go to the bathroom."

He didn't say anything, just watched while she unsnapped electrodes and wires and slid back into her jacket and shoes before padding off into the daylight beyond the tent walls. Looking around, he realized that it was quite bright inside the tent. But he couldn't be upset that she had stretched her awake time by another half-hour.

He dozed while she was gone but jerked awake at the sound of the Velcro ripping. Without a word, she slipped out of shoes and jacket and into wires and tubes and slid back between the covers, and began her restless tossing again.

His breathing evened and he felt himself slipping, just as her voice cut through. "Jordan. Wake up."

"Huh?" He used his legs to push himself upright and run his fingers through his hair. The daylight was the same shade and angle as he remembered it – only a few minutes had passed.

"Get up here. You're falling asleep in that chair and I can't." She held out her hand and waved him toward her.

It wasn't an invitation of the sort he wanted. It was Jillian, ever practical. But the thought wasn't unwelcome. "It's narrow, I can't have you rolling out."

"So put up the baby bar." Even as she said it, she pulled the release catch, tugging at the side rail. He reached out and, snapped the smooth metal easily into place. The back rail was already up, where he had left it to prevent him from rolling against the tent wall and thinking in his sleep that it was more solid than it was. The only option left was crawling up from the foot of the bed, and he made his way while Jillian shifted and adjusted the covers.

Within moments he curled behind her and draped his arm across her waist, waiting for her to protest. She didn't, just softly leaned back against him, probably completely unaware that he liked it. But she didn't curl into him because she wanted to, there just weren't other options in the tiny space.

With a few deep breaths he slipped off, consciousness growing frayed at the edges of his vision. Before he lost all contact he thought he felt Jillian's body relax, and he prayed that it was sleep.

Chapter 27

Becky stood just behind the first row of mourners, draped in her best black. Her parents and Brandon stood beside her, having shown up just to show up. They were using any excuse to see her these days-even Jillian's funeral.

Her eyes skimmed the crowd. The Brookwood women formed a solid front on the other side of the gleaming casket, Jillian one of only two family members they had lost. All this ascension talk had been most difficult on the families that lost one or two. How could they say that their loved ones had been among the damned?

They hadn't even been able to visit Jillian while she'd been awake. They lived on a mountain just north of the Georgia border and had been iced in the entire time. They had spoken to her on the phone once or twice but it was all that they had managed. Of course, they had gotten a warm front, just in time to throw the first dirt at their daughter's funeral. Sometimes God seemed cruel.

Behind the Brookwoods, under the shade of a tall oak, David lingered at the edges. He had been at the edges since Jillian had died yesterday. The funeral had been put together quickly, with the mortuaries running at full speed and processing body after body. Not all of them got a full funeral. There simply wasn't the time or resources. There were talks of mass graves for the unclaimed at the morgues. But no one would hear of it. The bodies would have to stay in the coolers until the religious right and wrong had a service for each of the damned.

Jillian was important though. And her funeral got precedence, just like Jordan's had. Becky had attended it, too, just like she had attended so many others.

She hoped this would be the last, at least for a good long while.

The preacher said the final words, not even looking to his scriptures. He had the whole thing memorized by now. And he read it like he had done this twenty times already this week. He probably had.

Jillian's family stepped back away from the hole in the ground, the light reflecting off the tears in their eyes as they turned to go. There was no reception planned – no time, no group of friends – simply this spot in the cemetery with too many shiny new stones and too many unmarked graves, waiting for the stone-cutters to catch up with demand.

As the mourners parted, David made a tiny salute to her and turned away to duck into his car. He had a flight back to Chicago. He had booked it for yesterday evening, but Becky had convinced him to stay for his lover's service.

She wondered now if he was fleeing because Jillian wasn't here, or if he really didn't care. Becky wasn't stupid; she wouldn't put either option past him. There was also the vague possibility that he had killed her. If you could call it that. He might have set her free on the other side.

But Becky didn't know. She couldn't speculate. So she simply smiled and watched as the black car pulled away from the curb at a sedate pace. He was only a block away before he spun the tires and high-tailed it out to the airport; even from here she could hear the rubber squeal.

A hand touched her arm. "I'm so sorry about your friend." Her mother's voice came over her like old quilts.

"She's in a better place now." Becky said the words, the same ones everyone said, but she *believed* in a way she never had before. "So are Melanie and Aaron."

Her mother offered only a tight nod, to say 'thank-you, but no more'.

Becky wouldn't take that though. "Mom, Aaron and Melanie are together."

"Of course." The hand patted her on the arm while her mother visibly disengaged from the conversation.

"Mom! Listen to me." She took a deep breath and let it all fall out. "When Jillian would go into a coma, she would be awake somewhere else. With Jordan, her lab partner. And she said a little girl hacked her way into the CDC phone lines convincing the staff that she was a Doctor Sorenson."

Her mother blinked, still not comprehending, still not wanting to. But Becky pushed, her mother was made of sterner stuff than this. "She talked to Jillian. Mom, it was Melanie. Jillian and Jordan drove out to the house and picked up the notebooks I left behind. They saw Aaron and Melanie."

"When?" Finally she had her mother's attention. Rapt green eyes, so like her own, fixated on her daughter.

"Three days ago."

"But they were already—"

"*There*. Mom, they're not here. But they aren't dead."

She felt the cold seep in as she watched her mother's spine stiffen and shield her from belief. The disconnect was more powerful now, now that she had less siblings to fall back on. Her mother turned away. "That's just silly."

This time it was her hand that grabbed at her mother's arm. But she wasn't gentle. She didn't follow the dictates of society. And she didn't care. "It's not silly, it's true. Jillian described Aaron and the house to a T. She said Melanie decided to go to the biology magnet *even if it meant riding the short bus.* How would she have known?"

Her mother's face took on the worried look of the convinced. "It's true Mom. They're just somewhere else."

"Then why aren't they here? Why did God split up a good family?" A glaze of tears threatened at her mother's eyes, and suddenly with that acceptance Becky knew what to do. Even though she didn't know she'd been deciding.

"God split up a lot of good families, Mom. I don't know why. But we're together and they're together. Aaron moved home to be with her." She sighed. "And I'm moving home, too, Mom."

"Rebecca!"

Arms were thrown around her with a joy that took her off balance. It made the other mourners stop and stare. But only for a moment. Things were odd these days and funerals were a dime a dozen. Black was getting a lot of wear, and a happy outburst at a funeral wasn't something to be too surprised about.

"I may not move into the house. But I'll be close."

Her mother's smile curved up, holding all the wishes a parent could have for a child.

"I'll see if I can get grants from the CDC to study the species here. Or maybe go back to the University. See if Warden is still there or not." Her mouth pulled up in a resigned grin.

If he was, she'd handle him. She had more clout now, maybe even some recognition.

She hugged each member of her family, then each member of Jillian's. She told them the same thing: that Jillian was in a better place. But she didn't elaborate. They looked like they wouldn't want to hear it. Like they all had sticks up their asses. Then she sent up a little prayer asking forgiveness for her thought. And followed it with a second prayer that the sticks be removed, before turning to catch the car that was heading back into Oak Ridge.

Three scientists shared the midsized sedan with her. In the same tasteful gold that all the CDC cars had been. She declined a front seat and spent the short trip to the center of town staring out the window at the landscape she knew so well – the patches of brown along the hillsides, the organic shapes of the Appalachian mountains rising up against the backdrop of too-blue sky.

And sure enough, even though no visible clouds rolled in, the color changed quickly and surely to grey during the short drive. When they exited the car they were treated to the first flakes of the first snow of the season.

With closed eyes, Becky stood at the edge of the high school field, and smelled the air she knew so well, felt the prickle of cold as it invaded her senses, and knew that she couldn't go back to Atlanta. Not for longer than it would take to pack her things.

She belonged here.

It was five o'clock, before her father managed to come get her. He simply hugged her and they were silent for most of the winding road home. But when they got there the front door opened to greet her with heat and laughter.

She went to put her things in Melanie's room, believing that Mel was here, even if she couldn't be seen. That by being in this house she was as close to her brother and sister as she could be. She took in a deep breath of the smells of little girl and clean ruffled curtains before heading out to have the spaghetti dinner they had held for her.

Jillian turned, or tried to turn, but something stopped her. She tried again, this time attempting to open her eyes as well. Neither worked. As she rolled forward, pins and needles shot up her right arm, as it reacted to being freed from her body weight. Her left shoulder hit something cold and metal. And, as grateful as she was that she could move, she jerked back, eliciting a grunt from the wall behind her.

Jordan!

"Jordan?" Her voice was mumbly, and right then she knew. She lacked the deep dry creak of waking from coma – she was *here,* where she had planned, hoped, to be.

"Jilly?" She smiled at the still asleep voice, and for a moment she could believe they were in a Florida hotel, checking out a little girl with a spider bite. But her IV tugged at the tape on her arm and her electrode snap stickers itched. And Jordan's voice became clearer. "Jilly!"

He shuffled his position and she shuffled hers to where she could smile at him. And he deserved a smile, damned if his hair wasn't sticking straight up and out.

He smiled again. "None of the alarms went off. And I set them pretty high. They'd have woken us both if you started slipping." Relief radiated from him in tangible waves. He didn't make any motions of resisting the urge to hug her, and before she knew it she was engulfed and squeezed, but she didn't mind.

But then his hands were everywhere, checking the pulse at her throat, then the radial pulses at each wrist, he looked into each eye separately then moved side to side to see if she was tracking him. She endured to make him feel better until he grabbed a stethoscope from the end of the bed.

She shoved at him, snapping one of the electrodes free, "Get your damn hands off of me! That's going to be cold as – " she didn't get to finish. The machine had reached its count and began wailing the alarm that its patient had dropped below reasonable levels, or removed an electrode, which was not acceptable.

Jillian slapped her hands over her ears, as Jordan scrambled to the head of the bed to disengage the wailing noise. The shrieking was loud enough that it just might have pulled her back had she started to slip away.

The sound stopped, leaving a ringing in her head that almost masked the sound of Jordan's heaved sigh. Just as she laid her head back down and felt some of the tension slip away, three techs ripped through the Velcro and burst into the room looking like white-coated avengers.

"Is everything okay?" They looked everywhere for the source of the alarm, stopping only when Jordan waved a hand from behind her and told them it was all fine.

It was then that their eyes stopped roving and settled on the two doctors sandwiched on one gurney. The taller tech with dark hair couldn't keep his eyebrows from raising. As Jillian turned her head away she saw Jordan's hand shooing them away, and the look on his face told them it wasn't any of their business.

The sigh settled deep into her lungs, making her grateful for the air even as she was frustrated. "Not again."

"Again?" This time it was Jordan's eyebrows that rose.

"Nothing." *Great.* On both sides now she had been found in the arms of one of her colleagues. It seemed life always had a way of catching up with her. But she fought the frustration by doing something. She yanked wires, freeing electrodes from their snaps and flat-lining all her readings. She sat up, rubbing her head and gently lifting the stickers there, before yanking the ones at the corners of her chest band-aid style. She gave little yelps while Jordan watched with a smirk on his face and a hand out that she slapped each used sticker into.

"I need a shower."

"I hesitate to let you go by yourself." He shook his hand over the wastebasket, freeing the stickers and letting them fall.

"Ahh!" She was a smart girl, she should be able to come up with a better protest than *that.* But before she could Jordan spoke again.

"I was kidding. It sounds like a good idea." He grabbed towels out of the cabinet and they bundled up, heading across the fields to the gym. She was thankful for the wave of heat that rolled over them when they opened the double doors and traipsed to opposite sides of the large wooden floor.

Only then did she realize that she hadn't brought a change of clothes, and she'd have to climb back into the scrubs she had slept in. *Not like anyone would notice,* it wasn't like she ever wore anything different anyway.

The hot water felt like a dream, and for a brief moment she let her eyes fall shut and stood quietly, thankful for the solitude. She hadn't been afforded any for over a week now. Everyone had been watching her with beady little hawk eyes waiting for her to slip back under.

After far too long she forced herself out from under the hot spray and tucked the towel around her torso noticing the red marks she had made from yanking the electrode stickers. As she padded carefully out to the locker area the door cracked just a little, no face showed, but she would have recognized Jordan's voice anywhere. "Jillian? What the hell were you doing in there? Surgery?"

"Enjoying the hot water." She waved her hand at him to shoo him back, even though he couldn't see it. "Now go wait for me."

She heard his chuckle as the door swung closed. She dressed and followed Jordan back out the door, where they were greeted by furls of tiny white snow attempting to warm itself in the heat of the gym. Everywhere outside the snow blew frantically. Up. Down. Sideways. It looked like Christmas morning, falling on the tiny tent town just down the hill from where they stood.

They walked through the flurries, Jillian with a soft smile on her cold lips, and as they got closer they could see heated discussions between people in bulky jackets. Jordan approached one of the people, and whether it was a man or woman, doctor or janitor, was all obscured by thick down and fuzzy trim at the hoods. "What's the problem?"

"We have to move everyone out of the tents. They won't hold the snow, and if it melts on the tops it'll pool and leak and we'll loose millions of dollars of equipment."

She and Jordan looked at each other, and she blinked. The other people disappeared at the edges of her vision, and she spoke clearly and happily, free for the first time in forever it seemed. "Let's go home."

Jordan simply smiled.

Side by side they walked back to the tent, and Jillian reveled in her footprints. Tried to track who went where from the pathways already marked by busy feet. Later, while they were packing. the phone rang. Hoping to distract herself, she waved Jordan back to gathering his things. "Jillian Brookwood, CDC Disease Lab." Well, that hadn't come out sounding quite right, but the person on the other end didn't give her a chance to change it.

"This is Dr. Greer Larson, I believe we spoke once before. I'm looking for Dr. David Carter, is he there?"

"Oh." She kicked herself after the word slipped out. She knew better than that – you should never act surprised. But now she had to step up and tell him. "David passed away yesterday."

"Yesterday?!"

She explained, and waited patiently while he asked why he hadn't found his friend on any of the lists. She mentioned the waking and falling under, and heard the deep disappointment in the voice on the other end. He asked if she could give him a moment, and Jillian realized that David's ticket out of here was the loss of a very real friend. And knowing David, one of a very small number.

He came back on the line and started in with a deep breath. "I finally think I have an answer to that question you asked."

She started to say something brilliant, like *huh?* But he continued, "The cretaceous die-out could conceivably have all happened from an illness. In a matter of days. There isn't anything that says the dinosaurs died over time." There was a brief pause, and Jillian couldn't think of anything intelligent or comforting to say. Again it was Dr. Larson who solved the problem. "I don't know if that helps. I'm sorry if it's too late. But I wanted to pass that on."

She nodded, even knowing he couldn't see her. Then spoke in soft tones, "I'm sorry about David. He spoke highly of you." She remembered. She hadn't realized it at the time, but this was the only other scientist David had ever quoted or deferred to.

They hung up and she settled the phone back in its cradle, then waited silently on Jordan. Without speaking, they left the confines of the tent and the heat, then a little further stepped beyond the edges of the tent town into an explosion of white.

Snow clung in thick pieces to her gloves and jacket, the wind lifted her hair and sent it dancing. "Will we be able to drive in this?"

Jordan bounced the keys in his hand. "I'm from Minnesota." They found the sedate CDC gold sedan in the parking lot and tossed the bags into the trunk before sliding into the seats. Jillian slammed the door and shivered, even through her jacket the leather of the seat felt frigid.

They warmed the engine for a few minutes. When Jordan didn't start a conversation, Jillian waited with him, silent even when he judged the engine ready and pulled out of the parking lot. She didn't need conversation, she was content just to watch the world float by in little clumps of white. Finally they merged onto the interstate, flurries blocking their vision even more.

She kept her mouth closed, not wanting to interfere with his driving, and let her brain wander. Although they were headed due south, the car's compass read 'north'. Even so, a cold, easy peace settled over her, a calm that had everything to do with the storm she left behind, so that even the storm she was in couldn't shake her.

After a while the flurries subsided to a world with clear air and a thin layer of white frosting. That gave way to a simple dusting of snow. And at last they emerged onto crisp, cold ground, with no signs of the winter they had left behind.

Not ten miles further, Jordan suddenly broke the silence. "We're getting close to Chattanooga."

She looked to him, startled. And this time it was he who replied before she could form words.

"Signal Mountain isn't that far out of the way. Do you want to stop to see your Dad?"

"No." *He remembered.* "We never really got along. The family I talk to is all on the other side."

Even while driving, he turned square to check her out for a moment. "Then why are you here?"

Her mouth quirked up in a way that she couldn't help. "Let me rephrase that. My blood family is there. You and Landerly understand me a lot better than they ever did."

He smiled.

And she laughed at him. "I think you two may even like me."

Again the flash of true grin, one she hadn't seen in a long while. "That I do."

For a few minutes she just studied him, taking in the charming profile, the straight nose and brilliant eyes. His smile had faded, taking the boy into man. The mouth opened and his voice interrupted her thoughts. "What about David? I thought you two were getting serious."

"Oh no. David is…David. He only really cares about David." She shrugged.

"I thought you liked him."

"I do. I just accept him for what he is, and isn't."

Jordan nodded, eyes still in tune with the road ahead, not looking at her face.

Her voice was small when she spoke, realizing what needed to get said. The first words were always the hardest, and after that it would flow. "Thank you–"

"For what?" He looked at her full on again, teal eyes full of concern for whatever he didn't know.

"For taking care of me. The way Landerly says it, you busted your ass to save my life."

He reddened a bit, but spoke with pride. "Yeah, I did. And I'd do it again…you owe me big time."

Her laughter burst out of her, filling the edges of the car, and she wasn't sure if she saw something when he looked at her again. After the giggles died down, she settled back, they still had several hours to go. So she started in, knowing Jordan was the only one who would understand.

"If everything changed when the poles shifted, and some species wound up on one side of the shift but not the other, won't they evolve differently? The whole ecological structure has altered."

"That makes sense." He nodded, but didn't give any other follow-up.

"So, in a thousand years our descendants will have evolved differently from David and Becky's."

"I don't think Becky will have him."

She almost punched him in the arm, but held back.

He spoke again, even as he swerved the car around a tire scrap in the road, "I don't think David should ever reproduce."

Jillian rolled her eyes and steered the conversation back to where she wanted it. "So probably the same thing happened the last time the poles shifted. Some species went one way and some went the other."

She waited until Jordan nodded, acknowledging her idea. "Does that mean that there are dinosaurs somewhere?"

It made perfect sense, but she just wasn't sure she could wrap her brain around it.

Read the first three pages of AJ's next novel

VENGEANCE

Chapter 1

The thick smell of blood wasn't a shock. He was used to it. What startled Lee was the woman. She was sitting at the dining room table, seemingly oblivious to the carnage mounted on the wall behind her. She was working over something, like she was writing, and deep in her work were she didn't acknowledge him.

A large red bow, the kind you would put on a three foot Christmas present, stole his attention sitting there on the table beside her. She wrote with precision, her head bent low, her rich chestnut hair worked into braids and wound round her head in a style that called to mind *The Sound of Music*.

Lee suppressed the boiling anger in him down to something in the range of a solid simmer and took a step toward her, wondering if she was in shock. Her right hand came up sharply, one leather gloved finger telling him to wait a minute, but the rigid control he saw in her told him she intended for him to wait as long as she wanted.

In that moment he saw what he had previously missed. She wore leather, in several shades of shadow, from her fingertips to her toes. The braids weren't cute, they were cop hair - the kind you couldn't get a hold on and use to yank a person around.

"There." Surprisingly, given the growing stench of death emanating from what Lee was now pretty certain was her handiwork, her voice was musical and held a low note of pride. She stood and turned to face him, holding the bow and what was apparently a large gift tag. And she smiled at him.

The smile reached her large chocolate eyes, and Lee felt the blood drain out the soles of his feet. She was insane. Clinically insane. There was no other reason a person would be truly happy here. Add in that she was armed to the teeth—a short dagger was sheathed at her waist, a pair of matched sais were slid into long thin pockets down each thigh, strange wood and metal sickles slipped gracefully through lined up loops so they didn't jangle when she walked—and the sweetness he had initially perceived fled like dandelion tufts.

She looked at him like she would a small puppy sitting at the edge of her living room, like he was cute and non-threatening. Lee's hand inched under his jacket to his hip, fondling the warm butt of the 9mm there. Given everything else, he wouldn't put it past her to be fast.

But she didn't say anything, just went about fastening the bow to the body and plumping it a little, like she was Martha Stewart off to a birthday party. The body was held to the wall behind it by serviceable unadorned throwing knives. At least he was pretty certain they were unadorned, only the last inch of the handle was visible on each of the six that knives that had crucified the man to the wall.

Lee thought he had seen lethal in his time, but it looked like the body had been alive when it had been pinned there, and the buried knives were sunk into wall studs. It was the only way that the heft of the large, muscular man wouldn't have come forward, bringing drywall with him. That took planning.

The face of the man on the wall sagged, eyes and mouth open, blood running in thin rivulets from the edges of each. He had suffered a thousand punctures and surface slices in his final moments, and the woman carried exactly the implements to do it. Although she must have cleaned them thoroughly before sliding them into their leather homes along her lean legs.

Stepping back she admired the tag. Lee, for the first time, read it.

In payment for murder, rape, and the destruction of families.

One by one, she used claw-like throwing stars to pin obituaries, newspaper articles, and pieces of police reports to dead flesh. After a moment Lee no longer cared what she was tacking to the corpse, he just wondered where in hell the stars were coming from. She would simply produce another and another, like a sick magician.

She turned to smile at him again, and his breath hitched. A wailing started deep at the back of his head.

He'd been wrong. She was just a girl.

VENGEANCE

COMING SOON

Visit AJScudiere.com for more information

About the Author

A.J. Scudiere has lived in Los Angeles for the past ten years and holds a Bachelor's Degree from New College and a Master's Degree from UCLA. A seasoned educator, A.J. has taught math, science and writing at every level from junior high through graduate level. These days A.J. is mostly found in front of the computer at work on the next novel.

Readers can visit AJScudiere.com
or email AJ at AJ@AJScudiere.com